Buried
In
Angst

David J. Pedersen

Cover art by
Alessandro Brunelli

Editing by:
Angie Pedersen http://www.angiewrites.com
Danielle Fine http://www.daniellefine.com

Angst font:
Comodore Paper by Reza Mfck
http://comodorepaper.blogspot.com/

© 2013 by David J. Pedersen
Odysia Press

ISBN 978-0-692-99115-2

Acknowledgements

When I wrote *Angst*, I needed to get something out of my system. I needed to prove to myself that I could do it. My first novel was another marathon to run, or mountain to climb, and I wasn't convinced I'd write another. So, I left *Angst* with an ending that could continue, or could be left alone.

I didn't leave it alone for long. Readers have been generous with their flattery and people who like *Angst* tend to really like it (the same goes for people who don't!) I've received more than enough encouragement to continue, but the great feedback set a high bar I found to be intimidating. I already knew how to continue this as a series, but I wanted to write something that everyone felt was at least as good as the first book. You'll have to be the judge if I was successful.

This is more than a novel, it really is a production. In my attempt to make it a good read, I involve a LOT of people. They deserve all the thanks and credit I can give. My lovely wife Angie is the first person that sees my mess. She edits, encourages, provides feedback and is amazingly supportive. When she is done beating me up, I send the chapters to my alpha team. They are the most patient people on earth, having to wait weeks between sets of chapters that sometimes end in a mini-cliffhanger. Matt is my oldest friend and provides me more encouragement than anyone, he is also quick to respond with great advice. Mike provides me with great suggestions and really solid feedback. Becky, who always has a different spin than the boys, has saved my story on numerous occasions. And Cristi, who, in addition to working full time and going to school part time provided me with some of the most fun feedback I've gotten, as well as some kick-ass recommendations. If you follow my blog, Cristi is also my spokesmodel at conventions, I couldn't do all of this without her!

After my alpha team finishes with their review, I make changes and give the book to my beta team. My brother-in-law BJ does an awesome job helping me fill in the geeky logic points that I tend to leave out. When Dusty reviewed *Angst* on his blog www.thedustyblog.com, I knew he got it. I'm glad I asked him to be on the team, because he provided me with excellent feedback. My mom read the beta and gave me the encouragement that only moms can, she's the best! Also, I have to mention Mitch who came back from basic training and asked if he could still be a part of the beta team - I've got to thank him for both his enthusiasm, and his service!

My wife edited *Angst* a second time after the Alpha and Beta teams were done, but she couldn't this time because she was busy writing *The Star Trek Craft Book: Make It So!* (Check it out, it's really cool!) Fortunately I found Danielle Fine. Dani added the polish to *Buried in Angst* that I really wanted. Her edits were thorough and her critiques were dead-on. If you are looking to hire an editor send her an email, you won't be disappointed.

Joshua Calloway provided the cover art, taking the scene from chapter 35 and making it his own. I really love the dragon!

I need to thank some very supportive friends and family. Holly is still Rose, she puts up with a lot and I'm grateful for her patience. Allie, an alpha reader for Angst, was truly an inspiration for this book. Brandon, Cristi's boyfriend and a friend of mine has been invaluable helping with my marketing efforts. (I'm thinking he needs a costume for cons too!) Marina helped me select the cover artist and cover art, which I really need because I have no taste! Joanne and James provide ongoing support that I need. And my dad for his encouragement and spreading the word.

Finally, I have to thank everyone who waited! I wrote this for you and I hope you have fun. Enjoy the show!

Books by David J. Pedersen

Angst Five Book Series:

Book 1: Angst
Book 2: Buried in Angst
Book 3: Drowning in Angst
Book 4: Burning with Angst
Book 5: Dying with Angst

Young Adult / Middle Grade Fiction:

Clod Makes A Friend

Map of Ehrde

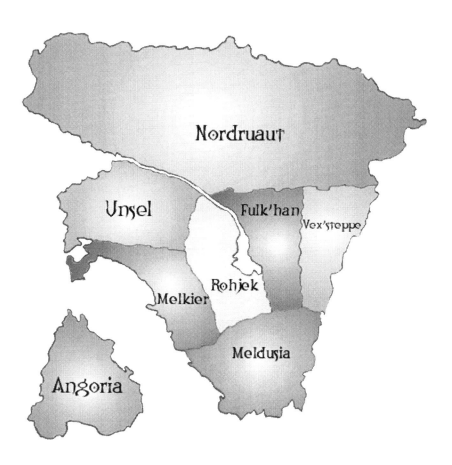

Prelude

A dark storm threatened the horizon, tossing the ocean about like water in a bucket. The waves came faster and faster, growing larger each time they crashed against the side of his fishing boat. They seemed to reach for the boat's edge, hungry to grasp and pull it down into the maw of darkness below.

Johnis wiped salty sea spray and loneliness from his stern face. His tan, weatherworn complexion made him appear a man of forty instead of a mere thirty-two—but one cost of spending so many days out to sea. The work was hard, the conditions unfriendly, but he wouldn't have traded the solitude for anything. His kaynarr boat could have readily held four men in comfort, but he preferred it empty. Nobody to trip over, or worry about.

Johnis closed his eyes and took in a deep breath of sea. He had but scant minutes before it would be too late to pull in his catch, but he knew the coming storm could reward his nets, so he waited. His breath caught as thunder shook the air, and a wary eye skyward revealed the storm had moved far faster than expected.

"By the cursed Vivek!" he yelled in his scratchy voice.

Johnis rushed to the nets and began pulling them over the rail, smiling at his catch. His arms were long and thin and filled with wiry strength, but the nets were heavier than they should've been. His timing had been off, the catch was too full, and his smile washed away in the heavy rain now pouring down. Thunder clapped the instant lightning covered the sky, and he knew the storm was directly above him. He tugged and fought as the net grew heavier still.

Turning his head skyward, he stared down the storm. He should've let go, but something felt wrong—he had to see what was in the net. Johnis struggled and wrenched with every ounce of his formidable strength to force the net to breach the surface. He cinched it to the side and leaned over the edge. The pale, panicked face of a beautiful young woman greeted him. Johnis stared in confusion as she stopped fighting the net and looked up at him. She was mostly hidden by dark water, but Johnis could make out her high full lips, deep blue eyes, and dark blue hair.

"Wait one moment, miss. I'll cut you free!" he yelled over the rain, which beat the water like drums.

Johnis moved to draw his fishing knife but paused when anger flashed across her blue eyes. She thrashed violently.

"I'm going to try to help you!" he called over the madness of booming storm, crashing waves, and pouring rain.

Before he could completely unsheathe the knife, lightning struck the bow of the ship.

Johnis was thrown into the air and dropped feet-first into the ocean. He kicked and clawed at the water until he broke free to sweet air. Struggling to keep his head above the thrashing waves, gasping for air, he glimpsed his burning ship in the distance, engulfed by the merciless waters.

"No!" he screamed, remembering the girl caught in his nets.

Though he was a strong swimmer, Johnis battled the stormy waves with every stroke to reach the remains of his ship. The net and its contents were gone, sinking to the bottomless depths. He took several quick breaths, pushed all the air from his lungs then drew one final, full breath.

The water was too dark to see, so Johnis grasped desperately into nothingness for the net. He thanked the lady of the sea when when his hands tangled in rough rope. He reached through the net until he felt cold, unmoving fingers. Together they dropped fast, as the ocean swallowed them deep into its gullet. He unsheathed his knife and cut away pieces of coarse netting until he could pull the hand and then the body of the young woman through.

His lungs wrenched in his chest, desperate for oxygen. Johnis swam and pulled forever, towing the woman behind him. His first breath was filled with life and burned his lungs. He gasped and coughed through sticky salt waves of cold ocean. The blue-haired woman was no more than dead weight in his arms but, miraculously, she began to struggle like any drowning person. Had she been a man, Johnis would have struck her unconscious, but he couldn't bring himself to harm her. Even in the dim fiery remains of his burning ship, he could see, almost feel, her beauty.

Johnis wrapped his long arms around her chest, just below her naked breasts. She kicked and pushed as he wrestled her back toward the wreckage.

"I'm trying to save you!" he screamed, exhausted and desperate for her to stop fighting. "I'm trying to find some flotsam we can hold onto…"

A large wave overtook them. They tossed and turned in each other's arms. Johnis feared for their lives, but the woman seemed calm as she fought against him. There was no panic or concern in her eyes, just curiosity.

"Please stop fighting…so tired…" he pleaded between gasps of sweet air. "I'll protect you."

Johnis wasn't even sure she could hear but had very little energy left to care. A quick look around showed that any remains of his boat were now lost. They were miles from shore with no boat, no floating wreckage, and she wanted to wrestle. Resolutely, he gripped her waist, and began to swim.

After several minutes, she managed to push away. They treaded water together, rising and lowering with the water.

"You don't understand!" he yelled. "I'm sorry for the net! I'm just trying to keep you safe!"

She stared deep into his eyes and smiled. He felt momentary relief as he took in her face one last time. It had been such a lonely life, and now after seeing such beauty, was he still happy with his decisions? Suddenly, his solitary life seemed a waste.

Life could have been worth living if he'd only gotten to enjoy those lovely blue eyes a while longer. The water swelled, and the ocean roared in anger. Johnis tore his eyes from hers and looked up.

"I'm sorry," was all he could say before an enormous wall of water ate them, pulling them deep into the ocean.

Johnis tumbled and flipped in watery chaos before his fingers touched sand. Sand? He would never make it to the surface if he'd reached the ocean floor. For a brief moment, he thought he saw the blue-haired woman swimming toward him then his head struck something hard and all went dark.

* * * *

His eyes and mouth and lungs opened simultaneously as life returned and the nightmare passed. Johnis looked around to find himself in bed—his bed—in his house. He propped himself up on his elbows for a moment then decided it was better to lie back down. Only moments before he'd been at the bottom of the ocean—finding himself home was too much to grasp. Placing his long fingers on his stomach, Johnis found his skin to be cold and clammy. Would he ever feel dry and warm again?

The door to his room slowly opened, and a thin bare foot stepped through, followed by the peeking face of a young woman. He read the hesitation in her ocean-blue eyes, but eventually she came into the room. His breath caught painfully in his throat. Little about her was left to the imagination. Her long hair curled lushly over full breasts, and she wore a string of delicate shells around her waist. The rest of her body was beautiful rosy skin that softly painted lovely curves. She finally made eye contact well after he remembered to close his mouth.

He wanted to say something—anything—so she wouldn't leave, but his deep breath turned into a painful wracking cough.

"You are a foolish hum…a foolish man," she chastised in a pleasant high-pitched voice, shaking her head in disbelief.

"I couldn't let you die," he whispered. Unsure if she could

4

hear, he whispered louder. "I'm sorry about the nets. How did you...how did we...?"

She sat by his side and touched his forehead with cold slender fingers. "You aren't better yet. This will take weeks, and I need to leave."

He put his hand on hers and gripped it as if she were his lover. "Please stay," he whispered. "I need to know you, to know how we—" Another coughing fit took him, and he could say no more.

"You are a good man, Johnis, filled with loneliness and love." She stared into his eyes, into his heart, and his mind, and his soul, and smiled. "Not for people. You have a great love for your mistress, the sea."

Somehow, she understood his need and, for the first time since waking, his shoulders relaxed. He nodded in agreement, still gripping her hand.

"I will stay with you, for a while. Maybe until you are healed and rested. But know this, I will never tell you how we got to your cabin, and you will never ask. Do you understand?"

He nodded weakly then rested his hand behind her neck and slowly pulled her toward him. Her blue eyebrows furrowed with curiosity.

"What is your name?" Johnis said softly into her ear.

"You may call me Selchia," she whispered.

He pulled her closer.

She acquiesced, wondering what could be so important for Johnis to say in his weakened state. He kissed her ear very gently then passed out. She jerked her head back in surprise, and his hand fell limply to his body. Blinking, she touched the place on her ear Johnis had kissed. The spot was wet, and she was filled with a warmth she'd never felt before.

She smiled broadly as she looked at his resting face and said quietly, "I will stay awhile."

* * * *

Selchia was still as beautiful as the day he'd found her. Her hair was the same length and the same deep blue without a single gray showing. Her pale skin smooth and soft. She seemed to maintain the same level of energy, strength and inner power typically boasted by younger women.

Johnis, on the other hand, carried those thirty years of labor and life within each wrinkle of his weatherworn face. His few remaining hairs fringed the edges of his head and made small white clouds over his ears. At sixty-three, he was still strong—stronger than he had any right to be. Most of his acquaintances had passed, but something kept his heart beating, and his mind sharp.

He never questioned, out loud, their incredible luck at sea. Every day they would fish and return with a winning catch. It was a hard, well-earned life that was often rewarding and fulfilling. He didn't even think to question Selchia's apparent youth, he was grateful for it. Johnis did not regret that they hadn't bore children. It wasn't for a lack of trying, and it was more time with his love that he didn't have to share.

They returned from fishing on the last day of summer to find a young man waiting by their front door. The youth gawked at Selchia with slack-jawed awe. She smiled coolly and took the message he held.

"Thank you, son." Johnis rolled his eyes and handed the youth a copper.

The young man stared at the copper then back at Selchia. "Sir, your daughter, is she...may I...?"

Johnis coughed to cover his curse, and Selchia smiled slyly. "You will stop gawking at my wife and be gone before I give you the front side of my boot!"

This shocked the younger man from his stupor and he began to stutter. "Your...your wife. Sir...ma'am, my apologies. Your wife? Yes, I'll be off." And with a final glance at the beautiful blue-haired woman, he sprinted down the road.

"Just lucky that I married such a beautiful woman." Johnis grunted, rubbing the back of his bald head.

"What does the note say, dear?" Selchia asked affectionately.

"Oh, yes," Johnis replied, having been distracted from the true purpose of the young man's visit. He mumbled as he read then squeezed his eyes shut to fight back tears. "It's my brother, Cahleb. He's dying."

Their eyes met meaningfully, and Johnis nodded in acknowledgment at her knowing look.

"We haven't been close since...well, in years, but he is family." He looked at her with concern. "I must pay my respects."

"I know, but I can't...if you are away I won't be able to keep you..." She chewed her lip.

"You don't have to explain. You never have to explain," he replied without a hint of question in his voice. "I know your...love for the sea keeps you close to the shore. I will go by myself and be back in a matter of days."

"No, I don't think that is wise." Selchia sighed deeply and rubbed her hands together with fret. "I will accompany you, but you must know that travel fatigues me greatly."

"I will gladly take care of you as you have always taken care of me," he replied, kissing her thoughtfully on the cheek. "I've been wanting to show you my birth home for years. It will be nice to have the opportunity."

She nodded but worry darkened her heart. Johnis had never understood, and never asked why she would not go inland. He had never seen her go further than several miles before turning back. Even those trips required a swim in the ocean or lingering walks along the beach upon return, which he never seemed to mind.

She smiled at the kiss, but concern still clouded her face.

* * * *

The trip was two day's ride by horse and carriage. The road was easy, the weather was fair, but Selchia showed signs of weakness mere hours into the journey. By the second day, her eyes seemed sunken, her blue hair, normally wavy and wild, rested heavy on her drooping shoulders, and she struggled to breathe.

"Selchia, let me take you home. I can come back alone," Johnis offered in a panic.

It was not his first offer, and the answer was always the same. A shake of the head followed by a firm, "No."

Eventually Johnis spied a tired farmstead and smiled, memories of his youth assailing him.

"I remember," he said, turning to face Selchia.

A pained smile lifted her cheek, and Johnis felt a great need to hurry.

"I remember much, and look forward to sharing it when we return home," he said with an apologetic smile.

They hastily made their way past Johnis's relatives and friends who waited with patience and impatience. They all despised him for not visiting, which made it easier to rush past them with Selchia's hand in his.

He broached his brother's sickbed and, leaning forward, whispered something in his ear. They made eye contact, firmly gripped hands and nodded. Apparently nothing more needed to be said.

Cahleb looked at Selchia fondly and reached for her hand. He whispered, and she leaned forward to listen to words meant only for her. "Thank you for being my brother's life, lady of the sea."

Selchia was surprised for a moment, and her eyes filled with tears she wiped away with a finger. She touched the wet finger to his forehead.

"May your passing be peaceful, Cahleb."

The room trembled, causing everyone to look about in concern. Cahleb's hat fell off the nearby nightstand, landing on the dusty floor as the quake became violent.

Selchia sucked in a deep breath and looked at Johnis in panic. "No!" she cried. "Johnis, run!"

They rushed out of the cabin and across the yard toward the horses. A whining noise, accompanied by sickening crunching sounds, became louder as the seconds sprinted by.

Johnis slowed to look in the direction of the odd noises. "Selchia, what is that sound?"

"Johnis, please! Just run!" Selchia begged.

The wall of trees standing before them blinked out of existence, consumed by a large beam of black light that reached up to the sky. Black lightning snapped around the edges, biting at the ground. Like a tornadic nightmare, everything behind it was laid waste.

Selchia pulled and tugged at her stunned husband. "Please, oh please! No!" she begged.

Johnis turned to his wife, his face longing and desperate. "Selchia, I love—"

And he was gone.

The beam slowed momentarily, as though mocking her, then sped through Cahleb's house and beyond.

She was too angry to weep, too stunned to scream. Who would do this? Who would let Magic free to run wild through the world? The beast that had been trapped for thousands of years was now able to run rampant across Ehrde. This would change all the rules. Who would be foolish enough to set Magic free of its host? Who was to blame for the death of her beloved husband?

Then she saw. Following close behind the raging pillar of black light, a short man raced by on a steel swifen. The enormous foci, Chryslaenor, rose high over his shoulder. In spite of his speed, he caught sight of the woman with blue hair and their eyes met. She saw remorse, and pity, and worry.

Selchia shook with anger, and reached out with her mind. Grasping for the man, for the foci, for some clue as to why this had happened. Every ounce of her yearned to destroy him for what he had taken away, but this far from the sea she was too weak.

She tried one final time to learn something about her husband's killer and found it. More loudly than humanly possible, she screamed, "*Angst!*"

Then her body formed into a tall swirling waterspout that rose into the clouds and disappeared.

1

Angst was frustrated. He paced the empty throne room, circling Chryslaenor. He paused for long moments to stare at the giant sword, *his* giant sword, which appeared to be dying. Thorny forks of black lighting cascaded across the flat of the blade, sputtering down the long edge, dripping to the floor, and disappearing on contact with the bright marble, like rain evaporating on parched earth.

He wanted to reach for the sword, bring it back to life, and bring himself back to life. The song from Chryslaenor was now so distant, he had to squint and concentrate to hear it. But he could just make out the firm warning that Angst should not even attempt to touch it. The sword that had so quickly made all he wanted come true was no longer his. The foci now entrapped the living element of Magic within. Angst had sacrificed his bond with the sword to save the two people he loved most, but the cost to himself was great.

He was no longer Al'eyrn, no longer able to do amazing heroics. Angst was left with nothing but greener grass, deep sighs, and a fleeting sense of accomplishment that he had done the good he'd always known he was capable of. Removing the bond with Chryslaenor had left behind an empty place that often ached and throbbed with pain. He'd heard stories of people losing hands but occasionally feeling as if the hand remained. Though two months had passed, he sometimes felt the bond with

Chryslaenor was still there, but he couldn't "wiggle those fingers." He sighed and turned away.

The throne room was still a mess. Cold and snow fell from the open ceiling to mark the wide path magic had sundered. The giant marble pillars surrounding the room reflected brief sparks of the dark and silver lighting that danced across the long blade of Chryslaenor. Work that should have already begun was lost to the continuous bickering of the queen and her staff, who were unsure whether to rebuild around Chryslaenor or move to safer grounds.

"Whad are you doing in here?" asked a thick shadow with a thick voice.

Angst blinked in surprise, unable to make out the intruder's identity. A tall, obese man entered the room followed closely by a smaller man. They stepped over and around scarred floor and fallen ceiling as they cautiously moved closer.

"Just assessing the damage," Angst lied.

The two men stopped mere feet away before Angst could recognize one—the co-assistant guild-whatever who'd been so rude to him in the file room. Angst inadvertently tensed as the man's fat greasy lip curled into a jowl.

"No one is supposed to be in here, we gots work to do," the big man said with a grunt, jerking his meaty thumb toward the door.

The smell from the man struck Angst, and he took a step back, closer to the sword. He shook his head in disbelief—the beast didn't know who Angst was, nor did he seem to remember their last encounter.

"It's not safe in here. You need to leave," proclaimed the co-assistant guild-whatever, with a thick air of self-importance and partial sobriety.

"Yes, you heard him. This place is tainted with magics." The thinner, balding man, who was even shorter than Angst's five-foot-eight, jerked his thumb over his shoulder, pointing to the entrance. "No one is allowed in here, so get out."

Angst focused on the annoying weasel. "No need to be rude. I have permission from Princess Victo—"

He was cut off by the finger conductor. The assistant guild leader stepped directly in front of him and pointed his favorite weapon right in front of Angst's nose. The menacing odor forced Angst back another step.

He wanted to ask if the man bathed in mead, but instead attempted to negotiate one last time. "Look, we don't have to go about it like this—"

"The queen has commanded that this room be emptied for ex...excavat...for cleaning."

Angst lifted his chin defiantly and raised his voice. "Then you go get Isabelle, and she can command me to leave!"

The scruffy little guy that followed the guild co-leader like a puppy snorted through his nose, and the bigger man coughed and stood back. Both appeared shocked and upset at Angst's casual use of the queen's first name.

"Did you not hear what Giff had to say?" The little man's eyes were wide, and he looked up to Giff. "Maybe he didn't hear you?"

As though he were suddenly ingratiated to the crown and personally offended, Giff's face grew red. He pounded on Angst's chest with his thick finger. "You get out of here or I'll drag you out of here."

Angst's hands glowed. "You may not remember our last *meeting*, Giff, but we've already gone over this. I suggest you leave now—"

The room shook and both men facing Angst stepped back. Bits of loose ceiling fell about them. The earthquake began as a gentle rumble, like any number Angst had mistakenly started before gaining control of his abilities. He hadn't caused a quake in years, but the glowing hands made him appear the criminal. The guildies panicked, grabbing at each other's arms and gripping tight. Ignoring them, Angst closed his eyes and concentrated. Using his ability to manipulate stone and minerals, he searched for the source. This earthquake came from something other than him. He held his hands out, urging the angry ground beneath them to calm. Just as the room stopped shaking, he felt something else.

Angst tilted his head to one side and glanced up as a large portion of marble ceiling cracked. Before he could shift his focus to anchor the stone and keep it attached to the rest of the roof, it pulled away.

"Giff, watch out!" the smaller man yelled. They pushed and jerked at each other in panic but otherwise remained in place.

The sky was falling. An enormous chunk of marble roof dropped quickly toward them. Without the foci, it required all of Angst's concentration to keep it from flattening the three of them. He held his glowing hands high and the loose piece of ceiling stopped abruptly, hanging mere inches overhead.

The two men were crouched in front of him, holding their hands over their heads as though that would save them from sudden death. Angst breathed in deep to renew his strength and smelled iron. A trickle of blood dripped from his nose as he drew in all his willpower and pushed the giant floating rock away. It crashed loudly, landing safely nearby—no longer able to squish helpless people.

"Giff, he tried to kill you!" the weasel said.

This perceived threat brought the large man to action. Giff's head whipped up. His drunken beady eyes narrowed warily at Angst. Weary from saving them, Angst took a slow step back. The larger man, who typically used a finger to warn Angst of his wrongdoings, balled up a beefy fist and swung it wildly. The power behind the strike knocked Angst back. He tripped over a piece of fallen ceiling and collided hard with Chryslaenor.

Light and sound disappeared. The room blinked as if time had hiccupped. Black and blue lightning shot from the enormous blade, tearing violently through the air. A fierce battle between Magic and Chryslaenor ensued as the foci struggled to maintain its hold on the element. Strands of lightning burst from the blade, reaching, grasping for something. Anything. They found Angst. For a moment, he was surrounded by the angry dark light. He writhed and roared in pain until he managed to roll away. Blue lightning pulled at the black, as though ripping out briars deeply embedded in skin. The lightning reluctantly left his body, returning to Chryslaenor.

His head throbbed painfully and, as the world began to fade, he watched the two guildies sprint out of the room in fear. It would've been laughable if Angst hadn't felt as though he'd done something terribly wrong.

2

Angst awoke at the precipice of madness. His body was covered in numbness or burning, a deep ache penetrating his muscles. Angst rolled to one side slowly then pushed himself up to rest on an elbow. He could only see out of his left eye and blood dripped freely from his nose. None of that mattered. His mind reeled from the vision before him.

He rested on the edge of a cliff, thousands of feet above an enormous chasm that didn't exist in Ehrde. A blurry pan of the horizon showed what had to be nightmare. It was miles across and thousands of feet deep, reminding him of a thousandfold Vex'kvette. A deep orange glow carved through its center, no doubt wreaking havoc with everything that made contact. Unnaturally warm, the air wafted with burning ashes and gaseous vapors that burned his lungs. Geysers of water shot into the sky along the canyon edges. The elements were going mad.

Angst took in a heavy breath and looked at the dark, starry sky. In the distance, enormous winged creatures floated through the air. A half-dozen of the beasts hung in the moonlight, patrolling the long orange path of the Vex'kvette. One passed a stone's throw away and the whoosh of wings on air almost pushed him over. A stream of flame poured from its open mouth. Was that a dragon?

"Hold still, Angst," said an old companion in a melodic, calming whisper.

He didn't listen. Rolling to his back, Angst looked up to see a woman his own age. Her skin was tan, she had a cute pug nose with a little mole on the end, and her long hair flowed about her shoulders like a mane. Aerella was alive.

"What have you done?" she asked in a husky voice. She shook her head, and tears streamed from her pretty eyes as she surveyed the madness surrounding them. Aerella floated several feet above the precipice, a beautiful specter, transparent against the night sky.

This couldn't be right. As Angst rolled to his hands and knees, he remembered just how much everything hurt. He stood, slowly, shakily, and took a deep breath of the heavy, sickeningly sweet air. Something was poking him in the arm and leg. Angst looked down to find his armor in shreds. One piece dug roughly into his bleeding thigh. Sharp metal bent outward from his chest piece and his arm bled freely.

The shock was beginning to wear off, and his stomach reeled from the pain. He collapsed to his right knee and winced, grunting noisily. Then Aerella was there, her touch like the gentlest of feathers. An uncomfortable tickle filled Angst with warmth.

"I'm not able to heal all of your wounds while I'm in this state, but this will keep you alive," she said.

He coughed up phlegm and blood, wiped his mouth, and peered at her. "Aerella, I don't understand any of this. I thought… I'm sorry, I don't mean to be cruel, but I thought you were dead?" Angst had barely gotten to know Aerella. She had escaped the curse of Gressmore Towers only to be killed by Ivan. Aerella didn't reply and Angst looked around. "Where am I? What is this place?"

"This is Ehrde, and you stand high over the heart of your Unsel." Aerella was stern, angry.

"No!" Angst reached up to grip her arm, but his hand floated through her as though she were merely a cloud. He yanked his hand back in shock and fear, her presence-or lack of presence-too much to fathom. He turned away and looked around, desperate to find a landmark.

17

"Look closer, Angst. Look at the ground, look at the entrance behind us."

He inspected the ground, and the weathered entrance behind them. Kicking dirt and rubble aside, Angst found he was not on the edge of a cliff but the ruins of a broken stone patio. What could have been planters, and several broken stone pedestals, had been thoughtfully placed around him. The pile he stood beside could have been a bench, and…

He looked up at Aerella. "The maidens' courtyard?" Angst swallowed hard and licked dry lips. "I need to find them. Where are my friends? Where's Heather? Aerella, where's Tori?"

"They're long dead and gone, Angst." Aerella's voice was heavy with sorrow.

"No…no, you're lying." Angst's voice cracked and his eyes grew wet. "I don't understand. Who did this? What did this?"

Aerella rested a small hand on his shoulder. "You did, Angst."

"What?" he snapped, wiping blood and tears and confusion from his face. This wasn't right. Angst felt detached-the words were his but seemed to come out on their own.

"This was wrought by your mistake, Angst. You cannot wield another. You don't know the dangers that will be unleashed."

Angst reached to his back instinctively, but Chryslaenor was still gone. He felt the empty place in his mind and found he held nothing. "I wield no weapons. No foci. I have nothing."

"You did, and you couldn't control them. Your egocentric, self-indulgent need for something more has led to two thousand years of disaster. This nightmare was wrought by you, Angst, and only you can make it right."

Aerella was fading. Everything around him seemed to fade with her into fog and shadow.

"I don't understand… I can't even touch my foci." Angst yelled. He felt as though he was being pulled away into a long dark cave of cool and reason.

"Don't do it, Angst. Don't wield another." Aerella's whisper chased him into the darkness.

CHAPTER TWO

He blinked his eyes rapidly to see his pretty friend with dark red hair and deep eyes looking over him. Angst reeled as pain from the nightmare faded, and the reality of the throne room returned. For the briefest of moments, he swore that a trickle of dark lightning flickered in Rose's eye.

"Right now, I hate you," she said sternly.

"You're such a flirt, it's embarrassing sometimes." Angst sat up and looked around the throne room.

All was as he'd left it. The two men were gone, snow continued to fall gently from the ceiling, and Chryslaenor remained in place, still surrounded by black and blue lightning.

"Just a bad dream," Angst muttered with relief.

Rose stared at him with a dumbfounded expression. Was she in pain from healing him or upset at him for passing out?

"Rose, thank you," he said warmly, hoping to calm her. Her face didn't change, and she continued to stare at him. "Are you okay?"

"You make me so angry sometimes, Angst." Her hands were on her hips, and Angst couldn't tell if she was going to yell or cry. She did both. "Do you ever bother to think about what you do? About the choices you make and how they affect everyone? You got lucky last time. Walk away...no, run away! You got to be a hero. Isn't that enough? Stop now before you do something stupid!"

"Rose, what are you talking about?" Angst asked in complete astonishment. "I know that I shouldn't have been in here, that touching the sword is bad, but everything is okay. I just had a bad dream, is all."

"Then why did Aerella say it was your fault?" Rose asked.

3

"What in Ehrde were you doing in there anyway?" Hector asked, his bushy eyebrows frowning.

Angst sighed deeply, feeling his age. He didn't want to talk about how much he missed Chryslaenor, how he longed for the bond, how much he missed being a hero. He could only admit to himself that it wasn't just the bond, or the power, it was the looks he'd get carrying that beast of a sword on his back. It was fun.

He looked around the Wizard's Revenge for some escape from Hector's piercing gray eyes. In spite of the storm, the inn was busy and bustling. The room appeared brighter than Angst could ever remember it being, and a certain pride and levity seemed to carry conversations now. Defending Unsel against unstoppable foes had made magic-wielders more valuable. Change was happening, like the tide washing away footprints in the sand—he could only hope that change was for the better.

Angst was separated from his thoughts by a crowd of young, boisterous men surrounding a table by the fire. A parade of mugs and pitchers floated to the table only to be emptied as fast as they had arrived. Nearby patrons flashed the youth annoyed stares, but the party continued.

"Go easy, Hector. That doesn't matter right now," Dallow said, obviously trying to temper the situation and regain Angst's attention.

"Enough of my drama… We really should be celebrating Dallow's return," Angst interjected, feeling somewhat guilty for ruining his friend's homecoming. He poured another draft of port, one of many that night, and handed a goblet to Dallow. "Tell us about your trip."

Dallow shook his head at Angst's attempt to change the subject. Dallow's long blond bangs hung carefully over squinting brown eyes that peered knowingly at him. "We have all night to talk about the Gressmore Ruins excavation," Dallow answered. "So, you both saw the same thing?"

"Not exactly," Rose said, glaring at the party-table with hate as though they were broaching her personal space. "I watched Angst speak with Aerella, who appeared as a ghost—it was creepy."

"I thought Aerella died," Tarness said in his deep voice. "After Ivan turned into the giant monster host of Magic, didn't he suck her up into his hand…or something like that?"

"Yeah," Angst said sadly. "She was with us such a short time after Gressmore, we barely got to know her."

"Other than your make out session," Rose taunted, sudden cheer around her large, dark eyes.

"It was a hug," Angst said, his grin becoming mischievous. "A long, meaningful hug."

Rose looked at Angst with her customary impatience, while he enjoyed the moment, taking in her prettiness. Rose was lean, yet curvy enough to make other women hate her, and the black leather bustier she wore accentuated this. Her long, dark red hair was pulled back into a tight ponytail, the end dangling over her pale bare shoulder. Rose's thin eyebrows narrowed, and her full lips pursed, warning Angst not to take in too much.

"Did you see anything else?" Dallow interrupted.

"I didn't see the giant Vex'kvette, nor did I see any dragons." She turned to stare down Angst. "Really, Angst, dragons? What next, flying pink unicorns?"

"They were wyrms, fire breathing and all," Angst said. "I didn't realize they were real, but now…I just don't know."

"We know dragons *were* real," Tarness interjected, stopping his giant-tankard halfway to his mouth. "Didn't we, at Gressmore…" He gripped the tankard and winced as he tried to remember.

"Best to forget that, Tarness," Angst said, resting a hand on the large man's shoulder. "Trying to remember what happened doesn't seem to be healthy."

Tarness nodded and shrugged, a deep draw of mead washing away the concern from his forehead. He towered over the others, easily a head taller and taking the width of two seats. Tarness's skin was a thick coating of dark black over large muscles and unforgiving age. His heavy eyebrows made him seem angry, but a wink at Angst said otherwise.

"According to the history books from Gressmore Ruins, wyrms, er, dragons did exist," Dallow said excitedly. "I have hundreds of books to go through. It takes a long time—for some reason, I keep having to relearn Acratic every day before I can read them—but the history is amazing. We've lost so much understanding of magic."

"I still don't believe you went on an archaeology dig this time of year," Rose said in annoyed disbelief.

"I needed to clear my head of things, is all." Dallow stared into her large eyes for a moment long enough to make everyone else uncomfortable. "And I didn't want the weather to do any more damage to those treasures."

Rose nodded but looked away. Angst had wondered on their last adventure if their relationship was more than sharing a horse. Dallow's marriage was the same mess as his, if not worse, but Rose was so much younger, it didn't seem as though it could work.

"My team will go back in the spring—we need softer ground to really dig deep—but I found enough to keep me busy for a while. The books will reform history as we know it. Why I can't believe…" Dallow's green gaze flicked around the table, looking in vain for someone who was still interested. He sighed deeply and brushed bangs from his eyes.

CHAPTER THREE

Tarness, Hector, and Angst watched the pretty barmaid check on the party-table, practically endowing everyone in the room with her ample gifts.

"Does she look thinner?" Hector asked with a little concern.

"...and I found these." Dallow dropped a handful of clear polished stones on the table.

"Rocks?" asked Tarness.

"Not just rocks," Dallow said with excitement. "These rocks seem to have magic qualities. If you look into them, you'll see little maps."

"Memndus," Angst remarked reflectively as he picked up one of the stones and stared at it thoughtfully.

"Memn... I don't remember hearing that word. I don't think." Dallow squinted in concentration as he tried to recall. "I thought we might be able to use them. I found a dozen or so."

Everyone else grabbed a souvenir from Dallow's trip and thanked him. They all looked into their stones with awe before once again being distracted by the raucous noise. A young, thin blonde was now standing on top of the table and dancing to the clapping of hands and pounding of feet. They were youth having fun, and Angst smiled to himself as he watched.

"Ahem." Graloon coughed to gather their attention. The portly barkeep stood behind them with a stern look on his face and his hands parked in the greasy apron that covered most of his ample belly.

Angst watched the young woman drop into the lap of a burly man, who seemed proud of his catch. He planted a deep kiss on the woman's pouty lips.

"Something the matter, Graloon?" Angst asked mockingly. "You haven't forgotten what it's like to be young have you? What it's like to dance?"

"Yes, yes I have," Graloon replied with a grunt. "I don't mind but, Angst, you'll want to take a closer look at this crew."

Angst looked around his own table in confusion, attempting to peer through the haze of drink. Dallow, Tarness, and Hector's jaws rested on their chests. Rose appeared disgusted, and Angst was certain he could see fumes rising from her eyes. She looked at him accusingly before jerking her head toward the other table.

Angst inspected the noisy youths. They were loud, and obnoxious, but otherwise causing no harm. The pretty blonde was attempting to pull away from the large young man who, it seemed, wasn't quite done eating her face. Angst stared closer at her long, curly blond hair, the pale skin that covered her high cheekbone, her thick dark eyelashes…

He stood so suddenly his chair flew back to the ground. Angst stomped over to stand behind the embracing lovers and gripped the large man's shoulder.

"Here we go," said Tarness with a sigh. He slowly got up and began moving tables and chairs aside to make room.

Angst placed his other hand on the man's forehead, wrenched him out of lip-lock, and continued pulling until the angry youth stood. The man continued to stand until he towered over Angst, his large wide shoulders level with Angst's forehead. The man's arms were almost as large as Tarness's. Angst ignored the oaf and turned his attention to the blonde.

"Tori, what in the Vivek are you doing here? What are you doing with that thing?" Angst said, jerking his thumb at his colossal opponent.

She merely giggled, obviously deep into the kegs.

"Do you have any idea who this is, you idiot?" Angst said, forcing his tongue around the words. He had one hand still on the man's shoulder, raised high over his own head.

The fist hammered Angst's face so hard, he flew over the table and landed at Rose and Hector's feet. Angst looked up in shock, suddenly a bit more sober and certain most of his teeth were now loose or missing.

"I've got this," Angst grunted reassuringly, still lying on the dusty floor.

"Angst?" Tori said in confusion.

"That's Angst?" the young man said with challenge in his voice. "Doesn't look like a hero to me. Let's see if he still is one."

"I think I've got this," Angst said sitting up. Hector pushed on his back to get him on his feet.

Angst approached the young man, only to meet hammers. His opponent was fast and powerful, his fists making violent contact with every other swing. Tori drunkenly gripped the back of the young man's arm and was knocked to the floor. In desperation, Angst reached out for anything stone or mineral, and found something he'd never considered. A blue glow surrounded Angst's hands as he connected to the mineral with magic. The man grabbed Angst's collar with his left hand and swung hard with his right.

The sound of cracking bone filled the room, followed by a loud scream. Everyone opened their eyes to find Angst remained standing, his face contorted in an angry scowl. The large man let go of Angst's collar to hold his own arm. It was broken between the elbow and wrist, hanging grotesquely as though snapped in half.

Angst proceeded to release that day's frustration. He smashed the man's face with his left fist then his right, and continued to pummel until he threw all of his weight into a final blow that knocked the man unconscious. It was more than the young man had deserved, but the fight was over.

The other youths around the table quickly scurried away from Tori. He pulled her to her feet and draped a dangly arm over his neck to balance her. Angst shuffled the princess over to his table of friends.

"Rose, do you think you could...you know?" Angst asked politely, wiping blood from his face with a free hand.

"What did you do? He didn't deserve this," Rose snapped as she knelt beside the young man and began to fix his broken arm.

"I weakened a spot in the bones of his forearm so it would break when he struck me," Angst answered, surprised at her reaction.

"Since when could you do that?" asked Dallow with concern.

"I think I'm going to be sick," Tori mumbled between her fingers.

Rose grimaced. The man's arm straightened, snapping back into place with an unnatural jerk. She cried out as her arm cracked noisily. As though a hinge had been added between her wrist and elbow, the top of her arm fell over. Within moments, it reformed to a natural position. Rose wriggled her fingers before balling up a fist. She stood, angry and hot as the sun, and disgusted with both Angst and Victoria.

"You are on your own," she snapped.

Rose stomped over to the pretty waitress and said a few words, before giving the other woman a long hug and leaving the bar. The waitress smiled and waved as Rose walked away then sat down for a moment to catch her breath.

Angst looked at his other friends, who all shook their heads as they eyed the hot mess of drunken princess hanging on the much older man. Tarness smirked while Hector stared down his nose judgmentally. Dallow rolled his eyes.

"Good luck with that." Tarness chuckled, nodding at Tori.

Angst sighed and attempted to cover them both with his red cloak before stepping into the storm. Even as they shuffled their way through the entrance, he was amazed someone so light and tiny could be so unmanageable.

4

"Why did you do that, Angst?" the Royal Princess Victoria slurred.

She wrapped her left arm around his neck and reached up with her tiny right hand to grip his heavy cloak for additional support.

Was she holding herself up, trying to get his attention, or both? Whatever the reason, he gracelessly stumbled over protruding cobblestones to compensate for her new position, and tripped them both. Quickly righting himself, he only just had time to catch Tori, wrapping both arms around her in the process. They were an unceremonious mess of awkward, but Angst held her for a lingering moment before letting go. Tori laughed so drunkenly, he couldn't help but chuckle himself. She stopped laughing to stare at him, her thin eyebrows coming together with sincerity and concern.

"What did I do now?" Angst asked innocently, attempting to smirk against the biting winds. He pulled the thick red cloak tighter about his shoulders.

"He was so cute!" Tori said very loudly, stomping a little foot. "You shouldn't break them like that."

"I think you need less cute boys in your life right now," Angst said in an attempt to sound playful yet stern.

"You're jealous… Why are you jealous?" she teased, her thin brows furrowing. "I'm sure you were cute once too."

The backhanded compliment sank into his wrinkled pores, making Angst feel old, though he did his best to ignore it. He had to question what he was doing. Shouldn't he be at home with his pregnant wife instead of tripping through the streets of Unsel with the young princess? But he couldn't leave Tori in the bar, not like this, and not with that young monster who had to be brimming with ill intent. Aside from that, Angst needed some time to sober up before the long ride home on his swifen. A brisk walk to the castle would clear his head and numb his fresh bruises.

"I'm not jealous," he enunciated slowly, so he wouldn't sound quite as drunk as the princess.

They were still standing very close—to hear each other above the burgeoning storm, of course. Cold wind whipped her curly blond hair about his cheeks, but he could still make out Tori's eyes as she peered at him.

"Don't pretend you aren't drunk. I know everything, remember?" The words sloshed out of her mouth, and she lifted an eyebrow in mischief.

"Shh," he said, cognizant enough to look around them with concern. Angst attempted to whisper over the wind. "You don't know everything. You have no clue what I'm thinking now."

Victoria leaned forward and pressed her cheek against his. Angst took in a deep breath of surprise and the strawberry scent of her hair, paused for a moment then pulled away, making her giggle. Tori's touch, that connection, gave her great insight into a person's wishes, plans, and future.

"I would never do something like that!" Victoria said in shock. "Well, probably never." She giggled.

He realized his jaw was wide open when his tongue got cold. Snapping his mouth shut made her giggle again. His cheeks flushed, and he grasped desperately for what he'd been thinking. He concentrated through the haze of drink to remember her soft cheek, and how fond he was of her, and how worried that his time with her in his life would be so very brief.

"You are so full of bark, Angst," Victoria said with a melodic giggle. "You were thinking about how much you love me, and how much you'll miss me when I become queen." Her eyes became sincere. "You are my best friend, and nothing will ever change."

Victoria tucked herself into the nook of his arm, pulling herself as close as possible, as though it were suddenly important to hide from blustery winter. "Now stop worrying and bring me home."

Angst smiled to himself, enamored by her youth and innocence of the future she knew so much about. He gave her a sort of side hug. "Yes, Your Majesty."

* * * *

They arrived at the servants' entrance late that night, or very early the next morning, depending on your perspective. A lone soldier "guarded" from a chair that leaned far back against the cold stone entryway. He was half-awake, resting his hands on his portly stomach, yet still alert enough to scan them up and down slowly through squinted eyes and tilted helm. A wry smirk lifted his left cheek.

"Evening, Cedric," Angst called out, behind a port-filled burp.

"Angst," the guard said with a nod. He eyed the leaning princess. "Fun evening tonight?"

Victoria pulled Angst down to whisper in his ear, "I don't like what he wants. It's gross." She gripped her stomach.

Angst nodded at her and patted her hand where it clutched his shoulder. "Pardon us, Cedric. Early morning tomorrow."

"Of course." Cedric kicked one foot out to block the entrance. He scratched at his scruffy pointed chin with two fingers then extended them outward in a beckoning motion. "With the rumors and all, it would be a shame if, well, you know…"

Angst rolled his eyes and sighed. He dug into his pocket and pulled out a gold coin stamped with Queen Isabelle's profile. He set it between Cedric's hungry fingers, which smoothly hid the coin as though it were magicked to another place.

"Enjoy the rest of your...evening," Cedric said through his nose, giving Angst an approving nod and the princess a leering stare.

Angst wanted to beat some sense into the ass, but it was probably best to help the struggling princess to her chambers. After walking several feet into the castle, however, Tori stopped, stood tall, and pulled together her last remnants of regal fortitude. She looked at Angst with determined, bloodshot eyes.

"Wait here for one second," she said, as clearly as she could.

She wobbled over to Cedric and stared down at him long enough that he sat up nervously. The princess pulled out a threatening finger as the queen might, leaned over then vomited on the guard's armor. Victoria wiped her chin and patted it clean on Cedric's shoulder. She turned away and stumbled back to Angst, whose eyes were wide. They walked slowly down the long hallway, holding each other up as they listened to the guard's disgusted remarks.

"Feel better?" Angst asked, barely holding back a chuckle of surprise.

She merely nodded and smiled as they crept up the stairs to the royal chambers. Guards stood along the hallway at attention, avoiding eye contact at all costs. Angst's heart raced as the lights under Queen Isabelle and Captain Guard Tyrell's chambers went dark. Had they been waiting up for the princess? How much noise were Angst and Victoria making? He could suddenly hear every breath coming from his mouth, and the click of each boot step. He did not belong here.

At the entrance to the princess's chambers Angst paused. What was he supposed to do now? He pushed the doors open to find her room spacious and, fortunately, empty of people. A jungle of flung-off clothes covered the floor except for a rough path from the door to her bed. Angst's heart jumped, her room appeared ransacked, then he realized it had to be Tori's form of housekeeping. Despite the mess, a fire in the fireplace and candles along the walls made her room warm and too welcoming.

"Could you have someone bring us water, please?" Angst asked a guard in the hallway who seemed desperate for Angst not to exist. The wild-eyed guard's head snapped up in what could have been a nod of confirmation, or a shooing gesture to rid an annoying fly.

As Tori pulled a reluctant Angst into her room, he was certain each step forward brought him closer to doom. In a final burst of cognizant energy, she kicked the doors closed after they entered. They tripped and shuffled their way to her bed where she flopped unceremoniously across the breadth of the mattress to lie on her back. He stared at her, rocking back and forth on his heels drunkenly, as if holding a newborn in his arms. Tori's arms and legs were spread akimbo, with total disregard for anything princesslike, or even ladylike. Her storm-dampened cloak bunched beneath her, and he could tell she was struggling to breathe inside her corset. He also noticed she was pretty.

Angst waited, and sort of paced for several minutes that seemed like an hour, hoping a handmaiden would arrive to assist his drunken friend. It was warm, and he let his traveling cloak drop to the floor in a wet heap. Victoria lay still, unmoving as though dead. Angst frowned, walked to stand over her, and leaned closer to listen for breathing. The princess took unnaturally short breaths in her tight bodice. He decided to remove her boots.

Nobody slept in their boots, he reasoned, and she wouldn't question him pulling them off. The laces were confusing but, after many long moments and a few complaining groans from Tori, he set her wiggling toes free.

Oddly, that hadn't helped her breathing. He scanned her for something else he could safely do to help. Her cloak! Angst realized that the wet cloak was spread over her comforter. He struggled to gently roll the princess over and found she was suddenly a thousand pounds of dead weight. Victoria made the sincere attempt to assist his efforts by trying to hug him. He tugged and pulled the wet cloak from under her until it came free and Tori was rolled over, sprawled on her stomach. Angst threw the evil cloak to the floor in triumph.

Having succeeded in his heroic duties, Angst gathered himself to leave when he was stopped by the princess's whimper. He frowned. Removing the cloak had done nothing to help either. Her short, rapid breaths must be painful. He sighed as he stared at the ties of Victoria's bodice. They were slightly out of focus and appeared incredibly complex. Couldn't Chryslaenor have left him with some small bit of knowledge that imbued him with bodice lock-picking and drunk princesses?

He leaned forward again and almost fell on Victoria. Up till now Angst had avoided getting on the bed at all costs, but it seemed prudent to place a knee on her mattress. He closed one eye to better his focus and began untying, which required patience and coordination Angst didn't possess at that moment. This was truly a battle of wits that must have taken hours of concentration and surely required several handmaidens. No puzzle could have been more complicated.

Just as he reached the last eyelet, Angst realized he was undressing the princess. He briefly panicked, looking around the room guiltily before noticing she had a blouse on underneath. Angst sighed with relief as he uncoupled the last eyelet, finally rescuing his friend from its confines.

Victoria took in a deep sleeping breath and rolled to her back with a smile, revealing that her blouse was quite transparent, even in the dim candlelit room. Angst immediately lifted his hand, shielding his view of more than he should've seen. He was almost done—after he covered her with blankets he could sneak out, ride home, and start apologizing to Heather. Angst wondered where he could pick up flowers this time of night.

Angst leaned over to fight with her comforter. She lay deathly still, a heaped mass of thoroughly unhelpful princess. Eventually, he gave in and climbed onto her huge bed, his knees sinking down into the soft mattress. After several moments of struggling, Angst wrestled Tori so she was straight in her bed with her head resting on a pillow. With a courageous breath, he straddled her awkwardly, grabbed the comforter from either side of her with the ingenious plan of tugging it out from under her. He hovered over Victoria, using every bit of strength and will not to fall, or peek too much at the see-through blouse. Just as Angst made his second tug at the blankets, Tori reached up and gave him a bear hug, pulling him close.

Her young breasts rose and fell against his chest, and her husky breath labored in his ear. She mumbled as their cheeks met again, and her hands wandered freely along his back. Angst was embarrassed at being aroused while desperately kicking the blankets from under her. The scents of strawberry and alcohol were overwhelming, and he wanted nothing more than to hold her, lie next to her, and sleep.

With his last ounce of willpower, Angst pulled away, kneeing and kicking the covers until they were clear of her feet. Tori reached down and gripped his hands. Angst freed one hand to reach wildly for blankets. With great relief, he found one and covered her. The ordeal was over, and he began to pull away.

Tori shook her head from side to side and moaned loudly. Angst was at a loss. Was this the drinking? A premonition? He felt so tired, and wanted so much to just hold Tori, calm her worries, and sleep. He really couldn't stay. Angst desperately scanned the room and found a nearby chair, which he clumsily hooked with his ankle and dragged closer.

The princess continued to rock her head as he sat in the prim high-backed chair, utterly exhausted. When she clasped his hand and pulled it to her chest, he leaned forward awkwardly, waiting for the moment to pass. It didn't.

Tori's eyes snapped opened, and she stared directly at Angst. "Don't do it, Angst! Not another! Please don't! I need you. You can't leave me!"

"I won't, I promise. I won't leave you," he comforted.

His response seemed to be enough. Victoria gazed at Angst from behind her dreams, and smiled with concern in her eyes before falling back into her slumber. Her right hand fell to her side, but her left held his in a death grip.

"It's okay, Tori. I'm here," he said to console her. The alcohol, and the evening, and the warmth of the room enveloped him, and Angst's breathing slowed. "It's really okay. I won't ever leave you."

He searched the empty room and realized he was warm, comfortable, and holding the hand of his best friend. Angst looked down at Tori and sighed as her face relaxed. She was finally resting, finally at peace. He was free to leave her, free to head back home to his angry, pregnant wife. He blinked slowly, his eyelids heavy with sleep. Tori stretched luxuriously, though she didn't let go of his hand, and Angst couldn't help thinking how young and pretty she was. He longed for youth, desperate to be younger than forty. Victoria was so…refreshing. He blinked ever so slowly. What had she meant, not another? Was it talk from drinking or talk from her ability to see the future? Angst's eyelids drooped. He gripped her hand once, tightly, and thought, or maybe whispered, "I love you" and indulged in dreams of dragonslaying and maidensaving.

5

Someone gently shook Angst's shoulder, and he adjusted his position. A sharp twinge of achy muscle in his back forced his crusty eyes open, reminding him once again why it was such a bad idea to fall asleep in a chair. He battled with bleariness, certain his eyelashes must have been tied together. A chair? He looked around the opulent pink and ivory room. A blindingly bright sliver of light carved a dusty path of air to land at the foot of an ornate bed. Princess Victoria's bed. Which contained Princess Victoria, who was still holding his hand.

Angst fought dry mouth with a loud smack of his lips and winced slightly at the port-induced headache, which tried to puncture his brain from the inside. Someone shook his shoulder again, and he peered over slowly to find one of Victoria's blurry handmaidens.

"Mr. Angst," the woman sort of whispered in his ear. "Mr. Angst, you should not be in here." She shook him harder, staring at the hand holding Victoria's. "Sir, you should leave now."

What had he done? Angst blinked the stupor from his eyes then wiped at them with his free hand. The plump young handmaiden continued shaking his shoulder. When Angst stood and tried to pull away from her, Tori gripped his hand once then rolled over to return to a dead sleep. The handmaiden gasped at this display of affection, and Angst shuddered at the thought that it could have easily been Rose waking him. Her being one of

35

Victoria's new handmaidens was a bad idea for so many reasons.

"Thank you," he croaked to the young woman in a dry scratchy voice, and she quickly turned away to hide from his breath.

He badly needed a glass—no, a pitcher—of water, and could really use a bathroom. He looked around and found neither. For some reason, he gently patted the handmaiden on the shoulder before shuffling to the door. Stooping to pick up his moist red cloak made him feel a bit woozy, and he braced himself for the hallway lights. He opened the door a sliver, and turned back to make sure the princess was still sleeping soundly. Her handmaiden shooed him out. Angst smiled fondly at his friend, backed out the door, and gently closed it.

As he turned to leave, Angst faced a wall of angry faces so intimidating he considered going back into the princess's chambers. Four soldiers, Captain Guard Tyrell, and Queen Isabelle formed a straight line on the other side of the wide corridor. Tyrell and Isabelle stood in the center, their arms folded, their stares piercing deep into his guilt. After holding his breath for what felt like an hour, he remembered to bow jerkily. As much as his churning stomach would allow, anyway.

Angst began to prepare an apology when he noticed Tyrell's wild eyes and briskly shaking head. Even the soldiers, all of whom he knew, seemed to offer Angst warning glances. His mouth closed slowly, as though connected with a rusty hinge, and he swallowed dryness while awaiting his fate.

Queen Isabelle looked him up and down with disapproval. She hadn't even taken the time to put on formal attire or paint her face—not that it would have hidden the seething anger in her eyes nor the red flush of her cheeks. The queen stood before him in a yellow nightdress, fluffy purple robe, and matching purple fuzzy slippers. The scars around Isabelle's fake right eye made her appear even fiercer. She grunted in disgust then grabbed his arm tight behind the elbow, led him down the hallway, up a flight of stairs, and into the busiest passageway of the castle.

"The guards should have already killed you, Mr. Angst, and I just may do it myself." Her high-pitched voice screeched and echoed throughout the corridor. Everyone within earshot stopped what they were doing to listen. "Only because you are a hero of Unsel, only because I saw you *not* sleeping with my daughter, am I allowing you your life, but that gives you no right to take liberties with my trust! If I ever see you in the princess's chambers again, your execution will be amongst the most frightening events ever recorded in history! Am I clear?"

Angst's cheeks flushed with embarrassment and frustration. Once again, he opened his mouth to speak but then noticed something odd. The queen's piercing gaze kept flicking to the ground, beckoning him to stare at the floor with humility. He wanted to argue that he had kept Victoria safe from unsavory predators but for once, wisely, he ignored his instincts and stared at the ground.

"Yes, Your Majesty." His voice scratched at the air hoarsely.

He continued to stare at the floor as the queen began admonishing Tyrell and the soldiers.

She flipped a long lock of disheveled white hair over her shoulder before shaking her thick finger back and forth. "How this…this…magic-wielder could possibly be allowed in the royal hallway, much less the chambers of the royal princess, is beyond my understanding, Captain Guard. Don't think for a second that I hold Mr. Angst," she said with much spittle, "solely responsible! Are my private hallways guarded by the masons' guild now?"

"No, Your Majesty," Tyrell said, his head also bowed.

"Discipline will once more reign with your guards, starting with a daily sunrise march!" she squawked loudly.

Tyrell's head whipped up. "In this weather, Your Majesty?"

"Did I stutter?" she screamed.

"No, Your Majesty!" Tyrell replied, eyeing Angst with contempt.

"You and your men are dismissed!"

Tyrell leaned forward to Angst and huffed an angry, "thanks," before turning on his heel to march away. The soldiers spun about stiffly and followed.

"You, I'm not done with yet!" Queen Isabelle gripped Angst behind the elbow once more, pulled him into a nearby antechamber, and slammed the door shut.

The room was quiet, for which Angst's head was eternally grateful. He looked up from the floor to see the queen completely calm, no longer the threatening beast who had dragged him into the room by his elbow. Angst rubbed his eyes and smacked his mouth open.

"Please have a seat, Angst." She beckoned to a table with every ounce of courtesy she would offer a foreign statesman. She poured two glasses of water and set one at the opposite end of the table.

His eyes went wide, and his heart tried to leap through his constricted throat. Maybe he was still sound asleep in the princess's chambers? Would he wake up soon and have to experience this nightmare all over again? He sat gingerly, letting his stiff muscles and joints adjust to yet another chair. Angst drowned his mouth with water while eyeing the other glass.

"From the smell of your breath, I would recommend sips," the queen stated, waiting patiently.

"Yes, Your Majesty," he said between gulps. Sweat formed on his forehead as last night's drink began seeping out his pores.

"Thank you," Isabelle said sincerely.

"Your Majesty? I, um…" He let the words trail off.

"Raising a teenage daughter is a daunting task," she stated matter-of-factly, completely ignoring him. "Raising the future queen of Unsel is almost impossible. You may not remember, but once, not so long ago, I was that young princess. I was also a teenager. It's not easy being both, and often the needs of a teenager outweigh the requirements of being a princess."

She sighed, staring at him, waiting for this to sink in. Angst took another desperate gulp of water to replace his quickly dehydrating supply. Isabelle pushed her glass to him as he set his empty one on the table.

"Thank you, Your Majesty," Angst said apologetically.

"I am not only the queen. I'm a worried mother. I knew this would be a challenging time, and I now know what my parents went through when I was a teenager," Isabelle went on, with a surprisingly human look of guilt on her face. "Last night, late after you arrived, I peeked in to check on my daughter. I was... You surprised me, Angst. Again. I saw you, passed out in the chair, holding hands with my daughter."

Before Angst could reply in his defense, the queen held up her ringless hand to stop him.

"It could have been far, far worse. Another man would have taken advantage of the situation to position themselves as a potential consort, or husband, or simply to be cruel to a young woman for their own base needs." She shook her head in concern. "But there you sat, holding her hand like a friend... I'm amazed, and grateful."

"But," he said before having to gulp down a bit of his stomach. "The yelling?"

"Oh really, Angst, don't be such a baby. This isn't the first time I've yelled at you," she said with surprising candor. "Half the castle was already talking about how you slept with the princess last night. As her mother, as the queen, I can't let anyone assume I think that's okay. The princess's chamber doors will not be allowed open to just any man—with or without good intent."

Angst nodded, speechless, before taking several more gulps of water.

"I assume you are well enough to make it home. I have no doubt your pregnant wife will have more...yelling...for you," she said with a chuckle.

"Yes, Your Majesty. Thank you," Angst replied with a respectful nod.

"I suspect next time you will find it within yourself to make it out of her room before anyone sees you?" the queen asked. "There is a servants' entrance—"

"The next time, Your Majesty?" Angst interrupted.

"Tori mentioned you were bright. I'm hoping this is just the alcohol talking," the queen snapped, her patience wavering. "Unofficially, of course, I want you to make certain the princess arrives at home, if you are to find her again. I have a feeling she will find you, no matter what I do, so I would rather have her home safe. Is that understood?"

"Yes, Your Majesty. I will always do everything in my power to keep Tori...the princess safe," he replied quickly.

She paused for a long moment, pursed her lips then nodded once. "I believe you, Angst. Now, if you will accompany me to the door, I need to yell at you as you leave."

Angst smirked at this before frowning for those lingering in the hall. "Yes, Your Majesty."

* * * *

The queen had rewarded Angst's heroism in defending Unsel against the element of Magic with land and a sizeable cottage. The "reward" was a half-day's ride from the castle—and the princess—by horse...and an exhilarating hour by swifen. Cold wind whipped through his sweat-soaked hair, refreshing him to his core. The early-morning bite was enough to freeze his nostrils shut but, in spite of the hangover, he welcomed the awakening.

Angst struggled to formulate a thoughtful tale that would be less painful for Heather to hear. She wouldn't want to know he had spent the night in Victoria's chambers, no matter how noble or innocent his intent—her animosity for the princess was palpable for reasons he couldn't fathom. But nothing came to mind, his thoughts were overwhelmed by the foggy memories of last night with Victoria, and the crystal sharp memories of this morning with Isabelle, as he arrived on the stone-pathed hilltop of his cottage estate.

Angst dismounted his swifen and looked at the spellbound creature. It seemed shorter than when he'd chased the beam of magic from Fulk'han, and several pieces of patched rusty metal had appeared on the swifen's belly and flank, as though it were eroding with Angst's confidence. He dismissed the swifen, walked to the door, took a deep breath, and braced himself for yet another battle.

His boots echoed on the hard tile entryway. The tile was dark, and the wood-trimmed walls gave the room a warm closeness. Scar's nails clicked as the lab pup approached, his tail wagging so hard his butt rocked from side to side.

After giving the lab almost enough love by scratching its ears, Angst walked down a small hallway to the sitting room. A cozy fire burned in the fireplace, casting light and shadow on his wife's face as she sat awkward and uncomfortable on a brown longchair near the fire. From the entrance, Angst couldn't tell if she was asleep or awake except that she didn't move. Regardless, she shouldn't be sitting in such an unnatural position as though she hadn't meant to fall asleep in that chair. Her hand rested on her four-month baby bump, and she breathed deeply.

Angst knelt before Heather and put his hand on her knee. She lifted her head with a start, and he brushed curly brown and gray hairs from her face. Even as she opened her blotchy eyes, she seemed on the verge of tears.

"Angst," she said quietly, "you're okay."

"I'm fine, Heather. Let me help you to bed," he said guiltily.

"You smell like the Wizard's Revenge," she admonished in a sleepy voice. "I'm glad you're home safe. What happened?"

"Well I...I drank too much... I had to walk Tori home... I passed out." Angst looked at her with worry. "I'm sorry, Heather. I didn't... It was just..."

Heather held her hand to his mouth. "It's okay. I'm just glad you're home with me."

Angst helped her up and walked her to their bedroom. He pulled the quilts back from their bed and she crawled under the covers. She sighed as he covered her with blankets up to her shoulders.

"Are you going to join me?" she asked hopefully.

"Of course," Angst lied. "Let me first get cleaned up so I don't get you drunk from my port breath."

Heather smiled and squeezed his hand before rolling to her side. Angst waited for several moments until her deep breathing became a gentle snore then snuck out of their bedroom and returned to the main-room. He kicked off his boots, let his damp cloak drop to the floor, and fell to the couch. Guilt was poor bedcompany, and Angst stared at the fire. The quiet of the room made his ears ring, and his stomach burned from his hangover and mistakes.

If only she had yelled. It would have been so much easier to justify his actions had Heather gotten angry, but she hadn't. Angst's thoughts were torn between his uncomfortably pregnant wife, who was usually upset, and his best friend, who was young, and pretty, and probably still drunk in her bed. His eyelids grew heavy as he stared at the flickering warmth and light in the fireplace.

Wouldn't it be easier if Heather hated him? Wouldn't it be easier if Tori wanted him? Wouldn't it be easier if he were younger? Wouldn't it be easier if he were bonded with Chryslaenor once more?

It was never easy, and neither was his slow descent into dreamless sleep.

6

Trepidation crept up Angst's spine and tickled the base of his skull as he entered the maidens' courtyard. He looked around to gather his bearings, and couldn't quite place what was wrong. His was an inside-out sort of déjà vu, having just experienced a future in which the courtyard was destroyed. Angst stepped forward slowly, cautiously. He heard the fountain bubbling instead of flame from dragonmaw flying overhead. He saw planters filled with out of season flowers and not a chasm at his feet. Everything appeared fine, for now.

Usually the first to arrive at the empty courtyard, Angst raised an eyebrow with concern when he saw a young woman sitting at the fountain. He avoided eye contact, frantically trying to recall if this was the right day. This place was always off limits to men, save for his weekly meeting with the princess, a reluctant "gift" from Queen Isabelle after he'd helped save her and Unsel.

His eyes flickered back and made contact. The young woman smiled wryly at his approach. She stood and sauntered over to him, unconcerned by his presence in the courtyard.

"You must be Angst, the hero my cousin's always talking about," she said, holding out a dainty hand that sported a rather large ruby ring.

Angst was taken aback by the cousin reference, but quickly composed himself as she was quite striking. He took her hand, bowed, and kissed it for an almost lingering moment, completely missing the ring.

"I am Angst," he confirmed with a genuine smile, trying as hard as he could to maintain eye contact and not take in the full view.

"It's a pleasure to meet you, Mr. Angst," she replied in an airy voice. She did not retrieve her hand. "I'm Alloria."

Angst failed; he had to look. Though it was hard to be certain, Alloria appeared several years younger than Victoria. She was just as thin, yet much curvier. Her long, light brown hair fell about her tanned shoulders in waves. Alloria's ice blue bodice fit snugly about her tiny waist, greatly accentuating her curvy hips and abundant breasts. Her thin eyebrows arched with intent, and her full pouty lips were painted dark red, seemingly poised to kiss at any given moment. Where Victoria was alluring, Alloria was arousing, and Angst couldn't hold back his blush or the intake of breath in awe of her youthful beauty.

Alloria did not shy away from his reaction. Unlike Victoria, she seemed to revel in it. Still holding Angst's hand, she pulled him to the nearby bench and sat. "My cousin's going to be several minutes. Please, join me."

Certain his palm was sweating, Angst tried pulling it gently away, but she wouldn't let go. She was royalty, she was beautiful, and Angst didn't want to be rude, of course, so he sat next to her. She rested their hands on her knee, which made him lean closer, and stared deep into his eyes. Angst drew in a deep breath of not-gawking-at-cleavage willpower and swallowed hard before leaning back.

"Victoria never told me what pretty eyes you have," Alloria said in her light voice.

"I think she's always been more impressed by my height," Angst replied with a smirk, desperately seeking the safe ground of humor.

Alloria chuckled, sat upright and tugged at her bodice to straighten it. "She mentioned you were cute, and funny—"

"That's because I am," Angst interrupted with a cocky smile, not understanding her game and beginning not to enjoy it.

Alloria's eyes widened in surprise, and she tried to cover his faux pas with an uncomfortable giggle.

Just as she began to speak again, Angst cut in. "I do that," he said with a smirk.

"You did it again! You interru—"

"Isabelle hates it," he said, letting go of her hand.

Alloria's face paled. "You speak of your queen like she's a commoner."

"I am the commoner, Alloria, though not a common one." He winked. Alloria might very well have been one of the most beautiful women he'd ever seen, so it required extra focus to realize she wanted something. "While it's very nice of you to wait with me, I have to wonder why I have the pleasure of your company."

Angst was happy to see he'd taken her off guard, though she recovered quickly. "The queen asked me to tell you not to use magic this afternoon during the ceremony," she said.

Angst nodded once, though surprised by this edict and by Isabelle's choice of messenger.

"Is it true, that you are inflicted...er, can do magic, with stone? That you can make things?" Alloria asked, looking at Angst with large, hopeful eyes.

Angst was still wary, but Alloria was cute and so he allowed himself to take the bait. He lifted his hand, which glowed with a faint aura, and a small stone bird grew from the ground at Alloria's feet. She seemed in shock as fine detail appeared on the bird's feathers. It blinked and hopped toward her as though alive. Angst laid his hand on the ground, and the small stone bird jumped onto his glowing palm. Alloria gasped, and smiled, leaning toward him for a closer look. Angst enjoyed her reaction and decided to play for a moment.

The bird's wings stretched open and fluttered. Angst concentrated on the stone, and the air surrounding it, and watched with pleasure as the bird flapped its wings and flew.

"Oh my!" she said with surprise. Alloria had forgotten about Angst and was completely lost in the moment. "It's so beautiful."

Angst smiled to himself, proud he'd figured out the balance between stone and air without the help of a foci. The small bird flew about the courtyard with grace—floating between pillars, rising high then diving fast to hover before Alloria's hand. Her palm was closed in a fist, unwilling to open. Angst urged the stone bird to bump her, and she lashed out, knocking it to the ground where it shattered.

"Oh Angst, I'm sorry, I'm not used to magics…" She sat up straight, her composure and control completely lost.

For a brief moment, Angst saw the young woman with her guard down. Exposed, she seemed more a person and less royalty, which made him like her for more than her looks.

"Nothing to worry about," he said with a smile. Angst walked over to the pile of broken stones and willed them back into the original shape. When he sat beside her once more, he handed the unmoving stone bird to her.

"Mr. Angst, that was amazing. Thank you," Alloria said genuinely, hesitantly accepting the gift.

She took a moment to smile at the small marble carving as though it were alive then gripped the bird tight in her hand. She appeared guilty, ashamed of something. Alloria looked about the courtyard as if in anticipation. Was she expecting an earthquake? Was Alloria trying to recreate the moment he'd had with Victoria so many years before? His control over magic was far stronger now. Even without Chryslaenor, he could use a great amount of magic without fear of side effects. It wasn't the same as being bonded to the foci—the raw power, the fountain of knowledge, and the companion were gone—but he could still do many things.

"Um, Angst?" Alloria pointed to his face.

Angst looked down and lifted his hand to wipe blood from under his nose. Of all the times to get a bloody nose…now? Angst was embarrassed, and began sniffing loudly and breathing in deeply, hoping to dry out the trickle. He looked at Alloria and shrugged, making her giggle, then wiped his hand on his trousers.

She took the hand that still had a bit of dried blood on it. "Are you okay?" she asked with genuine concern.

Angst nodded awkwardly, in spite of a dull thud beating the inside of his temples. "Really, I am. I don't know what Victoria did, or didn't tell you, but things are different without Chryslaenor," Angst said, unsure why he was suddenly comfortable enough to open up.

Angst shared highlights of his time with the great sword. He couldn't help but notice how close she sat, how full her lips were, and how she smelled almost too pretty. Aside from that, she listened, and seemed genuinely interested. Angst was a bit baffled why this young woman wasn't flirting with knights or courting with dukes instead of listening to him, but the concern was fleeting as her attention was on him.

As he finished his story, he noticed a tear dripping down her cheek and wiped it with the back of a finger. "Did I say something wrong, Alloria?"

"That was just... It's just that you sacrificed everything you'd always wanted," she said, disbelief in her wide azure eyes.

"That's what you do for the people you love, right?" he said matter-of-factly.

Now she really began to cry, and Angst held in a disparaging sigh. It had felt like the right thing to say, but it seemed to have upset her even more.

"Alloria, what's wrong?" Angst asked.

"I'm just...very alone. I lost my family last week when Cliffview collapsed into the ocean. I haven't been able to talk about it until now, but..." She gripped his hand tight.

"Alloria, I'm sorry. I hadn't heard," Angst said, patting her back as she leaned forward to cry on his shoulder. "What happened?"

"We were on vacation, getting ready to leave, when the entire city fell into the ocean. My parents died, everyone died. I was the only one who made it." She began sobbing again.

"I'm so sorry." Angst made soothing noises, while contemplating what could have caused such an incredible disaster.

Several moments passed as Alloria struggled to regain composure but eventually she pulled back and looked at Angst gratefully with her large, wet eyes.

"Angst, are you still in here?" Victoria stomped into the courtyard with stormy exasperation. "Whoever sent me clear across the castle with a fake message from my mum will be marched in the cold winter with Tyrell's guard!"

She charged to the bench where Angst sat holding Alloria's hand and gawked. In his entire life, Angst had never seen such a tornadic combination of emotions in any one person. Shock, dismay, frustration, anger, disappointment, and catty were all rolled up into a curt smile and squinted eyes that glared at the small marble bird resting in Alloria's hand. Alloria gripped the bird tight, as though it were the only thing she owned.

She stood, pulling away from Angst, and curtsied. "Your Majesty," Alloria said respectfully. She looked at Angst with surprise as he stared, at a loss for how to react.

"Thank you for attending my friend, cousin," Victoria stated sharply. She eyed Alloria's attire. "I'm sure he appreciated every moment."

"Yes, Your Majesty," she replied, staring at the ground. After several moments, Alloria looked back and forth between Victoria and Angst, apparently contemplating whether to say anything. "Thank you," she said to Angst with a smile before leaving the courtyard.

"It was nice meeting you." Angst stood and bowed politely.

Victoria smacked him in the chest. "Holding hands?" Tori asked with raised eyebrows.

"I thought it was a…royalty…thing," Angst replied.

"It's not," Tori said tersely.

"Too bad," he played, desperately trying to salvage the morning.

"Well, if you like, I can arrange for you to hold hands with my mother," Victoria snapped.

"Upset about something?" Angst asked, returning her raised eyebrow.

"No," Victoria replied too quickly, looking at the door Alloria had exited through.

"Look, I—"

"Don't," Victoria interrupted. "Don't worry about it. Do what you want, you always do. But I don't trust her."

"She didn't seem that bad," Angst stated in surprise.

"I'm sure," Victoria replied before saying more calmly, "She wasn't, but something's changed."

"I'll be wary," Angst said, frowning. He wanted to say more, but the moment seemed to have passed.

Victoria recounted her day, sharing in great detail her concerns of court and country. The burdens of title rested heavily on her shoulders. Angst wanted to hold her, and rock her, and take away the pain in any way he could, which meant he spent this time listening and nodding. It was impossible to be everything for everyone, and more impossible to be anything for her other than a shoulder.

At the end of her half-hour rant, her shoulders dropped a quarter-inch. Victoria had let it all out, and he could tell that, if nothing else, she had found more even footing.

"Are you okay? How do you feel?" the princess asked with concern.

With a deep sigh, Angst compressed his concerns and pain and frustrations into the five minutes he knew she could handle. Victoria meant well, but she was also only nineteen, without the experience and years Angst had struggled through. Still, he was happy with what he could get, and what she graciously offered.

"So, are we, you know, okay? Was it weird? Did I do anything I shouldn't?" Angst rambled on for several moments, attempting to share his concerns about stumbling drunk to her room, undressing her, and passing out while holding hands. His awkward query was met with a dumbfounded look.

"You're fine, Angst," Victoria said dismissively. "Thanks for seeing me home safe."

That was it? The young man beating him in the face, the queen screaming at him in front of…everyone? Heather's pure, unabashed hatred of their friendship? All she had to say was thanks?

"You're welcome," Angst replied simply. He sniffed, and could smell the iron in his nostril.

She looked at him and smiled warmly then gave him a long hug that he returned in full.

"So...are things still broken?" Angst asked quietly, looking around the courtyard.

"I just...I don't understand it, Angst. I can't see things like I did," Victoria said in frustration. "Some visions fit, and still make sense. But others don't. I can only see some of what you're thinking now, just bits and pieces. I can't read Alloria at all, but I can read my mom and Tyrell clearly. It's so frustrating."

The princess looked ready to cry and Angst hugged her again. "It's okay. There's a lot going on," he said consolingly. "I'm sure it's temporary."

Victoria nodded. "I need to go. Be very careful around Alloria. She doesn't have your best interests in mind."

"I promise," Angst said with all the sincerity he could muster.

After several moments of deciding whether his response was genuine, Victoria replied, "When you're done thinking about her giant boobs, please remember what I said."

Angst tried his best to look shocked, which made Victoria laugh out loud. "I'll see you this afternoon, at the thing?"

"Yes." He nodded somberly. "I promise."

7

Dignitaries, knights, the queen, and her advisors filled the large hall, which had hosted the banquet honoring Angst and his friends only months ago. The blanket of silence covering those attending made the room so quiet, Angst was certain he could hear a servant sweeping a hallway at the other end of the castle. His cough echoed throughout the chamber, and he swallowed loudly. Heather's nudge against his armor was louder yet, flushing her cheeks red and making her more upset at Angst.

Whatever forgiveness she had felt after he'd returned from Victoria's bedchamber faded when he arrived home after his morning meeting with the princess. As though she had suddenly come to her senses, Heather had given Angst a verbal beating that would have made the queen wince. As usual, it succeeded in doing nothing more than making him argue back until he was done and simply stopped. The swifen ride to the castle was tense as dragonhide, and as palatable as Angst's cooking.

Angst looked around the room warily. Sitting here for this occasion with these people was like sitting naked on a rocky shore. Everyone was surely staring and he couldn't adjust enough to find comfort, least of all with Heather beside him. Angst had tried pleading with the queen, and then Victoria, and finally Heather to let him stay away, out of sight, or possibly out of country. But they would have none, and so Angst sat in the front row, in armor that wasn't made for sitting, wishing some emergency could take him away from Ivan's funeral.

Six knights in full armor knelt and set a closed, empty casket mere feet from Angst and his friends. The knights stood to attention, bowed respectfully to the queen, and went to stand in line with other knights attending. Queen Isabelle's face was somber as she rose from her throne and slowly moved to the ornate gold and mahogany casket. She closed her eyes and rested her hand on the casket as though preparing to raise the dead. In her other hand, she gripped a large scroll tight to the point of shaking.

When Isabelle opened her eyes, they focused on Angst for but a second. Her mouth tightened, and he braced for a storm of words. Heather squeezed his hand, and a bead of sweat trickled between his shoulder blades. The queen and Angst sighed in unison before she stepped to Tyrell and handed him the scroll.

Tyrell unrolled the document and began to read. "We lay to rest a Knight of Unsel, Sir Ivan, whose deeds, accomplishments, and services will not be forgotten. Always, Sir Ivan fought to protect Unsel from foes and villains. His good nature, courage, and honor show all knights what they can achieve. For his legacy, and his family, we will recognize the titles and honors bestowed on Sir Ivan.

Knight of Unsel
Stalwart Hero of the Realm
Champion of the Vivek
Keeper of Unsel..."

Angst wanted to vomit. He looked at Rose sitting next to him, at her small, pale fists shaking with anger. Her fingernails dug deep into her palms, and Angst reached over to stop her. Rose seemed taken off-guard, not pulling her hand away from his as she normally would. She looked at Angst with large, dark eyes filled with bitterness and frustration. Still holding her wrist, he turned it over to look at the damage to her hands. There was blood, but the wounds had already healed. Rose jerked her hand away and nodded toward Tyrell. Angst wanted to ask what she thought she was doing, but turned to face the Captain Guard as instructed.

CHAPTER SEVEN

"Guardian of the Domain
The Exemplar Citation
Victor in the Battle of Hemsid
Feather of Valor…"

Angst adjusted once more, as respectfully as he could, and did his best to swallow a large yawn. There was one fortunate side effect of the armor—it wouldn't let him slouch. He looked around the room, which had a surprising turnout for a man everyone had to hate as much as Angst did. It just made no sense. Had Ivan really been this popular? Had this many people really liked him? More likely, this was some sort of pomp and bureaucracy Angst had no desire to understand.

His gaze found Victoria and Alloria, both of whom stared at the floor in respectful repose. What if Ivan truly had been as pretty as the picture Tyrell was painting? Was it possible he had started on a path of good intentions, no different from Angst? Could it be that magic and power had corrupted Ivan that much? Or was he really just an ass who happened to do his job, and the crown was giving a little credit to save face?

As though feeling his gaze, Alloria looked up, briefly making eye contact with Angst. She winked before returning her gaze downward. Even before he could smirk, Heather had let go of his hand and pinched it hard. Angst stifled a yelp and crossed his arms defensively.

"All of these things were accomplished and earned by Sir Ivan. His hard work and perseverance will always be remembered. A true hero to the end." Tyrell finished with a bow of his head. His tone had remained both sincere and unemotional throughout the eulogy.

Several knights and one duke stood to give similar, fortunately shorter, speeches. Each brought Angst closer to the abyss of deep nod though neither Angst nor his friends had any choice but to remain alert and respectful since the queen had placed them front and center. The final speaker was an old knight Angst did not recognize. His armor seemed ancient—polished silver etched in great detail with ornate golden leafy flourishes. His

53

height, chiseled features, and haughty nature made him so familiar that all Angst's friends tensed. Before saying anything, the
man stared each of them down with an angry scowl, finishing
with a sneer at Rose.

"No man wishes to outlive his son, but how could I be more
proud? Ivan once again proved himself to be the hero Unsel
needed. How could I ask for a greater honor than that which my
son has bestowed upon me?" Ivan's father took a deep, pained
breath.

"I didn't even realize old Vars was still alive." Hector leaned
forward and whispered between Angst and Rose. "The man is
crazier than Ivan ever was. I'd recommend ignoring everything
he says and find a happy place."

"He was the last of my bloodline to carry the family torch
through the ranks of knighthood. His death is a great loss, not
only to me but also to our entire kingdom. I taught Ivan myself
how to deal with the... undesirables, the criminals among us, the
true danger that is hard to ignore." He stared directly at Angst.

Angst's jaw clenched. He wanted to leave, but Hector's restraining hand on his shoulder kept him in place. He glanced at
Victoria, who was making shocked eye contact with a young
man standing nearby. Her gaze moved to Angst, and she shook
her head, pleading with her eyes for him to refrain from anything
foolish.

Vars smirked and looked about the room with wild wide eyes
that made most shift uncomfortably in their uncomfortable seats.
"I've heard many stories about my son's death. Many stories
about the magics," he said with a growly whisper. He stared at
Angst and Rose. "But I know my son! I know Ivan would have
died before becoming a pawn of that infliction!"

Tyrell was now standing behind the man, a sign that Vars's
moment to speak was over. "There is nary one man who can deny my son's heroism," he said loudly, pointing to everyone in
the crowd. "And nary one man who can prevent the wake of re-
sults from his charge to do right."

Tyrell pulled the larger man back, firmly yet gently, and ushered him to his seat. Vars stared at the casket with a lost expression, tears streaming openly down his wrinkled cheeks.

* * * *

Angst wanted to slap the man across the mouth for raising such a bully, and for being such a blithering idiot.

"He obviously wasn't told what actually happened," he said, pacing their corner of the room. "We came to the funeral. Do we really need to stay for the wake too?"

"It's polite to stay for a little while, Angst," Heather said apologetically.

Hector and Dallow were doing their best to calm Rose, who seemed poised to launch herself at Ivan's father. Tarness stood by Angst, gnawing on a turkey leg in one hand and gulping from a goblet of mead in the other. Angst stopped his pacing to look at his munching friend, glancing at the food, and the drink, and then at Tarness, who shrugged with a lopsided grin.

"What? Idiots make me hungry," Tarness stated without an ounce of apology.

"You're right, Tarness," Angst said with a nod and a chuckle. "Maybe I should shake this off. It's done. We risked everything to save Unsel, and probably the rest of Ehrde. That should be enough, right? Thanks for reminding me."

Angst smiled at everyone and, with a nod, left to wander the crowd.

"Is that really what I meant?" Tarness asked around a mouthful of turkey.

"Now I'm not sure who's crazier, Angst or Vars," Rose replied, shaking her head in dismay.

Angst ignored the crowd in search of Victoria. After the speech by Ivan's father, people made extra room for him as he waded through to seek her out. Wasn't it her job to save him from these things?

He exchanged his empty goblet of mead for a full one from a passing tray and continued wandering until he saw her long hair, which was black once again. The crowd shifted to make a clear path for him to his friend. Victoria was looking up, nodding, and flirtatiously patting the arm of a tall young man standing in front of her. Angst's face felt flush.

"That's the cutest thing I think I've ever seen," Alloria said behind him with a giggle.

Angst spun around to see the young woman sipping deeply from her goblet. Her funeral attire was form-fitting and low cut, and he could only hope his own funeral was honored with equal vigor. He once again willed himself to maintain eye contact and smirked.

"Your Majesty," he said, only a little mockingly. "What would that be?"

"Your ears," she declared, reaching up to touch the top of one with her finger. "They turn very red when your cheeks flush."

They became even warmer, and he looked at the ground, embarrassed. She giggled again and clapped her hands briefly as though she had won a contest.

"Your armor is different than everyone else's." She walked around him to look more closely, running a finger along the open spot behind one of his arms and making Angst shiver slightly.

"That's so I can make birds out of stone." When he saw she didn't completely understand, he leaned closer to whisper, "The armor is designed for people who do magic. Armor like this hasn't been worn for a very long time."

Alloria smiled at this and nodded, apparently impressed. "Well, you look very handsome," she said warmly. "I think what that man said about you, and magic, was just awful."

"I agree! That's not how it happened at all!" The words burst out of Angst. Alloria had triggered exactly what he'd been trying to repress. He did his best to rein himself in. "We didn't want this for Ivan, but he chose his path," he whispered harshly.

"That's exactly what Victoria said," Alloria agreed. "Though the queen seems to have mixed feelings about what happened."

"That doesn't surprise me," Angst said. "But it doesn't matter. My heroing days seem to be over."

"I wouldn't be so sure," Victoria said as she approached from behind Alloria with the young man in tow.

Angst smiled at her, until he realized she wasn't smiling back. He turned around to see that Vars had found his friends. Ivan's father was yelling at Hector while holding Rose at arm's length. Why was Hector being diplomatic when Rose was in danger?

"Hey, aren't you Angst?" asked the young man standing beside Victoria. He squinted at Angst as though he recognized the older man.

"Unfortunately, yes," Angst said with a sigh as he made his way to Ivan's father.

Alloria had moved to get a better look and now stood between him and his friends. It took several precious moments to set her aside gently. Angst was once again angry with Vars, and the familiar surge of power coursed through him. Moving Alloria reminded him he wasn't supposed to use magic, and he calmed that power, balling his fists as he stomped toward the group instead.

The tall man reached back with his free hand, winding up to strike Rose in the mouth. Angst grabbed the man's wrist, but without magic, or even the visible shock of wielding a giant sword, it simply wasn't enough. Vars swung wildly, pulling his hand free and punching Rose hard in the face.

As quickly as she reeled and fell to the ground, Tyrell and Tarness were on Vars, shoving him against a nearby wall.

"You killed my son!" the crazed man yelled at Angst. "It was your magics that tainted him."

Angst dropped to his knees by Rose and watched as she forced her broken jaw back into place. It didn't take long for the wound to heal, but he could tell it hurt all the same. Angst felt pangs of guilt for her tears.

The guards pulled Vars away, dragging the kicking man from the wake. Tyrell turned to Rose, his stern face actually showing concern. "Are you all right?"

Rose nodded, holding her jaw with her hand while she

opened and closed her mouth. Seemingly healed, she stood and dusted off her dress, avoiding all eyes with embarrassment large on her face.

"Rose, I'm sorry, I didn't think he..." Angst trailed off as he realized he didn't know what to say.

"Where were you when I needed you, Angst?" Rose asked angrily. She stared at him, waiting for an answer. When it was obvious he had none, she stomped out of the room.

Everyone was quiet, staring at Angst and his friends. He turned away from them and kept his eyes on the ground to avoid looking at anyone.

"It's okay, Angst," Heather said consolingly. "Maybe this just isn't for you anymore."

And with that, Angst's heart sank its last inch.

8

"I think it's time for you to leave," Queen Isabelle said thoughtfully, tapping her chin with a finger. "All of you."

Angst swallowed a bit of shock and confusion, wondering exactly what she meant by this proclamation. He stared at the queen, searching her face and form for a clue, but she gave nothing away. Even her clothes were carefully neutral. Her conservative, high-necked dark brown dress had long sleeves and only a bit of piping to accentuate the curves she wanted to share. The dress was not attractive, she was not attractive, but her outfit was smart and to the point. She looked every inch a queen whereas, after the events at the wake, he felt terribly silly wearing armor made for a hero in front of her.

He looked over at his friends instead, only to find his surprise and disappointment mirrored in their faces as they toyed with the breakfast that really wasn't a breakfast at all. A handful of yesterday's pastries rested in the middle of the table, visibly drying before their eyes. Whatever frosting or filling once decorated their delicate crusts had sunk and spread into an oily mess. Tarness had stopped mid-chew at Isabelle's announcement.

Finally, Angst sought out Tyrell, who stood behind Isabelle's left shoulder and nodded in agreement.

"Once again, we need your help," she said to everyone around the table.

"Of course, Your Majesty," Hector replied on their behalf

with a deep bow of his head. "We are at your service."

Tyrell walked over to the nearby door, opened it, and ushered in the young man Victoria had been hanging on at the wake. He had blond hair with dark roots, a firm jaw, and alert blue eyes that took note of everything. The man was in his younger thirties, and thin enough that his cheeks sank in slightly. Angst did not see anything about him that was flirt-worthy and immediately distrusted his presence.

"Cliffview is gone, and our friend Jaden was there at the time of its destruction," Tyrell explained.

Jaden looked at Angst for a long moment, apparently trying to understand the older man's obvious annoyance at him. He avoided eye contact with Angst for the rest of the meeting as everyone else seemed more than appreciative of his presence. Angst closed his eyes and listened as Jaden began his tale.

* * * *

Something shook Jaden to reluctant consciousness. He felt numb, cold to the core, and did not want to budge. Another jarring movement made him open an eye. His long arms and legs were sprawled across the ground as though he rested on a down mattress. He lifted an arm that was wiry yet muscular, and ran his hand through his wavy blond hair. None of this made any sense; he could barely remember his name. Everything else was hazy. He bent his stiff neck from side to side to see who was trying to wake him.

The frigid damp of the cobblestones beneath him seeped into his bones and joints, bringing with it the ache of old age or great exertion. It all hurt, he hurt, and he didn't have a clue where he was or what he was doing there. Jaden pushed himself up slowly to all fours, making sure the numbness in his elbows and knees wasn't damaging. There were eyes on him, and mumbles from a gathering crowd that watched from a distance.

Jaden had been asleep, or passed out, in an alley. He hadn't yet been asked, or forced, to leave—but despite the bitter cold, those passing by on the nearby road stopped to take notice. Jaden shivered and peered out the alley. Through the crowd, he glimpsed sea, or ocean. The ground shook violently. He rested his bare hands on the cold cobblestone and closed his eyes to concentrate for several moments.

"Oh, this isn't good at all," he muttered to himself.

Jaden worked his way onto his feet, forcing his muscles to move. Everything ached as though he were ill. There wasn't time to be sick, though he fervently wished for time to find warmer clothes. The sleeveless leather armor he wore offered little protection against the wet and biting air, and he definitely didn't have time to warm himself in other ways.

Jaden slowly moved out of the alley, pressing past the curious to approach a sturdy iron guardrail. Even the weather couldn't mar the view. He stood on the edge of a cliff and, far below, a body of water stretched forever into a gray horizon. On either side of him, along the u-shaped edges of the tall cliff, were rows and rows of buildings and houses. They surrounded the scenic view, built on levels carved into the side of the cliff like observers seated in a stadium, looking down on the ocean as though it was a mere show for their amusement. The buildings were high enough to be protected from the torrential onslaught of violent waters, yet close enough to hear the crash of the waves, the sounds of the sea. He breathed deep and took in the smell of sea air, thick and salty, and the cool dampness spread through his lungs, just as it seemed to cover the city.

Jaden turned to face the crowd with growing worry. Everyone shuffled about nervously, but they seemed more concerned with his shoddy appearance and choice of campsite than the earthquakes. A dozen or so businessmen and guildies had joined the ranks peering at the spectacle.

"You look lost, son," a blacksmith in a heavy leather apron said.

"Don't you understand? Can't you feel it? You're all in danger!" Jaden burst out frantically.

Another tremor made Jaden hold his hands out as though the

very air would assist him in keeping balance. Several of the gatherers laughed.

"It's been doing this for weeks, young man. A bad winter storm, nothing else. Go have some more mead and sleep it off," gruffed a surly overweight mason in patchwork clothes, waving Jaden off like a bug before walking away.

Jaden shook his head frantically. He turned back to the spectacular view of the violent violent sea and leaned far over the iron railing. The ocean pounded the cliff base with nearly palpable hate and disdain. Massive tidal waves crashed into the foundation, pulled back, then attacked again. He stared in disbelief and awe. The waves looked like open hands, reaching for the cliff and ripping it away. His mouth hung open and he pointed at the watery hands, peering at the people and their dumbfounded looks.

"This...this can't be normal?"

Tremor.

"'Tis a bad storm is all, lad. Now move along. You're scaring people," stated a calm and resolute middle-aged woman.

Jaden shook with frustration, or the ground shook with another tremor, or both happened at once. But this one was bigger yet, as the ocean continued to pound and dig away at the rock below. This time, the crowd looked at one another with surprise. A man who was too tall, standing a head higher than Jaden's six feet, forced an unconvincing smile onto his gaunt face and aimed it at Jaden. The man looked to be a hundred, or no age at all, with his bald head and hairless face. His long brown robes flailed about wildly in the stormy wind.

"What are you doing with your hands, son?" The ageless man nodded at Jaden's hands, which were still held out before him as though to keep himself from falling.

"My hands?" Jaden looked down at his hands, and guiltily pulled them back to his sides. "I... Nothing. I just—" His words were interrupted by a string of violent quakes, followed by a loud crack.

Several in the crowd stumbled and fell while others dropped

to their knees. The guardrail wrenched loudly. Jaden jumped away from the edge, landing by the man as a thin sliver of cliff behind him pulled away, dragging the railing down with it.

"These tremors were never this bad, not until you arrived!" the ageless man accused loudly. He grabbed Jaden in a fierce grip and pointed at his hands. "What were you doing with your hands? Is this your magics?"

At the end of town, several buildings resting along the edge of the cliff teetered, forward and back and forward once more, before giving way, yielding to the wrath of the angry sea. Houses and buildings and people fell to the watery darkness below, instantly consumed as storm and erosion washed away all signs of life. Within a held breath, they were gone, leaving nothing behind but naked stone.

The ageless man with the awkward smile pulled Jaden close and rasped in his ear. "You probably have time to save yourself," he said. "Probably."

Jaden didn't understand. He pulled himself free of the man's grip and looked at the crowd. Anger and blame were quickly replacing the expressions of shock. Jaden could sense the emptiness behind him—with the safety of the guardrail gone, any of them could push him over the edge with little effort. The ground quaked and, as the crowd braced itself, Jaden dove through it.

"Run," he yelled back as he sprinted as fast as his stiff joints would allow.

Ground crumbled beneath his feet and pulled away as he ran up the stairs to the next level of buildings. The screams he left behind were horrific as the sea claimed more lives. Jaden kept shouting his warnings, his heart racing in panic and exhaustion. He grabbed a broom handle leaning against a building and pounded on the doors he ran by, though there wasn't enough time to see if his warnings did anything more than startle occupants. His path ahead was unknown, and he was being chased by chaos.

"You have to leave now! You're all in danger!" he pleaded as he leaped up the stairs to another level and sprinted along a crowded road.

He passed people stunned by the utter devastation left in his wake. The city behind him was falling apart, and the fools stood and watched. Jaden was living a nightmare, unable to command anyone's attention. As though he were running past statues of people already dead.

Stone crumbled behind him as he struggled to find solid ground with each step. The cliff beneath him pulled away, forcing him to scramble on his hands and knees. With a final leap, he grasped an outcropping of stone and hung on the side of the cliff, his feet dangling freely beneath him. Jaden refused to look down at the ocean below even though the tremors had stopped. He heaved himself over the side and crawled away from the edge until he could no longer move. Jaden lay there for several minutes, shivering from the rush of fear and exhaustion.

He felt as though he had almost drowned in the madness of it all. As though the sea had purposefully eaten the entire city, stopping only after licking its plate clean. All that remained was an empty horseshoe-shaped cliff overlooking a calm sea. Jaden sat up and stared in disbelief. The ocean was calm. Maybe he truly had gone mad. He stood shakily and took a deep breath.

"Is anyone here?" Jaden yelled loudly. "Is anyone still alive?"

* * * *

"I spent hours walking back and forth along the edge of the cliff, searching for survivors, but found nothing. There were no signs of life, nor signs there ever had been life. All that remained was a spectacular view of calm waters from the edge of a tall cliff." Jaden appeared visibly flustered by the retelling of his story.

"I wasn't able to save anyone. Though they accused me of everything that happened, they didn't deserve to die. But I failed to convince any of them to escape to safety." He stopped, on the verge of weeping.

"It sounds like an awful disaster," said Dallow. "You're lucky to have made it out alive."

"It wasn't natural," Jaden said, swallowing hard. "After several hours, the crashing began again and there were more tremors."

"Were there more hands?" Angst asked in disbelief.

"I wanted to look, but didn't know how long the cliff would last," Jaden said with a distant look in his eyes. "So I came here."

The room was silent for several moments as Angst and his friends looked at each other in consideration.

"No offense, Jaden," Hector said. "But has there been any confirmation of Cliffview being washed away?"

"Yes," Angst replied, surprising everyone. He peered at Jaden with distrust. "But I thought Alloria was the only survivor."

"I don't know how I could have missed her," Jaden said, his voice rising in frustration.

"A disaster as terrible as this one can be a confusing time," Queen Isabelle declared. "But their stories are similar."

"Most importantly, they both independently confirm what has happened, that the great cliff city is now gone," Tyrell said firmly to get them back on track.

"We need you, and your friends, to investigate, Mr. Angst," the queen requested, though it obviously wasn't a request.

"Your Majesty, our resources are…limited," Angst said apologetically, glancing over his empty shoulder. "It just isn't the same since…well, you know."

"In spite of the loss of Chryslaenor, Angst, the queen feels that you and your friends' abilities are still key to the defense of our kingdom." Tyrell paused for a weighted moment to allow the significance of this statement to sink in. "You understand this stance is a major change for the crown."

And there it was. Any choice Angst and his friends had about accepting this "request" had been effectively whisked away.

"Thank you, Your Majesty," Angst replied dryly. "We will head out at dawn."

The queen nodded in acceptance before looking at Tyrell.

"That's good, Angst. Be sure to plan accordingly as Jaden and Rook will be joining you," Tyrell noted with finality.

9

"They should be here any minute," Angst said apologetically to Heather.

She tugged her drapey blouse over her pregnant belly and visibly struggled to put on a brave face. "Stop worrying, Angst. I'll be fine," she said, hugging him close.

Angst leaned over awkwardly in his armor and held her as gently as he could. She smelled like fresh air, and he smiled at the gray hairs wrapped inside curly browns.

"You're still pretty cute," Angst said, pulling back. "For an old pregnant lady."

Scar yipped several times before she could retort.

"It sounds like they're here," she said, still eyeing him with mock bitterness for his backhanded compliment.

"I would feel better if Scar stayed with you," Angst offered one last time.

"For a short trip like this? It's good for him to get out. Maybe the fresh air will help him grow a little."

Heather looked at Scar, the eternal puppy. The lab's tail wagged rapidly at the extra attention, and he circled himself several times, providing a full view of his namesake. Angst had used Chryslaenor to heal the dark spell of magic out of the lab pup, and the ugly scar still looked like a fresh wound.

"If he does "grow," the problem is big and this trip's going to last more than a few days," Angst warned.

"They usually do," Heather said with a sigh.

"I left you plenty of gold on the mantle," Angst said. "Don't hesitate to use it."

"I won't, and I know where there's more, so stop worrying!" She squeezed his hand in understanding before letting go. "Now let's get you on the road so I can get back to sleep."

Angst opened the door to find Hector, Dallow, Tarness, Rook, and Jaden standing on the threshold. Scar pushed his leg aside as he ran outside to greet the others, with absolutely no care or concern for the cold, damp air.

"What happened to Rose?" Angst asked in surprise as he looked over the group.

Hector, Tarness, and Dallow exchanged sidelong glances.

"She isn't coming," Dallow said, disappointment plain in his voice.

"Something about not feeling well," Tarness said. His eyes begged Angst to believe him.

"Sure," Angst replied. "Well, we have more than enough people for a scouting mission."

"Hi." Jaden approached Heather and offered his hand. "I'm Jaden."

She seemed pleased at this, taking a scant moment to appreciate the young man's good looks before accepting his hand. "It's a pleasure," she said, blushing as he kissed her knuckles.

"If you're done with my wife's hand, we should be leaving," Angst said snippily. "Where's your mount, Jaden?"

"You aren't going to believe this, Angst," Tarness remarked.

A beautiful orange and red marble gazelle appeared by Jaden's side as he summoned his swifen.

He chuckled at Angst's surprised expression. "It's my favorite, but I can summon something different if this one isn't to your liking," Jaden offered with a cocky smile.

"A different one?" Angst said, a bit bewildered. "No, um, that will be fine."

Dallow, Hector, and Tarness all gave Heather a quick hug, each of them looking forlorn as her mood inadvertently affected theirs. Rook waved awkwardly after seeing this and mounted his pinto as the others summoned their swifen. Angst gave her a final kiss before stepping aside to summon his ram. It took longer than it should have, and his nose was bleeding when he finally finished. He shook his head at Heather's worried look, and sniffed in deep to dry his nose.

"That's, well, that's a unique swifen," Jaden remarked. "I can probably help with that little problem."

The sides of Angst's swifen were once again a patchwork of metal, as though it were reverting to its original form. Angst sighed deeply, scooped up Scar, and noisily mounted the tall ram. It took several quiet steps forward, and Angst felt some relief that the rattle hadn't returned, yet.

"We'll be fine," Angst said, shooting down Jaden's offer. "Let's go."

* * * *

"She talks about you a lot, you know," Jaden said.

Jaden spoke to Angst with such familiarity it felt as though Angst should know him, but his accent was unrecognizable, and his voice buzzed annoyingly in Angst's ear. He gently petted Scar as they rode, trying not to let Jaden irritate him.

"Who would that be?" Angst asked, as though he didn't already know the answer. "Alloria?"

"Well, no, I don't speak with Alloria much," Jaden said uncomfortably. "Though, she's sort of young—"

"To be talking to me?" Angst said defensively.

"To be winking at you," Jaden responded, just as pointedly.

"I've found the secret to wooing young, attractive women," Angst said, raising an eyebrow. "Get old, gain weight, and start losing hair. It does wonders."

Jaden chuckled at this before becoming serious once more. "Aren't you married?" he asked accusingly.

"Happily, even, sometimes," Angst replied. His eyes thinned to peering, and he stopped petting the lab. "Remember? You met her hand."

"You seem defensive about everything I do," Jaden said, cocking his head to one side. "You don't like me much, do you?"

"What difference does that make? Whether I like you or not? You come out of nowhere bearing bad tidings and don't remember who you are or where you're from. Oh, and you wield magic."

"So you don't trust me."

"Should I? Would you?" Angst asked pensively. "I see how you look at her, and she's not ready for that look yet."

"From *other* men," Jaden challenged.

Angst pulled his swifen to a halt.

"You have no foci, I wouldn't recommend—" Jaden flew from his horse before he could finish his sentence, landing hard on the ground in a surprised heap of cloak and leather armor.

Angst calmly dismounted his swifen and placed Scar on the ground. He took a step toward Jaden. Before he could react, Jaden's glowing orange hand smacked at the air, and the magic lifted Angst high off the ground. Angst flew twenty feet to land jarringly in a pile of wet slush. His cheeks were now red with anger, and the snow quickly melted off his face. Angst pushed himself up, both arms glowing bright blue as he marched forward.

Within moments, Scar grew to giant size behind Angst and barked loud enough to shake everyone's armor. The monster dog prepared itself to leap at Jaden.

"No," Angst commanded, and the giant pup hunkered down, growling at the young man.

"Should we put a stop to this?" Tarness asked, bringing his great obsidian stallion around to face the battle.

"Please." Rook pleaded as he backed his pinto several feet.

"Wait, I want to see something," Dallow said, stopping Hector from dismounting. He glanced over at his friend, who was obviously disturbed by the outburst. "They won't kill each other, and if things get worse we can step in."

Things got worse. Balls of fire shot from Jaden's outstretched hands, creating a trail of smoke and drying the ground between them. Angst instinctively blocked the first fireball, surrounding himself with a shield of air. Fire struck the shield and wrapped around it. Snow at the base of the shield instantly melted to a boil. Angst lifted his glowing hands and continued advancing. The shield appeared to be shrinking, as every additional fireball struck closer to Angst. Finally, the shield was small enough to cover only Angst's hands and he batted the fireballs away as he approached Jaden.

Jaden's eyebrows furrowed with concern. He stopped throwing the fire, held both palms together and stretched out his fingers. Wind rushed from Jaden's hands, pushing against Angst, hindering his steps. The gust quickly became a gale, forcing him to stop. Angst concentrated, and his armor glowed blue as he forced the steel to take each step against the torrential onslaught of air being thrust at him.

Jaden was showing signs of exhaustion. He stopped pushing wind at Angst and stretched his arms far apart in preparation for yet another attack. Before he could cast anything, Angst blurred as though he wielded Chrysleanor and appeared directly in front of the young man.

"You know a lot of fancy tricks, but there's a reason I was chosen to wield a foci," Angst said with menacing calm.

With two glowing hands, Angst picked Jaden up as though the man weighed nothing then drove him into the ground like a fence post. The earth below the young man cracked and split to make just enough space for Jaden to be pushed into the ground.

Jaden, now waist deep in earth and snow, looked about in panic. He was breathing heavily with exhaustion, and struggled helplessly against the trapping ground. Jaden held his hands up in surrender to keep Angst from attacking again.

Angst leaned over and reached out a hand. "You have one chance, that's it. Are you with me or against me?"

He stared at Angst's offered hand, and the orange hue surrounding Jaden's arms disappeared. The young man took a deep breath to calm himself then reached out to take Angst's wrist. The earth surrounding Jaden relaxed and fell away like sand as Angst pulled the younger man free.

"I'm with you, Angst. I didn't mean…" Jaden looked genuinely apologetic. He once again stared at Angst as though he knew him. "Sorry."

Angst inspected the young man for a moment, still not understanding the familiarity. He sniffed and smelled the coppery scent of blood.

"Everything okay now?" Hector asked as he dismounted his panther swifen.

"If you two want to hug, the rest of us can turn around," Tarness mocked, unable to see the blood.

"I save all my hugs for you, big guy," Angst said, kissing the air mockingly.

He turned to face his friends, and they gasped aloud. Angst's face was pale and gaunt. Blood streamed from his nose and ears as though he had taken a terrible blow to the head. It was an eerie sight with Angst's broad smile and confused look at his friend's reactions. He pulled off his gauntlets and reached for his face to find it covered in blood.

"Great," he said simply. Angst pinched his nose with one hand and sat hard in obvious frustration. With the other hand, he grasped a handful of snow to wipe blood from his ears and cheeks. He could barely speak the words, "Peade don't tell Heather."

Scar had shrunk to his normal puppy size. He trotted over to Angst and yipped threateningly at Jaden before lying beside Angst as though suddenly filled with depression.

Hector gave Dallow an annoyed glance. "This is as good a place to stop as any. I was only planning to ride another hour anyway."

"Hey, at least we have dry ground," Tarness said with a smile.

* * * *

Angst felt light-headed but couldn't decide if it was from the battle or loss of blood. He rested by a generous campfire as everyone else tended to tents and dinner, ignoring his friends' worried looks. He felt guilty for not doing more to help, but he was drained.

The campsite was perfect. Jaden's fire attack and Angst's air shield had provided them a relatively dry spot of land to pitch their tents. Dinner included cured beef, honeybread baked fresh that morning, and a large bottle of port wine, which was handed around. The first day on the road was always the best for eating, and Angst quickly regained much of his lost energy. Scar, who had consumed his own healthy plate of beef in gulps, took a turn begging for more from each of them. Eventually he plopped himself next to Rook, who offered the lab more beef than the rest.

"Feeling better?" asked Dallow before taking a few gulps of port and handing the bottle to Tarness.

"Much." Angst eyed the bottle hungrily. "I don't know what's going on with the nosebleed thing, but it can stop now."

"I think you're allergic to setting up camp," Tarness said with a wink. He took a "sip" that Angst estimated drained half the bottle.

"You don't have any theories, oh learned one?" Hector asked Dallow.

"Now that you mention it," Dallow began, sounding relieved to share the thoughts swirling about his head. He accepted the bottle from Tarness, took a swig, and handed it to Rook. Everyone rolled their eyes and shared smiles as Dallow took a deep breath to explain. "It's not that complicated, really. Before bonding with Chryslaenor, you were good with minerals, very good actually." Dallow smiled and nodded encouragingly. "After bonding, you not only began expanding your abilities to other elements, but the sheer power you wielded was mindboggling. It makes sense that you still remember how to do some of what you learned, but you shouldn't be any more powerful than you were before."

"That makes sense." Angst nodded agreeably as he watched Rook drink from the port and hand the bottle to Jaden. Shouldn't it have been his turn?

"But you are more capable than you should be. Crushing the bones in that man's arm, for example? I have a feeling young Jaden knows more about magic than any of us, but when you two were—"

"Being stupid?" Tarness interjected. Both Angst and Jaden quickly shot him cool looks. Jaden handed the bottle to Hector.

"Yes," Dallow agreed with a wry grin. "You beat Jaden with brute force. These are signs, Angst, that you're wielding power you shouldn't."

"Why is it I'm always doing something I shouldn't?" Angst said in frustration. When his rhetorical question wasn't answered, he continued. "Okay, I do feel stronger, when I'm not bleeding out my head, but how am I able to 'brute force' magic without Chryslaenor?"

"I don't know," Dallow admitted. "But my best guess is that it's like widening a creek. If there's enough water it becomes a river."

"And if there isn't enough water?" Rook asked.

"The creek dries up," Angst replied staring at Dallow. "It's a sound theory… So how do I fix my little problem?"

"Try not to use up the water," Dallow replied. "I would try to wield magic like you used to."

Angst thought for a long moment, accepting the bottle from Hector. He hefted the bottle, expecting a swig, only to find nothing more than a gulp remained. Angst looked down the throat of the empty bottle longingly. He patted his leg and Scar scampered to him. While petting the lab, he contemplated and quickly jumped to a conclusion.

"So that explains the problem with my swifen," Angst said hopefully.

"Um, well…" Dallow looked to the others for help.

"Actually, I think that has more to do with your sword getting smaller," Hector said with a raised eyebrow.

10

The lack of dreams left Angst with a small headache the following morning. It beat against the inside of his forehead, like allergies not yet dulled by the first frost. Before becoming Al'eyrn, before wielding Chryslaenor, he'd had dreams. They weren't frequent things, but the ones he could remember were filled with color and adventure and, on occasion, they'd come true. Chryslaenor had replaced those dreams with its own visions the minute he'd touched the foci. Now it seemed all dreaming had been forcefully removed along with his bonding, leaving him with nights of sleep and little rest.

Angst kept his eyes closed and tried not to stir within his tent, hoping nobody would notice. Scar left his side, stretched, and crept through the tent opening, letting cold air nip at his nose and lips. He was lonely without Chryslaenor, without Rose, and he hated leaving Heather and Victoria behind. This was not adventure, this was annoying, and Angst didn't want any part of it...until he smelled bacon.

"I really miss Rose being here," he heard Hector say. "Not to do the cooking, but because she knew how to make it taste good."

"Me too," Dallow replied somberly.

"What you were saying...is that really the reason she didn't want to be here?" Hector asked in disbelief. "She wasn't just being mean for the sake of being...Rose? It wasn't for that boy

Angst injured in the bar?"

"I don't think so. She basically repeated what she said after Vars attacked her." Dallow whispered, though still loud enough for Angst to hear, "She said she didn't think he could keep her safe anymore."

"That doesn't sound like Rose at all." Hector was whispering now as well. "Don't tell Angst. He's going to have a hard enough time without her. Hearing that would kill him."

And it did kill him, a little, on the inside. That useless feeling had returned, and he expected that at any moment someone would ask him to start filing papers in the castle cellar again. The emptiness was worse than before he had wielded Chryslaenor—almost enough to make him insecure. He rolled over and pushed himself up. His sore muscles and tight tendons reminded him how long it had been since he had traveled, or fought, and he would feel it all day.

"That smells good!" Jaden said energetically. "Anything I can do to help?"

"You can clean once I'm done," Hector replied. "Thanks for asking."

"Aren't you cold?" Dallow asked.

"It's a little chilly…but, eh, I'm fine," Jaden replied breathing the cold air in through his nose. It then sounded as though he were hopping up and down.

Angst rolled his eyes and took a deep breath before crawling from the warmth of the tent into the painfully bright and crisp morning.

"Morning, old man," Jaden prodded.

Angst smiled politely then looked at Dallow with eyes that said, "that's enough sass to punch him in the jaw, right?"

Dallow responded with a smirk and a quick shake of his head.

Angst was obviously the last to wake, as everyone's tent had been neatly tucked away. He turned away from his friends and began packing up.

* * * *

The snow seemed lazy. Large flakes fell slowly and rested on the skin for a moment before melting, as though waiting for someone to notice their uniqueness. Even atop the swifen, Angst could tell the ground was soft. Each step of his ram's hooves crunched through a thin layer of ice before squishing into the mud below. Winter had barely decided to arrive, often making the daytime air cool rather than cold. They stopped their horses at the edge of a tall cliff with a breathtaking view of the shadowy sea.

"Nice place to put a house," Tarness stated as he stared out at the expanse of water far below.

"That's what the people of Cliffview thought," Jaden said forlornly.

"I'd never traveled there. To Cliffview, that is. Are you sure this was it?" Angst asked Jaden, striving for a non-threatening tone.

"Maybe," Jaden answered with concern. He looked at Angst's face to make sure there was no challenge in the question and relaxed when he saw Angst's worry. "I'm definitely not from around here, but I think we're close."

Angst and Hector looked at Dallow, who immediately searched through maps in his mind. Dallow's eyes flashed white as he scanned the vast library of books stored within his memories. Rook winced and looked away uncomfortably, but Dallow's eyes soon returned to their natural green.

"We are close. You did good, Jaden," Dallow said with an encouraging nod. "We're only a couple miles south."

They continued along the cliff edge at a cautious pace. After several minutes, Angst noticed that the distant horizon appeared cut off, as though ending too soon. There were no trees, no foliage, animals, or signs of life in general. Angst looked at Hector, whose keen senses were already scouting well beyond what the others could see. His older friend and mentor looked confused, his thick brow furrowed.

"What's that look?" Angst asked.

"Something isn't right," Hector said after another minute had passed.

"Is that all you've got?"

"That's all for now, Angst," Hector replied, his gray wolf-like eyes once again staring out far ahead.

Without another word, Angst urged his ram forward. Everyone followed quietly, on edge with knowing that something felt wrong while there was no outward evidence of danger. Ten minutes passed before they found the horseshoe carved out of the cliff. A 'U' shape had been roughly torn from an otherwise straight cliff wall.

"Just as Alloria described it," Angst said quietly to himself, drawing his red cloak about himself and Scar.

Jaden shot him a cool look.

"It still proves you're both right," Dallow said to Jaden, calming the young man.

"All those people, just...gone," Rook said sadly. "I had hoped that, well, maybe—"

"What's that?" Tarness interrupted the moment by pointing toward the middle of the crescent. "Is that another hole?"

They followed the cliff face for five minutes before coming to a gap. Halfway around the 'U' where Cliffview had sat, they found a circle. This circle met yet another circle, which met another as far as the eye could see. It was as if the number eight had been smashed into the ground back-to-back, creating new holes wherever it landed. But calling it a hole was like calling the moon a rock. Each circle was almost perfect and the size of a small city. The circle edges were sheer drops into forever.

"This wasn't here when I left," Jaden said in a high, worried tone.

"What in Ehrde could do something like this?" Rook said loudly to cover the deeper worry in his voice.

"It looks like an enormous sinkhole," observed Dallow. "But I've never heard of sinkholes this large. These must be thousands of feet deep."

"Let's follow the trail and see where they go," Angst suggested.

CHAPTER TEN

They rode for several hours, following ten of the circles end-to-end into a large snowy clearing.

"Wait," Hector said, holding up his hand for everyone to stop. "Do you hear that?"

Scar's ears perked up, and the puppy whined. Rook's horse snorted and stomped. A rumble in the distance grew louder.

"That's not good," Tarness commented on the animal's reactions.

A hundred yards away, a herd of creatures thundered through the openness. They were massive, twice the size of a large bear, and moved with incredible speed. The creatures didn't charge directly at them, but instead seemed to target the nearby cliff edge.

"Are they in a formation?" asked Rook in surprise. He drew his short sword. "They're almost in a triangle, like a flock of birds."

"Yeah, that's not right," agreed Tarness. "I've never hunted anything like that out here. It's always been deer or elk in this area, not green-colored herds of giant things."

"Maybe something left over from the Vex'kvette?" asked Dallow.

The approaching herd sprinted even faster toward the edge.

"What are they doing?" Dallow yelled in shock. "They'll die!"

Only fifty yards away, the green-skinned monsters were moving almost too fast to discern, but they appeared unconcerned by the edge of abyss that Angst hated his friends looking over. The creature in the lead leaped into the hole, making everyone gasp. The other monsters followed, as though they were all plummeting to their death, but just before they fell, the monsters spread their arms wide. Skin stretched from their wrist to their ankle and, still in formation, they glided northeast to the next sinkhole.

"They have wings?" asked Tarness in disbelief.

"Ugh," Rook replied.

Like a flock of geese, the almost-triangle of monsters glided deeper into the next sinkhole, skimming the darkness below like stones on water. They coasted gracefully for several long seconds, floating away in the air.

"How many of these holes are there in Unsel?" Angst asked.

"Let's go see," Hector said with a smile of wild abandon.

They charged forward, doing their best to pace the monsters while keeping a safe distance from the edge. Angst glanced around at his friends. Dallow was mouthing words to himself and appeared very focused. Tarness was so braced for action Angst was surprised his swifen was able to move beneath him. Rook had assumed knight-mode, his eyes keen, his training instinctively kicking in and preparing him to do his job. Jaden was full of cocky, had a smirk on his face Angst itched to remove, and his hands already glowed bright orange. Hector was almost drooling, a crazed smile of bloodlust on his face, his knuckles white on the swifen's reins.

And Angst? Angst thought cake sounded really nice. A big fat piece of cake and a warm fire to hide behind. Teasing with Victoria, flirting with Alloria, dodging stray smacks from Rose, or avoiding angry wife-glares from Heather. These distractions were much less intimidating than the unknown, and preferable, as he felt the weight of every expectation upon him. A battle of anticipation and waiting warred in Angst's mind. If faced with a fight, how he would perform without Chryslaenor?

They rode hard for an hour, as fast as Rook's tired horse could go, until they finally found the last sinkhole. They circled around to the end, where they heard the loud smash of crashing water below. Angst and Jaden were the first to dismount. Angst's swifen quickly walked into shadow and disappeared. The two men looked over the edge before Angst straightened to pull Jaden back.

"If you don't mind, please let me," Angst requested.

"What?" Jaden asked in alarm, looking back at the others.

"It's a...thing," Dallow tried to explain. "Just humor him."

Angst got on his knees, and the ground shuddered beneath him. He crawled forward, took a deep breath, and looked over the edge. Far far below, giant watery hands pounded and ripped out chunks of earth and ground.

"Giant hands," he said in disbelief. "Made of water!"

Angst looked up at Jaden, who shrugged and nodded before holding out a hand to help Angst up.

"How far are we from Unsel?" asked Hector warily.

"Maybe two days' ride by horse," answered Tarness.

"It only took two weeks for the sinkholes to get this far?" asked Jaden in surprise.

Dallow looked down thoughtfully before declaring, "That means we have about a month before they overtake Unsel!"

A blue aura surrounded Angst's hands as he lifted them high, aiming them at the sinkhole before him.

"What do you think you are doing?" Dallow asked in shock. "You don't have enough power to do anything here!"

"This is what I do. It's earth and mineral. Even without Chryslaenor, I should be—"

Without warning, one of the giant greenish beasts swooped in and landed in front of Angst with a bone-jarring thud. Two more quickly followed, landing on each side of the first. Monsters continued to land hard until the entire flock of thirteen towered over them. Like gargoyles on castle ramparts, they stood alarmingly still, guarding the cliff from any potential threat.

The creature in front of Angst quivered in anticipation. When its muscles shivered, its body rippled like a stone dropped in a pond. Its large scaly head had a snub nose and enormous webbed ears. Giant muscular arms reached all the way to its knees, and the folds of thick, leathery skin that allowed them to glide were visible. It seemed to struggle to stand upright, as though it would be more comfortable resting on its haunches like a wolf. The monster stared at Angst with deep black eyes, shuddering with excitement, waiting for a threatening move. It smelled like fish and seaweed.

With Chryslaenor, Angst could have quickly destroyed the lot. Without Chryslaenor, Angst was frustrated and growing angry. He pulled his stunted sword from its scabbard. The creature looked down at the sword and rippled like water, apparently laughing at him. Angst shook with rage and, using air, pushed the monster far into the emptiness of the sinkhole it guarded.

"Here we go," yelled Tarness.

11

"Don't you see?" Heather pleaded with Victoria. "How can you be queen without some sort of worldly experience?"

Tori looked down at her large carup of soup to avoid the question. Noodles floated around the edge, circling the one piece of chicken bobbing listlessly in the middle. She had never understood the luncheon tradition of soup in a bowl with two handles. Where a spoon would make more sense to capture the food, one had to hope that the noodles or, more elusively, the chicken, would find its way to one's mouth.

"Your hair looks very pretty, Your Majesty," Heather complimented Victoria's blond curly locks. "I'm surprised the queen agreed to letting you change it."

"Thank you, Heather. It's fun having blond hair," she replied politely while avoiding the other comment entirely. Victoria set her pale white carup on the tile-covered wood table and looked around the room.

The sitting room of Angst and Heather's new house was charming. In spite of the cold outside, there seemed no need of a fire in the fireplace, which was empty of wood and ash. But the room felt warm and cold all at the same time. Victoria sensed the comforting presence of her friend, and the cool distance of his wife. She tried to disregard Heather's frosty looks and brittle comments as formality of title, but it was hard to ignore and, without Angst here, she had nowhere else to go.

"Didn't your mother travel to other kingdoms before she became queen?" Heather asked.

"I honestly don't know that my mother has ever left the castle," Victoria said, her thin eyebrows furrowing. "But she is, well…you know." Victoria waited for polite recognition of her mom's disposition.

Heather's eyes were cool, though one eyebrow was raised high.

"Okay, she's pretty amazing when it comes to politics and ruling," Victoria said, nodding hard in the hope that Heather would nod with her. "I'm sure she had to learn it somewhere, along with being mean," she muttered under her breath.

Heather calmly set her soup on the table and placed her hand on Victoria's knee. "Angst has said many times what a great queen you'll be," she said to the princess, who smiled and blushed, hungry for more praise. "The real question is, are you ready to rule?"

Victoria's shoulders dropped as though all hopes were dashed. It certainly wasn't the praise she was looking for, and Heather waited for an answer. Victoria could only reply with a doe-eyed shrug.

Heather nodded slowly and reached for her milk and tea. She desperately needed less Victoria in her life. The young princess was almost certainly the reason her husband was so distracted, and separating the two of them would surely give her the time needed to strengthen their relationship. Time away would also help Victoria become a better queen—traveling and meeting other diplomats, other kings and queens, could only bolster her position. So, she pushed.

"Your Majesty…Victoria…we believe in you. Angst believes in you," Heather said hopefully, and the princess looked at her with hope. "To become a great ruler, a great queen, you need to experience life. Now more than ever."

Victoria was smiling and nodding, seemingly drawn to what Heather was saying like a moth to a bonfire.

"By going away, by visiting other countries…other leaders…you'll learn what should, and shouldn't, be done," Heather said. She pushed and willed in ways she never had.

Heather's ability had always, briefly, brought compliance, or agreement to her wishes. Whatever she was feeling, her immediate company experienced with her. Now, however, she wanted more. Heather wanted these feelings to last, to be a part of the princess—for a while, anyway. With Victoria gone, and her pregnancy, Angst would want to be home. She was sure of it.

"Would I be safe?" Victoria asked hesitantly, obviously entranced by the moment. Her hand paused in mid-air, stuck in the act of reaching for her carup of soup.

"Does safety matter?" Heather asked with another nudge. It felt different, pushing like this. Heather had only tried it this hard once before, and it had worked with Angst. She wanted the princess to go away, more than anything else in the world, and that was the sum of all her emotions. "It's for your kingdom. It's for Unsel."

There was a long moment where time seemed to halt, and Princess Victoria stared past Heather into the distance, her hand still hanging abandoned in the air. For the briefest slice of time, Heather wondered if pushing like this was wrong but, before she could change her mind, it was done. The princess shivered then focused on Heather.

"You're absolutely right," Victoria said with certainty. "I need that experience to be the queen Unsel deserves."

"Yes," Heather said with an infectious smile. "I know you can figure out a way to be safe, a way to experience the world and still be safe."

Victoria stood suddenly, pushing the small tile table with her knees. Heather's carup of soup fell. The porcelain shattered into many pieces, and the remaining soup splattered.

"Heather, how can I ever thank you?" Victoria gushed, as if completely unaware of the mess she had made. "I always know I can turn to you for advice when Angst isn't here."

"I am at your service, Your Majesty…Victoria," Heather replied, trying hard to will her guilty conscience away.

"You don't know how he speaks of you. How fond he is of you." Victoria looked at Heather intently. "I truly admire you, Heather. If you don't mind me saying so, I look up to you. I want the sort of relationship you have with Angst."

"I'm sure you do," Heather replied as warmly as she could, biting back sarcasm with all her strength. "You can have that sort of relationship. You just need to find it."

With someone else, she thought then immediately shook off the unbecoming bitterness.

"I will!" Victoria said with finality. She stood and gave Heather a sisterly hug. "Thank you so much!"

"It's my honor," Heather said with a curtsy as she watched the princess rush from the room.

* * * *

If she'd been a wolf, Victoria's hackles would have risen when she received her mother's summons. All guards had been informed to "advise" Victoria on her return from…wherever…to attend her mother in the study.

The queen's private study was spacious enough to make the clacking of her hard-soled shoes echo off the marble. Victoria walked across the parlor toward the enormous greymaul desk, suddenly annoyed she hadn't worn slippers. Isabelle barely lifted an eyebrow at the young princess's loud entrance. Noisy steps and loud sighs were quickly followed by a huffy flump into a cushy brown leather chair. Victoria squeezed every exaggerated display of impatience and impertinence she could into the two or three minutes she was made to wait for her mother, the queen.

Queen Isabelle ignored the noisy onslaught and palpable impatience of her daughter, the disregard for protocol, and the bitter, resentful gaze she could feel trying to bore through her forehead and directly into her brain. Isabelle held back her deep, hidden desire to sprint around her desk and hold her daughter tight. She wanted to throw her crown aside and tell Tori how proud she was. Instead of doing what any good mother would, what she truly wanted to do, Isabelle took a deep breath and reminded herself she wasn't raising a teenager, she was raising a queen.

"I knew I was going to make it home safe that night," Victoria said, as though reminding her mother that people use forks to eat, wake up in the morning, or that magic was mostly forbidden.

"I'm supposed to make that same assumption?" Isabelle said in a tone of haughty frustration.

"Yes, of course you are," Victoria replied confidently. "You know what I can do. That should be enough."

"You knew some man was going to be spending the night in your chambers?" Isabelle's words spat righteously from her bright-lipped mouth.

Victoria leaned her head to one side as she stared at the dark floor. She did a poor job of hiding a smirk. "Angst isn't *some man*." Victoria's words dripped with defiant emphasis.

"You may be able to see what's ahead of you," the queen said, judiciously ignoring Victoria's reply. "But I don't believe for a second you use that insight to actually think ahead, Victoria."

"I don't understand." The princess shook her head.

"Did you *envision* that the castle would be abuzz with rumors about you and Angst?" Isabelle spittled as she forced the embarrassing words from her mouth. "Did you 'see' the effect this could have on his pregnant wife? Or were you just that selfish with your own…needs?"

Victoria continued staring hard at the floor. Surely exceptions should be made for the princess? Not everyone in the castle had to understand, as long as she did. As long as Angst did. Angst understood, right?

"I just can't stand being locked up in this castle any more, mother!" Victoria pleaded, desperate to change the subject. "I know nothing about the world outside! How could I ever lead if I don't—"

"I'm trying to keep you safe. You're being irresponsible with the crown you will bear. I don't even know what you do with your time. You're always in the library, or sneaking out of the castle, or bringing men to your room. And since young Jaden arrived, you've spent hours and hours with him." Isabelle waved her ringed hand as though shooing away gnats.

"I like Jaden," Victoria said in a small voice. "He's cute."

"You will marry royalty, have no question."

Victoria looked through the window behind her mother, staring far off into the cloudy winter. She nervously ran her fingers through her hair, which was once again straight and black, waiting for Isabelle to continue.

"Tomorrow, I will be naming a second," the queen stated, watching Victoria closely.

"A second what?" Victoria replied with great concern.

"Princess, of course," Isabelle snapped. "If you are unable to bear the responsibility of title, if you end up in a situation where you cannot be whisked away and flown to safety, if you leave and don't come back... I need someone else that can take on the responsibility."

It was like a hard cold slap to the face—not only the threat, or the unprecedented solution, but also that Victoria hadn't seen it coming, and she should have been able to envision the queen's plan. The distant future was becoming too worn a gossamer thread to be understood.

"Wh...who..." She cleared her throat. "Who did you have in mind?"

Isabelle fought back a smile. She had finally acquired her daughter's attention. Her daughter's flurry of brash self-indulgence had finally been set aside. The queen could only hope Victoria could see the prize, and would fight for it.

"Alloria, of course," Isabelle replied as though reminding Victoria that people use forks to eat, wake up in the morning, or that magic was mostly forbidden.

"Alloria?" she repeated quietly. "Why... Is she the next in line... Would she be?"

"Coincidentally, her family *would* be next in line to the throne," Isabelle confirmed. "In spite of their tragedy, the timing of her arrival is ideal. I've asked the scholars to confirm her lineage, but if necessary, I will make her my ward."

Victoria was dumbstruck, absolutely shocked at the possibility that *the tramp* had even the slightest potential of being absorbed into the family.

"You know, for a short time after the crisis struck Unsel, the kingdom was overwhelmingly supportive of you becoming queen," Isabelle stated. "Your choices in friends, your gallivanting, your blatant disregard for protocol and responsibility have left me with no other choice. Bringing a known magic-wielder to your bed was the final straw."

"It wasn't like that, he wasn't in my bed. I don't think. He was keeping me safe," Victoria said quietly. There was a very long pause before she finally said, "I would like Angst to be my champ—"

"Don't you dare say that!" The queen cut off Victoria's words. "That title has never been held by a magic-wielder!"

Tears trickled down Victoria's cheeks as she struggled to control her frustration. She wanted to scream at her mother, kick her in the shins, get through Isabelle's thick skull that she was making a terrible mistake. Even worse, she had wanted to warn the queen about her growing concerns regarding Alloria, and couldn't now without sounding as though she had ulterior motives.

"I've told the guards you can now come and go as you please. The choice is yours, Victoria. You can leave to become an adventurer, or meet your responsibilities and become queen," Isabelle declared with a nonchalant wave of her hand. "You now have the comfort of knowing that if you seek adventure, everything here will be...taken care of."

Victoria stood, staring at her mother in disbelief, but the queen gave her no ounce of comfort. Without a word, Victoria stormed out of the room. She tried slamming the heavy door to the queen's private study behind her, but it was so large it gathered air, losing its ferocity. Behind the slowly closing door, Victoria was surprised to find a somewhat nervous Alloria.

The beautiful young girl smiled with her full lips and blinked innocently with her large eyes and Victoria stared at her in disbelief. Could this person actually become queen in her stead? Was she as naïve as she appeared, or hiding plans and malevolence behind a pretty face?

They looked at each other for a long time.

"I've always wanted an older sister," Alloria said.

Victoria screamed in frustration and stomped down the hallway.

12

Angst instinctively lifted his sword arm to protect his face as a ball of heat and light rocketed past. Dallow had unleashed whatever he'd been preparing earlier, and it seemed he'd chosen well. The ball of fire had grown to engulf two of the creatures, leaving behind small green puddles as it continued across the sinkhole. As if sentient, the puddles merged and slowly oozed toward the nearest gargoyle.

"Was that a spell?" Angst snapped, daring a glance over his shoulder. "You could share this stuff with the rest of us once in a while!"

"I didn't know it would work!" Dallow said in disbelief, his green eyes wide with surprise.

"Oh, that's a comfort," Angst muttered to himself.

Scar was once again the giant beast. Two additional legs had sprouted from his sides, and his four eyes shone red as he sought the nearest prey. The bony protrusions that covered him like fur formed hackles as he pounced and chomped into the gargoyle in front of him. The monster dog tore and gnawed at the top half of his green adversary until it came free. The bottom half of the gargoyle liquefied, falling from his mouth like gooey rain. A second gargoyle attempted to grab Scar's three tails, but its hands fell to pieces on contact. Scar spun around and barked so loudly the gargoyle's skin rippled just before he removed a chunk of it with a ferocious bite.

Hector swung his longsword across the chest of his challenger. The blade slipped through it as if slicing curtains. Bits of watery gargoyle flew from the tip of his sword to land on another monster and the second creature absorbed them, as if the gargoyles were giant sponges.

"We've got a problem!" Hector yelled, wielding a pair of very broad short swords. He struck the gargoyle with the flat of both blades, gouging out sloppy chunks of the creature.

"What are these things made of?" Tarness yelled. Having given up on his sword, Tarness was now grappling with the giant beast. It was twice his size, yet Tarness forced it toward the cliff edge.

"That one I knocked over hasn't returned," Angst said loudly.

"I don't think they actually fly. They must just glide," Dallow said in exhaustion. A much smaller ball of fire flew from his palms, only disintegrating half its target. The gargoyle shrank to man size. It roared in frustration and stormed toward Dallow when Scar came up from behind and gobbled it in one bite.

"Yearrgh!" Rook screamed as a gargoyle ripped off the metal legging of his armor, taking layers of skin and muscle with it. The burly man collapsed in pain.

In a tantrum of annoyance and anger, Tarness pulled his hands free from grappling and grabbed his gargoyle by its wrists. With a yell, he spun around, lifting the giant gargoyle from its clawed feet. As though he were twirling a child at a picnic, Tarness whirled about several times. He let go, tossing the gargoyle into the one hovering over Rook. Both fell over the ledge, lost into the sinkhole.

Jaden stepped forward, completely focused on the remaining monsters. He held one hand before him, palm up and fingers tight together as though preparing to spin a ball on them. With his other hand, he drew quick circles in the air around his fingers. Faster and faster, one hand circled the other. His hair lifted, soon followed by dirt and puddles of slush at his feet, until a thin vortex rose from his fingers, no wider than his hand though it reached high into the sky.

He had everyone's attention, and the remaining gargoyles thundered toward him. His face was filled with fierce determination. With the hand holding the vortex, he reached back then thrust forward, as though throwing a ball at the gargoyles. The thin tornado flew at the approaching onslaught. It struck the first gargoyle, which immediately disintegrated, pieces flying into the other gargoyles, which quickly grew as they absorbed the first. This happened again and again, until there was one final, gigantic gargoyle. Four times their size, it rippled with watery power. The vortex pushed up against the giant, but the gargoyle resisted. Only small bits and pieces were reluctantly pulled away.

"Scar!" Angst yelled as he willed air to lift the gargoyle off the ground. "Fetch!"

Scar wagged his tail as he leaped to the falling monster. He took a large bite out of its center then spun around on landing to return to Angst. The dog's three tails splattered even more of the creature. The gargoyle shrank with each strike until it was too small to defend against the waiting tornado. Bits of gel and watery goo shot everywhere, drenching them all.

Dallow and Jaden dropped to the ground in a sprawl of exhausted arms and legs.

"Bring Rook here. I'll do what I can," Jaden said between heavy breaths.

Hector and Tarness picked up Rook and laid him next to Jaden, who sat up wearily. He winced at the piece of meat that used to be Rook's leg then reached over with a glowing hand and gripped the exposed muscle. Rook promptly and mercifully passed out.

Scar, still in monster form, cried loudly. He circled the area, sniffing the ground in a desperate search for the right spot.

"Is Scar okay?" asked Dallow. "He looks like he...overate."

"Or overdrank. What's he going to do with all the..." Tarness stopped and squinted as he watched.

With a loud sigh, Scar arrived at the edge of the sinkhole and lifted a leg. After several very long moments and a few whimpers, the last of the gargoyle dribbled away. The emergency over, he became a lab pup once again and pranced to Angst.

"Yeah. That's a good dog!" Angst said with enthusiasm, rubbing Scar behind the ears. "You peed so good!"

"That's just...gross," Jaden said from his seated position.

"Dogs." Angst shrugged. "Is Rook going to be all right?"

"Mostly," Jaden shrugged. "I'm not a healer. He'll be able to walk, and he won't be in much pain, but it looks a little messy. He'll need to take it easy for the next several days. It's the best I can do."

"You did fine... Better than fine," Hector acknowledged.

"I agree, but I've had enough of this nonsense," Angst said in disgust, tearing his gaze from Rook's mangled leg. He returned to the edge and held out his hands.

"What do you think you are doing?" Dallow yelled.

"I'm going to fill this sinkhole," Angst replied with determination. "And when I'm done, I'll fill the next until everything's back to normal."

"Angst, that's a terrible idea! You don't have that kind of power!" Jaden warned.

"I don't? I still channel power from Chryslaenor," Angst said.

"That sounds like an easy way to die," Tarness shook his head. "Didn't Dallow say—"

"I don't have time to argue with any of you," Angst snapped. He pointed at Rook. "This can't happen to anyone else. I need to stop this now so we can get him to safety."

Angst closed his eyes and took a deep breath, seeking for calm inside himself before reaching deep into the earth. He searched for the bottom of the sinkhole and then deeper. It was strange to go so far into cold and unfamiliar ground. His mind felt as though surrounded by cold wet stone, and thick hard clay. Angst pushed, and the water filling the sinkhole bubbled and roiled. After several incredibly long minutes of struggling, the sinkhole floor finally budged. His lip and chin quivered, and a bubble popped in his ear that felt warm and wet as it trickled down his cheek.

His friends gasped, and his eyes snapped open. Cold, unyielding hands grabbed Angst's wrists and wrenched them to his sides. The giant statue, the element of earth, stood before him.

"That's enough, young human," she said. "If I cannot do this thing, you will do nothing more than die trying."

* * * *

Rose sighed as quietly as she could, hoping she wouldn't be heard over the brushing of hair, the filing of nails, or any other bit of nighttime primping Her Royal Highness deemed necessary. The Princess Victoria spent more time readying herself for bed than most people did for a night out. Rose watched Victoria's long black locks fall from her brush to land gloriously on her perfect pale shoulders. Her shoulders curved into her perfect collarbone, and her delicate pink camisole top barely hid Victoria's perfect breasts, which were younger, perkier, and twice the size of Rose's. Not that she'd noticed.

Not that she was jealous either. She was far more attractive than the princess. But Rose was often frustrated that so much of what others thought of as "perfection" was wasted on Victoria. The package didn't meet up to expectations. "Tori" seemed ditzy, distracted, way too interested in court gossip…and then there was the talking. The non-stop chipmunk chatter that ate away at Rose's senses until she snapped, often forcing her into an argument with Victoria. She fought the urge to reach up and press her eye, which was beginning to itch.

"…I couldn't believe she said that about her sister. What is it with some people?" Victoria gossiped. She took a vial of lotion from her vanity and handed it back to Rose before staring into the mirror again.

Rose shrugged and reluctantly rubbed lotion into Victoria's shoulders and the back of her neck. Rose was supposed to spend another hour with the princess before bedtime but the very thought of it made her head throb in pain. She was half-tempted to draw the tiniest bit of health from Victoria. Push her headache onto the princess, who would then need to go to bed immediately. The thought passed quickly as Victoria jerked her shoulder from Rose's hand.

She spun around in her seat to face Rose. "Thanks for the lotion. That should be enough," Victoria said shortly.

"But I didn't get everywhere," Rose replied in surprise.

"Would you grab my shawl?" Victoria asked, pointing to a hook only steps away.

The shawl was so lacy it seemed pointless to Rose, but she walked over to grab it, sighing with every step.

"So, why didn't Angst want you to come with this time?" the princess asked, in an effort to keep Rose at a distance, out of touching proximity.

The words stung enough that Rose's back arched and her shoulders pinched together. She stared at the shawl without reaching for it. "This time I chose to stay behind, Your Majesty," Rose replied, fighting every inclination to lash out at the implied snark.

"Why on Ehrde would you wish to do that?" Victoria asked. "Are you sure you aren't just saying that?" Victoria's voice teased, but hit close to home all the same.

The pain in Rose's head continued throbbing until it met the itch behind her eye. She lifted a hand and pressed her palm against it, only mildly relieving the pressure. "Yes, I'm sure he just wanted me to keep you from sneaking out and getting pregnant," she said quietly, still facing away.

"What did you say?" the princess asked in shock.

She should have stopped. Rose knew deep inside that she should hold back everything. Something felt different, though. There was a sense of urgency, a great need to leave, to push the princess away. There was an urging, a nudge from somewhere, which placed her past that safe crossroads of something she shouldn't have said and deep apology.

"Someone's got to keep you from tramping around the city when Angst isn't here to watch your backside. Or your front side," Rose snapped flippantly, finally turning to face Victoria.

Rose waited for tears, or sobs, or even shocked stutters, and was quite surprised that Victoria turned slowly to look at her with very, very cold eyes.

"Or maybe you were left behind because they are sick of you and your nasty attitude," the princess said, looking Rose up and down with contempt. "It goes well beyond your stormy nature, Rose. You're thoughtless. You never say thank you. Not to me, and especially not to Angst." Her eyes narrowed accusingly. "I'm very grateful for Angst's friendship. Are you?"

"Gratitude isn't sharing your bed," Rose judged.

"We didn't—" Victoria bit off her words with a deep breath. She attempted to steer the subject away from rumors. "I am grateful for Angst, and I trust him to always do right."

"You're using him because he's vulnerable, and it makes me ill," Rose admonished. "His broken relationship with Heather, losing Chryslaenor…his life is a mess and all he has left is saving the 'attractive young princess.' You may think you know him to always do right, but it's not like you can read his mind. He would bed you in a heartbeat if he could get away with it."

"You know nothing, and you are dismissed." Victoria waved her off and turned to face her mirror.

Rose began to stomp out of the room, but stopped before reaching the door. Her eye was now on fire, and she knew she had to say one more thing. She had to get in the last word. "You're right. Angst won't do anything with you because there's someone else now," Rose said. "Being a tramp is the only way you can keep his attention."

"What?" Victoria crossed her arms in front of her chest as though taken by a sudden chill.

"It's true, isn't it?" Rose said triumphantly, stalking back toward the princess. "You're so afraid of losing him to your cousin, who's younger and more attractive than you, that you'd do just about anything to keep him under thumb."

"He doesn't feel that way about her. It's not true," Victoria said, but her tone was worried.

"You've been replaced, Victoria," Rose said, standing directly behind her. "The only way you think you can keep him as your friend is to dress like a tramp, and put yourself in danger right under his nose."

"He's my best friend, not hers and—"

"Is that why he doesn't stop talking about Alloria?" Rose put her hand on Victoria's bare shoulder. She let the young princess's health trickle through her hand like warm running water.

"No!" Victoria yelled. In a fluid movement, Victoria pulled a hidden dagger from the vanity, spun about and stabbed Rose in the hand.

"Bitch!" Rose yelled, jerking back her hand. Blood shot from the puncture, splattering onto the floor. She stared at Victoria accusingly and looked back down at her hand, which continued to spill blood. It wasn't healing. She ran toward the door, leaving a trail of blood behind her.

"Rose, wait! I'm sorry," Victoria called after Rose.

But the angry, scared redhead had already pushed through the door and was gone.

13

The element of earth towered over them, her long arms held out in warning. She shook her head, causing waves of her short stone-carved hair to flip back and forth. Every movement she made was loud, like rocks being crushed in steel gears. Angst stopped what he was doing so, if for no other reason, that she would quiet.

Angst had only seen her briefly in the castle months ago, and now stared at her speechlessly, stunned by her presence. The element of earth was twenty feet of beautiful statue but, as before, she'd appeared quickly, like a seed grown to tree within seconds. In the castle, she'd been white marble, seemingly formed from the floor itself. Now she was made of sand-colored limestone. Hair, fingernails, toenails, irises, eyelashes—all were all accentuated by dark crystalline quartz. She wore thong sandals, and a gown thrown over one shoulder and cinched at the waist.

The blue glow around Angst's hands faded as he lowered them. She suddenly stared off beyond them, as though her focus was somewhere else entirely. Angst looked at Hector, who shook his head briefly in disbelief. Dallow shrugged, not even attempting to find reference of this in his mind. Tarness seemed concerned by her presence. Jaden winced and squinted his eyes, as though struggling to remember something. Rook completely ignored her and chose instead to stare down at his mangled leg. His complexion was pale and greenish, and he couldn't seem to decide whether to pass out again or vomit.

Scar's tail wagged fiercely. He pranced up to the statue and loosed several ferocious yips, and the earth maiden's focus returned to the group. She bent over low and picked up the pup, which sniffed at her hand. With her every movement, grains of the limestone shifted like sand beneath a footstep.

"Aren't you an interesting amalgam," she said to Scar in her light, gravelly voice then gently handed the puppy to Angst. "Please don't try this thing again."

"I don't understand," Angst replied. He'd brushed her hand as he took Scar, and it was cold, like touching the side of the castle in winter. "Don't try what thing?"

"I'll show you and hopefully you'll understand." She lifted her arms out as though preparing to steer a horse and carriage.

There was a grinding sound as the earth around them tore away from the ground, and rose several inches into the air. This platform was like the one Angst had created when battling the Magic-infused Ivan, but much larger. It hastily moved toward the edge of the cliff. The earthly maiden turned away from them to face the direction they were going.

"Angst, I can't move my legs," Tarness yelled fretfully.

"I'm ready to go home," Rook stated, holding his hand to his mouth.

His friends struggled against the earth maiden's hold, but Angst knew this trick and, with great effort, forced his bones and armor to pull away from the ground, defiantly taking several steps toward the statue.

She shook her head and appeared to sigh before looking at him over her shoulder. "It's for your own safety." They could all hear her clearly, despite the rumbling ground beneath them.

The platform of earth crossed the cliff edge and went over the side at the same quick speed, as though they were on a giant dumbwaiter without ropes. It was now an outcropping that would've looked natural had it not been descending the face of the limestone cliff.

The roar of crashing waves grew louder, and the air smelled

of wet earth and salty seawater. The increasing moisture made the wintery chill even colder, and his cheeks numbed.

"Where are you taking us?" Angst shouted.

"To show you what you've started," she replied.

They stopped ten feet above angry dark waters, low enough for the waves to slap the underside of the stone platform. Angst could now move his feet without effort, making it easier to look about the enormous sinkhole. Dallow gripped Angst's shoulder and pointed to a hand the size of their platform. It rose from the water and balled into a fist before solidifying into a crystal.

Angst shot Dallow an inquisitive look. "Ice," Dallow yelled.

The fist of glassy ice crashed into a breach already dug out of the cliff base. Bits of ice and limestone shattered on contact, and Angst threw a shield of air around everyone on the platform. They continued to watch as fist after icy fist smashed into the side of the cliff.

"Do you see what you have done?" the earth element asked.

Angst shook his head. How was this his fault? He eyed his friends for feedback, each of whom tried to say something. The thundering onslaught of waves and the giant, icy hands ripping away limestone made it too hard to hear them.

"I think we've seen enough," Angst yelled, placing his armor-covered hand on the statue's hip and pointing up with his other one. She neither reacted to his hand, nor chose to acknowledge his comment.

"This has been going on for over a month," the earthly maiden said. They could all hear her clearly, as though the sound had travelled through the ground, up their bones and directly into their skulls. "You can only see a small amount of the damage from up here but, far below, the undercurrents are pulling away at the limestone foundation. It won't be long until there is another sinkhole."

As the sound came to them through the earth, Dallow rubbed his temples vigorously, while Jaden pressed the palm of his hands against his ears.

Angst yelled again, this time rapping on Earth with his

knuckles as though knocking on a door but she didn't even look at him. After nothing happened for several moments, Angst tired of waiting and decided to act. He lifted glowing hands and concentrated on their stone platform. It began to rise up the cliff side, returning to the top. The statue quickly turned in surprise. Her shoulders reared back and she tilted her head in apparent frustration with Angst, while at the same time smirking slightly at his persistence. The stone stopped moving, and pain sliced through Angst as she resisted his push.

"I will return you to the surface when I am done," the maiden said. The platform began to lower again.

"We're done now," Angst said, setting his jaw as he braced himself.

With a deep breath, he used air to push the stone platform away from the cliff, and the maiden's face contorted in pain. They were now floating high over the water, their platform no longer making contact with the ground. This took all his strength, and he wouldn't be able to maintain it for long.

"Don't!" There was panic in the maiden's voice, and he looked up to find her eyes wild with concern. "I can't... You need to stop this, Angst. You're hurting yourself!"

A slight burden lifted as Dallow's eyes turned white with concentration. An orange aura surrounded Jaden's hands as he also began to push. Together, they moved the platform out of the sinkhole and back onto solid ground. On contact, the platform exploded, throwing everyone away from the edge.

"*Air!* You dare to use *air* against *me*?" the maiden roared. She held her hands in front of her, as though braced for attack, and the ground around them shuddered in fear of her anger.

Hector landed lightly on his feet while everyone else crashed hard back to the ground. Hector sprinted toward the statue, a large steel hammer swinging in his hand.

"Hector, no!" Angst yelled, and Hector skidded to a stop. "That won't be necessary." Angst walked up to the stone maiden until they were almost toe-to-toe, and looked up. "What's going on? What's all this about?"

CHAPTER THIRTEEN

She seemed torn, as if deciding whether to continue her attack or answer Angst's question. Eventually, she shook her head and dropped her hands. "Humans," she said to herself. She kneeled, lowering her giant head to make eye contact. "I'm actually here to ask you the same thing."

"Ask me what?"

"What is going on? What have you have done to make the element of water so angry?"

Angst shook his head in disbelief, his eyes wide with surprise. He didn't know the answer, and attempted to shrug in his armor. He looked back at his friends still scattered about and picking themselves off the ground.

"Maybe if you explain what this is about, what you are..." Dallow stood, brushing himself off. "If we understood, maybe we could figure out why water's angry."

"What I am? You already know that. I am the physical embodiment of everything earthly." The maiden sat and crossed her legs as though preparing to tell a campfire story to children. She held out a hand and a miniature mountain grew from it.

Angst took several steps back to stand with his friends and take it all in.

"I am the mountains that keep volcanoes from erupting in Vex'steppe. I am the ocean floor," she explained, while a tiny version of everything she said appeared in her hand, "and the shore that contains all the water in the world."

"She's not doing a very good job of that," Angst whispered to Dallow.

She raised an eyebrow but continued. "I am the largest diamond and the deepest cache of gold in Ehrde." An enormous diamond appeared and was quickly replaced by a stream of gold embedded in her palm. "I am that which is coveted by all nations more than anything else. Land."

She stared off again, seemingly absent from their story time. The maiden winced slightly, but otherwise said nothing.

"How is this even possible?" asked Rook. "We've all heard of elements. But element people? That's absurd."

Her focus returned after several moments. "Yet here I am, to fight the battle once more."

"Battle?" asked Hector.

"The elements are always at war, young human. Waves and wind erode my walls, wildfires eat oxygen, magic wreaks havoc on everything, and I change over time, adjusting to their warring ways." Her carved face seemed upset as she continued. "Every two thousand years we find ourselves in corporeal form and the war escalates. We have always had our warriors. Water always fought with her gargoyles. Fire attacks with dragons. Air uses the cavastil birds you fought so adeptly in Unsel. Magic...well, that depends on the day. Most recently, magic attacked with the Vex'kvette. I have my gamlin."

A gamlin—three feet tall and covered in rocky quill-like protrusions—hopped out of the ground and into her palm, its long claws clicking loudly as it landed. Scar immediately began yipping, the hair on his neck and butt hackling, and Angst shushed and petted him reassuringly. The gamlin's strangely human face scrunched as it made a loud horting sound at the pup before diving back into the ground like a fish returning to water. Scar ran over to the spot, his tail wagging cautiously as he sniffed with intent.

"Since the arrival of humans, the battles have become more...interesting. Millennia ago, we agreed that when we became corporeal, we would imbue hosts with great abilities, allowing humans to fight the battle for us."

"Hosts? Like Aereon?" asked Rook.

"And Ivan," Angst added somberly.

"Yes," the maiden agreed with a loud, grinding nod, "but when you destroyed Ivan, when you captured magic, it changed everything."

"Of course it did," Angst said with a sigh.

"The others are no longer fighting the battle with their hosts," she said sadly.

"That doesn't sound like a bad thing," Tarness said. "Now you have to fight the battle yourself instead of using us humans to do it for you."

"You do not seem to understand. When I am in this form, fighting the other elements, I attack with mountains. I split the ocean floor wide open to drain the seas. Fire creates volcanoes everywhere. Air becomes unbreathable, changing to smother fire. Water becomes glacier and spreads across the lands," Earth said, wild-eyed. "We choose to fight with humans to keep Ehrde from being destroyed. This battle will be the end of everything you know."

Tarness whistled low and loud. Dallow and Hector shook their heads with incredulity. Rook lay back down and stared up at the sky. Jaden seemed unconcerned—his fingers were spread and cupped on the ground as he focused on something else entirely.

"Then how do we help?" asked Angst.

"You have caused enough problems already," she replied. "Anyway, you do not have that long to live."

"What do you mean?" asked Dallow, the shock on his face mirroring their friends.

The earthly maiden stared at Angst for several moments, as if waiting for him to answer the question. Angst squeezed his eyes shut and lowered his head. Somehow, in the back of his mind, he already knew.

"Removing his bond with the foci is killing him," Earth stated. "Without it, he will be dead before the battle has begun."

"No," Hector said in disbelief. He marched over to Angst and gripped his friend's shoulder.

"You're saying there's nothing at all we can do?" yelled Tarness, his face filled with anxiety.

"This is beyond your human abilities," she said dismissively. "You should go make peace with your loved ones and prepare for the end of all things."

"Wait one minute," Angst said, holding up a defiant finger. "If you think we're just going to lie down and die, you're mistaken."

"What exactly do you think you can do, human?" she scoffed.

"I've taken out one element," Angst growled. "I'll re-bond with Chryslaenor, find more foci for others to bond with, and we'll bring the battle to you and yours."

The ground about Earth vibrated, and the giant statue winced as a palm-sized chunk of stone popped out of her arm. It landed with a mucky splash and quickly melted into the ground. Left behind was an ashen, smoldering lesion framed by several cracks. She blinked, her eyes widening in surprise as she covered the wound on her arm.

"It looks like you may need our help after all—" Angst said.

As if struck by lightning, Angst roared in pain and grabbed his head with both hands. Scar yelped as though someone had stepped on his tail, and they collapsed to the ground, writhing.

"It has already started," the earthly maiden said in a crispy voice.

14

Rose tripped down the dark hallway, cradling her bleeding hand at her waist and pressing her other hand against her eye. She hated arguing with the princess—it felt like betraying Angst—but Victoria could be such a bitch. Their arguments were becoming more frequent and, after each fight, her headaches got worse. This time it wasn't just a headache though. It felt like someone had crawled in through her ear and was trying to push her brain out through her right eye.

Rose stumbled as her feet led her down the hall, but she had to get away from Victoria. Away from the look in her eyes. She hadn't meant to try to steal the princess's health, but it was nigh impossible to control the hunger gnawing at her mind. The pain throbbing behind her eye had almost pushed her to violence. She'd come within moments of knocking Victoria to the ground and forcing her to give up health. The princess had barely saved herself. When Victoria had stabbed her hand, she'd looked at Rose with shock as if she knew…something. That was impossible, of course, but then why stab her? It made no sense.

Rose whimpered at the wrenching pain in her hand as blood streamed from the wound. Why wasn't it healing? The castle walls were her friends just then, propping her up when she felt like collapsing. Rose didn't know where she was going, and didn't care as long as it was away from Victoria. Minutes passed, and the pounding in her skull continued. She braced herself against a stone corner and looked back to make sure the princess wasn't following. Maybe she was there and Rose couldn't see her—a thought that made her panic and stagger down the hallway faster.

She turned a corner to arrive in what used to be the main hallway before Magic tore through the castle and destroyed everything in its path. This was the place. This was where she needed to be. The pain subsided, and Rose was able to stand upright, though she still held her eye. She walked through the large entrance.

Chryslaenor looked weary. Angst had knocked the giant blade askew, and it leaned heavily to one side. The black lightning was gone, as though someone had put out a fire, leaving only the faintest blue hue—the light the sword used to emit when Angst was in danger.

Why was she here? There was nothing for her here. She turned, taking a step from Chryslaenor, and pain exploded from every pore. Two steps closer to the sword and the pain abated. She licked her dry lips. Nervous sweat from her palms made the cut sting. If she could only steal a quick heal right now, she would have the strength to pull away.

"Are you lonely? You could've just asked," Rose said mockingly to Chryslaenor. She inched closer and felt even better. "I suppose a brief visit couldn't cause any harm." Rose shook her head and rolled her eyes. "Ugh, I'm starting to sound like Angst. 'What could possibly go wrong now?'" She would never admit it aloud, but she wished he were here. Rose leaned away from Chryslaenor experimentally, and the pain tickled the inside of her skull. "No, this really isn't a good idea. I should go find the crazy physician. Maybe talk to Dallow when he gets home."

Rose tried to move away again but, after a single step, grimaced in pain. Even so, she took another, fighting the unknown assailant. She whimpered with every inch, but, in the back of her mind, she hoped that if she could get just far enough, she would break free. With a deep breath, she leaped toward the entrance, but was stuck. An invisible wall barred her path, and she screamed in anguish and agony. It pushed her closer to the sword.

"You couldn't just ask nice?" she shrieked at Chryslaenor.

A loud clatter at the entrance preceded two soldiers.

"What's going on in here? We heard a scream," said the taller soldier.

"Miss Rose, is that you?" asked the short, stout soldier. "You shouldn't be in here. It's dangerous."

Rose reached out to the soldiers for help. Her arm felt as though it was on fire, and she tried to explain but the only thing that would leave her lips was another scream of pain. She turned away from them as the wall pushed her within ten feet of Chryslaenor. The blue glow seemed to dim as a cloud of darkness hovered near the floor. A low dangerous hum resonated from the sword. No longer under her control, her hand reached for Chryslaenor. Black lightning stretched from her eye to the end of her fingers, tickling and burning as her arm as it hungrily sought the great sword.

The soldiers moved toward her with caution. "Please, Miss Rose. Please come with us."

She gritted her teeth in pain and determination but, no matter how hard she fought, she couldn't stop the dark lightning from wrenching her hand open. It blazed and burned through her finger bones, curling them tight around Chryslaenor's hilt. The dark lightning shot in streams from her eye, wrapping around her arm and embracing the blade. Blue lightning from the foci grappled with the dark, exploding on contact and showering the floor with bright balls of glowing debris. Rose was petrified that she might be bonding with Chryslaenor, but this was nothing like Angst had described. This was a battle, as though she held together two magnets that didn't want to meet. The dark lightning and dark cloud had encompassed the blue light, snuffing it out. Rose wanted to vomit as her body convulsed, rejecting the darkness. The fight was brief—the old sword seemed weak without a true wielder. Slowly, ever so slowly, she was forced pulled the blade free from the floor.

"I'm sorry, Miss Rose, but we have to stop you!" the tall soldier warned. He looked over at his partner. They hesitated, but then nodded and ran to tackle her.

The hunger was now all consuming. The battle had sucked her will dry, and she could feel her life fading away. She wanted to collapse, but the darkness wouldn't let her. The lightning that forced her to heft Chryslaenor now turned her to face them. She didn't want this. Rose wasn't close to either of the men, but she knew who they were. Knew their families. When the men leaped at Rose, she held up her free hand like a talon.

With a thunderous crack, the dark lighting leaped from her fingertips and froze them mid-jump. The shock on their faces turned to pain. They screamed as their cheeks sank into their skulls, and the skulls collapsed into their armor. Their energy and life flowed into her like a prisoner's first taste of sunlight. Bits of burnt soldier, bones, and armor clattered to the floor. Acrid smoke wafted quietly. Rose stood straight, once again healthy and strong. She took a deep breath and closed her eyes as she lowered her hand.

"That was just the heal I was looking for," she said in a gruff voice filled with relief.

Rose shook her head, horrified by her own reaction. This wasn't right. Where had that come from? Had the darkness affected her so much that she'd enjoyed killing them? Those men hadn't deserved to die.

She tried to let go of Chryslaenor, but her hand remained attached to the hilt of a blade she couldn't even lift. The darkness inside urged her to the doorway, and with each movement, drank her strength. Her life trickled out to become the lightning that wrapped around the heavy weapon and drove them both forward.

Rose took a reluctant step, and then another, until she was finally walking at a somewhat-normal pace. The sword dragged loudly behind her, the tip of the blade ripping up bits of marble flooring as it was forced to move.

She wanted to cry for help, desperate for her friends, but she knew what would happen to them if they came. How long would it be until she needed another heal? She was already becoming hungry. She had to get as far away from Unsel as possible before more people died.

* * * *

"Chryslaenor!" Angst yelled, still clutching his head. "Rose!"

Dallow rushed to Angst's side and dropped to the ground. "What's going on, Angst? What happened to Rose?"

"We need to get home now," Angst said, shivering in spite of his armor and feebly trying to roll to his stomach.

Angst looked at Scar, who was shaking and whimpering loudly. The pup had a glazed look in his eyes. When Tarness rushed over to pick him up, Scar snapped at him before passing out.

"Something terribly wrong has happened." Angst got to all fours slowly and took several deep breaths. "I don't know what it is, but Rose is in trouble. Chryslaenor is in trouble. We need to leave."

Dallow stared at his friend, waiting for more, but Angst was currently more concerned with breathing and living, so Dallow turned to Hector instead.

"Are you going to stop us from leaving?" Hector asked the Earth elemental.

"I will not stop you from returning to the castle," she said. "But do not get involved in my war. This is not open to negotiation."

Hector turned away from her without another word. He looked over his bedraggled team, focusing lastly on Rook. "You could probably join one of us on our swifen."

"I'll get back myself. Don't worry about me," Rook said stoutly.

"I don't think you could fight off a herd of cats much less survive another attack by those green monsters," Tarness warned as he summoned his swifen.

"I should come with, you can use me, but I'll see Rook home

safe," Jaden offered. "Do you want me to take Scar too?"

"No," Angst said as he stood. "No, thank you, but he has to come with us."

"Good man," Hector said, clasping arms with Jaden. "Thank you."

Angst nodded in agreement and attempted several times to summon his swifen. It finally appeared as the rattled patchwork ram he'd first created. The others were already mounted by the time Angst crawled weakly onto the ram, bringing it about to face Earth.

"Leave me and mine alone," he warned, his voice tired but sincere. "Or I'll blow you to pieces."

Angst continued staring at the earth maiden, who said nothing in reply. He nodded once to Jaden and Rook before departing with the others.

"I take my leave of you, young humans. Enjoy what remains of your brief life," she said to Rook and Jaden.

"Wait, I have a question," Jaden said.

"What is that?" she asked with her last grain of tolerance.

"How were you able to talk to us when it was so loud?" Jaden asked. "It felt like you were communicating through the ground."

"You mean earthspeak?" she asked.

"Can you teach me?"

15

They traveled as fast as Angst's swifen would allow, but what should've taken mere hours of pushing their swifen to their limits stretched into a tedious day-and-a-half long trip, interrupted by stops and starts. The pain rolled over Angst in waves. It wasn't until a six-hour break that included actual sleep that most of it subsided. Angst was weak and shaky, but no longer felt like his intestines were being torn out by hands of ice and fire.

Scar, however, was not recovering, or was recovering more slowly. Dallow had draped the limp puppy across his swifen. He did his best to pet and comfort the pup, but there was little else he could do. The only reaction Scar would give to the attention was an occasional raised eyebrow and pathetic whines.

"How could anything that happened to Chryslaenor have caused this?" Tarness asked, his low voice filled with concern.

"I guess I understand how Angst could be affected, but why the dog?" Hector questioned in a rough voice testy from travel. He was a mess of wild hair, dirt, and sweat. He looked itchy.

"I healed Scar with the foci," Angst observed. "Chryslaenor is in enough trouble, enough pain, that we're both affected."

"That doesn't make any sense, Angst," Hector growled. "How could a sword feel pain?"

"I don't know," Angst replied simply.

* * * *

When they arrived at the castle grounds on the second day, clouds had already brought on an early dusk. Without pause for formality, or guards, they rode their swifen past the castle entrance, through the castle, and into the broken great hall. Shocked soldiers grouped near the doorway, many of whom hadn't seen the strange-looking swifen before. After Angst and his friends dismounted, the swifen disappeared—making the soldiers jump back in surprise. Angst wanted to calm everyone, but didn't have the patience to gloss over the appearance of magic.

He stood over the place where he'd driven Chryslaenor into the ground, trapping magic, and saving Unsel. The giant sword was gone. Angst looked around in panic. Hector and Tarness were already on their knees, analyzing the scorch marks left by the lightning strike and the deeply scarred trail of broken floor.

"What happened here?" Angst asked a young, fresh-cheeked soldier near the door.

"It was Rose, Angst," Victoria said as the soldiers made way for her to enter the room.

Angst walked to her and gave her a full-armed hug that he cut short when he remembered where he was. As he pulled away, he could see the worry painted on her face. That brief embrace had been enough to show her that he was in pain. Dying. He bowed in an attempt to correct his error, quietly admonishing himself for both the breach of protocol and causing her to worry.

"Your Majesty," Dallow interrupted as he walked over and bowed briefly. "I don't understand. You said Rose did this?" Victoria nodded, avoiding his eyes. "But that's impossible. Where is she?"

"We need to talk, Angst," Victoria said under her breath, avoiding Dallow's questions.

"We need to talk right now," Isabelle screeched as she stormed into the room, followed closely by Captain Guard Tyrell. "Everyone leave! If I find any of you within hearing distance, you will lose your ears."

There was a great racket as full-armored soldiers did their best to sprint from the old throne room.

"How could Rose have done this?" Angst demanded, turning away from Victoria to face Isabelle.

"No, Angst. You first. What is happening to my kingdom?" the queen squawked loudly. "What happened at Cliffview?"

"Yes, Your Majesty," Angst replied snappily, his jaw set in frustration. She was right—Unsel was more important than one person, or his sword—but he worried about Rose.

"Ehrde is at war, and we didn't even know," Angst said. "The physical embodiments of the elements—Earth, Air, Fire, Water, and Magic—are preparing to battle. Water directly attacked Cliffview and has been eating away at Unsel—creating giant sinkholes that are filling with water."

The queen looked at Angst in disbelief. She scrunched up her nose and turned to Tyrell, who shrugged.

"The sinkholes are heading straight for the castle," Angst warned. "And there's nothing we can do to stop them. At least, not right now."

"What else?" Tyrell asked, not sounding convinced.

"They're protected by giant water guardians and, according to Earth, will be here within a month," Tarness added.

Based on Isabelle and Tyrell's shocked looks, this wasn't what they were expecting. Victoria stared at her mother in exasperation, shooting her daggers of 'I told you so.'

"Rose didn't bring you the sword?" Tyrell accused.

"Bring me the...? What are you talking about?" Angst snapped, taking a step forward defensively.

Queen Isabelle straightened and patted Tyrell's arm to quiet him, as though sweeping his theory under a rug.

"You said sinkholes and the creatures will be here in a month?" Isabelle asked. "And there's nothing we can do to stop it?"

"Nothing right now," Angst corrected.

Isabelle sighed in resignation, looking from Tyrell to Victoria to Angst's friends and then finally at Angst. "What do you need?"

"I need my sword!" Angst roared, making everyone lurch in surprise. "Without a foci," Angst went on, forcing his voice to calm, "there is nothing I can do to protect Unsel."

"Which brings us back to my question," Dallow said, finally seizing his chance to speak. "Where is Rose?"

"Something…happened to her," Victoria said. She covered her hand with her mouth and spoke through her fingers. "She attacked me and I was forced to defend myself by stabbing her hand."

"What?" asked Dallow.

"I felt awful, Mr. Dallow," Victoria said, looking apologetic, "but I had no choice. I think something happened to her. She was behaving very strangely, and when she ran out of the room, her hand was bleeding and she was holding her eye."

"How exactly did she attack you?" Dallow asked accusingly, but at everyone's stares added a hasty, "Your Majesty."

Victoria made eye contact with Angst, not wanting to have to explain how she knew Rose was preparing to steal her health.

"She must not be in her right mind," Angst interrupted, resting a hand on Dallow's shoulder. "Does anyone know how she stole away with Chryslaenor?"

"There were few witnesses, Angst," Tyrell answered. "The blade was surrounded by a dark lightning that killed anyone who got too close. Though one person said the lightning actually seemed to come from Rose."

"It was her eye," Dallow said, looking at the queen. "When Rose healed you she must have absorbed more than your injury."

Isabelle instinctively reached up to the scars around her right eye and shivered, obviously remembering the horrific attack by the steel-beaked birds, and the cursed eye the host of Air had given her that almost took over her mind.

"We don't know where she is," said Tyrell, finally answering the question. "Her trail went cold outside the castle."

The room quieted as everyone contemplated the significance

of the day's events. Angst looked up through the broken ceiling to see dark clouds churning above. Nausea coursed through him, pulled by a wave of pain.

"What are we going to do without Chryslaenor?" Hector asked Angst. "You need a foci now!"

"What do you mean without Chryslaenor?" Dallow said in surprise. "We find Rose and get it back!"

"Dallow, there may not be time," Hector said apologetically.

"Of course there is—"

"Angst, you once said you had an idea about what to do next," Victoria interrupted.

"At the party you threw, when I first wielded Chryslaenor, King Gaarder of Melkier said there was another sword," Angst answered, swallowing hard to keep his stomach in check. "I believe he knows where Dulgirgraut is."

Dallow stared at him, disbelief in his brown eyes. "You want to go to Melkier?" He shook his head and clenched his fists. "Angst, if we go to Melkier, how will we find Rose?"

"You cannot leave. We need you to stay and defend the kingdom from the threat of water," Tyrell stated firmly.

At this, his friends began arguing with Tyrell.

"That's enough," Angst yelled as loudly as he could. A small piece of ceiling dropped, shattering as it struck the dirty marble floor. "I need to speak with Victoria. Alone."

"What?" Hector asked in surprise.

"This isn't the time," Tyrell snapped.

"I agree that we need a private conversation with Mr. Angst," Isabelle said firmly in her high-pitched voice. "Tyrell and Victoria, please stay. The rest of you can wait outside."

In a loud mass of grumbling and discontent, Angst's friends stomped out of the room, leaving behind a frustrated wake that could only be soothed by apologies and mead. Angst sighed deeply at their departure.

"Thank you, Your Majesty," Angst said, bowing his head before turning to peer intently at Victoria. "I need to know what you see."

"No, this isn't right," Tyrell snapped, gripping his sword. "You aren't supposed to know!"

"Don't be a fool, Tyrell. Of course he knows," Isabelle said, crisp as a thin sheet of ice. "Shut up or you can leave too!"

Tyrell was barely contained at the end of his leash, bitterly upset at Victoria's secret being spoken of so casually, and out loud. Angst ignored him, keeping his focus on Victoria. She seemed to pale as her eyes flashed between Angst and her mother, worried now that he could be in danger. The queen nodded at the young princess without a hint of disappointment or concern.

"I know it's hard for you to 'see' around the foci, but I'm not bonded to it now. I need you to tell me about my future. I need you to try," Angst encouraged.

Victoria's hands were trembling as she glanced at the queen and Tyrell one last time before looking into Angst's eyes. She reached out and took his hands. The queen rested hers on Tyrell's arm once more to calm the Captain Guard. Victoria breathed deep, trying to let herself fall into a trance-like state.

"I can't do it!" she said, attempting to get away from Angst. "It's too much. I'm scared now, that they might…"

Angst kept holding her hands. He moved closer, too close, as close as she normally stood when her mother wasn't right next to them.

"I'm in no danger from your mother or Tyrell, Tori," Angst said quietly. "I know you can do this."

He continued pulling her until his chest touched hers. Until her cheek rested against his. The queen clicked her tongue and sighed loudly in disgust, but said nothing further.

Minutes crawled by as Victoria tried sifting through Angst's futures, pushing aside thick cobwebs of what he wanted, what could happen, and what she wanted. She could see so many paths that lead directly to his death; it was everything she could do to keep from pulling away. But he held her close, helping her stay calm and focus. Finally, she found it: a thin trail that led to survival, to success, and to something that made her shudder to her core.

She knew it was the only way.

Victoria let go and inched back, tears streaming down her cheeks. Angst eyed the tears with concern—the future had never made her cry before.

"What did you see, Tori?" Angst asked hopefully, his voice a gentle whisper.

"Dulgirgraut," Victoria said as she pulled her hands from Angst's and swiped her cheeks. "We need to go to Melkier. There is a chance that will work. A chance."

"Thank you, Your Majesty. That's what I'll do. I'll… Wait. You said we," Angst said, his face suddenly panic-stricken.

"Yes." Victoria nodded, now smiling innocently. This was her one opportunity to leave, just as Heather had suggested. She swallowed hard and looked at Angst bravely. "You need me, Angst. You'll die if I don't come with. There's only one path and—"

"Oh, this is absurd!" Tyrell roared, starting toward Angst. Once again, the queen held him back. He looked at her in shock, but she nodded at Angst.

"I agree with Tyrell," Angst said, verbally stamping out Victoria's hope. "There's absolutely no way I would bring you on such a dangerous trip."

"Dangerous?" Victoria said defiantly. "King Gaarder adores me! There's no danger in me visiting Melkier."

"No!" Angst growled.

"But you'll die!" she wailed.

"*I said no!*" Angst shouted in panic. He hated this. He had never hurt Victoria in any way before. "Don't you understand? Look at what's happened to Rose. If anything happened to you, I—"

Victoria slapped him across the face as hard as she could and ran out of the room in tears.

Angst adjusted his jaw, moving it left to right before making embarrassed eye contact with the queen and Tyrell.

"I'm sorry, Your Majesty. I just couldn't bear it if she were hurt," Angst said, looking down at the ground. "I meant no disrespect to your daughter."

"Go now, Angst," the queen said. "Make haste. Go find your foci so you can save Unsel once more."

"Yes, Your Majesty." Angst stood up straight, bowed to the Queen and nodded once to Tyrell before striding out of the room.

"That was the first thing he said today that made sense," Tyrell said as Angst left the room.

"I'm not sure about that, old friend," the queen remarked, looking about her broken throne room longingly.

* * * *

Angst jogged down the empty corridor to find his friends. Hoping to take a shortcut, he turned into a small, dark corridor that servants used when the throne room was active. In his rush, Angst crashed into her. He grabbed her arms to steady himself and to keep her from falling over.

"Your Grace," Angst said in surprise to Alloria. "I'm sor—"

He broke off to goggle at her. Her nightshirt was short and low cut. It covered very little, and where it wasn't baby pink, it was sheer. Every breath she took left little to the imagination, and it was so jarring to see her like this, after his last several days, that Angst feared his reaction was offensive. Until she giggled and made a vain attempt to tug her nightie down, exposing even more of her breasts.

"Are you okay? I didn't mean to…" He kept looking from her eyes to her ample cleavage, to the rest of her. Angst was pretty sure he was still too weak from the ordeal with Chryslaenor to face the young woman as she was right now.

"I heard you're leaving me. Again." She bit her full bottom lip. "Were you going to say goodbye?"

"Of course," Angst lied, and she leaned her head to one side in disbelief. "I'm sorry, Alloria. Standing here and talking would be a lot more…interesting than what I have to go do, but I don't even have time to explain."

Alloria looked restrained, as if there were something she wanted to say but couldn't. She lifted up one bare knee and stomped gently on the ground.

"Are you okay?" Angst said, worried that something might be wrong. "I do have to go, but I've got a moment."

Alloria reached between her full breasts and pulled out a ruby ring that hung from a necklace. Where had that come from, and how she could have possibly hidden it within the little she wore? His cheeks heated. Being here with her, especially like this, was very wrong, which made him restless and in a hurry to leave. She hesitantly slipped the necklace from her neck, stood on her tiptoes and leaned forward to place it around his.

"I can't take this from you," Angst said with a dry throat.

"This ring was a gift from my parents. I believe this is the reason I made it safely out of Cliffview." She looked at him hopefully.

Angst swam briefly in her large eyes, where the water was very warm.

"Please bring it back to me," she said.

She gave him a long hug before leaning back and kissing him quickly on the lips. Alloria smiled mischievously, as though she'd gotten away with something, then ran off, her bare feet pattering down the empty castle corridor.

Angst held one hand to his lips and the other to the ruby ring now dangling around his neck. He stood there for a moment, like a deer dumbly eating an apple and staring off at something he just couldn't understand.

"Wow. What do I do with all of that?" he whispered to himself before dizzily turning around to find his friends.

16

"Are you sure you aren't angry?" Angst asked, still stunned by Heather's quick acceptance of his upcoming journey.

"Not at all, Angst. Not if this is what it takes to save your life," she said sincerely, though the small wrinkles at the corner of her eyes were pinched with worry. "Not to mention Rose. Poor thing."

Heather seemed to be the only one not upset to the point of fury. Hector, Tarness, and Dallow all seemed put out. Angst couldn't decide if they were angry that he'd asked them to leave the room before consulting with Victoria, or if it was simply the prospect of another mission so soon after returning.

Tori probably wouldn't speak to him again. When he'd told her she couldn't come, she'd been so angry it was like she was channeling Rose.

Rose...

He was so worried about her his stomach cramped every time she crossed his mind. Angst felt responsible and he couldn't stop wondering about the unpredictable dangers she was facing. He was clueless about how to help her, especially without a foci, and was desperate to find one. Angst would bond with any foci if it meant he could find her and keep her from further harm. He hoped the trip to Melkier would quickly lead him to Dulgirgraut. It would be nice if just one thing would be easy.

He'd told Heather everything...well, everything except the

long cheek-to-cheek embrace with Victoria while she'd tried to see his future. And the kiss from Alloria, which was flattering and confusing and made him blush when he tried not to think about it. So, he'd told Heather almost everything.

"Is it warm in here?" Angst asked, thinking on these things. There was no fire in the fireplace.

"I'm always warm these days," Heather replied, resting her hand on her pregnant tummy.

Angst smiled and couldn't help but rub her belly. Above all else, this made him not want to leave. He was far more excited about being a father than he was about wielding another foci. Heather's changes throughout her pregnancy were amazing, and he couldn't stop wondering if the baby were a boy or girl.

"I was thinking about names—" Angst started.

"I thought we'd decided already, Angst," Heather said in exasperation.

"Yes. If it's a girl we name it after your mother and if it's a boy your father, it's just—"

"Quit saying *it*," Heather said firmly. "You can say *baby* or *he* or *she* but *it*?"

"Sorry," Angst replied quietly.

"Both family names are strong, but it's too early to decide." Heather sighed in frustration. "We can't really know what our baby's name will be."

"What do you mean?" Angst asked.

"We'll know our baby's name when the time comes." Heather patted her belly.

"You mean we'll know when *he's* born?" he teased.

"Yes, when *she's* born we'll know *her* name," Heather replied with a full-lipped smile.

Despite the smile, Heather looked tired, and not from their banter. He pulled her close, embracing her as though he was leaving soon, or she was pregnant.

"I've asked the queen if she would send Rook and Janda to stay with you. Rook's still capable, but he could use some down time after his injuries," Angst said. "And I'm pretty sure Janda can keep you safe from just about anything."

"They're a couple now?" Heather asked, her mouth open wide with surprise. "I thought he was wary of magic, especially after what happened to his leg."

"He is, very much so, but she's pretty and I think that makes it an easy decision," Angst said with a wink.

"So you're leaving your pregnant wife with a pretty woman, an injured man, and a sick dog?" Heather teased, giving him the furrowed brow "wife look" which made him laugh and shy away at the same time.

"Um, yeah," Angst said with a broad cocky smile. "I'd hate for you to be bored."

"I'll be fine," she said, raising an eyebrow. "The company will be nice, Rook is cute, and Scar's in no condition to travel."

The lab pup's ears perked up but his head remained on the floor. He wagged his tail once before giving up. Scar looked pathetic and he sighed miserably.

"Rook's cute?" Angst asked in surprise.

Scar made a lame attempt to rise, yipping hoarsely before settling back onto the floor.

"I think your friends are here," Heather said, coyly changing the subject.

Angst looked at her wryly as he got up to open the door but she merely batted her eyelashes innocently in response. His friends remained on their mounts, looking bedraggled and irritable. This "life of adventure" was not one they craved—they were here solely to save his and Rose's lives. Hector, Dallow, and Tarness appeared so weary at the idea of travel that he wasn't sure they even cared about the danger threatening Unsel.

Heather peered over Angst's shoulder and noticed immediately. She left the warm house and walked into the cold, approaching them. When she stood beside Hector's panther, she held her arms out for a concerned hug. "Please take care of my husband and save Rose," she said. "I'm so worried."

It took only one glance at the overly-concerned pregnant woman for the three to dismount and take turns embracing her.

Their icy moods broke, her hugs a gentle reminder of how important their mission was.

"I'm sure we'll return him healthy, if not happy, within a week," Hector tried to promise.

"Then I'll see you in a month," Heather replied knowingly.

Heather turned to Angst and held him for as long as she could. The embrace contained everything she wanted to say. She was sorry they continued to argue, she wanted him and needed him, she loved him and wanted him to hurry home safe. He replied with an equally meaningful embrace, a kiss, and a nod before summoning his own swifen, which was becoming more of a mismatched patchwork each day.

"Please come home safe, Angst," Heather asked as they rode off.

* * * *

"If we push the swifen we should arrive in Melkier by tomorrow night," Hector stated stoically, avoiding eye contact with Angst.

"That's not a good idea," Dallow replied. "With Angst's condition, we should pace ourselves."

"My condition?" Angst asked in denial.

Everyone turned to stare at him with deadpan expressions that told him quite clearly it was time for him to stop talking. He held up his hand to fend off the dirty looks.

"It's for your own good, Angst. We need you healthy when we find Dulgirgraut, and the foci will help us locate Rose," Dallow said without emotion, trying to fight off his concerns with more planning.

"It's nothing," Angst said dismissively, patting his hobbled ram. "This *is* for Rose. We should push on until I can't."

"Um, Angst, have you seen your swifen?" Tarness asked, his thick eyebrows raised high.

"I'll be fine," Angst argued. His nose itched, the coppery smell of blood already filled his nostrils, and he breathed in deeply to ensure no blood dripped out. "Don't you think we should push a little, just to test?"

"Let's ride awhile and we'll see how you feel by the end of the day." Dallow patted his shoulder encouragingly. "We can push tomorrow if you're feeling better."

Angst disagreed, but felt it best to acquiesce. It wasn't the ideal time to argue—even though his friends were trying to help, he could tell they were frustrated with him. Maybe a few hours of casual travel would help smooth over any resentment his friends harbored toward him or their journey.

* * * *

The clouds were dark and low and appeared ready to slush at any given moment. His friends trudged along, with their heads tucked in against the malicious wind, and the tension seemed to grow with every step. Now would've been the perfect time for Hector to break out in story, ease things up with some manly levity, and Angst desperately sifted through memories to find that one anecdote that would trigger some great prose or minor jest.

"Does anyone remember Izzy?" Angst said in attempt to get things started. "The pretty girl who followed me around before the Wizard's Retreat burned down for the last time? She—"

"We're being followed." Hector drew a short sword.

"I'm pretty sure we aren't in any danger on the open road like this." Angst stopped his swifen and looked back down the path. "From here it looks like a messenger. See the red cloak and cowl?"

"Don't tell me you're getting another love note from your girlfriend." Dallow rolled his eyes.

"Which girlfriend? I can't help but be amazing like that," Angst replied, desperately flippant. "Anyway, the last time we got a message it turned out well." It had been delivered by Rose, and she'd joined them on the road. "Maybe it will be good news."

"I miss Rose, but at least with no women here to distract us, we'll get this done faster," Tarness said in his deep voice, trying his best to sound convincing. "What could possibly go wrong?"

"After we find out what the messenger wants, we'll push our swifen until dark," Angst said. "I'm feeling pretty good at the moment."

"Oh no." Hector's back suddenly stiffened, and he sheathed his sword. "We should ride now. As fast as we can."

The messenger's cloak was red, identical to the one Angst wore, the cowl lifted to cover the courier's head. At a distance, the small rider appeared to be a young man on a white filly. The horse stopped a hundred feet from the group. There was no message in the dainty hand that reached for the cowl and pulled it back. The long, curly blond locks that fell out revealed the rider's identity instantly.

Angst's breath caught while everyone else sighed with frustrated annoyance.

"Hi Angst," Victoria said with wide, excited eyes and a broad smile on her lips.

Everything that could go wrong, just had.

17

"No!" Hector said loud enough to startle the birds from nearby trees. "No. No. No!"

Much to everyone's surprise, he dismounted his swifen and grabbed the reins of Victoria's horse.

"What do you think you're doing?" Victoria asked incredulously.

Hector didn't answer, he just tugged and pulled on the horse's bit until it faced Unsel. He walked behind the horse and swatted its rear, evidently hoping it would head home. It didn't move. He smacked it several more times in vain and yelled something that only succeeded in making everyone else jump. The horse did not move.

Much to Hector's dismay, Victoria dismounted and approached him. He was easily a head taller than the young princess, which didn't seem to bother her.

"I've had this horse since I was a child. It won't move for anyone but me," she said, staring up at Hector. "Not even for grouchy old men."

"You are *still* a child," Hector snapped, ignoring her insult, "which is why you're going straight home."

Victoria crossed her arms stubbornly, narrowed her eyes and lifted one thin eyebrow to challenge Hector's own bushy furrowed brows. Their eyebrows dueled for several seconds as everyone else watched in amazement.

"Get back on that horse right now, Your Highness," Hector commanded, pointing in the direction of her horse and Unsel. "And I'll show you how I can make it move!"

"You mean like this?" Victoria asked. She pulled a strap on the horse's back, releasing a small duffel which fell to the ground. She then whispered in the horse's ear and it took off toward Unsel. "See, you don't always need to beat things for them to obey. Not always."

Hector's mouth gaped open as wide as his eyes. When he finally turned back to the others, he saw they all had the same look. All but Angst who didn't bother to cover his smirk with his hand.

"This is your problem, Angst." Hector jerked his thumb toward the princess.

Angst dismounted and walked over to his friend. He leaned his head to one side for a better glimpse of what she wore under the heavy winter riding cloak, making her blush. Her outfit was similar to the one she'd once given Rose—tight black leather riding pants, thigh high boots, and a very tight leather corset. He wanted to pull the cloak back for a better look, but knew he would never hear the end of it. Even though she knew every thought passing through his head, he couldn't help but smile and gawk.

"Tori, what do you think you're doing?" Angst finally asked, as gently as he could.

"I told you, I'm coming with," she answered with wide eyes, silently pleading with him to keep her secret.

Angst looked over his shoulder and nodded at his friends reassuringly. Hector wouldn't make eye contact. Tarness rested his chin on the palm of his hand, apparently waiting for the inevitable. Dallow just shook his head in disapproval.

"I know you want to come with, but it's going to be dangerous," Angst warned.

"If I don't come with, you're going to die," she whispered so quietly Angst could barely hear her.

"But, if you were hurt—"

"I know you'll keep me safe," Victoria said sweetly.

"You've got to be kidding me," Hector mumbled as he kicked at a stone in frustration.

Dallow and Tarness sighed loudly behind him, and his cheeks and ears warmed with flush. Victoria smirked ever so slightly. She was enjoying this. He was tempted to give in, but put on his best stern face.

"This isn't going to be just some trip to Melkier. We also have to find Rose, and save Unsel," Angst said firmly. "It's going to be dangerous," he repeated.

"You said that, Angst," she said, her patience wearing thin.

"Why did you send your horse home?" he asked.

"I'm riding with you, silly," she replied as though it were the most obvious thing in the world. She turned and addressed the others' dumbfounded looks as though speaking to children. "My horse can't ride as fast as your swifen."

"But how will you get home without your horse?" Angst asked in frustration.

"On your swifen," she answered. "When we're done with our adventure!"

"Tori, we don't have time to go back to Unsel!" Angst's voice rose along with his frustration. "We have to—"

"Why would you go back to Unsel," she shouted back, "when we are going to Melkier?"

"No!" Hector barked from his swifen.

"I'll handle this," Angst said back over his shoulder. He turned to Victoria and yelled, "No!"

"Yes!" she shouted, stomping her foot with finality. "I order you!"

"There is absolutely no way I'm letting you come with!" Angst said resolutely.

* * * *

The first two hours of riding with Victoria were frustrating on several levels. Angst wanted her to sit behind him, but she complained about his armor being cold, and that he couldn't always hear her, which made her repeat herself. When she sat in front of him, he was distracted by the smell of strawberries, the way she settled back into him "for warmth," and her hair that was always in his face. He finally gave in, and did his best to pay attention while riding with his arms around her.

The ceiling of clouds was dark with storm, and seemed to press cold air down onto them. The tiniest pieces of snowflakes fell on occasion, threatening a greater storm. Hector rode far ahead of everyone, so angry Angst was certain he heard a non-stop verbal onslaught of ugly cursing trailing behind Hector.

"You realize your mother is going to kill us," Angst said quietly. "And if she doesn't kill you, she's going to make you watch the rest of us die."

Victoria giggled.

"I'm serious," Angst tried again. "You're going to feel really bad!"

"Why aren't we going faster?" Victoria asked, changing the subject.

"I'm...not up to full strength after the Rose ... Chryslaenor ...thing," he said, embarrassed.

"Well, my being here will make you feel much better," she said confidently.

He didn't want to say it out loud, but he hadn't thought about the pain since she'd arrived. Victoria was a welcome distraction from the others' bitterness. Having her with him lifted his spirits, despite his worry for her safety. He really did feel better.

"See, it's working already!" she said, commenting on his thoughts.

"What?" he asked then whispered, "Are you going to do that the entire trip?"

"Do what?" she replied innocently, looking around to make sure the others didn't hear. "You know I wear the strawberry because you like it? Enjoy it while it lasts, I didn't bring any with."

Angst couldn't help but laugh.

"So why's Hector riding so far ahead of us?" Victoria said in a normal tone.

"He gets upset when he doesn't get his way," Angst answered quietly. "He's acting just like Ivan did."

"I can hear you," Hector shouted over his shoulder. "Both of you."

Victoria turned to smile at Angst, and he realized she'd done that on purpose. After several minutes, Hector slowed to join the rest of the group.

"I didn't think it was supposed to thunder when it snowed," Tori said.

"It's unusual," replied Hector curtly, staring forward and not looking at the princess once.

"Why does he hate me?" she whispered to Angst.

"Actually, right now he hates me. You're just getting the overflow," Angst said loudly enough for Hector to hear. "I'm used to a bit of hate, so no need to let it bother you. All Hector needs is a draft of mead or a kick in the pants. Or both."

Hector sniffed loudly. "Without your cheat...I mean, sword...I don't see that happening." Now he turned back to face them, his voice thick with judgment. "And I have no intention of taking you two anywhere near a bar. Ever."

"Don't act like you're in charge, Hector," Angst said sharply. "You aren't."

As Hector lifted a warning finger, Tarness and Dallow rode between them, cutting off any chance of a rebuttal.

"It's getting late. We should find a place to set up camp," Dallow advised, changing the subject.

"I'll go off trail and see if I can find a clearing for the tents." Tarness's large obsidian swifen leaped gracefully over a log and trotted into the forest.

"Tents?" Victoria whispered to Angst.

"For sleeping in?" Angst replied snappishly, still defensive from his argument with Hector.

"I'm not stupid, Angst. I brought one, I just hoped we would stay at an inn," she said wistfully. "And, well, I... It's just that

I..."

"You've never been camping?" he asked with a wry grin.

She shook her head sheepishly.

"You'll be fine," Angst whispered. "We'll pitch your tent close to mine so my snoring drowns out any noises from the woods."

"Noises?" she asked warily.

"You'll be fine, really. It's fun," Angst said, trying to sound positive.

* * * *

The discussion between Hector and Victoria at the campsite was less than cordial. He threatened to leave if she didn't. She said that being princess meant she outranked him and he would do as he was told. They were both red-cheeked and spitting by the end of it. Angst finally separated them when Hector threatened to bend her over his knee. Victoria stormed off to set up her tent, and Hector left camp to "collect firewood" for over an hour.

Tori clumsily began assembling her new tent next to Angst's, making high-pitched grunting noises when her rope-lines wouldn't cooperate.

"Can't I just stay with you?" Tori asked in frustration.

"What?" Angst said, louder than he'd intended, making her start in surprise. "No! I mean, I'm sorry, Tori, but that wouldn't be appropriate. These tents are very small and—"

"Fine!" she said, turning her back to him. Her long blond hair, wet from the now-sleeting snow, whipped around, slapping her in the cheek and eye. She seemed to be shivering, or crying, or both. Angst couldn't tell and he felt helpless.

"Tori?" he pleaded, resting a hand on one of her shoulders.

She yanked her shoulder away and began to wrestle with her mess of a tent once again. Angst waited several moments before shuffling over to the others. Dallow was on a knee, digging bread and cheese from the food pack.

"We don't really have time for dinner before the storm

comes," Dallow said, looking up, "but personally I'm not that hungry."

Hector returned, without wood, and quickly put his tent together. When he discovered Victoria's mess, he grunted in frustration and stomped over to her.

"You're doing it wrong. You need to take this," he grabbed a tent stake roughly from her hand, "and put it there."

Rather than crumpling in tears, she spun on Hector. "Give me that!" she ordered, yanking the stake out of his hand. "I didn't command you to help me, so go be useless somewhere else, hater."

Hector's chest filled with air as he prepared to argue, but then he apparently reconsidered. "Of course, Your Highness." He spun on his heel and returned to the others. "I'm going to bed."

* * * *

The storm dumped windy sheets of icy rain and sleet on them, chasing everyone to their tents soon after dinner. Angst loved this—sleeping outdoors, listening to rain pattering on the thick canvas. He always felt he was getting away with something, that the thin layer of cloth safety shouldn't be enough to keep him warm and cozy.

But, just as he began to fall into snoring, he heard something. At first, he tried to ignore the noise, but then he recognized the sound outside his tent as whimpering. Before long, the whimper became a cry, and finally a voice.

"Angst?" Victoria asked from the other side of the tent flap.

His eyes snapped wide open. He pulled back the flap and was rewarded with a slap of cold wet air. He could barely see more than a shadow of Victoria.

"Tori, why are you out of your tent?" he asked with sleepy concern. "It's pouring."

"It…it," she sobbed. "It collapsed an hour ago."

Angst sighed deeply. "We can't get it back up tonight." He was still groggy with almost-sleep and trying to understand.

"Please, Angst, can't I just…stay in here?" she said with a whimper, her teeth chattering in the cold, sleeting rain.

"No, Tori. There's no way that would work," he replied firmly.

Her cries became louder as the thunder made her jump.

"Okay, okay. We'll just…" he thought for a minute. "We'll figure it out."

"Thank you," she choked out, still sobbing.

"Look, you're going to have to get out of your wet clothes." Angst tried his best to sound like this was a normal everyday sort of thing.

"What?" Tori asked. "I'd be naked."

"If you don't, you'll get sick," he said. "I've got a towel, a dry tunic, and I can't see a thing. Hurry up."

He sat up to dig through his pack and could hear her wet clothes slapping the mud outside the tent as they came off.

He handed her his small towel. "Do your best to towel off as you come into the tent. We don't want anything getting wet."

Tori toweled herself while entering as quickly as she could, awkwardly climbing over Angst in the process, and plopped herself at the other end of his sleeping pad. He could only assume she was naked as birth.

"I am naked, and cold, so please try to stop thinking about that," she replied between chattering teeth.

Angst swallowed hard. "I'm doing my best." He looked away as he handed her the shirt.

Victoria started to chuckle as she dried herself off more thoroughly.

"What?" Angst asked.

"You turned away, and you can't even see me." Tori took the shirt. Her teeth clicked together loudly as she shivered her way into it.

Angst chuckled a little before realizing he had only one mat to sleep on and two blankets to sleep under. Trying his best not to think about it, he lifted up the blanket as she shimmied into the space next to him. She shivered violently as he did his best to inch away, placing an invisible wall between them.

"Angst, please," she pleaded between shallow breaths. "Nothing's going to happen. I'm freezing."

"All you've got on is my shirt," he said, still pulled away in his safe place.

Victoria's shivers worsened into shaking. Angst finally gave in and inched his arm under her head so it rested on his chest. She draped herself over him. He rubbed her back and shoulder vigorously to help generate heat.

"You *are* freezing," he said with a shudder. "You should go back outside before I get sick."

"Ha ha," she said. "Just lie there and be warm."

18

His dreams were gone. Immediately after bonding with Chryslaenor, Angst's dreams and visions had been replaced with lost histories of those who'd wielded the foci. He forgot most of the dreams shortly after waking, but he always had the sense the stories were trying to teach him. After Angst removed the bond with Chryslaenor, his nights had once again become restless, or useless. Originally, he'd hoped the foci stories would continue, but when he'd realized they were gone, he'd hoped his own dreams would return. There was nothing. When Angst could fall asleep, it felt as though he would only doze a few minutes in spite of hours passing. Without dreams, remembered or not, there seemed to be no passage of time, and thus very little rest.

After settling in as best he could next to the young princess, Angst was both surprised at how quickly he had fallen asleep, and relieved to find himself here. Wherever here was. Angst lifted his hand and saw right through it. His fingers, his toes, his entire body was transparent and unable to touch anything, including the ground. Angst did not feel hungry, nor tired, he was merely there to watch. It was exactly as he remembered his foci dreams, and Angst readied himself to observe a story while he slept.

Early morning sunlight peeked through the trees surrounding him. Frost had bitten the leaves on the ground, leaving white tooth marks wherever it fed and making Angst grateful he couldn't feel the cold in his present state. He spied an old moss and ivy-covered cottage missing half its roof, long abandoned by residents or caretakers. Without taking a step, Angst found himself inside, looking down at Rose.

His young friend lay in a fetal position on the grimy floor. Her left hand gripped Chryslaenor by the hilt as though she were ready to fight. A very dim blue glow surrounded the great blade, as if some part of the foci was trying to protect her. He felt a twinge, an ache inside himself, in that place where the bond had been. Angst reached for the foci but, before he could touch the hilt, the sword pulled away.

"Who's there?" Rose asked, sitting up with a start.

Angst instinctively tried to pull back but merely jerked awkwardly as he floated overhead. Had he moved the blade? He reached for Chryslaenor once more but it was now too far, and Angst tore his gaze from the blade to watch Rose. Even in the dull light of the foci, he could see she was a mess. She had always been thin, but now appeared sickly, as though wasting away. Rose's pallor and sunken cheeks gave her a haggard gaunt look, and her large dark eyes protruded unnaturally. Blotchy circles had formed under her eyes, and her long red hair was thin and reedy.

"Do we always have to get up at the crack of dawn?" she grumbled.

Rose stood shakily, the sword hilt lifting with her hand as though by a puppeteer's strings. She took several purposeful steps forward to the entrance, the heavy burden attached to her hand dragging behind. The tip of Chryslaenor carved a deep gouge into the cabin floor, and Angst could see that every movement took its toll on her.

"How about eggs and bacon this morning?" Rose asked with sarcastic cheerfulness, obviously mocking the situation. "Did you ever think I may want to actually chew and digest my food?"

Angst didn't understand the question but, looking around

quickly, realized she had to be talking to his sword. He followed her out of the cabin and into the wintery morning. Rose moved so slowly, Angst assumed she still had to be near Unsel—though he didn't recognize these woods or even these trees. Rose drew in a deep breath of morning, and frosty air escaped her chapped lips.

"At least I'm warm. I suppose that's your doing," she said, looking down at Chryslaenor. "Attract something quickly, will you, so we can get wherever we're going and I can kill the bastard doing this to me."

A loud roar sounded from the woods. Instinctively, he reached over his shoulder, and then to his side, only to find himself weaponless. He felt naked, and helpless, as something far down the trail rushed toward Rose on four massive legs. The creature ran past an opening in the trees, and sunlight reflected off thick burgundy fur. It was a giant red bear, easily nine feet high on all fours.

"Rose, run!" Angst called out in frustration, though his warning was useless.

The beast's every step landed with a terrifying thud, shaking the nearby forest floor. The monster had to weigh two thousand pounds or more and looked as hungry, and almost as upset, as Rose. As it approached, the red bear stood on its haunches, raising its large clawed paws high in the air, ready to swing down and rip the life from his friend.

"We didn't have to wait as long this time," she said fiercely, licking her lips.

Rose dragged the reluctant sword about to face her attacker. Black lightning trickled and beaded along the blade's edge as though Chryslaenor had been pulled from a lake of oil. The bear loosed a ferocious roar as Rose took a step closer. Dark lightning now completely encompassed the blade, and small dark bolts struck the ground, kicking up debris and scorching the earth. When the red bear was within arm's reach, black lighting shot out of Rose's eye and through the sword to wrap around the giant monster.

Rose held Chryslaenor aloft, and bands of the dark lightning rippled between her and the animal, lifting it into the air as it howled in pain. Strength and life drained from the bear and—to his amazement—it compressed, as though all the air in it was being sucked out. Rose breathed deep, her vitality and health visibly returning. Rose's sunken cheeks filled, she stood straight, and her pale complexion no longer appeared sickly.

As Rose smiled, the dream began to fade.

"Wait, no!" he yelled, reaching out for Rose.

Angst felt a hand on his transparent arm and jerked it back in surprise. He looked over to see a ghostly vision of Victoria staring at Rose with worry and sorrow in her eyes. In a surreal moment, she turned her head to face him.

"At least we know she's safe," Victoria said.

Before Angst could reply, the dream was gone, and he returned to his dreamless slumber.

Back in the woods, Rose's brow furrowed. She lowered the sword and looked from side to side. For the first time in days, she felt a tiny bit of hope.

"Angst?" she called out into the empty woods.

* * * *

Queen Isabelle no longer slept well. Since the attack in her room, she did not feel safe in her own home. The steel-beaked cavastil bird was not only to blame for the loss of her eye, but seemed a harbinger of the change she could feel coming. Her deceased husband, the king, had put great trust in intuition—his had been uncanny in its depth and knowing—and she could only honor him by trusting her own. The changes in Ehrde caused her great fret late into every night, forcing her to cram sleep into the three or four hours before sunrise.

This lack of sleep wore on her, requiring her to put a great amount of effort into her attire and makeup so no one would have a clue how weary she truly was. Unfortunately, the dark navy velvet dress she wore fit her heavy figure like a glove. Piping accentuated her breasts and waist, in a somewhat flattering manner. The dramatic light red gem she wore hung heavily from her neck, complimenting the red gems in her crown. Every ounce of fabric, every piece of jewelry weighed greatly as she considered her own intuition. The magics had invaded her daughter, they had invaded her, they had invaded Unsel, and now she felt this was only the beginning.

She refocused. This overly thorough briefing by Rook confirmed everything Angst had said in painful detail. Isabelle did her best to appear interested and alert until she could take no more.

"Lieutenant," the queen said, concluding the conversation. "Thank you for your comprehension explanation, and your sacrifice."

"Yes, Your Majesty," Rook replied, doing his best to bow, in spite of the tightness in his leg.

He reluctantly leaned on Janda, who had insisted on joining him. Was bringing her a mistake? The crown had formally recognized and rewarded Janda's efforts during the crisis, but she was still a magic-wielder. Even now, it was obvious the queen had little patience with her presence. Isabelle had made scant eye contact with Janda throughout Rook's detailed retelling of his recent adventure. He felt bad for how the queen treated her, but when he looked into Janda's eyes, Rook saw only pride and strength.

She stood tall, her strawberry blond hair framing a face sprinkled with freckles. Sparkling green eyes met Rook's with encouragement.

"My queen," Rook began, ignoring her dismissal. "There is one more thing."

"That is all, Rook," the Captain Guard said sternly.

"No, it's okay," the queen corrected Tyrell before turning back to Rook. "You've earned your audience, Lieutenant."

Before he could go on, Alloria hustled awkwardly into the room and past Janda and Rook, stopping within feet of the throne. The young woman was out of breath and appeared un-comfortable in her formal attire. Her dress looked new, and mimicked everything the queen would wear. Fashioned of dark purple velvet, the high-necked dress dripped with beaded accents and piping that unnecessarily accentuated her curviness, much like Isabelle's. Alloria looked stifled, and pressed her hand to her chest as if holding her lungs in while she bowed.

"Angst and the others fought bravely, and many other magic-wielders would be honored to defend Unsel." Tyrell bristled, and the queen raised a warning eyebrow, but Rook plunged on. "I couldn't do anything to defend against these creatures, but they could." Rook did his best to sell the idea. "We need them, Your Majesty. A guard comprised of magic-wielders could be of great service."

"Thank you, Lieutenant. That is all." The queen nodded to the exit.

"Yes, Your Majesty." Defeated, Rook did the only thing he could—he bowed respectfully.

A glare flashed in Janda's eyes as she bowed curtly before helping him toward the exit.

"What do you need, my dear," Queen Isabelle asked a gasp-ing Alloria.

"Your Majesty, she's gone," Alloria exclaimed between deep breaths. She walked to the queen and handed her a note. "The princess went with Angst."

The queen noted that Rook and Janda glanced at each other before leaving the room. Alloria should have waited for their departure. Isabelle took the note with her ring-laden hand, and skimmed the page quickly. She handed the note to Tyrell, who read it slowly, his cheeks flushing more by the second.

"It seems Victoria has made her decision," Isabelle stated. She looked sad and tired. "We will need to proceed with my plan to make you the next in line. The throne needs a successor." The queen nodded toward the empty seat next to the throne.

Alloria lifted her dress and hastily moved to sit beside Isa-belle. She appeared nervous, and her eyes were wide and as she did her best to be attentive without showing excitement.

The queen tapped a finger to her lips as she thought. "Alloria, did you hear Rook's proposal?"

Tyrell turned to face her, and Alloria knew it was a test. She studied them both for a moment before furrowing her perfectly plucked eyebrows in thoughtful concern.

"I believe that would be a mistake, Your Majesty," Alloria stated sincerely. "The soldiers of Unsel have been defending the kingdom for…for a very long time. Putting too much reliance on those inflicted with mag…I'm sorry, magic-wielders…will undermine our authority. We should send out our soldiers to defend our kingdom. Your Majesty."

The queen smiled broadly at Alloria. She looked over her shoulder at Tyrell, who nodded in agreement, then back at the young princess-to-be. Her eyes combed Alloria's attire, her jewelry, her poise, and approved.

"You will do wonderfully, dear," the queen avowed.

19

"Angst! The princess, she's gone!" Hector called, yanking the flap of Angst's tent open.

Angst blinked rapidly at the brightness of morning. He looked over his forehead to see Hector staring, jaw dropped at the sight of Victoria entangled with Angst. One naked leg was wrapped outside the covers around Angst's right knee, and her arm was draped across his chest. She nuzzled further into Angst, pulling the blankets over her head, avoiding the noise, the bright light, and the cold air. Hector let the tent flap fall and silently walked away.

Angst lay there sighing, his heart racing from being woken. He breathed in deeply, smelling the fresh cool air Hector had let in, and strawberries. He smiled, despite feeling like he had just been caught. This was so many levels of wrong and inappropriate he didn't know where to begin. Nor could he believe how quickly he had fallen asleep or how restful that sleep had been. In spite of the upcoming confrontation with Hector, Angst couldn't help but peer down at Tori and think for the briefest of moments that this was nice.

Nice was fleeting, as he thought about Heather being home and pregnant, as he worried about Rose. Hector was probably packing up to leave and encouraging the others to join him. He was so stubborn, and Angst didn't know what it would take to make him stop.

CHAPTER NINETEEN

"I liked your other thoughts better. Can't you go back to nice?" Tori asked in a tiny voice muffled by the covers.

"No... Well, maybe for a second." He gave her a quick side-hug. "But I'm going to have to deal with this."

"Fine," she said, rolling off his chest. She pushed up and looked at Angst, studying his face fondly. "Thank you for saving me last night."

"You're welcome," he replied, trying not to look at the expanse of young exposed skin.

"I was practically naked all night and now you think you're being respectful by not looking?" She laughed at this before becoming serious. "Go find me some dry clothes and stop worrying. I'll handle Hector."

Angst awkwardly slipped out of his old nightshirt and into leggings and jerkin under the covers, hoping Victoria wouldn't notice his belly or sag. It didn't help that she giggled and poked his side several times, making him scramble out of the tent. Angst tripped over the pile of muddy clothes she had left at the entrance. As he leaned over to pick up the garments, he could feel their stares. He closed his eyes tight, took a deep breath, and stood straight.

"Good morning," Angst said, bright-eyed and cheerful.

The salutation wasn't enough of a shield to block the glares. Dallow seemed disappointed as opposed to Hector, who refused to even make eye contact with him. Tarness smirked mischievously, obviously impatient to find out how Victoria had ended up in his tent but hesitant to ask. When Hector flashed Tarness a disapproving glance, his mouth lost the smirk but his eyes didn't.

"Whew. Cold out this morning, isn't it?" Angst said with more glee than his voice had mustered in ages.

He tore his eyes from his friends to stare into the small camp-fire that seemed reluctant to share its heat. A quick look around the campsite showed tents already packed, ready to be strapped onto swifen.

Angst pulled Victoria's clothes out from under his arm, dripping with mud and snow. Tarness's eyebrows raised high on his large dark forehead, and Dallow shook his head slowly. Angst shrugged and squeezed the mud out. Hector finally looked up at Angst, taking a deep breath in anticipation of a good yelling match.

"Next time her tent collapses, I'll let her sleep outside," Angst said with considerably less cheer.

"Really? She was naked, Angst?" Hector snapped.

"Really? She should sleep in her wet clothes, Hector?" Angst replied. "You were the one who taught me about surviving in the woods. And she *wasn't* naked, she had my shirt on! Oh, in case you didn't notice, I wasn't naked either."

"Oh, that makes it all okay!" Hector bellowed.

"I didn't say it was okay. I just didn't see another option in the dead of night and the middle of a storm!" Angst was red-cheeked and spitting now. "What else was I supposed to do with her?"

"We would've gotten up to help with her tent, Angst," Dallow said.

"She shouldn't even be here!" Hector continued, his wolf-gray eyes flashing with anger. "In case you don't remember, the queen already hates you. If she knew about this, we would all be hung by our entrails. And don't forget your pregnant wife back home!"

"The princess being here is a bad idea on so many levels," Dallow began, trying to inject some reason into the argument.

"See what you can do with these," Angst interrupted, handing the mess of muddy clothes to Dallow while still staring down Hector.

"I'm done with this *adventure!*" Hector said with finality, slashing the air with his hand. "It's *me* or *her*! Decide!"

"That's enough," Victoria said in a voice that commanded attention.

She stomped barefoot through the mud, wearing nothing but Angst's ratty nightshirt. Dallow and Tarness stared at the ground, though Tarness glanced up on occasion to glimpse her bare legs. This time, Angst didn't shy away. She was right, what was the point? She stopped inches in front of Hector, staring up at him and staring him down at the same time. The outside of her wrists were shoved into her tiny waist, and bursts of cloudy air puffed from her mouth.

"Not you *or* me, Hector," the princess threatened, holding up a tiny fist. "You *and* me! Let's go!"

"Wha…what?" Hector stuttered, completely taken aback.

"That's right. I've had enough of your complaining, and your nonsense," she declared, pulling out a threatening finger. "Your friend saved my life last night. Tell me I could've lived through that storm without stripping down and climbing into his dry tent?"

"Well, it's not that," Hector said more quietly. "It's just…" He shuffled his feet and rubbed one hand through unkempt hair.

"It's nothing, Hector," Victoria continued. "I didn't set up my tent right because you made me so angry! I was forced to get naked and crawl into Angst's tent because you aren't getting your way—and your way doesn't even make sense!"

Angst had never seen Victoria so riled up, so angry and determined. Her voice was filled with command and confidence, and he was proud of her.

"Shut up!" she screamed before Hector could even get speak another word. "Let me make this clear. You agreed to come with, but you aren't in charge! You don't get that. It's just not good enough for you. So I challenge you."

Victoria looked at Dallow and then Tarness. She reached over and tugged at Tarness's gauntlet, which he loosened so she could pull it off. Victoria threw it to the ground at Hector's feet. It struck the mud with a loud splat.

"I challenge you! You duel me, with whatever weapons you choose," she challenged. "If you win, I leave. I go back to the castle and never speak of any of this."

"Wait a minute," Angst said, his voice filled with concern. She reached back and grabbed his arm, instantly quieting him.

"This is ridiculous," Hector said with an awkward smile as he looked around at everyone. "You're not serious, are you?"

Victoria continued staring at him, shivering in the cold but otherwise unwavering.

"Fine. If I lose?" he asked with a half-chuckle.

"Then I come with, you treat me like the rest of the team," Victoria listed her demands. "And you stop hating me!"

Hector's eyes widened with surprise. He looked at Dallow and Tarness in disbelief, but they both shrugged.

Victoria's hand was still tight on his arm, and Angst used that to pull her around to face him. "Are you crazy?" Angst whispered. "Hector is one of the best fighters in Unsel. Possibly in Ehrde. Tyrell may be the only man who could beat him."

She looked frail, shivering in the cold, goosebumps covering her arms and legs. Victoria released his arm and pushed blond curly hair from her face so he could see her eyes. Angst wanted to continue warning her of the dangers in dueling Hector, since he had fought Hector so many times himself. Victoria's eyes, however, narrowed knowingly. A cocky smile crept up the corner of her mouth so only he could see and understand.

"Oh, really?" he whispered in surprise, and he knew it would be okay. He nodded once at Hector.

"Then let's hurry up and get this done with," Hector said, agreeing to her terms. "We need to save Angst, and we need to save Rose."

20

"Your Majesty knew she was going to leave with them?" Tyrell asked incredulously.

Alloria had been dismissed, the doors were closed, and they were now alone. Tyrell wiped a bead of nervous sweat from his forehead as he paced back and forth before the throne. He suddenly felt old, and out of control.

"Of course I knew. I am her mother," the queen reminded him. "And the guards notified me right after she left the castle."

"They...they notified you?" Tyrell asked, his normal stoic nature cracking. "They didn't stop her?"

"I told them not to," Isabelle said matter-of-factly. She seemed completely nonplussed by his panicked state.

Tyrell stopped pacing and moved very close to the queen. She tried to rear back in the throne, pressing her head firmly into the cushioned chair. Tyrell leaned in and stared intently at her glass right eye.

"It looks normal," he said quietly to himself.

"That's not very funny," she said.

"It wasn't meant to be," he replied, straightening. "I just don't understand, at all, Your Majesty. You just let her go? With them? With...him?"

"I didn't want to," Isabelle said, crossing her arms. "But she'd become foolish, and I truly believe she was heading down a bad path. A journey like this will require more vigilance and character than she has shown since the crisis."

"But with Angst?" Tyrell asked. "Of all people, him? A magic-wielder?"

"She wants that man to be her champion, and tests him to save her all the time," she answered with a discouraged sigh. "At the same time, he wants to be her hero. There's little I can do but hope they fit."

"But the dangers out there..." Tyrell fretted. "She flirts with disaster. They flirt with each other!"

"Is it any less dangerous here?" the queen asked, touching the damaged skin around her eye. Her voice grew quiet. "If Angst's story is correct, it wouldn't be safe for Victoria to stay in Unsel anyway. She has a choice to make, Tyrell. Either she wants to be queen, or she wants to be an adventurer." Isabelle looked into the distance, her face wrought by concern.

Tyrell patiently observed her. It was a rare occasion when her guard was down, when she stopped being queen and allowed herself to be a mother instead. He could see that worry, and in many ways felt the same way. He sighed in resignation.

"If it is of any consolation, Your Majesty," Tyrell began. "I have prepared her well."

* * * *

It was cute, at first. Princess Victoria, clad in her tight riding pants and bodice, still filthy and wet from the storm, her long blond hair pulled back in a loose plait. She crouched, poised to attack with two unique slender shortswords, shivering from cold and anticipation.

"I'll bet a silver that Hector sends her home," Tarness said with a wink.

"You're on," Angst said, shaking Tarness's hand.

"You seem pretty confident," Tarness said.

"I believe in her," Angst replied without pause.

"Two swords?" Hector asked, one thick eyebrow raised high.

He drew a shortsword and held it aloft. "You won't mind if I just use one?"

"Use whatever weapon you want to be beaten with," Victoria said with a cocky grin as she circled the older man. She blew a lock of blond hair from her eye. "When I win, I get to come with—"

"When *I* win, you go home," Hector corrected, also circling his opponent.

"—and you apologize to me," Victoria taunted.

"Wait, what?" Hector said. "I don't remember agreeing to that."

She jabbed at his stomach with her left sword. As he parried, she swung her right toward his unguarded side but Hector was quick enough to parry the second swing. Victoria pulled back then jabbed neatly with both swords before quickly stepping back. Surprised at her control, Hector instantly began reassessing her abilities as he swung at her side.

* * * *

"How safe do you think she would be?" asked the queen. "If she were attacked?"

At this, Tyrell smirked with an almost-fatherly pride. "Of that I have no concern, Your Majesty." He arched his back and took in a deep breath. "She has been my pupil since she could stand."

* * * *

Victoria crossed her blades to hold Hector's sword in place. She lifted her arms and, in a half-circle motion, pushed his sword to the ground.

"Are you holding back or are you just that old?" she taunted, smacking his sword loudly with one of her own.

"All right then," Hector replied to her challenge, his hackles rising.

He swung his shortsword fast, every blow a vicious attack

from a new angle. Hector grunted in frustration as the princess ably met and blocked each strike. After several minutes, Hector slowed his attack to catch his breath.

"Did you want to make a bet too, Dallow?" Angst smiled smugly at Tarness and Dallow's shocked faces. Dallow shook his head without taking his eyes off the fight.

"What are those things?" Hector pointed at her swords with his own. "Foci?"

"Nope." She giggled, and her face filled with confidence. "Just me."

* * * *

"She's incredibly adept with the sword," Tyrell continued. "I've taught her almost all of my signature moves."

* * * *

The princess crouched and jabbed with her right, nicking Hector's sword hand. As he let go, she caught his hilt with her left sword and tossed his blade high into the air, disarming the veteran warrior.

"That had to have been one of Tyrell's moves," Angst said, slapping Tarness and Dallow on the shoulder as their jaws dropped.

Hector leaped ten feet in the air, doing an impressive backflip while grabbing his sword mid-flight. Before returning to the ground, he spun around mid-air to face Victoria on landing.

* * * *

"But it's more than that, Your Majesty," Tyrell added. "With her magic-wielding, she seems to have an instant intuition of her opponent's attacks. It's been years since I've been able to beat her."

"You, Tyrell?" the queen asked in surprise.

"Without something like a foci, I can't imagine there is a person in Ehrde who could win a duel with Victoria."

* * * *

Hector landed in the mud, expecting to see the princess standing before him. As he sought his footing in the slick, the back of his knees gave way to her foot. He slipped and landed hard on his back. Blinking rapidly, he found her boot firmly planted on his solar plexus, and a sword pointed at each eye.

"Say it," she said, breathing hard.

"Fine," he said reluctantly, knocking both swords from his face. "You can join us."

"And?" she said, stepping on his forehead with her muddy boot.

Rather than getting upset, Hector barked out a laugh. Victoria removed her boot so he could sit upright then gave him her hand and helped him stand. He nodded admiringly at her as he caught his breath.

"And...I'm sorry...Your Majesty," Hector said sincerely, with a little bow. "I'm impressed. Tyrell has taught you well."

Victoria squealed and pounced on Hector, surprising him with a hug and a kiss on the cheek. She quickly pulled back to bow dramatically to the others. Angst, Dallow, and Tarness applauded.

"One more thing," Victoria said to everyone. "While I appreciate the formality, we don't exactly want to advertise who I am, so please call me Tori while we're on the road."

* * * *

"So there is a chance?" asked Isabelle. "That my daughter will be safe?"

"While I hate to admit it," Tyrell said, "Between Angst's magic and Victoria's innate abilities, she's probably safer than we are. All things considered."

* * * *

"Now I just need to wash these things," Victoria said in disgust, pulling the muddy clothing away from her body. "I feel gross, and I'm freezing."

"Hector, didn't you say there were hot springs in the woods over there?" Tarness pointed to the south.

"Yeah," Hector said angrily, shaking his head.

"What?" Tarness asked.

"Perfect," the princess said, squealing with delight. She took Angst's hand and dragged him toward the woods. "Come on, hurry up."

"That," Hector said to Tarness. "Let's gather more wood for the fire. They're going to need to dry off afterward."

"I don't understand. Why they?" Tarness asked.

"Wait, why am I going with?" Angst asked with a half-smile.

"You really expect me to go out there alone?" Victoria asked with another giggle.

Angst looked back at his friends with a shrug before running after Victoria.

"Need I say more?" Hector asked Tarness.

"Shouldn't one of us go with?" Dallow asked.

"What do you think the answer to that will be?" Hector replied. "While we're looking for firewood, maybe you can come up with a spell to dry them off. And make it a fast one."

21

"You never told me you trained with Tyrell," Angst remarked as he stepped over a fallen log, still in awe of her triumph. "That was just...really...wow. You really did it."

"I never mentioned it because I thought it was stupid," Tori said, vigorously rubbing her damp sleeves in an attempt to keep her arms warm. "Since my ability to see the future has been...off, I wasn't sure it would work."

"Wait," Angst said, stopping suddenly. "You dueled Hector even though you could have lost?"

"That's what you would do," she said, pushing him forward. "Now keep moving. I'm cold!"

Their feet crunched on the frozen ground, echoing noisily through the empty woods. Victoria's lips were becoming bluer with every step. She'd been able to ignore the cold during the fight, but her damp clothes did nothing to warm her now. The longer they trekked through the woods in search of the hot springs, the more she suffered. He slowed and put his arm around her.

"How far away are these springs?" Tori asked through chattering teeth. "We've been walking forever."

"Knowing Hector, they could be a ways off. He moves pretty quickly, especially when he's upset." Angst ducked under a branch then held it up for her.

"Thank you, sir," she said as she passed under the branch unhindered. "Hopefully that nonsense is over."

"With Hector?" Angst stepped around her to take the lead again. "I doubt it. He has control issues."

"How can you be friends with someone like that?" Victoria asked.

"You mean how can I be friends with someone who gets upset when they don't get their way?" he replied with a wry grin. "Gee, I don't know."

"Don't make me beat you up too," Tori said, flicking the back of his ear. She peered over his shoulder and sighed with relief. "Finally."

These weren't mere hot springs. They were an oasis of heat and life buried in the middle of a frozen, sleeping forest. Steam hovered lazily over the dark waters, occasionally giving way to a cold wintery breeze only to rise again from the large pond. Moss-covered round stones framed the edge of the pond so precisely it seemed they had been placed there by hand. The entire area felt warmer by at least ten degrees, and Angst immediately relaxed.

"This could be the most restful place I've been in—" Something wet slapped the back of his head and fell to the ground behind him. "What was that?"

Angst spun around to catch a glimpse of naked princess leg before turning on his heel to face away. She giggled through her chattering teeth as she peeled off the rest of her wet clothes and plopped them unceremoniously in a sloshy pile before hastily tiptoeing over the mossy stones.

After a pleasant, albeit brief, glimpse of her backside, Angst turned to watch the surrounding woods as she waded noisily into the spring. Every movement created gentle splashes followed by a grateful moan or sigh.

"Sounds like the water is nice," Angst said, attempting to make conversation.

"Ooh, you're so brave," she teased Angst to his back. "Are you afraid of a little naked girl?"

"I saw what you did to Hector," he retorted. "Quit making me spin around or I'm going to get dizzy."

"Wait. You aren't joining me?" Victoria asked in genuine surprise as she immersed herself in the warm waters.

"Are you kidding?" Angst asked incredulously. "Of course not. I'll just keep you safe from right here."

Victoria stuck out her tongue and made a raspberry sound.

"How are you supposed to watch over me when your back is turned?" she argued playfully. "I am surrounded by water...ooh, and rocks! I could be in great danger!"

"That's not funny," Angst said, almost seriously. "You just keep talking, *Your Majesty*, and I'll know you're fine."

There was a sudden moment of awkward silence. Angst shuffled his feet and sighed loudly. The first moment became a second, and then a third.

"Tori?" Angst said.

The forest was dead silent—even Victoria's splashing had stopped.

"Tori, this isn't funny!"

He listened for anything, hoping to hear breathing at least, but there was nothing. Angst's cheeks and ears flushed red with frustration. Not knowing what else to do, Angst spun around and immediately met with her laughter.

Tori stood ten feet into the pond, a trouble-making grin spread wide across her face. Angst was angry, but within moments was chuckling and shaking his head, until he finally found himself mesmerized.

Tori was completely nude and completely wet. Her curly blond hair was now straight and matted to her cheeks and bare shoulders. The cold air and warm water had made her full lips incredibly red. Water lapped just below her hips, exposing her long flat stomach. Her hands cupped most of her breasts but, as she laughed, her stomach muscles tightened and they jiggled under her fingers. In spite of their friendship, Angst couldn't help but take in her beauty and youth. With a deep breath, he finally closed his eyes and turned away.

"That was not funny," he said, articulating every word.

"Your cheeks…sooo red," she said between chortles. It took several moments for Victoria to compose herself. "I thought you were going to pass out."

Angst had worried about the same thing. He leaned over and picked up her wet clothes. Holding out a hand, he waved to the ground, motioning her to submerge.

"Just…let me know when it's safe so I can rinse these out," Angst said.

"Go ahead," Tori replied, though there was disappointment in her voice. The water lapped as she sank deeper into the spring. "I just don't see why you're so embarrassed. It's not like I haven't seen *you* naked before."

"Of all the things I'm grateful for," Angst said, patting his roundish belly with his free hand, "One of them is that you haven't seen me naked."

He turned slowly, peeking over his shoulder to ensure she wasn't pranking him again. Victoria rolled her eyes but remained immersed enough to cover some of her breasts. Angst sighed and got down on his knees, resting them on the soft moss. He rinsed the mud from her pants, keeping a close eye on her to ensure she wouldn't pull him in.

"Oh, stop that. I'm done teasing with you. Mostly. You're no fun, anyway." She stuck out her tongue. "And I did so see you naked, silly. During our dream last night."

"Our…what?" Angst asked with wide eyes, almost dropping her pants into the water.

"You really don't remember?" she asked in concern and confusion.

Victoria made her way over to him on her stomach, crawling across the shallow floor of the pool's edge. As she got closer, the small of her back and part of her bottom rose out of the water. He skittered away from the edge.

"Would you stop that?" she said. "I'm being serious. Come here. I need to see something."

She was as close to the edge as she could be without getting out. Angst lay on his stomach and crawled forward so she could reach him. A pang of guilt was quickly overcome with excitement, and he could hear his own breath over the lapping waves. Lying flat, the only thing he could see was her face, and that was enough. She inched closer so they were almost nose-to-nose. Her lips looked so—

"Stop that," she said with a quirky smile.

Steam rose from Victoria's hand as she reached up to his face and closed her eyes. Angst felt it appropriate, for whatever reason, to close his as well.

"I should, you know," she whispered.

"What's that?" Angst whispered, licking his dry lips.

"Kiss you," she giggled. "Then you really would pass out and I could enjoy the pool all day."

"Tori!" Angst pulled his face back.

"Shh," Victoria said in an almost serious tone, still holding onto his cheek. "It doesn't always work. I don't always trust what I see, so I need to focus."

"But the thing you just said, about the kiss?" Angst asked quietly as he wiggled toward her again. "How did you know—"

"I didn't have to read your mind to know what you were thinking," she said, opening her eyes to peer at him. "We're best friends, remember?"

She closed her eyes again, and Angst followed suit. He thought about last night, about how fast he had fallen asleep, about his foci dream, and about—

"Rose!" he said. "She's okay!"

"You remember now?" Tori asked.

"Yes. No. Well, some of it," he contradicted himself, focusing his thoughts on what had happened. "There was a giant red bear, and...she ate it? Wait, was I naked?" he asked, his eyes wide in horror.

"I told you!" Victoria giggled. She licked his face before pushing away from the edge of the pool.

Angst splashed water at her then got up to his knees. "I don't remember everything. Do you?" he asked, wiping her spit off his face. He grabbed her discarded pants and returned to rinsing them. "Even more important," he said in concern. "How were you there?"

"Now I'm in your dreams, Angst. That's not a good sign," the princess taunted as she turned over and pushed away, floating on her back.

"Stop it," Angst said, slowly forcing his eyes to look down at the pants he was washing.

"Sorry, that was an accident," she said sincerely, rolling back over onto her stomach. "Honestly, I don't know how I was there, but I remember the entire thing."

Victoria did her best to remember to stay submerged while she recounted their dream, and Angst finished with her pants as he listened. He squeezed out the excess water and rolled them up before attempting to clean her bodice...thing.

"We should head back and tell the guys," Angst said as he looked off in deep thought, thinking about the dream.

"We can't! They can't know about me, about what I do," Victoria pleaded as she swam toward the edge.

"No, of course," Angst said, still looking thoughtfully into the distant woods. "I'll tell them I remembered during your bath."

"Right," she said sardonically. "They're going to believe you were thinking about your dream while I'm bathing naked?"

"Well..." he said as he finished cleaning her bodice. "I'll think of something."

"Um, Angst?" Tori asked, once again floating at the very edge of the pond.

"Yeah?" He suddenly noticed most of her steamy backside hovering over the dark waters.

"You may want to turn around so I can get out," she advised. "I don't mind, but I don't want to carry you back after you faint."

"Oh, yeah, right," Angst said apologetically. He stood and faced away from the pool.

Her departure from the water was noisy, and seemed to last quite a while. Angst could only assume she was upset he'd ushered her out.

"I guess what I don't understand is how Chryslaenor could have done that to the bear?" Angst asked. "I just...I don't ever remember it being able to absorb life. We were bonded for such a short time, but I didn't think it was capable of..."

The noisy sloshing of water stopped, and the forest was quiet again. There was no teasing commentary, nor the struggle of putting wet clothes on wet skin. Angst couldn't even hear breathing.

"Tori, please, let's just head back to camp," Angst said in exasperation.

Nothing.

"Victoria, I mean it! That's enough teasing!"

There was a loud slurp of water as though the pond behind him had choked. Angst spun about quickly and found an empty pool. No water. No Victoria.

"Tori!" he yelled in panic.

His voice echoed through the woods. There was no answer. Angst listened intently, until he heard a bubbling sound from the middle of the spring. Bubbles appeared listlessly in the muddy gloop, as though someone had pulled a plug from a tub, allowing all the water to drain away.

Angst's hands flashed blue and glowed bright as he held them out. He stormed into the mud thick remains of the oasis. Before his feet could sink in the muck, he forced the top layer of the silt to solidify and provide better footing. Angst reached with his mind deep into the earth, just as he had when attempting to lift the sinkhole. He breathed quickly, his stomach wrenching in panic. Searching for Victoria through the wet ground below the surface was like sifting through a bucket of mud in search of a small seed.

"Please," he whispered.

Angst was tiring, magic was harder to wield and control. The glow around his hands began to fade. His energy leached into the sucking mud, sapping him, and he fought desperately against a growing emptiness.

"There!" he said.

A small pocket of air and mud and water. It felt different from everything around it, and he could only hope it was the princess. He tried to tow the pocket to the surface, but the mud surrounding her fought him, resisting his pull. This had to be an attack by Earth, the element trying to scare them away! Angst reached beyond that wall in his mind, opening that stream of magic only the foci could provide. Blood poured from his nose and ears as he forced solid ground below the mud to push the pocket back to the surface.

In a loud, muddy burp, Victoria emerged, as if birthed by the spring. She was unconscious, and Angst rushed to her. Each step was an exhaustive struggle and, as he kneeled to pick her up, Angst felt lightheaded. His nose continued to spew blood, and the world began to spin. Muddy hands reached up from the spring bed, grasping at her legs, dragging her back into the earthy grave.

"No!" he yelled, wrapping his arms around her slippery naked body. "That's enough!"

His arms and chest were now glowing so bright he could barely see her. Power coursed through his veins, uncontrolled and unleashed in his desperation. The muddy floor of the pond sank further into the earth, pulling deep into the bowels of Ehrde. Angst held Tori close as he fought against the hands and, pushing with his legs, forced his way back to the shore. He glanced over his shoulder to see what he had wrought. The pool was now a bottomless pit, almost a sinkhole. All that remained was the outcropping of stone which had been his path out.

The glow surrounding his arms dimmed and disappeared. Dizzy, and sick to his stomach, Angst dragged one foot forward and then the other.

He had to get Victoria to safety.

22

"That was close," Hector said, clapping Dallow on the back with a heavy thud. "You did it."

Angst forced his eyes open to the familiar scene of worried friends looking down at him. It took every ounce of energy just to breathe. He couldn't even raise an arm.

"T...Tori?" he asked weakly.

He heard a cough to his left and rolled his head to see Victoria lying next to him. Her eyes were closed, but he could see her breathing under the blanket. He was tired beyond exhaustion and still frantic with worry. He thought he had lost her. Angst wanted to reach out to her, but couldn't.

"You're okay," Dallow assured him, patting his chest. "You'll both be okay."

"I found her things," Tarness said from the woods. Twigs broke under his feet as he approached. "I don't understand how he could have carried her all that way."

"Are we in any danger if we stay here?" Hector asked. "I think they're going to need another night before we move on."

Dallow sighed in frustration. He stood and began pacing, but said nothing more.

"I think we're fine. You said there was a hot spring back there?" Tarness asked Hector. "You should go see what Angst did to it!"

Angst rested his eyes.

163

Buried in Angst

* * * *

"Welcome back," Tarness said from above Angst, his smile beaming from ear to ear. "No wonder you're hurting! I'm not sure you could've done that when you had Chryslaenor!"

His back was cold from the ground, but heat from the large campfire warmed Angst's bones. A blurry Tarness came into focus as he leaned over to give Angst a sip of water. Angst still couldn't lift his head, or his arms, but he was able to grunt something he hoped would pass for a thanks. It was hard to tell how much time had passed—the sun was mostly hidden behind clouds.

"Tori?" Angst asked shakily.

"She hasn't woken yet," Tarness said in a worried tone. "But she's restless, so I don't think it'll be long."

"Rose," Angst said weakly, remembering the dream.

"It's okay, Angst," Tarness said encouragingly. "We'll be on the road by tomorrow. Hector is hunting for food and Dallow's looking for roots to make medicine. He's worried that you aren't shaking this off faster..."

With a tired nod, Angst closed his eyes.

* * * *

"Angst, you're awake," Victoria said in relief. She reached out from under her blankets to grab his hand. "You did it, you saved me. You were amazing!"

Angst smiled until Dallow shoved something awful and chewy into his mouth. It was bitter and minty at the same time and bile rose in his throat, but Dallow held his jaw shut. Angst tried lifting his arms to fight his friend off, but realized Tarness and Hector held them down.

"Sorry, Angst, but we're losing you and this is the only thing that will make you better," Dallow apologized. "After seeing what you did, Hector wants to get out of here, and I agree. This is the only way."

Angst swallowed the last of what had been forced into his mouth. His arms and legs shook violently in reaction to Dallow's "medicine." When his body stopped moving, Angst watched his friends stand and look at each other with concern. Dallow shrugged in response to Tarness and Hector's unasked questions.

Everyone turned to watch Tori stand, holding blankets up with one hand and gripping a bundle of clothes in the other.

"Everyone turn around so I can get dressed," the princess declared. "Nobody should see me naked."

* * * *

"Ahhh, ouch!" Angst said as pins and needles woke him. "What is that?"

It felt as though his arm had fallen asleep. He sat up and grabbed his chest to find that it felt like his entire body had fallen asleep. A prickling numbness covered every inch of his skin. Everything hurt from the odd sensation, but he was awake, and alert.

"It worked!" Dallow declared, punching the air triumphantly.

"What worked?" Angst asked with concern. "What did you do?"

"I poisoned you," Dallow said proudly.

"You what?" Victoria screeched, sounding much like her mother. She cleared her throat before continuing. "You told me it was medicine!"

"That was the only way to get you to shut...to calm you down," Hector reassured her.

"I translated a book from Gressmore ruins," Dallow continued excitedly, ignoring the princess. "It gave me the spell I needed to create the poison. You should be at almost full health after eating some food."

"Why a poison?" Angst asked as he rubbed his arms and legs in an attempt to get his blood flowing.

"I poisoned Death, Angst," Dallow said nervously. "You were so close to dead after what you did, and then carrying the prin…Tori all that way. We couldn't revive you. I looked through everything I'd ever read, so it took me awhile. Poisoning Death was the only thing I could do to keep it away. One in a million chance it would work."

Angst propped himself up on his elbows and looked at Hector and Tarness, who shrugged and shook their heads.

"Originally, I didn't understand the old Acratic tome because I saw death as an equation," Dallow said with a smile and raised eyebrows, obviously excited to give more in-depth details of his hypothesis.

"Of course you did," Hector said wryly.

"I thought about how the five elements can take human form, and realized that life and death might as well," Dallow pressed on, ignoring his friend. "If they are anything like the other five, they can be destroyed or injured."

In spite of several distracting coughs and some curious looks, Dallow was so proud of his solution he continued.

"Angst was almost dead, and we've all heard the phrase 'when death comes.' I thought it was figurative, but what if it was true?" Dallow wiped his blond locks out of his face. "I went through the text again, thinking of Death as an entity, and then it made more sense that he could be stopped, or held off.

"When Death tried to take Angst, he must've gotten sick to his stomach! He couldn't take you away, he probably couldn't take anyone!" Dallow laughed aloud, sounding quite maniacal. "Don't you see? It gave Angst enough time to heal, and I bet people around Ehrde stopped dying for hours!"

Everyone shared nervous glances, as if expecting greater ramifications from Dallow's experiment. When he finally realized he was the only one laughing, Dallow looked slightly lost.

"Um, thanks, Dallow," Angst said weakly, not knowing what else to say. "I'm sure you're the only one who could have done that."

* * * *

CHAPTER TWENTY TWO

"That's the most unbelievable story I've ever heard," Hector insisted.

"No, really, Hector," Angst said defensively. "That's exactly how I remembered it."

"There is no way," Hector said, "you had your back turned the entire time!"

"Very funny," Angst said as everyone else laughed loudly, including Victoria.

"So, you were attacked by Water?" Hector asked.

"Not by Water," Angst disagreed. "It was Earth! Those hands coming out of the pool were made of mud!"

"Angst, as far as you know it could have been Magic," Dallow interjected.

"Does it really make a difference?" Victoria said loudly, trying to speak over everyone else. "Shouldn't we get out of here?"

"What's the point?" asked Tarness.

They all looked at the large man in surprise.

Tarness shrugged nonchalantly. "We're talking about earth, right? Or water, or magic," he said nodding at each of his friends. "Those elements are everywhere. We are just as safe here as we are ten miles down the road."

"You're right," Hector said after a thoughtful pause. He looked at Dallow's worried face and continued. "I want to catch up with Rose too, but if we push too much and Angst gets worse, we'll just have to wait longer."

"You're right, of course," Dallow said sadly. "But, we don't even know—"

"Yes, we do," Angst said. "Rose is alive, and she's doing fine. I had a foci-dream about her, and she seems more or less healthy."

"Why are you telling us this now?" asked Dallow. "Not to mention, I thought you didn't remember your foci-dreams very well."

Angst looked dumbfounded.

"He...well, he talked in his sleep all night," Victoria said, blushing.

Everyone's shoulders dropped. Hector rolled his eyes.

"It was loud. I'm surprised you didn't hear it!" Victoria said defensively.

"It was raining pretty hard," Tarness said to appease her.

"Angst, you also said we were headed in the right direction?" Victoria encouraged. "And something about us not being far behind?"

Angst was slow to pick up on her verbal queues until she pinched him, hard. This wasn't information he had shared with her; it must've been something she had seen.

"Yes, that's right." Angst did his best to sound genuine. "Dallow, we are very close. I don't know exactly where she is, but I could tell, because of Chryslaenor, that we are very close."

The princess nodded fervently, and kept nodding until Angst nodded with her. Hector looked over at Tarness, and then Dallow, with squinted eyes that screamed suspicion, but Dallow didn't notice. He seemed so relieved to have some news, no matter how sketchy, that they were suddenly all at ease.

"Good," Dallow said. "That's good, right?"

"Yes, Dallow," Tarness said, patting his shoulder. "Your Majesty, would you be offended if I were to set up your tent?"

"Um," Victoria said hesitantly, seeming extremely disappointed. "No, of course not. Thank you, Tarness."

"It's my pleasure," he said with a wink.

* * * *

Hector and Tarness's hunt provided ample portions of meat for their dinner, and Angst could feel his strength return with every bite. It was the first night that everything seemed to fit. His friends were in good spirits, nobody was fighting and, in spite of their recent ordeal, he was completely relaxed. Victoria excitedly took a bottle from her satchel and handed it to Angst. He took a long draw of thick port and passed the bottle to Hector.

"So, what is this?" Victoria asked as she gave up on ceremony and ripped meat from a leg bone with her teeth. "It tastes amazing!"

"That one would be giant rat, Your Majesty," Tarness said, winking at Hector.

"Really?" Victoria said, squinting unbelievingly.

Both men nodded as they watched her closely. Victoria grinned at their challenge and took another bite.

"Well, I think your rat is excellent," she declared. "I shall make sure it is on the table when I am queen."

Everyone laughed, and Hector handed the bottle of port to Victoria.

She took a long draw and winced. "I think I like the rat better," she said with a cough. "What did I steal?"

"Port, Your Excellency," Hector teased. "Freshly made too. Sure to grow hair on your chest!"

"Just what I wanted," Tori said wryly before chugging several more gulps from the bottle. She hit her chest until she burped loudly. "So, what was Angst like...before I was born?"

Angst sighed, reaching for the port while everyone laughed at him.

"Your *boyfriend* and I grew up together," Dallow said a bit drunkenly. "And you'd probably be surprised to know he used to be a flirt!"

"Boyfriend?" Victoria said, sticking her tongue out at Dallow. "No, I'm not surprised at all. But, really, you guys had to have...adventures...you know, before?"

"Well, there was this girl that sort of had a thing for Angst. What was her name?" Tarness asked. "Izzy?"

Everyone but Victoria laughed so loudly they didn't notice her wide eyes or how she'd paled.

"I remember Izzy. She was sort of cute," Angst said. "That was the same time the Wizard's Retreat burned down. When we finally met Tarness."

Tarness beamed with pride as Hector recounted the story in greater detail than he had ever done. Inspired by a new, and royal, audience, he thoroughly embellished the events leading up to the Wizard's Retreat burning down three times until it was finally rebuilt by Angst and other friends to become the Wizard's Revenge. Wrapping up the story with the reluctant kiss Angst had landed on Izzy before she'd run away forever, Hector was particularly inspired by Victoria's continued looks of shock and surprise. When he finally finished, all eyes were on the stunned, wide-eyed, jaw-dropped princess.

"I...I don't know what to say," she stuttered.

"I'm sorry, Your Majesty," Hector said in genuine concern and respect. "Did I offend?"

"I think Izzy is my mom!" she pronounced.

There was a moment of silent shock before the laughter began. They all laughed to tears. Whether it was the port, or the story, or the overwhelming stress of their situation, it lasted until their bellies were sore.

"You kissed the queen," Tarness accused Angst with a pointed finger.

"You kissed my mom!" Victoria squealed, gripping her stomach. "No wonder she hates you."

Angst looked defeated, bringing more laughter. Tori grabbed the bottle of port and pouted when she found it empty. Hector and Tarness stood.

"I'm glad you're here, Tori," Hector said respectfully with a polite bow. "Good night all."

Hector and Tarness walked to their tents and crawled in.

"Well, I'm on first watch," Dallow declared, running both hands through his blond hair and pulling it away from his eyes. He stood and poked at the campfire with a stick.

"Right," Angst acknowledged. "Thanks, Dallow. Hopefully I'll feel better soon and can help."

Dallow merely nodded, walking over to the pile of wood to grab several more branches. Angst looked over at Victoria. She seemed sad, or worried. As they approached their tents, he leaned over.

"You okay?" Angst whispered.

"I don't want to sleep alone," Victoria blurted out, sounding embarrassed.

They were facing away from the campfire, and she looked around the dark woods surrounding them anxiously. She leaned against Angst and gazed at him with large, pleading eyes.

"No," Angst said firmly. "We've put my friends through enough. Look, Tarness put your tent right next to mine. They're practically touching. You'll be fine, I promise."

"But what about Rose?" she whispered hopefully. "What about our dream?"

"Tori, no," Angst said as politely as he could. "Dreams are dreams. We'll have them whether or not we share a tent. Goodnight."

Angst gave Victoria a firm hug, which she barely returned. They crawled into their respective tents. Angst undressed and lay still for almost an entire minute. He couldn't find a comfortable spot on the ground and finally gave up, deciding he was just restless from the day's events. He could hear Victoria dressing, shuffling, moving in her own tent. It went on, and on, and on, well after he stopped.

"Tori," Angst whispered. "Are you okay?"

"Please," she pleaded. "Can't I sleep in your tent again tonight?"

"For the last time, no," he said firmly.

"But didn't you like it?" Tori said in her most convincing voice. "You said you slept better with me there."

"Of course I did," Angst whispered loudly. "It's just not appropriate"

"Since when did we need to start being appropriate?" she asked.

"Not to mention, it upsets Hector," Angst reminded her.

"I can just beat him up again," Tori suggested.

"I can hear you," Hector said from the other side of the campfire.

"We can all hear you," Tarness yelled in frustration. "These tents are made of cloth, not stone!"

"Please," Tori pleaded in spite of the audience.

"Would you both just go to sleep?" Tarness pleaded. "You sound like a couple of teenagers."

"But I am a teenager," Tori said.

Everyone grumbled loudly.

23

The street that hosted the Wizard's Revenge was a blemish. A sore thumb that stuck out amidst other, more traditional, buildings found in the busy heart of Unsel. The Revenge was in a monolithic structure neither large nor inviting. The bar and inn was a two story, stone block crammed between fat storefronts made from aged and weather-beaten wood. Dusty windows in one old boutique featured an even dustier "For Rent" sign. The other shop, providing massage services, seemed to have regular traffic at all hours in spite of its undesirable location.

Rook had promised Janda he would meet her at the bar before leaving for Heather's, but he hesitated just outside the door. Angst always spoke so fondly of his favorite tavern, but Rook had yet to feel the love. From the silence his entrance caused, to the lonely corner where he would sit and wait, the few times Rook had visited he'd felt like an outsider. Was this what it was like for Angst, his friends, or even Janda in the castle? Is this how they felt outside of the Wizard's Revenge? It was too cold to ponder, and he pushed his way through the heavy wooden door.

It took several moments for his eyes to adjust from the late morning sun. Even in that short time, Rook was certain the room had grown. It now appeared bigger inside than out, which made his brain wince, and he shivered a little at the unknown power behind such illusions—real or not.

He looked about and saw several familiar faces, all of whom nodded politely when he made eye contact before returning to their "breakfast," but no Janda. The bosomtastic waitress sashayed her way toward him, forcing a hard swallow and glance around the room to make sure his date wasn't waiting.

"Can I help you to a table, Mr. Rook?" she asked in a happy singsong voice.

"Um, sure," he said, removing his cap to free his light curly hair, "if you don't mind, that is. I'm waiting—"

"Everyone is welcome," she said while guiding him to a nearby table. "And Janda should be here soon. She mentioned you were coming."

Six mugs of ale floated in front of them, making Rook step aside unnecessarily. The waitress waved them off like gnats, setting them on a less direct path. She looked back with a full smile, as though attempting to let Rook know she would keep him safe from the foul floating mugs of *eeeevil*. She pulled out a chair for him to sit, which he did. He coughed with embarrassment as she leered at his broad shoulders.

"Did you want something while you wait?" she asked, leaning into the question.

"A mead would be great," he said, making eye contact several times. "If you wouldn't mind…delivering it by hand?"

She rested a hand on his arm and chuckled. "I would be happy to, doll." She smiled again. "I'm Heidi. Just call if you need something."

Rook watched as she sauntered away and, for a brief moment, felt welcome at this tavern of magic-wielders. There were twenty-odd people scattered about the room, though from Rook's perspective they were actually all-odd. The nearest table hosted a card game played by two older men, a young man and a young woman, all of whom mostly ignored his wandering eyes. The oldest member of the party had long, dark gray hair and a twinkle in his eye as he focused on the deck of cards shuffling itself in mid-air.

Since the crisis, many magic-restricting laws had been lifted, and there were obvious signs of this at several of the tables. Most noticeable was the ball of water that appeared above tables as food was delivered. Table-dwellers nonchalantly reached into their hovering globe then wiped their hands on a napkin before eating.

"I figured it'd be nice to keep the ragamuffins clean," Graloon said with a grunt, setting Rook's mead on the dark sticky table. "Dallow helped me work this out last week. Smart lad, that one."

Graloon pulled a hand from a greasy apron pocket and rested it palm down on a small, round metal plate at the center of the table. A head-sized ball of water rose from the plate and hovered expectantly in front of Rook. His eyes grew wide at the sight, and his back arched instinctively.

"Go ahead, it won't eat your hand," Graloon said, reaching into the water then pulling his hand out. He wiggled his fingers, letting several drops of water fall to the table.

Rook didn't want to be rude so, with a deep breath, he plunged his hand into the floating ball. The water was warm. He jerked his hand out, clenched a fist nervously then submerged both hands.

Graloon handed him a towel. "Heidi hasn't been well for months. Normally, I don't...clean. Dallow thought this might help," Graloon said with a shrug. "Maybe it does. As you can see, she's doing much better. I hate to see my niece falling ill."

"Nice try, but Hector told me. She's not your niece," Rook said with a wry smile, grateful Graloon would be welcoming enough to tease.

"I'll have to take that up with Hector when he gets back," Graloon said with a grunt. "Have you heard anything from them yet? Or the princess?"

"You know about Her Majesty?" Rook asked with a whisper, peering at those around them cautiously.

"She's gone off with Angst, right?" Graloon asked. "If that man does something foolish and hurts Heather in the process, I'll show him where he can stick that sword."

Rook didn't know what to say, and quickly camouflaged his lack of response with several gulps of the sweet mead.

"If you don't mind me asking, is it going to be made official?" Graloon asked, almost respectfully.

"What? I'm sorry, is what going to be made official, Graloon?"

"Magic-wielding soldiers. From what I understand, Unsel needs them." Graloon wasn't being coy or quiet, and those at the nearby table turned to face him.

"You're right, we do need them," Rook said, squeezing his hands together in irritation. "I asked the queen myself, and was told...I was told not yet."

"That's crazy!" the young woman clamored from the nearby table.

"I agree, Birgitte. I don't understand why they would want to wait," said a balding, burly man sitting next to her.

"John, Mitchell, Rahvin, Birgitte, and half the people in here are waiting to enlist," Graloon said with a wave of his hand. "They want to help, and they need the work."

"If I get another chance, I'll ask again," Rook promised as he dared a lingering look at Heidi.

"You dropped something," Janda said, smacking him in the back of his head. "Your jaw?"

The table of magic-wielding soldiers broke out in laughter. Rook looked up at Janda out the corner of his eye while rubbing the back of his head. She hugged Graloon, avoiding Rook's apologetic looks.

"I see your waitress is still earning her tips," she said dryly.

"She brings in the boys," Graloon said, jerking a thumb at Rook.

Rook stared at Graloon with eyes that screamed, "where is the brotherly bond between men?" Janda wacked Rook again, making the table of onlookers laugh even more. Birgitte raised a glass to toast Janda's disciplines, and Janda winked at the dark-eyed brunette before smiling at Rook as though nothing had happened.

"We were just talking about magic-wielders enlisting," Rook said, hoping to start their conversation on better footing.

Graloon nodded in confirmation.

"It's true? Your boy there recommended us to the queen?" Mitchell asked in disbelief, wiping a bit of ale from his scruffy face.

"He didn't ask," she answered, making everyone's faces turn sour. "He insisted, practically demanding the queen and her Captain Guard look into it. Rook told them they were fools for not wanting to protect Unsel. I'm surprised they didn't throw him into irons for insubordination!"

A brief pause was followed by loud cheers from all nearby. People stood to shake Rook's hand or slap him on the back. Rook's eyes were wide with surprise as he looked from the throng of supporters to Janda. She winked slyly and emptied the rest of his mead.

"See, son, the non-wielders aren't all bad," Rahvin said, slapping Mitchell on the shoulder.

"Fine job, Rook," Graloon said enthusiastically. "That one is on the house. You come back and tell us more, okay?"

"Yessir. Yes, um, thanks!" Rook said, dumbfounded.

"Let's get out of here, my dear. Jaden is waiting to go visit Heather," Janda said, taking Rook's hand and leading him to the entrance. She continued in a whisper, "And we don't need your head getting any bigger."

* * * *

The path to Angst and Heather's cottage was almost a road, barely wide enough for two horses, as though the pretty country view on either side of the path was desperately trying to meet once again. Rook had heard rumors that the queen was attempting to keep Angst away from the princess by awarding him a homestead so far away, but in Rook's eyes it was truly a gift. The castle was only a half-day ride by horse—far enough away to be free from the city crowds he proclaimed to hate, and close enough to be quickly available for young princesses.

Rook stared off at snowy fields protected by a tight, soldier's row of trees. The week of adventure with the magic-wielders had been wearing, and his nerves were on edge. His leg felt tight and his side hurt from trying to overcompensate for the injury. Even worse, he was certain he had to be going mad. Rook was falling in love with one of them, with a magic-wielder.

He looked over at the beautiful Janda. Long curly red hair framed her pale face. Tiny freckles covered her cheeks, which were blush red from the cold air. Her lips were thin, yet full enough to kiss, and they smiled like she knew what he was thinking when she turned to look at him. She was amazing, and he felt warm and calm in her eyes until she winced and looked up again.

"Ouch," Janda hollered over her shoulder while holding her fingers to her ears. "That was too loud!"

Janda quickly reached up into the sky and a fist-sized ball of flame shot from her fingertips. The fireball tore a hole in the ceiling of clouds, exposing blue skies above them as it continued to space and beyond.

"That's how far away I am!" she yelled fiercely. Her one-sided conversation seemed to be that of a crazy person. Janda jerked her head quickly to look over at Rook, her hair whipping around violently. She smiled warmly, trying to continue the brief moment that they had just shared.

"I hate this," Rook said, shaking his head in anxious frustration. "Why did Jaden have to come with?"

"I'm sorry, butter," she said sweetly. Before he could take off and ride ahead, Janda reached over and rested her hand on his arm. "He wanted to practice earthspeak, and it requires another wielder. You saw Earth try to teach him how, and it takes a lot of practice. I can't do it, and he can't do it right. We're trying to prepare...in case—"

Janda let go with a wince, holding both wrists firmly against her ears. Her top lip lifted in an angry sneer. She forcefully threw a larger ball of flame down the road behind them. Rook could feel the heat diminish as it moved further away.

Janda turned her head to smile sweetly at Rook again. "No matter how many fireballs I throw, he can't judge how far away I am, and it's pissing me off!" she growled. There was an indignant yelp from the trail behind them. "Hopefully that ass will start paying attention."

Before Rook could speak, a giant lizard bearing Jaden landed gracefully in front of them. It was an odd beast with six legs and a long tail. Scales of rough gray granite gave the creature a frighteningly cold and harsh appearance. Its long forked tongue licked and flicked at the path before retreating into the creature's mouth.

"What was that for?" Jaden snapped. "You singed my cheek!"

"It felt like my ears were going to pop!" Janda roared. She urged her swifen, a glassy red lioness, over to inspect the damage on his cheek. "You big baby, you'll be fine."

"It shouldn't have been that loud," Jaden said with less vehemence, rubbing his reddened cheek. "This spell is unlike anything I've tried. I know the practice will help."

"That's why I'm agreeing to do this," she said. Janda nodded her head toward Rook. "But it's time for a break from magic."

The rock and dirt road suddenly transitioned into a beautiful carved stone pathway. The hooves of Rook's horse clacked loudly, and he pulled the reins to dismount. Rook inspected the road ahead, rubbing off the dusting of snow with his hand. The stones were mostly flat and varied in color, all different types of limestone, flint, granite, and other indeterminate minerals. It was a beautiful mess that succeeded in both widening and fortifying the path ahead.

"Angst mentioned he was working on this, but I wouldn't have thought it would be so...pretty," Rook said in surprise.

"We must almost be there, right?" Jaden asked, unimpressed by the sight. "How much of this could he have gotten finished?"

"It's my understanding that he stopped fifteen miles from his house," Rook said.

"He did all this in under a month?" Janda asked in surprise.

"If nothing else, the guy is a work horse," Rook said, shaking his head.

"I wish the stones weren't covered in snow. I bet this will be amazing in the spring," Janda remarked.

"We should keep moving," Jaden said, doing his best not to look surprised. "Heather's expecting us."

The colorful stone road widened enough for the three to ride next to one another, and within ten minutes, the cottage came into view. As they came closer, the snow no longer covered the pathway and surrounding grass.

"That's odd," Janda said, commenting on the lack of snow. "Is this something Angst did?"

Rook merely shrugged then sighed with relief at reaching their destination. He was wary of imposing on Heather, but his leg was increasingly uncomfortable. He was also wary of Jaden. They still knew little about the young man—his intentions, his abilities, or even his origins. He was only here because he needed to practice earthspeak, and Tyrell wanted Rook to observe him and pass along what he could.

The cottage was much larger than one found in the city. Originally made from logs, it seemed Angst had fortified much of the structure with stones similar to those along the path. Unfortunately, what made the path oddly attractive didn't quite work for the house, and Rook wondered if Heather had the heart to mention it.

Rook dismounted his pinto and knocked on the door. As Janda and Jaden dismissed their swifen, Heather opened the door.

She smiled welcomingly at her dusty guests, and tugged at her heavy dress to cover her pregnancy. "Thanks for coming. I'm glad you're all here," she said, giving Rook a friendly hug and beckoning them inside.

Scar ambled toward them with his head hung low and his tail wagging slowly. He trod halfway down the hall then waited for Rook and the others to come to him.

"He looks awful," Rook said, picking up the pup and analyzing him. "How is he even alive?"

Heather's lip began to quiver, and Janda rushed to take her hand while shooting an angry look at him. Rook was at a loss and looked to Jaden for understanding, but he was in the same stupor. A sudden sadness overtook Rook as Heather's ability to influence others' emotions affected him.

"It's okay, Janda. Thank you," Heather said, taking a deep breath. "Scar and Angst seem tied together. When Angst fell ill, so did Scar, so he's the only sign I have that Angst is alive. But he's getting worse, and so...I worry."

"Heather, I didn't know. I'm sorry," Rook said in surprise. "I don't always understand this stuff. I'm glad Angst is okay."

Heather wiped the corner of her eyes and patted Rook on the shoulder. She nodded and smiled bravely. "Angst is always okay. Come in and tell me of goings-on at the castle," she asked. "It's quiet out here."

They followed Heather to the sitting room where everyone found a chair. Tea and biscuits waited for them on a table. Rook and Janda said grateful thanks through mouthfuls of biscuit.

Jaden stared at his tea. "It's cold."

"I didn't know when you were coming," Heather said apologetically, gripping the arms of her chair to stand.

"I can take care of Mr. Rude," Janda said, waving Heather back down. She took Jaden's cup of tea, unceremoniously placed her finger in it and concentrated. Within seconds, the tea was boiling. Janda flicked tea off her finger into the cup before handing it back to Jaden.

"You wield magic. Next time you can do this," she proclaimed, staring the young man down.

While his eyes appeared apologetic, Jaden said nothing, quickly setting the hot tea on the table.

The silence was deafening, and Rook decided to revisit his conversation from the Wizard's Revenge. "It seems the crown still has no plans to recruit magic-wielders as soldiers," Rook said, sounding disappointed. "I tried to convince Her Majesty and Tyrell, but they wouldn't budge."

"That's no surprise. Angst can't seem to convince Isabelle of anything either," Heather stated. "But you would think after the crisis, and with the looming threat of another, they would want to be prepared this time."

"Exactly," said Rook. He took an angry bite of biscuit.

"The queen seemed more interested in adopting Alloria than fighting the monsters around the sinkholes," Janda sniped.

"Adopting Alloria?" Heather asked in a chilly tone then muttered under breath, "I like her even less than the other one."

"What?" Rook asked around a mouthful.

"Have another biscuit," Janda said, winking at Heather. "Some say that after Princess Victoria ran away, the queen wanted an heir. Alloria is royalty, and next in line, so—"

"Victoria ran away!" Heather said loudly, almost jumping from her seat. She began breathing rapidly. Had it worked? Had she done this? Panic set in. "How…who? Is she…is she safe?"

"Heh, couldn't be safer," Jaden said snarkily.

"I'm sure if Scar is still healthy, she's just fine," Rook said with a smile.

"I don't understand," Heather said, gripping her heart and looking about guiltily. Her mind ran through the possibilities. She had never meant to put Victoria in danger.

"I figured you, of all people, would know," Rook said gently.

"Know what?" Heather asked. She couldn't control her breathing. She was starting to get dizzy.

"Everyone knows by now," Jaden said. "The princess went with Angst."

"What?" Heather screeched then promptly passed out.

24

Victoria wandered around the swifen while the others waited in awkward silence. She touched each one, studying them as she scratched behind their ears or patted their flanks. Dallow's tawny wood-carved gazelle had dark eyes shaped like his. The swifen pawed at the ground anxiously with its front hooves. The shadowy panther Hector rode appeared as though made from wet sand. Victoria had been reluctant to touch their swifen at first, but she'd found the skin warm and soft. When she finished stroking its back, the creature quivered like a cat shaking off water. She stepped toward the majestic stallion Tarness summoned. Obsidian marble with soft accents, the swifen was as sturdy as its rider.

"It's amazing how lifelike they are," she remarked, doing her best to stall. "I wouldn't have expected them to be warm to the touch. It's like they're alive."

"Yes, Your Maj…yes, Tori," Dallow replied.

"Your swifen always stay the same and Jaden's able to change his, but they always work." Victoria held her hand in front of the marble stallion, and steamy air puffed out of its nostrils. "Why is Angst's such a mess?"

"It's my understanding that the swifen is a reflection of you, a part of who you are," Dallow answered. "Angst's seems to be tied to his health, or his confidence. Or both."

"And Jaden?" she asked, unsettled by Dallow's response.

"I would say Jaden is overconfident," Tarness observed. "That, and maybe he's trying to be more than one person."

"As for us, we can't help but be perfect," Hector said with a smirk and sly eyes.

"Maybe," Tori winked. "But I'd definitely say steadfast."

Everyone's backs straightened with pride at her remark, for she was still the princess.

"Are you sure he's all right?" Dallow asked with worry and impatience.

"Are you sure he's coming?" Hector added.

A roar of frustration followed by a loud hacking cough burst from their campsite. Even from a hundred feet away, they could hear Angst stomping around in anger. They all turned around to look at Victoria with raised eyebrows.

"He'll get it, it just seems to be getting harder each time he tries," Tori said apologetically. "And no, I don't think he's all right."

"As much as I hate the idea of waiting," Dallow conceded, "he still needs more rest after your attack."

"He needs a foci as fast as we can find one," Hector corrected. "I think it's a mistake to wait any longer."

Victoria pondered these options as though they'd been presented directly to her. She twirled a lock of her blond hair around a finger and frowned. Pulling the strands in front of her eye she uselessly tried to line them back up where they belonged. Victoria sighed at the mud and oil that seemed ground into her pretty blond curls.

"I agree with Dallow. I'll convince Angst we need to stop at the nearest town." She thoughtfully placed a hand on Hector's arm. "You're also right, but if we don't give Angst a chance to catch his breath we'll have to move slower to compensate."

"Camfeld is on the border of Melkier," Hector offered reluctantly. "At a snail's pace we can make it there by early afternoon."

There was a loud rattle, and a sigh of relief followed by a hacking cough. They stopped talking as the clanking sound of

CHAPTER TWENTY FOUR

Angst's swifen approached.

"Sorry that took so long," Angst said, slightly out of breath.

Angst looked pale and sickly, his face drawn. Gaunt. He looked like Rose before she had fed on the bear.

"What?" Angst snapped at them as he stared down everyone's worry.

"Nothing," Hector said with gruff concern. "Um, Tori, would you like to ride with me?"

"No, I'll ride with Angst, thank you," she replied, without an ounce of worry in her voice.

Tori smartly used a bent metal plate on the swifen's shoulder to lift herself onto the saddle and swung her leg over the ram's neck. She settled back into Angst, who sighed with relief and gave her a brief hug before heading down the road. The others mounted and followed in silence.

"Angst, I'm still shook up by that whole thing," Tori said in her most fretful voice. "I'd like to stop at an inn tonight."

"I was hoping we could push past the first few towns so we're closer to the capital," Angst said, already sounding as though he had lost the argument. "If we make the swifen—"

"Please, Angst?" She jammed a lock of crusty hair into his face. "Look at this!"

Angst sighed deeply, exhaling exhaustion and concern. He knew his friends thought they should be in Melkier by now, and he agreed. He had delayed them enough. They needed to hurry and get Dulgirgraut or they would never find Rose, and who knew what kind of danger she was in.

"Angst, I know you're worried about Rose, but she's fine. And she's on foot," Tori said convincingly, several thoughts ahead of him. "This is the best time to get some rest before things really get messy. Please. Trust me."

"Okay," Angst conceded without further argument, though he was surprised the others remained silent.

"Is that what you see?" Angst whispered. "Things get messy?"

"We'll be fine," she lied, glad she was facing away from him.

* * * *

The road was busy enough throughout the year that it remained well kept even during winter. Water and slush drained away from the raised center, leaving a somewhat ice-less path and a pleasant ride, in spite of the cold. As noon approached, they faced a constant blast of cold air. Victoria pulled her cloak over her head as the trees surrounding them created a tunnel for the wind.

Hector lifted his nose into the air.

"What is it?" Tarness asked, recognizing Hector's attentive nose.

"Smoke," Hector said. "It is winter, so probably nothing."

Still, Hector's concern did not leave his face as they passed a *Welcome to Camfeld* sign. When they could finally see the small town, the icy wet sounds of their swifen's hooves and paws changed to crunching noisily on dry dirt.

"How did they dry the road?" Tori asked.

"They didn't," Hector said, instantly wielding a shield and broadsword.

"You want to ride on ahead?" Tarness asked as he pulled out his sword as well.

"No, I think it's a good idea to stay together," Hector said, looking back at Angst and Victoria.

The dry ground darkened with ash and soot as they crossed the threshold into what had been Camfeld. They stopped at what could have been the inn and looked around. Proud buildings and old cottages were now burnt-out husks of stone foundation and jagged boards that jutted only inches from the earth.

"What...what happened?" Victoria asked, her eyes wide as she looked around the charred destruction.

"We've seen this before," Angst said sadly. "Wyrms."

Victoria glanced over her shoulder with a questioning look.

"Dragons," Dallow clarified.

"I didn't think they existed," Victoria said as they brought their swifen to a halt in the middle of the dead town.

"Neither did we." Hector hopped off his panther and landed lightly in the wet ash coating everything. "This happened only hours ago. The air's still raw, so I would cover your mouths."

Everything around them smelled like cooked meat and last night's campfire. Grateful for Hector's suggestion, Angst lifted his cloak over his nose. Victoria shivered, and he gripped her shoulders supportively.

"If this is like last time…should we even bother?" Tarness asked the others.

"Always," Angst replied as he and Victoria dismounted. "This time, let's split up. Except for Tori. I'd feel better if you were with me."

Victoria nodded in agreement and stood very close to Angst as everyone else went in different directions. He watched as his friends wandered the newly-made graveyard with weapons out and shoulders heavy.

"Which way?" he whispered to Tori, hoping she could feel a life, a future, amidst the useless death surrounding them.

She gripped his hand and held it tight.

"How will that help?" Angst asked.

"I'm scared," she pleaded.

"Oh…right," Angst said, feeling stupid.

Victoria continued squeezing as she led him past a row of trees without bark, each of them painted black by fire's paintbrush. Ugly cracks appeared in several trees and the ground was littered with shards of splintered wood like teeth spat out of a mouth. She touched one's smooth surface and pulled back fingers covered in soot.

"According to Dallow, when a tree gets hot enough it can explode," Angst whispered somberly in explanation.

Victoria nodded, gripping Angst's hand so tightly it throbbed. She led him along a tall brick wall, partly destroyed and blemished in char. They followed it until they reached what appeared to be an entrance. Tori looked over her shoulder, seeking a bit of strength. Angst nodded that it would be okay. They turned the corner to find an artist's nightmare.

A hundred shadowy human shapes, frozen in horrific poses, stood in the courtyard as though seeking sanctuary from death beyond the walls. The roughly carved statues came in all sizes— babies curled in their mothers' arms, children hiding helplessly behind men taller than Angst. Some were grouped together in the back of the courtyard while others stood at the entrance. It was the shadowy representation of the seconds before a lost battle. Every likeness, whether attacking or retreating, seemed in terrible pain.

"It's grotesque," Victoria said, appalled. "Who would make statues like these?"

"Nobody," Angst said warily.

He approached the closest one, his stomach clenching anxiously. The statue was only slightly taller than him, and leaning back with its arms held out defensively, as though protecting itself from attack. Its mouth was wide open frozen in a scream. Angst ran his hand along one of the arms. The stone was rough under his palms, like volcanic rock. He gripped the end and shook. The entire statue wobbled.

"What are you doing?" Victoria asked.

"I don't understand why these are here," Angst said as he circled it.

They split up, wandering through the statues in their various disturbing poses. Victoria held her hand over each extended arm, as closely as she could without touching.

"Angst," she said fretfully. "Some of these feel...alive."

"How can you tell?" he asked.

"It's hard to see, but once in a while I get a glimpse of something very dark," she replied, her voice distant as she focused on the statue standing before her.

"Hey guys," Angst shouted. "You need to see this!"

Before they could hear even the distant clink of armor or rustle of movement from their friends, an arm on the first statue jerked. There was a loud crunch as the creature struggled to break free of its confinement. It pulled up a reluctant leg, as if ripping out a tree root, and then the other leg, until there was shaky movement forward. The statue took slow lumbering steps toward them.

With loud grinding sounds, the remaining statues swiveled their heads toward Angst and Victoria. Tori screamed.

"Now would be best!" Angst yelled to his friends.

25

Angst drew his long sword. Victoria leaped away from her statue as if launched from a slingshot. She landed behind Angst, brandishing her short swords.

"My heart's racing," Victoria stated between breaths, apparently on the verge of hyperventilating. "Is it always like this?"

"Yes," Angst said, swallowing hard against the dry soot and trying to sound calmer than he felt. "You'll be fine. We'll get through this."

They continued stepping backward to the courtyard entrance as the statues lumbered toward them. Angst looked down at his long sword in frustration. Chryslaenor would have given him everything he needed—the power, the size, the raw knowledge required to take out the sheer legion of monsters approaching them. As Angst and Victoria backed toward the entrance, the statues followed.

"They're stone, Angst," Victoria reasoned. "Can't you stop them? Keep them from attacking?"

Angst reached out and tried to anchor the minerals as he had done so many times before, but the statues felt slippery in his mind, like a watermelon covered in oil. Was it something he didn't recognize trying to protect the stone, or did his exhaustion keep him from grabbing hold?

They were all moving now, albeit slowly. Angst and Victoria retreated through the courtyard entrance.

CHAPTER TWENTY FIVE

"No. Something's resisting me," he replied in frustration. "Maybe I'm just—"

Hector arrived, quickly assessed the situation, and pulled two long-handled sledgehammers from nowhere.

"I hate using these. So cumbersome," he complained, holding the two large hammers aloft.

Hector stepped in front of Angst and Victoria, spinning the hammers threateningly. The statues were easily twenty feet away but, with every step, they moved faster. Angst and Tori rushed back, but Hector stayed at the entrance.

"This is a good place to hold them," Hector advised. "Only two or three can get through at a time."

Dallow and Tarness arrived, out of breath. Their eyes widened at the sight of a hundred living statue-monsters shuffling toward their friends but they positioned themselves on either side of Hector. Dallow spun his staff, nervously warming up for the oncoming battle. Tarness held his shield and longsword at the ready, towering intimidatingly over the others.

"It's obvious Earth doesn't want us here," Angst complained loudly.

"I don't think a wyrm attack would have anything to do with Earth, Angst," Dallow corrected. "Hector?"

"I don't like to think on it at all," Hector admitted. "You talk about the elements like they're people. They aren't."

"It's Earth!" Angst said. "She hates me!"

"This is a lot of hate!" Tarness snapped.

Tarness swung hard as the first statue crossed the threshold, exploding it into pellets of stone and dust. Angst tried to erect an air shield to protect them, but it failed, forcing everyone to cover their face from the dangerous debris.

"I'm sorry," Angst said in frustration. "I can't—"

"Just stay back," Hector said. He turned his head to give Angst and Victoria a quick wink. "We got this!"

Angst and Victoria held cloaks over their faces and listened to bits of monster statue patter against their protection. Tarness, Hector, and Dallow grunted. It sounded more like they were digging a hole in hard clay than battling a horde of angry creatures.

"This is too easy," Dallow complained. "Well, not easy, but still."

"I agree, this isn't even a workout," Hector grumbled.

There was a muffled scream.

"Oh no," Tarness said. "Wait, stop!"

Angst lowered his cloak. Hector and Dallow had stopped chiseling away at the animated statues to stare at the monster nearest Tarness. He'd cut off parts of the statue's arms, and blood poured from them.

"No," Angst said in a panic. "Tori, don't look."

But she'd already seen. She was pale and clutched her stomach at the sight.

"Finish it!" Hector yelled at Tarness. When Tarness didn't move, Hector swung a hammer with all his might and crushed the statue's head.

Victoria turned away to vomit. Angst reached with his free hand to hold back her long hair.

"These aren't statues," Dallow confirmed in revulsion.

"Are they...are they all alive?" Tarness asked. His large dark face was filled with guilt and worry, and he dropped his weapon.

"They can't be," Hector said. "This was the first to bleed. But there's only one way to tell. We have to stop them from moving and figure out how to check if someone's inside."

Angst patted Victoria on the back. She stood and wiped her mouth then took Angst's hand and looked him solidly in the eye, nodding in acknowledgement.

"I can do both," Angst offered. "I can keep them from moving, and feel for life."

"How?" Dallow pulled at his mouth, his eyes filled with concern.

"There isn't time," Hector said. "Better get started."

"You can do this, Angst," Victoria urged, then whispered, "We can do this."

From deep inside, Angst mustered the remnants of strength

stored in that place usually saved for desserts after a full dinner. It hurt so much he wanted to stop, or cry, or hide. Instead, he held her hand and concentrated. With a loud crunch, the statues stopped their march. Angst took several shaky breaths and stepped forward with Victoria in tow.

"Squeeze my hand twice when you find a live one, once if it's dead," he thought, hoping she would understand what he wanted. *"We'll do this together."*

He knew Victoria was scared, but she squeezed in acknowledgement and he was filled with pride. When the stones started grinding again, Angst redoubled his effort and the angry noise stopped.

"I can feel through the stone and know if they're alive," Angst lied through gritted teeth. "Tarness, you need to destroy the ones that...that didn't make it."

"I don't know," Tarness said weepily. "After that, Angst, I don't know."

"I'll do it," Hector said.

Angst led Victoria to the first statue, pulling her along reluctantly. He hoped it would get easier because he wasn't sure if he could keep them in place and drag her from statue to statue at the same time. He placed his hand on the first statue and she squeezed once.

"Hit it," Angst said coldly as he reached for the second statue.

Hector grunted as he swung down with both hammers, shattering the brittle statue into rubble.

"Hit it," Angst said again after touching the second statue.

Minutes crawled by as they destroyed another seven statues. Angst felt depleted of all energy and emotion as he went from person to person. Hector was breathing hard from the workout, but said nothing. Dallow consoled Tarness as the large man gently wept for killing what seemed to be an innocent. Angst placed his hand on a statue and waited for Victoria, but she hesitated. His hold on the statues slipped and took a deep breath. Still, she hesitated.

"Tori!" he yelled.

Hector looked at them quizzically but said nothing. Victoria squeezed once.

"Hit it," Angst said confidently.

Hector swung down hard with his hammers and they were splashed with blood.

"*No!*" Victoria screamed.

Angst jumped in front of her. Without hesitation, the statues surged forward.

Hector grabbed their cloaks and pulled them back. "It was dead," Hector said. "There was no scream! No sound at all! It was dead!"

Victoria nodded in acknowledgement then took a deep breath and lifted her chin. She stopped moving away from the approaching horde—an action that must've taken every bit of strength she had.

"Hold them, Angst," the princess said firmly. "We have to finish this."

Angst took a deep breath and concentrated. He winced, gritting his teeth as sweat beaded on his forehead. He grunted loudly, and the statues stopped their methodical march, becoming still again. Angst and Tori moved quickly now, knowing that Angst had little time left. This window of opportunity was shutting on their fingers.

Hector was a sweaty, smelly mess as they approached the last three statues. They were small, child sized, and had been put off for last. Angst placed his hand on the first and Victoria immediately squeezed twice.

"Not this one," Angst said hopefully.

Angst touched the other two, excited with the thought that they could be alive, only to have to tell Hector that both required his hammers. With his eyes squeezed shut, he reluctantly destroyed the other two statues.

Hector collapsed to the ground, his hammers gone. His normally ragged hair was wet and matted down. He mopped the sweat from his forehead and took a long draw of water from his flask. Tarness and Dallow joined them quietly, Dallow's hand resting on his large friend's shoulder.

"I guess this is me again," Angst said warily as he reached out to the small body.

He placed both hands on the statue's shoulders. At first, he didn't know what to do, but the coarse stone made him think of sand. Angst concentrated and the stone slowly fell away from the face as though it was weeping sand. They heard a desperate, crying gasp as the top half of the statue disintegrated to reveal a face.

Angst lowered his hands as Victoria stepped forward to catch the young boy under his shoulders. When the encasing was finally gone, the boy collapsed into Victoria's arms. She kneeled slowly so he could lie in her lap. Blisters and sores covered his body, but he breathed, barely. He couldn't have been older than ten.

"What happened here, son?" Hector asked as gently as he could. The boy took several swigs from Hector's flask.

"The dragons," he said distantly. "They were killing us, destroying everything, and then...the stone."

He struggled in Victoria's lap, twisting back and forth in panic as he remembered. Blood and pus from the sores stained Tori's leather pants, and she swallowed hard as she held his shoulders to calm him.

"We were covered in stone, we couldn't fight it!" The boy sounded crazed. His voice rasped hard with every breath. "It was worse than the fire. The stone covered everyone, made us fight. And then..."

He looked up into Victoria's eyes and reached for her face.

"And then what? What happened?" Hector encouraged.

"The fire cooked us in the stone like...like an oven," he cried.

The child continued rasping and wheezing in pain. Tears welled up in Victoria's eyes as he rocked in her lap.

They watched helplessly until he stopped.

26

"You fought the element of Air all by yourself?" Alloria asked, suitably impressed.

She leaned forward, providing Tyrell with an ample view of her cleavage. She was tucked into a low-cut navy velvet dress reminiscent of the queen's wardrobe. It seemed the court tailors had finally found her, for this dress fit better than the others, putting Tyrell at a dangerous disadvantage. Her light brown hair was held back by a dainty tiara that sparkled like her young blue eyes. She placed a ring-laden hand on his chest and pushed him away playfully.

Tyrell swallowed hard and cleared his throat several times before continuing. "Not exactly," he said, straining to sound less impressive. "He was just a host for the element of Air. I don't completely understand how it works."

"I thought the hosts were supposed to fight *for* the elements," she informed him smartly. "So he should have had almost all the abilities Air would. Which means it truly was an impressive feat."

"Well, um, thank you. I had plenty of help, from the element of Earth, and then Angst," Tyrell said stoically.

"But you don't wield magic, nor do you have a foci!" Alloria responded to Tyrell with thin, knitted brows. She stood on her tiptoes, mimicking his height and sincerity. "That's what makes it so impressive!"

"Which is why he makes such an excellent Captain Guard," the queen interrupted as she strolled into the room, the short train of her green velvet dress following closely. "And the very reason he is the Queen's Champion."

Alloria winked at Tyrell who shuffled aside and straightened his white tunic before bowing to Isabelle. Alloria curtsied as though she hadn't just been standing too close and flirting outrageously with the older man.

"I've heard Princess Victoria refer to a champion several times," Alloria said, her eyebrows raised in curiosity. "But I thought she meant it as a compliment and not a title."

The queen nodded to Tyrell, confirming he was free to discuss it as she took the throne.

"It's more than a title," Tyrell stated in his most staunch prose. "It's tradition, honor, and a privilege bestowed upon one person. The Queen's Champion is a secret keeper, a defender, and an advisor. He, or she, must be willing to sacrifice everything to protect the crown, and Unsel. Very few are aware of this title."

"Victoria wants Angst to be her Champion," Alloria said, sounding quite bored. She smiled slyly at the queen's grimace then, with a gleam in her eye, she quickly added, "Could Tyrell be my Champion?"

"I'm sure he would enjoy that," Isabelle said dryly with a raised eyebrow.

Alloria clapped quickly while Tyrell fought the urge to roll his eyes, smiling politely instead.

"When it is time, you will know the right person to choose," Tyrell said wisely, casting a knowing smile at the queen.

"Please excuse us, Alloria. Tyrell and I have several things we need to discuss," Isabelle commanded before Alloria could ask more questions.

"Yes, Your Majesty," the young woman said without hesitation. She curtsied, smiled at Tyrell, turned and strode out the room with regal confidence.

The queen smiled as she watched her young understudy depart before turning a stern eye on Tyrell, who reeled back in surprise at Isabelle's glare.

"Your Majesty?" he asked in disbelief.

"She's a little young, don't you think?" Isabelle asked, her voice quite sincere.

"Well...I... no, it was nothing like that. I would never..."

"No, you wouldn't." The queen smiled to herself. "Which is good, because I would hate to replace my Champion at this age."

"You know that won't be necessary," Tyrell said more firmly.

Isabelle chuckled briefly. "You certainly seemed to be enjoying your conversation with her," she said with a tight smile.

"I can see why Angst enjoys them so much," Tyrell said, looking at the door through which Alloria had exited.

"What's on our schedule today, Champion?" Isabelle asked, interrupting the Captain Guard's distraction.

"I have fifty ready men prepared to face the sinkhole monsters," Tyrell replied. He stared at his tunic and removed a long brown hair. "They will ride on your command."

"Fifty?" Isabelle arched her back and squared her shoulders. "I thought we had agreed on one hundred."

"Well, after Rook's report, I'm concerned that sending one hundred men means losing one hundred men."

The queen paused for a long moment, tapping a finger against her pursed lips. As she thought, Tyrell waited, staring at the green gem attached to that finger. He had known Isabelle for a very long time—long enough to wonder if this was for show. Not just the ring, or the tapping finger, but the very pause itself. He knew the answer, and wished at times that she would just be straightforward. But if that were the case, she wouldn't be his queen, so he waited.

"Do you think she will make a good queen?" Isabelle asked.

"Your Majesty?" Tyrell frowned, cocking his head to one side.

"Alloria," she said dryly. "Do you believe she will make a good queen?"

"Your Majesty has chosen her to be the heir. I'm certain you know—"

"Oh, posh!" Isabelle spat. "Stop this nonsense, Tyrell. Since when haven't you spoken your mind to me?"

"Since you've stopped listening to reason. My reason," Tyrell snapped. He took a deep breath. "Your daughter should be queen when you are done. Victoria is bright and capable, and her abilities will give her an edge no other ruler has possessed. When she returns, she will be wiser and more ready than when she left." Tyrell paused for a reinforcing breath. "While I'm at it, we shouldn't be sending a single solder to the sinkholes. The team of magic-wielders that defended Unsel during the last crisis would be better suited for this situation. I feel we are sending men to the battlefield naked."

"Thank you, Tyrell," Isabelle said with a wave that dismissed almost all of his concerns. "But you didn't answer my question."

"I believe she is manipulative, calculating, and too forward," Tyrell said, placing his hands behind his back. "While Alloria is very young, I would not care to wager with her in a game of roobles. I'm afraid I would lose my pants, as they say."

"Literally?" the queen asked then laughed at Tyrell's surprised look.

"My concern is that I don't believe in coincidence," Tyrell said with great sincerity. "That she is the only survivor of Cliffview, and it coincides with Victoria's departure? It is too much coincidence for my palate, Your Majesty."

Isabelle stared at her Champion for several minutes. Analyzing his long nose, strong jaw and short gray hair. Like a statue, he did not waver under inspection—as though he expected the occasional on-the-spot review.

"Send one hundred men," Isabelle commanded heavily. "There will be losses, but the crown needs a win, Tyrell. A win without magic-wielders. Do you understand?"

"Yes, Your Majesty," Tyrell replied, his face stony. "As you wish."

"See them off. And send a flag boy bearing my gold and green with them. I want them to know they carry the hopes of

Unsel," she stated solemnly. "Do this now, and when you return we will discuss Alloria's coronation."

Tyrell did not depart.

"Did I misspeak?" the queen asked sharply.

"Several visitors have arrived within the last twenty-four hours, Your Majesty," Tyrell answered. "Representatives from Rohjek and Melkier, unique-looking guests who say they are from Meldusia, a Nordruaut woman, and several Fulk'hans."

"I was expecting ambassadors from Rohjek and Melkier," Isabelle stated with a concerned look on her face. "But the others... What do they all want?"

"They are requesting help from Unsel," Tyrell said. "Specifically asking after your team of magic-wielders, and Angst. It seems troubles abound in all corners of Ehrde."

"The Fulk'hans want Angst's help?" Isabelle asked in surprise.

"Well, not unless by help you mean Angst's head," Tyrell replied with raised eyebrows.

"Can we provide that?" Isabelle asked hopefully.

"I don't believe so, Your Majesty. Not if he is to be a Champion," Tyrell said, smiling to himself at the queen's grimace. "The Fulk'hans. have changed. They are quite formidable, and angry. I would advise keeping a watch on them at all times."

"Please see to that," the queen replied, suddenly looking tired. "The Meldusians look unique now? More than before?"

"It seems the Fulk'hans weren't the only peoples affected by the Vex'kvette."

27

The town was small and tidy, tucked away in a grove of snowy fir trees. There were no signs of angry statues, burning pyres, or malevolent hot springs. A collective sigh went up from the group, quickly followed by relaxed shoulders. The inn, located in the center of town, was large and well-tended. A neat stone path framed by hibernating bushes beckoned weary travelers to the entrance.

"Are you sure you want to stop already?" Dallow asked Hector while avoiding looks from Angst.

"Are you really asking?" Hector asked dubiously. "Have you seen him? His swifen? Is Angst holding onto his ram or is the prin…is Tori keeping him upright?"

"What? I'm fine," Angst snapped from over Victoria's shoulder. "Just a little tired. We can keep going."

Angst felt like the bottom of a shoe, or his swifen's hoof. His silver ram swifen was now so far beyond repair it was impossible to keep track of its deterioration. The metal plates holding the swifen together now curled from almost every corner.

Tori looked pleadingly at Hector, who nodded in agreement.

"This is perfect," Victoria proclaimed. "I need a bath, now!"

"Tori, I'm sure we could make it to the next town before nightfall," Angst implored.

"You promised!" She pulled at a strand of curly blond hair, now matted with mud and soot. "They have baths here?"

"Yes," Hector said. In answer to Angst's frustrated gaze, he quickly continued, "I've stayed here before. They do have a bath, and there isn't another one to be found for several more towns."

"This is the most bathing I've seen someone do in my entire life," Dallow mumbled to himself.

"I've been meaning to talk to you about that," Tarness said with an obnoxious grin.

"If this is where you want to stay, then by all means," Angst said to Victoria with a tired sigh.

He wouldn't let the others know, but he was relieved. A warm meal, some mead, and an actual bed would help him get past the new bout of emptiness consuming him. Everything was sore, and helping Victoria dismount without being cut by his own swifen made his back twinge. His right shoulder popped loudly, making him jerk his hand back after she reached solid ground. He sat for a moment, contemplating the best way to dismount when he finally decided to take an easier route. The ram disappeared beneath him. Angst landed with a thud, straddling the travel packs that had been secured to his swifen's side and belly.

"Clever," Dallow acknowledged with a smile.

"We should've dismissed the swifen earlier," Hector remembered. "Magic is completely outlawed in Melkier."

"I have several documents from 'Izzy' that should prove useful if that becomes an issue," Angst said, digging through various pockets to find the right one.

"Just be cautious," Hector said with concern. "They aren't like us."

"I'd be careful about calling mom 'Izzy,'" Victoria said in a similar tone.

"But of course, Your—" Angst's mock-formal bow was cut off when a burly woman opened the inn door.

"You wanting to stay here?" she asked with a hairy raised lip. "I'm not sure we have rooms."

The woman was not even handsome. She was as wide as Tarness but the same height as Angst, essentially making her a very solid-looking square. Her skin was dark, and her gray hair curled short and tight against her skull. She scowled at Angst as he approached. He pulled his coin purse free and shook it several times to present its volume.

"We would love your company, lords and lady," she now said with a pained smile and one eye on his purse. It was as though Angst had paid for a bad performance. "Come in, come in."

They followed her into the dimly lit inn, which felt warm and oily. The smell of cooking grease, burnt meat, and stale mead hung in the air. Victoria visibly winced at the stench, while Tarness smile widened in anticipation.

He breathed in deeply. "Bar food," the large man whispered. "I can't wait!"

"We'll need three rooms, please," Hector requested politely.

Victoria's nod was as friendly as she could force it to be. Angst nudged her with his shoulder, and she nudged him back and smiled. In spite of his exhaustion, and her demands, Angst was glad she was with them and winked fondly as the innkeeper dug through a drawer. Eventually, the unfortunate-looking woman handed a key to Hector and another to Tarness. She held out the third key, offering it first to Angst then to Victoria.

"This is for you two," she said with a sneer, waiting for one of them to take it.

"Um, no. We need separate rooms," Angst said in concern.

"Oh? You could have fooled me," the woman huffed. "She isn't your honey?"

"No, she's..." He looked at the guys to find them thoroughly enjoying Angst's fretting. "She's my niece."

"Right," she said, handing the key to Victoria. "Do you want your uncle to have a spare key?"

"It's my understanding you have a bath?" Victoria asked, changing the subject. She pulled two gold coins from a pocket.

"Oh!" the woman squealed. It was more than the combined cost of the rooms, and she gripped the coins greedily. "I'll have my daughter, Hedrynn, start up the kiln. Would milady be wanting fresh water?"

"Yes, please," Victoria said, worried that it was even a question.

She gripped Angst's cloak tight, and he could tell her courtesy required every ounce of resolve.

"But when he takes his bath he won't require fresh water," Victoria said nodding toward Angst at the same time informing him that he, too, was taking a bath.

"You're with me, uncle," Tarness said to Angst.

Victoria and Angst sighed in unison as everyone else laughed, including the innkeeper. Angst picked up Tori's things and followed her to the stairs.

"Dinner is in an hour, and entertainment's in two," the innkeeper called after them.

"Entertainment?" Victoria asked with a smile and sidelong look at Angst.

"Yes, a local bard," she said. "He's not very good, but he'll sing all night for some coin."

Angst smiled broadly at Victoria, his eyebrows raised in anticipation. Victoria smiled back and let out a little squeal before running up the stairs to get ready.

Hector grumbled in frustration, and was about to say something when he noticed Tarness smiling.

"What?" Tarness said defensively. "It sounds like fun."

"I thought Angst needed rest," Dallow said, discouraged.

Tarness rested his hand on Dallow's shoulder. His voice was deep and serious. "Everyone finds relaxation in different ways, my friend. You'll see. Angst will be a new man come morning."

"What about my rest?" Dallow asked.

* * * *

The bard became more talented with every gulp of mead. His singing was fair at best, but he wielded the kendagar—a complicated ensemble of instruments that never ceased to amaze—better than Angst had once swung Chryslaenor. He would blow into the horn attached to his left hand between refrains, blaring in time with the staccato rhythms of his right. The bard held a small piece of metal attached to the palm of his right hand which he slapped somewhat spasmodically against blocks of wood, pieces of ceramic, or rubbed against his corrugated plate chest piece, making for an entertaining racket that sometimes sounded like music.

Hector's sensitive ears sent him upstairs after the first round of drinks, while Dallow lasted for two full drinks, seeming utterly fascinated by the bard's presentation and rhythm. Still, he quickly gave in to travel and mead and, after a warning, fatherly look that told Angst he too should go to bed, left for his room. Tarness didn't seem to enjoy the music at all, but still waited patiently.

Most of the tables in the generously-sized room had been pushed together for some unknown reason. Locals and travelers sat around the tables, clapping in time with the bard's music, but everyone turned as Victoria entered the room. Angst had never seen the dress she wore before. It was low cut, and showed more breast than he was comfortable looking at. The white silken cloth was light, flowing with every step. The dress also featured a high-cut slit, which exposed enough leg that Angst had to take another draw of mead.

The innkeeper's daughter, Hedrynn, followed Victoria. She wore a low cut peasant blouse, tight black leggings and thigh-high leather boots. The young woman was about the same age as Rose, and thinner, but without the curves. She was not exceptionally pretty, but her confidence was contagious and Angst couldn't help but smile at the young woman's dramatic entrance. Her mother rolled her eyes as Hedrynn swaggered in, but said nothing.

For the first time since the music began, Tarness smiled in anticipation, almost as much as Victoria. Tori clapped in excitement when Hedrynn flipped a coin to the old bard. He winked knowingly and changed tunes to play another something Angst had never heard. The song moved at a dizzyingly fast pace, and Angst was clueless how the man was able to keep up with so many instruments.

Victoria had finished her third mug of mead and waved for another while sipping on Angst's. Her cheeks were bright red, and her eyes looked drunkenly sleepy. She handed Angst his drink and proceeded to magically twist her hair into a ponytail the way girls did. The music continued to improve as Angst drank more. Hedrynn climbed onto the conglomeration of tables and beckoned for Tori. The young princess squealed, hopped up from her seat, and joined her new friend for the dance.

Angst was dumbfounded at how quickly Tori was able to emulate the other girl. They gyrated in unison, swinging their hips hither and fro in time with the beat, which Angst found himself attempting to mimic from his seated position as he slapped the table with his hand, almost in time with the song. Someone tapped his shoulder.

"Where did the princess learn to dance like that?" Tarness asked, his low voice surprisingly audible in the loud room.

Victoria and Hedrynn paused long enough to take steins of mead from a slack-jawed serving boy. The girls interlocked arms and chugged their drinks, staring at each other in challenge to see who would quit early. Neither did, and they handed the empty mugs back to the boy to continue with their captivating dance.

Angst looked at Tarness, who nodded at him briefly before staring at Hedrynn again. His friend was almost drooling. Angst waved at the serving boy, who hustled over. He held up four fingers and tossed the boy a coin, which sent the young man scurrying off with a smile. He returned quickly with four large steins of the cheap mead then proceeded to hover nearby, ready at a moment's notice for more mead and more coin.

When the song finally ended, Angst waved the boy over to fetch a drink for the bard. Tori and Hedrynn approached them, walking across the tables arm-in-arm. Hedrynn fell into Tarness's lap with a giggle, and Tarness nuzzled her neck with his nose while she grabbed a mead and drank deeply. Tori watched, and seemed to like the idea. She fell onto Angst. He panicked then relaxed as much as he could as she landed awkwardly, but safely, on his lap. He'd forgotten how light she was, and gripped her waist to give her a fond hug. Victoria's eyes widened, she smiled drunkenly and kissed him sloppily on the cheek before quenching her thirst with the mug.

"This is sooooo much better than tents!" Victoria slurred in his ear, the smell of alcohol thick with her every breath.

She kissed Angst's cheek again, making him blush and her giggle. He looked over to Tarness who was deeper into nuzzling Hedrynn (Angst wasn't sure if it was passionately or desperately). He avoided looking at Victoria's eyes or lips and turned to face the bard, who was wiping his mouth with the back of a tattered sleeve. The old man nodded gratefully for the mead, as well as the break. Angst tossed him a gold coin along with a hopeful gaze. Would that the bard was ready before Tori got tired of Angst's cheeks. This thought made her giggle, and he sighed that, even drunk, she knew every desire in his mind.

"Chicken," she whispered huskily in his ear.

"Whenever you're ready," Angst called out to the old man, doing his best to ignore Victoria's taunt.

She practically bathed in his awkward reticence, and wiggled provocatively in his lap before downing the rest of her mead. Angst looked pleadingly at the tired bard, who smiled at him. The old man took a deep breath then started a new, quickly-paced song with his kendagar. With a loud squeak, Victoria found Angst's cheek once more, kissed it for too long then stood on his lap. He winced while holding his hand out so she could brace herself. Hedrynn removed herself from Tarness's lip lock and stood tall on his sturdy muscular legs. The girls leaped to the tables and once again began their hedonistic dance.

"You didn't have to do that so quickly," Tarness said slowly.

"Yes, yes I did," Angst replied, his tongue thick from mead.

"Chicken," Tarness challenged, slapping Angst hard on the back.

"You're one of those men," the innkeeper said from behind them. She set down two more mugs of the sweet tasty mead.

"Who, me?" Tarness asked in fear.

"I know what you are," she said, staring him down over her jowly cheeks. "My daughter's a grown woman and can make her own decisions. You just treat her well or answer to me."

"Yes, ma'am," Tarness answered compliantly as he reached for a new mug of mead to hide behind.

"I'm talking about the other one!"

"Um, me?" Angst asked thickly.

"Uh huh," she said judgmentally. "Niece, huh?"

"Well…" Angst said with a smirk. "Most people don't understand that—"

"Oh, I understand all too well," she said, shaking a forbidding finger in his face. "Fifty-year-old man with an eighteen-year-old girl. You probably promised her her own kingdom while your pregnant wife sits home all by herself."

"His wife *is* pregnant," Tarness confirmed slurriedly.

"Shush," Angst said to his friend. "You don't understand. I'm forty!"

It wasn't coming out right, and his gaze kept left the innkeeper's judgmental glare to lose itself in the dance of joy continuing on the tabletops nearby.

"Ahem," she said to get his attention. "I understand exactly what's going on. Do you?"

With that, the innkeeper stalked away to a back room, thankfully out of sight. His thoughts were too blurry to absorb the deeper meaning of her insight. Angst shrugged at Tarness, who smiled as though all was right with the world. Angst drank deeply, which seemed to make everything comfortably fuzzy, and smiled as he watched his blurry friend dance to her heart's content.

28

"No!" Heather yelled, sitting up in a panic. She clutched her chest over her racing heart. "No."

Heather breathed quickly and looked around the sitting room, her eyes wide with shock. Janda rushed from the couch to kneel beside her. The younger woman held Heather's shaking hand with one of hers. It was all coming back. Had she really done it? Had she sent Tori away? Had she sent the princess to Angst? Janda handed her a cup of water, Heather nodded gratefully and took a long sip. After a brief coughing fit, she let go of Janda's hand, looking around the room for Rook and Jaden.

"I'm so embarrassed. How long was I unconscious? Where is everyone?" Heather blurted.

"You've been out for several hours," Janda answered, placing the cup of water on the table. "You were obviously exhausted."

"I haven't been sleeping well since Angst left," she said quietly, "I keep having a nightmare I can't seem to remember."

"I'm sure you just miss Angst. Not to mention being pregnant and home alone. It's completely understandable," Janda said with a broad smile. "As for the boys, after screaming at Jaden almost to the point of making him cry, I sent that idiot back to the castle."

She did miss Angst, and worried for his life, but now she also had to worry about the two of them out there, together. She wrung her hands together as though squeezing the concern out of her fingers. Heather saw the younger woman balling up her hands as though Janda was also on the verge of worrying. She reined her emotions in as best she could.

"Oh, that wasn't necessary. I'm sure he didn't mean anything," Heather said, forcing a smile.

"After you passed out, I thought he seemed to enjoy your reaction a bit too much," Janda said through clenched teeth. "He's arrogant and rude, and I have no patience for thoughtless people."

"Thank you, Janda. I'm glad you're here," Heather said gratefully. "What about Rook?"

"I sent him to fetch firewood." Janda smiled broadly and nodded at the crackling fire.

The stone fireplace in the middle of the room matched the stone path and stone exterior of their house. Heather looked at the fireplace and smiled thinly. It was ugly, but Angst had created it and that made her miss him more.

"But I thought Rook needed rest?" Heather said.

"This is rest for him!" Janda said with a laugh. "Rook is a dear, but he was in a panic when you fainted. Now he'll come back in, eat something, and then snore us both out of the room."

Heather chuckled politely and shook her head. Her thoughts battled between the guilt of putting Victoria in danger and the jealousy of Victoria and Angst spending so much unguarded time together. She crossed her arms and sank back in her seat.

"May I ask you something, Heather?" Janda asked, her face looking overly concerned.

"Of course."

"I guess, well, I didn't realize you hated the princess so much," Janda said carefully.

"I don't hate Victoria." Heather avoided eye contact with Janda. "I don't hate her at all"

"But your reaction to the news…" Janda let her question trail off.

"It's complicated," Heather said as she considered how to avoid discussing her part in Victoria's departure. "I don't hate

Victoria, I just don't particularly like Angst and Victoria. They're so close. They spend so much time together. He adores her, too much, and that sort of concentrated time together... It's just trouble, and it makes me angry."

"You think that bastard is cheating on you!" Janda stood abruptly, knocking over the mug of water. Her red hair shone bright as the nearby fire blazed in response to her ire.

"No, no, not at all." Heather held out her hand to stop Janda from causing more damage or storming out of the room to hunt Angst down. She took a deep breath to calm her emotions so they wouldn't affect Janda's. "He wouldn't cheat, like that, it's not in his nature. He just... I just... I wish sometimes he would talk about me the way he does her."

Janda sat back down. "I'm sorry for overreacting. I do that." She rested a finger in the puddle of water on the table, and it quickly evaporated. "Maybe he just needs to tell you more?"

"What do you mean?" Heather asked, her cheeks flushed. She took a deep breath and concentrated so Janda wouldn't become tearful as well.

"The few times I've been around Angst, mostly at the Wizard's Revenge, he didn't stop talking about you," Janda informed her sincerely.

"Really?" Heather asked, almost hopefully. "But he does that about Victoria to me. Every time he meets with her he can't stop talking about her."

"Really? He says a little about the princess, but I assume that stuff is confidential because, you know, she is royalty and such," Janda said. "He always talks about how beautiful you are, about his projects for your home, and about being a dad. Some of it is small talk, but it's always about you."

Heather swallowed hard and dabbed the corner of her eyes. Rook walked into the room, his pale cheeks red from the cold and a pile of wood in his arms. He looked with concern from Heather to Janda, who was patting at the wetness in the corner of her own eyes.

"Do I need to go get more wood?" he asked in a tired voice.

211

"I really don't want to cry right now."

"No, butter, come on in," Janda said sniffling. "Do you ever hear Angst talk about Heather?"

"All the time! He doesn't stop," Rook said rolling his eyes. He put the logs in a stone box next to the fireplace. "No offense."

"None taken, Rook, and thank you," Heather said, now smiling and happy.

"For the wood?" Rook replied, misunderstanding her gratitude. "Of course. I had to keep your fire going."

"My fire?" Heather said in surprise, looking at Janda. "That's not mine. The house is always plenty warm without one."

"That's the one fire I haven't started today," Janda said. "Maybe the ass did it before leaving."

Rook looked forlornly at the empty biscuit plate as his stomach growled loudly, but he flopped into a seat without saying a word. Heather gripped the armrests of her chair and began to pull herself up.

"Where do you think you're going?" Janda asked sternly.

"I was going to start making dinner," Heather said. "I've got chicken ready to cook."

"I'll take care of that. I promise I can cook anything much faster than you can," Janda said with a wink. "Besides, I'm sure Rook will soon be providing you with loads of entertainment."

They both looked at the man already nodding off in a nearby chair.

* * * *

Time seemed to slow as she stood and waited on the snow-dusted woodland trail. Branches creaked as the cold gripped them, attempting to strangle the life from them. Rose shivered, but not from the chilled air, as something unnatural always kept her warm. She appreciated privacy but had never felt as alone as this. The magic within Chryslaenor had forced her into exile, driving her away from her friends. Solitude was poor company, and this made her shiver.

She concluded there were three different forces at work. What she wanted, which seemed not to matter, the black lightning that fed her, dragging her in every direction, and Chryslaenor, which seemed to be losing its battle. The black lightning often looked like blood coursing through the metal filaments, at times she heard the echo of a distant, painful song, and Chryslaenor no longer stopped Rose from lifting it. The sword wasn't resisting; it merely felt heavy.

"You're taking longer than usual to provide me breakfast," Rose said aloud. "Don't we have somewhere to go?"

As though on cue, the black lightning leaped from the blade and struck the ground. A burst of light surrounded Rose and spread out to the trees as though a rock had been dropped in water, rippling out in waves on the ground. The circle of dust expanded, kicking leaves and snow into the air as it sought prey.

"Very fancy," she yawned, "for whatever good it does."

Something clicked in the distance, followed by a loud crack. Chryslaenor dragged itself along the forest floor, turning her to face the direction of the noises.

"Finally, something to eat. I just wish it were something normal," she said warily. "It should really be bread. I miss bread."

"Help!" cried a voice that sounded young and scared. "Please someone, help!"

"No," she whispered in panic to the sword.

Two small legs pumped desperately as a curly-haired girl ran toward her. Rose was bad at guessing kids' ages, but she looked about seven. Maybe eight? Certainly too young to be alone in the woods. The girl's dark curls bounced about her shoulders with every step and she wore layers of burlap to fend off the cold. Balls of steam puffed rapidly from her mouth as the run stole her wind. She tripped over her own feet, stumbling as she slowly regained her pace.

Chryslaenor rose into the air, black lightning licking hungrily from the tip.

"Please, no. Please!" Rose begged. She tried pushing and then pulling the hilt in any other direction but it was like trying to swing a mountain, and she couldn't.

The girl stopped suddenly in front of Rose, clutching her chest, tired and panic-stricken. There was a desperate moment of helplessness, when the black lightning charged the air around the sword and the tip pointed directly at the young girl. Her eyes were large deep pools, just like Rose's, and they widened in fear. She stood very still, entranced by the sword's hungry baiting. Rose looked into those eyes, her eyes, and deep inside decided she wouldn't let this happen.

"*I said no!*" Rose commanded.

With all of her strength, and all of her will, she fought and pulled and slowly forced the blade back to the ground. Angry lightning leaped from the tip of the blade to surround Rose like a swarm of vengeful wasps. Each strike created black sparks that bit her, punishing her for attempting to fight, and the blade inched up toward the girl again. In spite of the pain, Rose knew she would heal and continued willing the sword back to the ground.

"Please stop!" the girl squealed, confused and frightened by Rose and her sword. "It's coming!"

She could barely hear the child, but the warning was enough to make her look up and see it. A grotesque abomination of failed living ran toward them. Two long stick-thin legs struck the ground, soon followed by the other three legs, giving the creature an odd, lopsided gate. Its torso was a transparent cocoon that provided horrific glimpses of dinner and breakfast. The monster had two ape-like faces that met at a deep indentation, like a crease in a pumpkin. In spite of its four eyes, the monster had one enormous mouth, which wailed loudly at the sight of its next meal. The creature looked like it was in pain just to be alive, and Rose decided it shouldn't be.

"That's what we'll eat for breakfast," she said to the black lightning, licking her lips in hungry anticipation.

Without urging from the sword, she lifted it, pointing Chrys-laenor at the raging monster. The creature was held mid-leap, its five long spider-like appendages flailing desperately as the black lightning surrounded it. The monster's life drained into Rose, feeding her great hunger and quieting the lightning's rage. When she finished with her meal, the lightning stopped, and a husk of flesh and goo fell to the ground.

She lowered Chryslaenor slowly and looked down to see the girl attached to her leg. The child pulled back slowly, her fear of the monster now seemed directed toward Rose, but Rose wasn't hungry and knew the girl was no longer in danger.

"I'm Rose. You're safe now, I promise," she said as calmly as she could. "Are you far from home?"

"I left the house to get water from the well," the girl said between sobbing breaths. She pointed a tiny finger down the path. "I feel like I was running forever."

"I think that's the way I'm headed. I'll see you home safe," Rose said, hoping it was true, trying to pry the kid from her leg.

"What was that thing?" the girl asked, unwilling to let go. "What did you do to it?"

"Probably another monster from the Vex'kvette," Rose said, despite wondering the same. She looked at the kid's confused face and smiled. "What does it look like I did? I ate it."

"You...you..." she stuttered in fear, jumping away from Rose. In a very small voice she asked, "Are you going to eat me too?"

"Not if I get you home before lunch," Rose answered, realizing just how honest her statement was. "We'd better hurry."

The girl nodded and took Rose's free hand, quickly leading her down the path. Rose was dumbfounded—was she gaining some control over the foci? Had she actually just made the giant sword move?

The girl stopped suddenly and turned to Rose with a quizzical look. "Did the monster hurt you?" she asked, pointing at Rose's ear. "What is that?"

"No, I'm fine." Rose reached up to her ear and felt a small trickle of something warm and sticky leaking out. "It's probably just blood."

"Then why is it orange?" the girl asked.

29

"Rose!" Angst and Victoria said at the same time as they both sat up in bed.

The abrupt awakening from his alcohol-induced coma, followed by sudden movement and the shock of his dream, brought his throbbing head into precise focus. Angst wondered for a moment if he was going to be sick. Victoria flopped back onto the bed with a *fwump* and rolled to her side. Angst took a deep breath and swallowed hard, fighting an alcohol-thick burp and forcing his stomach to stay in place. He smacked his dry mouth and squinted at the painful light sneaking in through the curtains. The room was becoming clear, as was his predicament.

Victoria's hair was mussed by sleep, her golden curls a tangled web that caught his eye, pulling his view to the smooth skin of her back.

Skin?

Angst's heart stuttered. Fearful to look down, he frantically grabbed at his chest and was grateful to find a shirt. Without being overly conspicuous, Angst reached down to his legs and felt that he was wearing linens. He sighed deeply.

"You're silly," she admonished. "We didn't do anything. I helped you to your room then passed out."

"With your shirt off?" Angst asked accusingly, his voice dry and raspy.

"What? I passed out," Victoria said innocently. "I don't re-

217

member the details."

He lay back down and pressed his palms to his forehead, forcing his throbbing brains back into his head. He looked over and saw her shrug.

"Victoria, we can't...you can't do that," he pleaded.

"Suddenly you don't like seeing me naked?" she said, rolling over to face him.

"It's not a matter of what I like, or even want," he explained, staring up at the ceiling after a helpless glance. "It's about what's right and wrong, and this is not right."

"I don't understand," she said, resting her hand on his chest and mostly ignoring him.

"You're not listening to me." Angst groaned. "And I feel awful! I should still be sleeping this off. What time is it?"

"It's dawn...and I need your help. Come on." Tori shook his shoulder. "We need to get up."

"The guys won't be up for hours. Just let me sleep," Angst whined. "Can't it wait?"

"Angst, this is important. I can't do this alone," Victoria said sincerely.

"Why do I feel sick and you don't?" Angst said, trying to stall the inevitable.

"Because you're old, and you drank more than me. Now get up!" She had rolled over and was now on her knees, and was now pressing against his arm in a weak attempt to shove him out of bed.

"Please?" He squeezed his eyes shut. "You...you can even stay here. You can sleep here the rest of the morning if you promise to be quiet. And stop pushing me. And put on a shirt."

Victoria's hands slipped off his shoulder and she flopped onto his chest. Her breasts squished into him as her long blond hair fell across his face. Not daring to lift his hands for fear of what they might bump into, Angst tried blowing her hair away from his mouth. She pushed herself up, and he could only imagine every inch of young flesh from her neck to her navel was exposed. Angst's cheeks warmed as he opened his eyes and forced himself to look at hers.

She stared at him for a moment then smiled fondly. "You really are a good man. Any other guy…" The side of her face lifted with a half-smile.

"I supposed that's a good thing… most of the time," Angst said, not quite able to keep the disappointment out of his voice. "You don't make it easy."

"That's not my job," Victoria said seriously, still hanging over him.

"Can you hide back under the covers now, or go put clothes on, or something?" Angst pleaded, attempting to beckon her into action with his head.

"Are you going to get out of bed and help me?" she asked, shaking his arm.

"No. I want to sleep!" he said, as emphatically as he could.

"Then no." She flopped back on top of him and rolled to her back, stretching across his chest like a cat in the warm sun.

"Okay, okay, I'll get up," he said. "Please, before I lose the few morals I have left!"

"You didn't close your eyes that time," she said with a giggle, hopping out of bed.

Angst rolled to his side with a sigh and a grumble, doing his best to avoid looking at what else she wasn't wearing.

* * * *

They crept out of the room to find Tarness lying on his back in the hallway, arms and legs splayed out as though he were dead. Angst couldn't help but smile, though he had no idea how the thunderous snores from the enormous man hadn't woken everyone. When Angst stopped to wake his large friend, Victoria tugged at his arm. Angst held up a finger, walked back into his room and grabbed a blanket to cover Tarness.

They tiptoed around him and made their way out into the frigid early morning. Hints of sunlight sleepily reached out across the icy grass, each gentle footstep betrayed by a frosty crunch.

The cold air helped clear Angst's head. In an attempt to squeeze out the mead, he pressed his hands against his temples and pulled fingers through his short graying hair. Did it feel a bit thin? Angst pulled his hands away and looked at them—they seemed thin, as did his gut. He smiled at the thought of finally losing weight, then sighed when he realized he appeared sickly and emaciated. It seemed a cruel trick that was soon forgotten, lost in a wave of nausea.

"I still feel awful." He grunted, rubbing his hands together for warmth.

"You know, whining isn't your most attractive quality," Victoria chided.

"Do you just choose to remember what you want?" Angst said in a discouraged voice. "I'm dying!"

Victoria huffed at this, creating a small cloud around her mouth. "You aren't going to die, probably," she said with a giggle. "Remember? I know these things?"

"I thought you weren't *seeing* clearly?" Angst asked, sniffing deeply through his quickly numbing nose.

Victoria waved him off with a "whatever" sort of dismissal.

"Fine, then why are we outside, in the cold, at the crack of dawn?" Angst asked, staring at her in frustration.

He followed her to the back of the inn where they found a clearing of frost-coated grass glistening in the early morning sun. Victoria examined the area quickly, as though her brief glance would hide their mischief from spying eyes then looked at Angst in utter excitement.

He smiled, in spite of his headache. Her cheeks and nose were beginning to redden from the cold, making her look completely adorable.

"Pay attention," Victoria said with a smirk, interrupting his line of thinking. "You need to show me how to summon my swifen!"

"What?" Angst said, a little too loudly. He whispered, "What are you talking about? You getting caught summoning a swifen would be worse than someone finding us in bed together…again."

"That's why we're out here so early, silly," Tori said, as though stating the obvious. "So what do I do first?"

"This really isn't a good idea," he warned. "Anyway, Dallow would be better at this. I'm an awful teacher. Not to mention, you've seen my swifen-thing these days. Or what's left of it."

"Obviously, we can't go to Dallow, can we? They can't know what I do. Mom would have them put to death," she said, clearly losing patience. "Please, Angst, it's important."

He sighed. There were so many different levels of "important" with Tori. It could include everything from "it's important I get there in time to see a cute boy" to "it's really important because Unsel will be destroyed if we don't." Still, he couldn't deny that it would be good for her to know how to summon a swifen, so in spite of his wariness and weariness, he nodded.

"I promise, Angst. It really is important." She bit her bottom lip in anticipation.

He made her watch as he struggled to summon his swifen. In a way, his inability to immediately call forth the creature was an advantage, because it gave her the opportunity to see his movements and hear the Acratic phrases repeatedly. Finally, the patchwork steel ram appeared in all its noisy splendor.

"I think it's cute like this, Angst," Victoria said, patting his arm. When his shoulders drooped with discouragement, she quickly added, "Um, in a manly way, of course."

"Right," he said, deadpan. "Now it's your turn."

Angst reached up and plucked a strand of her hair.

"Ouch!" Tori yelped. "Why did you do that?"

"You have to the first time," he said. "I'm not sure, but I think it requires a piece of you. Anyway, quit complaining. Aerella took out a lot of hair before I was able to do it successfully, and I don't have as much to lose."

She scrunched her nose while rubbing her head. Victoria took the long blond strand and whispered to it in Acratic as Angst had done. She was deliberate and methodical, focusing hard on her first summoning, speaking slowly and moving her arms with precision.

The swifen appeared immediately, taking them both by surprise. Angst patted her on the shoulder while at the same time letting out a little air in disbelief. Not only because she'd summoned her swifen on the first try, but because the creature itself was a sight to behold.

The unicorn was bright pink. Its horn and hooves shone gold in the morning sunlight. It was shorter than a horse—a comfortable height for a petite princess. Victoria squealed in delight and clapped her hands together quickly. She hopped up to hug the poor beast around the neck. It smartly patted the ground with a shiny hoof.

"And look!" she proclaimed. "My unicorn is covered in feathers!"

"I noticed… You did great, Tori," Angst acknowledged. "I'm not surprised, but I am impressed at how quickly you were able to figure this out."

"I'm good like that," she said proudly. "I'm glad we stopped at this inn. I summoned my first swifen, and I got to sneak into your bed so I wasn't alone again."

"Wait, I thought you passed out?" Angst swallowed back a surge from his stomach.

"Maybe I didn't pass out," she said with a wry smile. "But I was right."

"About what?" Angst asked, resting his face in his palm.

"We only share dreams when we sleep together," Tori said, her eyebrows rising triumphantly.

Angst looked at her in surprise. She was right, but was this the only way he could remember his dreams? He shook his head in disbelief as he considered the best ways to dissuade her from bedding with him in the future.

"What is that?" asked a deep voice behind them.

Angst and Victoria jumped in surprise and spun about to face a soldier dressed in full armor. The armor was black as Angst's, but where reflecting sunlight it shone the darkest of blues. Angst shivered in the presence of the armor; even a hundred feet away, it felt wrong, like a void. The man tore his eyes from the unicorn to peer at Angst and then eye Victoria.

"What is...what?" Victoria asked, looking about as though a pink and gold feathery unicorn had never been there. She had dismissed her swifen the instant the soldier had looked away.

"That...um, I..." The man looked surprised then peered at them both with distrusting eyes. "Over here, I found them!" he yelled.

30

Angst barely held himself up, muscles throughout his body spontaneously twitching from exhaustion. He felt dizzy, his right cheek throbbed warmly as blood trickled down his chin. Victoria stood to his right, one hand resting on his back to provide support, the other balled into a tiny fist. She glared at the dozen soldiers observing them as though they were pets. Dallow yawned loudly, looking about with sleepy eyes, scanning from Victoria on his left, down to Hector on his right. Hector was slightly crouched like a spring wound tight, and every soldier eyed him with trepidation. Steam shot out his flaring nostrils into the frigid morning air. Tarness was still at the inn, snoring in the hallway. Three soldiers had been unable to wake him, or move him outside.

"Magic is illegal in Melkier." A large man paced in front of them, his hands clasped behind his back.

The man's size and presence were only overshadowed by his dark beard, which was so great and meticulous it seemed to have a personality of its own. Angst tore his gaze from the beard long enough to inspect his new opponent. His face was mostly hidden by the beard, but it was clear the large man's nose had been broken at one time, which sounded like a good idea. The man's full set of plate armor was so blue it was black, like the armor of the soldier who'd found them. The dark blue broadsword waiting on his back was small in comparison to Chryslaenor, but rather than radiating power, it was a cold and empty void.

"Magic-wielders are not welcome," the man continued in his deep booming voice. "They are either put in irons or put down. The only reason you live—"

"Is because, in spite of that fancy armor," Angst countered weakly, "any one of us could kill your detachment in the time it takes you to groom your beard...thing."

A dozen soldiers standing at ease nearby stirred angrily at the insult. The man grimaced, the leather of his gloves creaking noisily as he clenched his fists. He spun on a heel and stormed back to hover over Angst and stare him down.

"I know of you," the bearded man sniffed. "You don't seem much without your sword."

"Good," Angst said with a cocky grin. "I like being underestimated."

"My soldier didn't seem to underestimate you when he bloodied your nose." The large man nodded, his beard bobbing up and down.

"Sure," Angst said as his head bobbed up and down with the beard. He smiled wryly. "Let me know when you dig your boys out of that hole and they can try that again."

"He punched you in the face?" Hector asked, his fists clenching as he crouched lower.

"I let my guard down," Angst admitted from the corner of his mouth. "I was attempting tact."

"That's why he was hit," Victoria said to Hector.

"Shut your mouth," the large man said, raising a hand to the princess.

The ground rumbled loudly, making the soldiers brandish their swords. Angst grunted, and an oval of earth slightly larger than Mr. Beard sank directly behind him. Before his opponent could react, Angst stepped forward and pushed. The large man fell back, tripped over the newly created ledge and landed on his rear in an embarrassing and noisy heap. A collective gasp rose from the soldiers, two of whom leaped forward to assist their leader.

As Angst reached for his longsword, Victoria shoved him,

forcing him to step aside as an arrow sunk into the nearby ground with a thud, barely missing his leg. Angst looked behind him to see the glint of steel from another arrow pointed directly at him. A man in brown leather armor was crouched on the inn rooftop, his stance unflinching.

"Hold!" barked Mr. Beard.

The arrow whistled past Angst's ear to land at the foot of the freshly created hole. The bearded man glanced at his soldier on the rooftop and smiled. He dusted himself off and walked toward Angst, sneering as he eyed the princess.

"Fancy this one, do you?"

"You're welcome to find out," Angst replied coldly. The blood from his nose was now dripping off his chin. "How deep do you want that hole to be next time?"

"What's that?" the man roared, pointing at Angst's chest. The necklace bearing Alloria's ring had slipped out from under his tunic. The ruby seemed to reflect too much sunlight, as though it were glowing. Mr. Beard's face contorted with anger. "I said, what is that?"

Angst eyed Victoria warily and tried not to think about its origins. "A gift from a friend," Angst hastily tucked the ring back into his shirt. "Nothing more."

Mr. Beard's face clouded with concern. Victoria reached for Angst's hand to get a better sense of where the ring came from, but he pulled back before she could. She frowned, and her jaw jutted forward.

"What are you hiding?" she asked.

"I don't hide anything from you," Angst lied.

"Then where did it come from?" Victoria pressed.

"Now really isn't the time," Angst said, with a forced smile. "If you like it, I'm sure I could get you one."

"No, I don't like it!" Victoria said, visibly upset. "I think it's ugly."

"Then why worry?" he asked.

The man's head turned from side to side as they bantered. "You two need to shut up while I decide—"

"I'm not worried," Victoria said to Angst. "But you are. Why is that?"

The bearded figure looked at Dallow and Hector, who shrugged, neither of them surprised.

"Why would I be worried?" Angst feigned, filling his mind with thoughts of cats.

"Because you hate cats!" Victoria cried out, pointing her finger at Angst threateningly.

The soldier pulled his dark broadsword from his back, instantly disrupting the argument. Angst, Hector, and Dallow took a step back, bracing for a fight.

"This is nonsense. We're getting nowhere," Victoria said, turning her glare on Angst. She visibly steeled herself, taking several rapid breaths, then announced, "I am the Royal Princess Victoria of Unsel, and I seek counsel with King Gaarder of Melkier."

The detachment of soldiers made noisy comments, looking to one another in surprise. Mr. Beard's thick brows furrowed, and he stared at the princess in disbelief. Angst and his friends turned to her in surprise as Victoria met the bearded man's gaze, her eyes avoiding everyone else. She pulled a sealed parchment from a pocket in her cloak and handed it to the man.

He stared at the seal.

"You could open this, but I wouldn't recommend it," she said tartly. "This is eyes only for your king."

She gasped as the man broke the seal and read the document. He pursed his lips in contemplation then handed it back. The beard reluctantly nodded to the princess before bowing. She suddenly seemed very tall as the other soldiers followed his lead and bowed accordingly.

"Your Majesty, I did not realize," the man said with feigned regret. "You travel with magic-wielders...I would never have assumed."

"These are unusual times," the princess stated in her most formal tone. "Was Melkier not affected by the Vex'kvette?"

"It was, Your Majesty," his deep voice boomed proudly. "But we have our armor, and weapons, which are unaffected by magics."

"Magic-wielders are not wholly illegal in Unsel and were paramount in the defense against the Vex'kvette," Victoria said with great pride. "I would not travel without them, and these are the best."

An angry grumbling rose from the regiment of soldiers as they shuffled restlessly. The bearded man held his hand out, and they calmed instantly. A tight, thin-mouthed smile stretched across his face. He waved the archer from the roof. The man scaled down the side of the building in a Hector-like fashion, making Hector peer and raise a bushy eyebrow.

"Of course, Princess Victoria," he stated oilily. "I am Crloc, Captain Guard to King Gaarder. We shall accompany you to the capital."

"We would be honored by your company, Captain Guard Crloc," Victoria stated carefully. "To what do we owe the honor of your presence, so far from His Majesty's right hand?"

"I lead the Rehmans' Charge, milady," Crloc said darkly. "When given word, we are sent to hunt loose wielders."

"I trust mine will be allowed safe passage," the princess did not ask.

"They will remain unharmed, Your Majesty," Crloc promised. "If they wield no magic."

"They will respect your laws, Captain Guard," she said with royal constraint. "As long as we are safe."

"And your large friend who still sleeps?" he asked.

"Waking him abruptly would be a mistake," she warned. "Not even your great armor would keep you from harm. I'll make certain my men rouse him in due time."

"As you wish." Crloc bowed his head. He turned to the archer. "Please help them as needed, Kansel."

* * * *

The reaction had not been good when they summoned their swifen. Every sword was unsheathed and at the ready and, faster than the eye could see, Kansel had notched an arrow in his bow. Crloc commanded the unnatural beasts be dismissed but, as horses were unavailable, Victoria successfully negotiated a temporary pass until they could be acquired. She now rode behind Crloc and attempted conversation while Angst stared on in anger and frustration.

"Did you know, Angst?" Hector whispered. "That she was on official business?"

"No," Angst said coldly.

He wanted to lie and say yes, say that his closest friend would confide in him about everything, including state matters. She hadn't, and he felt emptiness in the pit of his stomach as he wondered what else was truth and what was lies. They had shared so much, he felt so close to her...too close to her. She trusted him with everything, even lying in his bed naked. Was that simply an extension of her trust, or did she mean something else by it? Victoria muddled his emotions, yet insisted they were only friends. He'd never asked for anything more, barely even considered it, but Tori...she didn't just cross lines he wouldn't— she trampled on them, jumping up and down on the line until it couldn't be seen.

Angst was conflicted, more so than usual. It took every ounce of energy just to stay in his saddle, and now he had to remain alert in case Crloc and his Rehmans' Charge mistakenly tried to kill his friends and abduct the princess. He was in poor condition to tackle the confusion she had left him with, but he felt used, and stared bitterly at her back, which was arched and tense. Had he been a fool this entire time, or was this a test? She had to have reasons for keeping this secret. That was it, she had to have reasons. He didn't like it, but this was about Unsel and had nothing to do with him. More than likely.

"No," he stated once more. Angst shook his head and forced a smile. "I'm sure she meant well, or was commanded by Isabelle, or something in between. Either way I believe in her, and support what she's done."

He watched as her shoulders and back relaxed at his conclusion.

Hector nodded and said nothing more.

* * * *

They rode at a steady pace the first day, stopping at an inn where Angst got less rest than he had the night before. Despite Crloc announcing they were guests and guards weren't necessary, every two to three minutes, the antsy soldiers casually walked the hall where Angst and his friends slept. How could they sleep while she could be in danger? Unable to contact the princess, Angst worried desperately for her safety. Every time he opened the door and peeked into the hallway, Angst was met by cold eyes and strangled courage.

"Do you need something, Mr. Angst?" the soldier said, his voice dripping with disdain.

"The princess…"

"She still dines with the Captain Guard," he stated. "I can pass another message to her."

"How long has it been? She doesn't eat that much!" Angst said in frustration, his lip curling slightly.

"I can pass another message to her."

"No, that won't be necessary."

Late into the night, a note appeared under his door. He grabbed it hungrily. It was in Victoria's handwriting, and written with her temperament.

"I'm fine. I'm doing my job. Get some rest."

The note didn't help his disposition, but it was enough to make Angst remove his armor and lie in bed. He worried about Victoria, and fretted over Heather. Maybe he was in the wrong place, after all. Maybe he should've been at home, tending his wife and preparing to be a father. Guilt was poor bed company, but without any distraction, he fell asleep early the next morning.

31

"It's hard to explain, Paul. I don't hate the magic-wielders," Myreb said in a less-than-convincing tone. "It's just...well, they're unpredictable. All that power makes them dangerous."

The fifteen-year-old nodded in agreement, as he felt he must, but this didn't seem like a complete answer. At least not the answer he sought. He sighed, knowing it was pointless to argue with his father. He squeezed his legs tight against the saddle fender and stirrups as he struggled to remain on his horse while simultaneously gripping the large flagpole set in a saddle sheath near his left foot. His slightly oversized steel helm bounced in time with the flag.

"Do you need magics to carry the gold and green flag of Unsel?" Myreb beamed at him with pride, eyeing the flag Paul held.

"No, sir," Paul said.

"Exactly! Nobody here wants to rely on something...unnatural to do their job," Myreb continued to explain. "Do you?"

"No, sir," Paul agreed.

Paul looked around to see the hundred soldiers on foot following in tight formation as they made their way through a path framed by thick woods. It felt as though every one of them was listening to this conversation. The men were tired and cold, their faces grim, but those nearby nodded amicably at Paul's father.

"We don't want the magic-wielders to hold our flags, or fight our battles!" Myreb stated, now loud enough for more men to hear. "Relying on *their* magics to defend *our* borders means we're defenseless without them. That gives them more power than the magic they wield."

"But what if they want the same things we do?" Paul asked.

"Well, they may seem to want the same things, Paul," Myreb replied, seeming surprised the conversation wasn't over. "But they just aren't like us, and their needs are different."

Paul's shoulders dropped in obvious discouragement and, for a moment, it looked as though he was going to let go of the flag. His leather gloves squeaked as he gripped tight to the pole and held it close. The gold and green flag now leaned at a slight angle toward the young man.

"Just be proud of who and what you are, my son," Myreb declared. "One day you'll understand."

A knight in well-decorated plate armor quickly approached them from the path ahead. Vapor shot from his mount's nostrils as the horse strove to catch its breath.

"Captain?" the knight stated as he pulled his horse next to Myreb's.

"Report," Captain Myreb commanded.

"Good news, sir. There are only a dozen of the creatures guarding the sinkhole," the knight stated in a deep voice. "A mere mile ahead."

"Excellent!" Myreb said with a wink at Paul.

He held a balled fist up in the air. Soldiers readied their weapons and braced for battle. The low murmur of excitement seemed to warm them as they finally approached their quarry. The forest opened to a clearing encompassed by snow-covered trees. A cloudy haze of frosty air hovered close to the ground, lingering over clumps of kneegrass and small bushes.

Thud-dum.

Thud-dum.

"What's that?" Paul asked, looking around the forest for the source of the sound.

Myreb swallowed hard and dismounted his horse. It pranced

nervously, and he patted the beast to calm it. He could hear the men shuffle as anticipation made way for fear. The steady *thud-dum* continued, like the footsteps of a mountain, or the heartbeat of Ehrde. Anxious soldiers looked about, seeking the giant beast. Myreb listened for several minutes then, finally, turned to his regiment.

"Steady men!" Myreb yelled. "Just the sound of the monsters tunneling echoing off nearby trees."

The voice of reason was hard to hear over the reality that filled their ears.

Thud-dum.

They walked an anxiety-laden quarter mile, surrounded by blustery winds and the loud heartbeat. When the sinkhole came into view, the soldiers stopped moving forward without being commanded. Where the surrounding forest met, there was an unnatural gap. A mile-wide hole had eaten every bit of tree or brush, and behind that, another enormous sinkhole had devoured more of the old forest, going back farther than the eye could see.

Thud-dum.

"Nobody does this to Unsel!" Myreb shouted. "Nobody does this to my country!"

Soldiers yelled in agreement, and they marched forward to the dozen gargoyle creatures guarding the cliff edge. Steam rose behind the creatures, and water dripped from their slick bodies as though they were sweating profusely. The gargoyles stood like enormous statues, in spite of the soldiers' approach.

"You ride over there," Myreb told Paul, pointing to distant brush. "No fighting, just watch how it's done. Hold that flag high!"

Paul looked at his father. He wanted to stay and help, or wish his father luck, or say something heartfelt, but knew he couldn't in front of the other soldiers. Paul nodded in understanding, and rode a hundred yards away so he could watch the battle from a safe distance. He dismounted and pulled the large flag from its saddle sheath. Paul held the flag high, as commanded, and watched, and listened.

His father gestured at the monsters as if scolding them. Paul could soon hear yelling as Myreb pointed a threatening finger then shook a fist. The creatures took no heed, as though participating in a rude prank. After a final warning, the veteran soldier wielded his sword and swung. His blade passed halfway through the gargoyle he faced then stopped.

"By the Dark Vivek," Myreb said loudly.

The gargoyles seemed to smile as their heads simultaneously turned to face the soldiers. The gargoyle in front of Myreb backhanded the man so fast its arm was a green blur. Myreb flew high into the air. Even before the captain landed, the gargoyles smashed into the troop of soldiers like an avalanche covering a small village.

"*No!*" Paul screamed as he ran toward his falling father.

It took Myreb a full minute to land before finally crashing to the ground in a loud, broken heap of armor and twisted limbs. His father pushed himself up then rolled over onto his back. Paul ignored the screams of soldiers, the horrific wrenching of metal and crunching of bones. There was only his father. When the young man arrived, he could see that Myreb's left arm was nothing more than a shattered mess of destroyed armor and torn flesh. His father's bloody face was almost unrecognizable as it began to swell from the two impacts. Myreb coughed blood as he tried to speak.

"Help me to see," he spat through blood.

Paul kept holding the flag with one hand and offered his free hand to his father. Myreb winced and grunted as he positioned himself to view the utter ruin that used to be one hundred good men. Gargoyles ripped and stomped on the few remaining soldiers, leaving behind dying screams and dead bodies.

"Paul," Myreb choked out the last of his life. "You must warn the queen! Tell her what happened. Quick, run before—"

A gargoyle landed nearby with a solid thud, followed closely by the others. The dozen monsters appeared unharmed from Unsel's attack, and they towered over Paul and his father.

"Always be proud of who you are, son," Myreb commanded

as a large, webbed foot landed on his chest and crushed the remaining life from him.

"Father?" Paul questioned in disbelief. "Father!"

Paul turned to face the creatures, tears streaming down his cheeks. The gargoyles stared at him with dull, uncaring eyes. He shook with fury. He let go of the flag. A painfully white aura of bright light surrounded Paul's hands and forearms as he aimed them at the two closest. Before the flag hit the ground, four of the gargoyles were destroyed.

* * * *

"*She actually screamed before passing out. Can you believe that?*" Jaden said through the stone.

"*Um, no. Of course, that's awful. I felt terrible for her,*" he lied in response, glad she wasn't there to admonish him.

Jaden had wandered the long hallway toward the old throne room, hoping another investigation of the spot where Chryslaenor had been taken would turn up something. Events were unraveling, and the alien surroundings overwhelmed him. His thoughts were so cloudy, and he wanted more than anything to remember who he was and where he came from. His only distraction, his only ounce of relief, came from time spent communicating with the earthspeak taught to him by Earth.

"*You look nice today,*" he said, trying to change the subject. "*Of course I can't see you. I just know...you always look nice.*"

"*Now that I've got this mostly figured out, are there any messages you want me to pass along... Wait, I hear something.*"

Jaden stopped moving. With tiny steps, he made his way to the wall, inching closer to the noise coming from an adjoining servants' hallway.

"Yes, I gave it to him. I don't care what you think!" a young woman's voice whispered loudly. "I don't answer to you, only to—ouch!"

"You do answer to me until I'm told otherwise," an older man said. "Believe me, young woman. You would prefer my disciplines over his!"

"You are a disgusting old man!" she squeaked, sobbing as if in pain.

"As old as death, just like you!" he replied. "Don't forget where you came from. I'll gladly send you back!"

She squealed louder and then cried out.

"You will be wise to remember this, girl," the old man snapped. There was a loud thump as if a body had fallen to the ground. "Get it back when he returns, *if* he returns. Understand?"

"Yes," she replied in a pained voice so quiet Jaden could barely hear it. "Do we have to do this?"

There was a loud crack, perhaps of hand against cheek. Deep sobs sounded from the corridor.

"Ask one more time, and I will tell him every transgression," the man said. His voice dripped with disgust. "And you call yourself royalty."

Noisy armored footsteps stormed down the servants' hallway, leaving behind a young woman's wracking sobs.

Jaden peered around the corner to find Alloria in a heap on the floor. Her purple satin dress was torn from shoulder to chest, as though she had been lifted up by her wrist—which was red and swollen. Jaden rushed in, wielding his shortsword.

"Your Majesty!" he said. "Are you okay?"

Alloria sniffed loudly between sobs and stood. Shivering, she wiped tears from her cheeks. She appeared disoriented, unable to decide what she should say. Her large eyes widened in panic, and she looked down the hallway to make sure her attacker was gone.

"I'll get that bastard," she said, still gasping for air. "Tell no one of this!" Gripping her dress tight to her chest, she rushed down the hallway.

Jaden stared after Alloria, dumbfounded.

"*Victoria, are you still there?*" Jaden said through the stone. "*You won't believe what I saw.*"

32

The next morning, Victoria joined Angst on his swifen, and he was comforted that she rode with him instead of Crloc. Something about the man made his jaw set and his teeth grind. Crloc was a bully, and Angst had no tolerance for those people. Her attentions toward Crloc, no matter how politically motivated, made him want to lash out. This couldn't be jealousy, he was just being over-protective, but he couldn't help but feel something was off.

All morning she appeared lost in thought, occasionally giggling to herself. She cocked her head to one side as though listening to something far away, occasionally giggling to herself.

"So, did you have a nice time last night?" he asked, attempting to snap her out of it.

"What?" she asked. "Oh, yes, Crloc. He's sweet, and sort of cute."

"Of course," Angst said, rolling his eyes. "I supposed you'll be *dining* with him again tonight."

There was another long pause as Victoria seemed, once again, lost in conversation. Angst remained quiet until her back arched stiffly.

"Everything okay?" he asked.

"I think so," she said distantly.

Angst rolled his eyes in an arc so wide his neck followed. It was as though she was talking to someone else even though he was the only one nearby. He wanted to know about the dinner, about what she had learned, and if they needed to prepare for anything. He also wanted to know about the lie, or the omission. Why hadn't she told him this was official business? Why bother fighting Hector when she could have commanded an official escort? More than anything, he wanted Victoria to share openly rather than making him ask.

"Why didn't you say something?" Angst finally blurted out. "I didn't know this trip was official business."

"I'm sorry, Angst. I can't tell you everything." Victoria said, this time more direct, as though she sat in front of him.

"Since when?" he asked.

She reached for his hand, tucking her fingers under his gauntlet, making contact with his skin. Angst jerked his head back in surprise; they didn't hold hands. She must have been worried that he was upset—which was unusual, but sweet.

"Where did the ring come from, Angst?" she whispered, now clutching his hand.

"Wait." He tried to jerk free, but it only took a moment to think of Alloria standing in front of him, pulling the little night-shirt down before leaning forward to kiss him.

"I don't believe it," Victoria said loudly, looking for an armor-free place to slap him. "Stop right now!"

"Victoria?" Angst asked in disbelief. "You're joking, right?"

"Here they go," Hector said shaking his head and glaring at Dallow and Tarness. "It's getting worse!" He sped up to ride ahead of Angst and Victoria.

"It will pass," Dallow called after him.

"They've had more verbal foreplay than I've gotten real foreplay in years," Tarness admitted, galloping to catch Hector.

Dallow soon followed, and they were left alone.

"I don't *believe* you're thinking about kissing her," Victoria screeched, spitting like her mom did when angered. "I'm sitting right here, in front of you, and you're thinking of kissing *her*?"

"Who, Heather?" Angst deflected with feigned innocence, knowing all too well he had been thinking of Alloria's full lips and full—

"I'm talking about my whore cousin," she said sharply.

Tarness looked back with a grin, and Hector shook his head in defeat. Dallow grimaced as the soldiers in front of them turned their heads to watch.

"That's strong language from a princess," Angst teased, desperate to make light of his thoughts. "Would you rather I thought about kissing you?"

"Eeuw! No, of course not," she said testily. "I don't kiss old, married men."

"Eeuw, neither do I," Angst replied, trying to deflect once more.

It wasn't working. Victoria pushed back with her rear, nudging Angst to the flank of his swifen. In a surprisingly acrobatic move, she spun on her tailbone while lifting her left leg across the front of his chest. She now rode backward, facing him. Her legs were over his, forcing him to sit very close. She peered at him, staring into his eyes, and Angst couldn't help but blush guiltily.

She breathed in deep from shock. "You weren't just thinking it? It really happened?" Victoria whispered angrily, her eyes wide with surprise and her brows furrowed with hurt. Victoria stared at him, focusing on his thoughts and seeking out the truth. "That little slut."

"It wasn't like that," Angst started. "Hey, what are you doing?"

Victoria reached into the top of his chest piece and pulled out the ruby ring dangling from his necklace.

"Really, Angst?" she said with zero tolerance. "You kissed her then she gave you her ring? What did Heather think of this?"

"Oh, now you're on Heather's side?" Angst said in embarrassed surprise. "Look, I didn't kiss her, she kissed me."

"What's the difference?" Victoria said. "You didn't even fight her off."

"It happened so fast," Angst said weakly. He didn't know why he should feel guilty, or be defending his actions to Victoria, but he did, and he was.

"She isn't even half your age, Angst," Victoria said with an unforgiving stare.

"Yeah!" Angst said. He meant it to sound like he, too, was in shock, but it sounded more like he was proud. It was the wrong answer.

A loud clatter beneath the swifen made Angst jump. When he looked behind his ram, he found one of the patchwork plates holding the creature together had dropped to the ground.

"Huh," Victoria said, spinning around to face forward once more. "Please catch up to the others."

Angst was now shivering as though the cold air coursed through his very veins, feeding the emptiness eating away at him. He wasn't sure why, but he tried apologizing. Every plea for understanding was met with tiny "hmm" noises. He felt completely lost, and alone, and as they caught the others, she finally answered his thoughts.

"When you understand why I'm upset, I'll ride with you again," she hissed.

"What?" he said with a shrug she couldn't see. "Can't you just tell me?"

"It seems the *lover* here can't stop going on about his kiss with my *younger* cousin, Alloria, and I'm fearful of losing my virginity," Victoria announced loudly. "Can I ride with someone else for a while?"

Heads and ears perked up as Angst tried to slip deeper into his armor. It wasn't working. Nearby soldiers from the Rehmans' Charge stared at Angst accusingly, as if they had an ounce of a clue as to what was going on.

"You kissed Alloria?" asked Tarness. "Fine work, old man."

"Uh, well, actually, she kissed me," Angst said under his breath.

"There's a difference?" Hector asked shaking his head.

"Exactly!" Victoria said, hopping off Angst's swifen. "I'll ride with Hector."

"Hey, don't I get a turn?" asked Dallow playfully.

"You got your turn last trip," Tarness replied.

"What?" asked Dallow in an uncertain tone.

Tarness coughed out Rose's name. Dallow rolled his eyes.

"That's not something I thought to see," Tarness commented on Hector and Victoria as they trotted away.

"How did she find out?" Dallow asked Angst.

"I…" Angst stopped to think. He had to be careful not to let them know her secret. "It sort of slipped."

"Ohh," Tarness said, shaking his head, "bad mistake."

"As good as you are with women," Dallow advised, "you're an idiot."

"What do you mean?" Angst felt dizzy.

"What makes you think Victoria wouldn't be jealous of that?" Dallow asked.

"I'm married to Heather," Angst stated. "Victoria and I are just friends."

"Right," Dallow drawled, clearly not believing a word. "Friends that sleep together? Friends that take naked baths together?"

"Wait, it's not like that," Angst said guiltily, looking back and forth between Dallow and Tarness. "Well, it's not sex."

"Sure," Tarness remarked, not believing Angst.

"I didn't say sex," Dallow continued. "But just friends? So when are you and I going to start taking naked baths?"

"I…I couldn't do that," Angst said with wild eyes.

"Then why is it okay to do it with her?" Dallow asked pointedly.

When it was obvious Angst had no reply, Dallow sped up to join Hector and Victoria, leaving Angst with Tarness.

"Did you have sex with Alloria too?" Tarness asked, resting his chin on the palm of his large hand as though waiting for story time.

"I didn't have sex with either of them," Angst said, clearing his throat several times.

"Why not?" Tarness asked in surprise. "That's what I don't get about you. You go through all the trouble to woo them, to the

241

point that they're kissing you. I know you aren't happy with your marriage. Why not just leave that and enjoy all...this?" Tarness waved his large hand about as though including all attractive young women everywhere.

Angst had never thought of it that way. He had never thought of women as being so available. It had never been his goal to sleep with them, or have sex with them, or even see them naked. This stuff just kept happening, and he was comfortable enough with it that it all seemed okay at the time.

"I don't know," Angst said finally. "I think these things happen because of what I won't do, not because of what I will do."

Tarness nodded at this, seeming to understand.

"Then maybe you can tell me something," Tarness said with a deep sigh. "What kind of carrot are you dangling?"

This made Angst chuckle. "Carrot, Tarness?"

"Rose almost died just to ride with you the first trip. It looked like Victoria had given up her crown for a jaunt to Melkier." Tarness shook his head. "And *Alloria*? Now they're all throwing themselves at you naked and kissing you and—"

"Wait, hold on Tarness," Angst said seriously. "What's this about?"

Tarness looked weary, his thick brows drooping over his dark eyes. For a moment, his face filled with sadness. "I'm alone," he said quietly.

"Oh," Angst said in hushed surprise. "You can have one of them if you want," he offered helpfully.

This made Tarness snicker. "I'll take Alloria," Tarness said a little too sincerely.

"I kid, big man. She's not mine to give. Not to mention, I think you'd break her."

"I would," he said proudly.

Angst waved him away dismissively, and they laughed again.

"I just can't find *her*, Angst," Tarness fretted. "I don't know if it's my size, or the magic. I know it can't be because I'm black. Nobody likes pale...no offense."

"None taken," Angst said with a smirk. "What about Maarja?

She might break you, but…"

"I think about her," Tarness said, smiling to himself. "But I don't know where she is now."

"So…and…go look for her!" Angst said. "What are you waiting for?"

"I happen to be here trying to help my best friend not die," Tarness said. "Oh, and save the world. Again."

Angst's heart warmed. Tarness had never said anything so affectionate, at least about Angst. It was almost enough to distract him from Victoria's anger and disappointment.

"I really think she's the one, Tarness," Angst said. "I've never seen you connect with someone like that before. If there is a world left when this nonsense is done, I'll help you find her."

"Yeah?" Tarness asked.

"Yeah," Angst replied with a smile.

"I guess you can have Alloria back," Tarness said grinning. "And keep the rest too."

Angst sighed deeply, a bit of pain creeping into his heart. He was still angry with Victoria for not confiding in him, and couldn't understand why she was so upset that Alloria had kissed him.

"They're all crazy. You know that, don't you?" Angst asked.

"So are we," Tarness replied with a knowing smile. "We're the ones who work so hard chasing them."

They rode on silently. Angst wanted to fall off his swifen and sleep. He felt weaker than usual, like the growing emptiness eating away at him was now filled with Victoria's anger. He refused to show any sign of this while surrounded by the Rehmans' Charge, but in spite of his resolve another piece of plate armor crashed to the ground. Angst clutched his stomach, swallowing hard to keep it down.

As the morning became afternoon, Hector slowed and assisted the princess off his panther.

"Thank you, Hector," she said sincerely.

"Any time, Your Majesty," Hector said with a deep bow of his head.

Without a word, Victoria used the bent armor of Angst's swifen to pull herself up and sit in front of him again.

"What did you talk about?" Angst asked.

"You'll know when you can read my mind," Tori replied. "I hate you right now."

"I know," Angst said with a sigh, grateful she was riding with him once more.

33

A low-pitched hum filled Angst's ears, and he had to wonder if Chryslaenor was singing to him once more. There was a second, higher note then a harmony of sounds followed quickly by the higher note again. Angst shook his head, took off his glove, and wiggled a finger in his ear. How could they possibly have caught up with Rose? He had no idea where she was.

"It's okay. I hear it too," Victoria whispered to Angst. She looked over at Dallow. "What is it?"

"I've always wanted to see this," Dallow said in anticipation, smiling at their reactions. "Or, I guess, hear it."

The distant echoing tones became louder and never stopped, like unkempt music from a crazed composer.

"This has been an annoyance of mine for years," Hector grumbled, his sensitive ears twitching with every new note. The lower tones made him wince. "I hate coming this way."

Angst looked at Dallow nervously as his friend rode closer to the edge. Dallow squinted as he did his best to see clearly and catalog everything. There was a tall stone wall on their left, and a thousand-foot-drop to the Bliss River on his right. In spite of the distance to the bottom and the loud musical notes, Angst could hear the waters raging far below.

The music made him think of Chryslaenor and, like an open wound, the emptiness drew energy from his very pores. But every time it crept in, the hold on his hand got tighter. Angst's right hand was almost numb from Victoria's grip as she looked straight ahead, avoiding any glimpse of their surroundings. He felt odd, holding hands with his friend, but she didn't care and Angst wasn't going to tell her to stop—it was much better company than her cold shoulder.

Angst did his best to ignore Dallow so close to the edge of the cliff, watching the procession of soldiers before him. Their dark helms and polearms led the way around a bend in the path.

"Do you see, Your Majesty?" Dallow asked. "It looks like they constructed the bridge in rows. First making a standard archway bridge, then stacking another atop the first, like blocks. They just kept going until the bridge reached all the way up here."

Angst gasped as the sight unfolded. The Great Bridge of Melkier lived up to its name. A monumental feat of engineering, it crossed a chasm easily three hundred yards wide and a thousand feet deep. The cliff-side road they followed provided a beautiful view of the expanse, and the structure. Low-hanging clouds hovered nearby, captive between the mountains held together by the Great Bridge. An ever-changing cascade of rainbows surrounded it, leaping from cliff walls to dive into a thick mist. The bridge appeared afloat, surrounded by clouds and rainbows.

"I don't need to see, Mr. Dallow," Victoria snapped brusquely, reeling and leaning back into Angst. "Your description is more than enough."

Dallow looked at the princess briefly and shrugged. "Whoever built the bridge also dug tunnels along the canyon—seven on each side—that have an opening upstream and an exit downstream. Water from the river pours through the tunnels at random. The air forced through the tunnels by water creates music, and rainbows."

"Rainbows?" Victoria said with sudden interest, looking up as though awakening from a long slumber.

Her grip on Angst's hand couldn't have gotten any tighter as she braved a peek. Water continued shooting out from the large holes directly beneath the Great Bridge. Steam and spray pouring out the tunnels combined to create a cascade of colors dancing about the structure as the river randomly chose which path to follow. Tori's cheeks lifted in a smile, and she let go to clap excitedly in spite of her fears.

"All created without magics," Crloc declared behind them.

"How do you know?" Dallow asked curiously.

Crloc's head whipped about in anger, and he looked ready to beat the curiosity out of Dallow, until the princess stared him down. She raised a thin regal eyebrow and cocked her head to one side thoughtfully, her fear of heights replaced with defensiveness for her friends. Crloc winced as a thin smile fought its way across his face.

"You brought it up, Crloc," she chided on Dallow's behalf. "It's a fair question."

"It's common knowledge," Crloc mumbled into his large beard. "Well documented in history books."

"History is always written by the winners," Dallow retorted. "Either way, as long as it's safe, I don't really care."

"Speaking of safe, you wouldn't want to edge away from the side of the cliff a little, would you, Dallow?" Angst pleaded nervously.

"A little too close for you, Angst?" Tarness teased.

"A little too close for him, actually," Angst said, trying to avoid explaining his fear of others-near-heights.

Victoria's head tilted back suddenly as she looked up into the sky, high over the bridge. She focused on a single point, as though trying to make out a star through high clouds.

Angst glanced at Crloc and Dallow, concerned they might have noticed her sudden distraction. "What is it?" he whispered.

"Something's coming," she whispered over her shoulder to Angst. "We should get across the bridge quickly."

"Can we hurry? I want to get to the other side, now!" Angst shouted without questioning her. He decided to make it sound like he was the one afraid of heights. "I'd like to get this over with."

"Your boyfriend is spineless without his giant sword," Crloc bullied.

"He's not my boyfriend!" Victoria snapped defensively.

"I'm worried for her safety," Angst said, ignoring Crloc and Victoria.

"Are you insulting The Great Bridge?" Crloc asked, obviously looking for a fight.

"I'm insulting the great fall, something I don't care for the princess to experience."

"Coward," Crloc snapped. He yelled loud for the entire watch to hear, "we will ride across quickly, for the princess and her spineless champion."

Victoria looked back at Angst apologetically. He merely shook his head and rolled his eyes.

"I'm used to bullies," Angst said, loud enough to be heard. "Luckily, they never get used to me."

Three-quarters of the way across The Great Bridge, Kansel pointed to the sky with his longbow and shouted, *"Dragon!"*

A dark shape emerged from the exact spot at which Victoria had been staring. The beast dropped from the sky, glided toward them shakily then fell once more. It was like a doe trying to walk for the first time but, while the flight path was unsteady, the dragon was still hurtling directly toward them.

Angst, his friends, and the group of soldiers rode forward at a gallop in a desperate attempt to cross the bridge before the dragon crashed into them. As it came closer, Angst could hear it: a roar that sounded more like a scream. Did dragons scream? The sound was horrific. As the creature approached, he could hear the desperate flapping of wings. A blast of dragonbreath scorched the air over him, and he wondered if it was actually the sun crashing on top of them.

"Almost there," Victoria yelled as they approached the bridge end. "When we cross, keep riding another fifty yards!"

"Kansel, shoot it down before it hits the bridge!" Crloc commanded.

"Faster, Angst!" Hector roared.

CHAPTER THIRTY THREE

Angst wanted to see what was happening, but there was no time. He could hear the music and the rushing water below the bridge, the screams of the falling dragon, and the twang of arrows loosed from longbow. It was a maddening blur, and his heart raced. Angst urged his swifen faster, sprinting past his friends and the Rehmans' Charge soldiers to seek higher ground. He continued along the road even as the dragon crashed into the bridge behind them.

34

Gushing wind blew salty ocean water at Rose's face, biting at her with cold sharp teeth. A great battle of water raged before her as the sea thrashed against itself under the gray cloudy sky. Though Chryslaenor somehow kept her warm, goosebumps rose on her skin, and she shivered in spite of herself. As if gripping onto her deer swifen would stop the shivering, she clutched the sapling branches that wrapped around the swifen's neck before branching upward to form large antlers.

The swifen was her first reminder of home and friends since being abducted, and its presence comforted her. Being able to summon and dismiss the creature was also a sign that she now had the tiniest bit of control over this nightmare. Saving the girl from the black lightning had taken all her effort, but it had also made her wonder what else she could do. Rose hadn't thought it would happen, but her swifen had appeared when summoned, scaring the girl as she'd leaped forward to hug it. Rose reluctantly dismissed it to calm her, and was elated she could summon it again after seeing the kid to safety. If Chryslaenor was forcing her to a destination, the only way to end this was to get there as quickly as possible. With the sword as her guide, she'd ridden hard for the entire week, resting only when necessary.

After the long trek of endless trails, unkempt hair, dirty clothes, and tasteless meals, she found herself on this cold beach in front of the raging ocean. Rose could only imagine she was on some empty coastline in Unsel, or possibly Melkier. On foot, she had traveled south for days, but after summoning her bramble-and-flower-covered swifen, she had veered east. Finally, she'd found herself here, but for what purpose?

She looked down at her swifen, grateful it hadn't decided to drag her across the dark, deep waters. Rose had been sitting and staring at the ocean long enough to be irritable. She was frustrated with waiting, and upset that Angst hadn't shown up to rip this monster from her hand. This foci-thing was something he wanted, and he should do his job. Rose didn't know why he wasn't here, and it made her angry enough to punch someone in the face—someone like Angst.

She needed to stretch her legs, and dismounted her deer swifen awkwardly, dragging Chryslaenor over the top. Rose didn't believe the swifen was alive but, in spite of herself, she petted several soft flowers on the creature's back. The swifen nuzzled her as if it appreciated the attention, which made her wonder if there were more to it than sticks and flowers.

Chryslaenor slowly pulled Rose's arm toward the sea. She rolled her eyes and reluctantly followed before stopping at the water's edge. The wind blew so hard Rose was grateful for Chryslaenor as an anchor—any harder and she would become a flag. The waters were calming. In spite of the gusting wind, the waves were now lapping where moments before she'd seen only whitecaps. She looked across the ocean, squinting to see, trying to find what she was being forced to wait for.

There was a sloshy thud behind her. Rose tried to spin about, but Chryslaenor no longer seemed willing to budge. She craned her neck around to see an enormous green creature with a scaly head and large webbed ears. Swallowing back a scream, she continued fighting the giant sword to turn around with her. Her right hand was locked in fierce combat, and she was quickly tiring. This was no time for a meal. Or maybe it was.

"I swear, once I get this sword turned around," she threatened, "you're lunch!"

The monster reached for her with large slimy green arms. Its great muscles rippled as it gripped her beneath the shoulders and around her chest with cold, clammy hands. It flapped leathery wings, launching off muscular haunches into the air, lifting Rose and a reluctant Chryslaenor from the safe ground. This time she did scream.

The gargoyle used the chaotic winds to gain height and momentum, diving back and forth with jerky sudden movements. The longer they flew, the heavier the sword became, and Rose's scream of panic became yelps of pain. Chryslaenor did not enjoy flying and weighed so heavily on her arm that willpower was the only thing keeping it in its socket. With her free hand, Rose pushed helplessly against the monster's arms as they crushed the breath from her lungs.

"Put me down!" she screamed.

The panicked abduction continued, and Rose gripped her right arm with her left to keep the sword from completely ripping it off. The creature took a final sharp turn before diving fast toward the ocean. Her insides lifted, and she swallowed hard, dreading the thought of vomiting up the contents of an empty stomach. The gargoyle finally landed with a bone-jarring thump, setting her on a leathery gray surface. Rose tried maneuvering Chryslaenor to point it at the creature, but the blade didn't move.

Rose stood on a squishy island far enough from land that she could barely see shore. She tried walking away from the gargoyle, toward the edge for a better look—hoping to figure out a way back—but, once again, Chryslaenor wouldn't budge. She fought and strained until the sword finally moved, sinking into the ground with a burp. Green ooze bubbled from the incision and, with a loud moan, the island moved. The gargoyle appeared to laugh in silence, pressing its hands against rippling stomach muscles.

As the gargoyle turned away from the shore, a dozen thin, hairy tentacles reached out of the water to slap at the annoying foci. Rose screamed a curse as she jumped behind the wide blade, barely escaping the dark green appendages. The gargoyle stopped laughing when a tentacle landed on its shoulder. Immediately, the other seeking tentacles stopped their search, darting to the intruder.

The gargoyle roared in panic as thick hairs sank into its arms and legs. It struggled and fought, but its enormous muscles could barely move as the thin tentacles continued sinking their hungry feelers into the green-scaled body.

"Sucks, doesn't it!" Rose yelled bravely from behind Chryslaenor.

The gargoyle's wings spread wide and, with a mighty leap, it launched itself away from the living island. Its final attempt at freedom was stopped a mere foot above the leathery ground. The creature screamed in silence as the tentacles ripped it apart. Green innards sprayed in every direction, covering Rose's right arm and slapping her in the face.

"That was…the most…disgusting thing yet!" she said, hyperventilating.

She kept her right eye shut, as it felt completely covered in goop. Rose reached up to her wipe her face, and stared at her shaking hand. It was covered in mucky bits of gargoyle. She was only able to flick off the larger pieces, and her clothes were too slimy to wipe her hand clean. She felt completely violated and out of control.

Unable to stop herself, Rose began to cry. "Please, please stop. Angst? Dallow? Anyone, please!"

A few feet away, the dark gray ground opened to reveal a red oval. Seven or eight feet across, the oval was glossy wet, pointed at both edges, and enough to distract Rose. Her crying slowed and she took a deep calming breath.. She felt embarrassed at the outburst, but it was all just too much. With her free hand, Rose did her best to wipe green gargoyle slime from her face and her long red hair.

She wanted to move closer to the giant red opal—which was horrifically beautiful, somehow—but she feared wiggling Chryslaenor would invite more tentacles. Instead, Rose leaned forward.

The dark gray expanse surrounding her became larger…*much*

larger...as the island lifted out of the water. More red ovals appeared along its edge—so many that Rose lost count. She looked at each one as the island went faster and faster. Her chest heaved, and she was hyperventilating again as the world spun and lurched around her.

Rose locked her legs defiantly. Staring ahead, she watched the ovals simultaneously blink.

35

There was a terrible crunching sound followed by muffled screams as stragglers from the Rehmans' Charge were crushed under the dragon's landing.

"Hold here," Crloc yelled, pulling a black broadsword from his back. "There is only one. Kill it fast and bone it!"

Angst reared his swifen around and did a quick check to confirm his friends were safe. Tarness and Hector had already dismounted and were at the ready with swords and shields. Dallow held his staff to one side, muttering to himself in Acratic.

"Keep your people back," Crloc barked. "Watch! We do this without magics!"

Angst briefly inspected the throng of soldiers before finally laying eyes on the dragon. The reddish brown lizard was larger than the bridge was wide. Hard bark-like scales armored the dragon from tail to belly and up its long neck to a rigid triangular head. It flailed about in pain, tearing at its chest and stomach with sharply-clawed talons. Enormous leathery wings flapped helplessly, creating a storm of snow, and dust, and leaves. Bursts of lava shot from the creature's mouth, splashing the ground with wet fire and dissolving everything it touched. This close, the dragon was a vision of horrific beauty, as awe-inspiring and dangerous as a volcano or tornado.

Dragons were creatures of legend, of story. Fear overtook him, tightening his throat, and Victoria once again gripped his hand in panic, not knowing if she should run, or scream, or hide. Angst tore his eyes away for a brief moment to find his friends panic-stricken. In all their adventures, none had seen a real, live dragon. Tarness stood with his jaw wide open, looking ready to drop his shield. Hector leaned against Dallow to steady himself, while Dallow shook his head in amazement, too shocked to categorize or catalog the great beast.

The dragon arched its back in a sudden, comical dancing leap, roared one final time then flopped onto its side, where it remained, unmoving. A hush fell over them, leaving only the sound of the bridge music and rushing water. The Rehmans' Charge soldiers looked to Crloc for guidance. He nodded to his second, silently urging Kansel to investigate. Kansel sniffed and wiped his nose before inching forward to poke the creature with his longbow.

"Looks like you didn't have to do it at all," Tarness called out, "with or without magic."

"Something is wrong here," Kansel stated, tapping at the creature's stomach. He leaned in to investigate. "I hear something."

"Kansel, step away," Crloc commanded. "Without the armor..."

Kansel looked down at his dark leather armor and shrugged, ignoring Crloc's command. The dragon's belly stretched and contorted, pressing outward then pulling back. The red scaly stomach and chest writhed like a sack of snakes. Liquid fire dripped from the monster's mouth, falling to the wet, snowy ground in angry hisses.

"Maybe it's pregnant?" Kansel shrugged as he turned back to Crloc for guidance.

"He's in danger," Victoria whispered.

"Get out of there, Kansel!" Angst yelled.

"I give the commands here, coward," Crloc snapped. "Make sure it's dead!"

Kansel turned back to the dragon, poking it one last time. The stomach stopped moving, and he stepped on top of the dragon as if it were a hill. As he notched a black-tipped arrow and aimed at the creature eye, there was a loud, slurpy pop. Kansel screamed in pain as liquid fire sprayed out of the dragon's belly. Fortunately, the scream was cut short as the fire burned completely through the man's face and chest, and he collapsed to the ground.

"No!" Crloc yelled, running toward his friend. He gripped the remains of a leg and pulled what was left of Kansel away from the dragon. "What is this madness?"

Long, thin claws poked through the dragon's stomach. They stretched and pushed until the small human-like face of a gamlin peered through the opening. The creature fell out of the dragon's belly, covered in liquid fire, like a grotesque birthing. Another gamlin crawled out, followed by two more. Beady red eyes blinked behind the liquid fire as they inspected the soldiers curiously, brushing off the lava like a cat cleaning itself.

"What are these creatures?" asked Crloc.

"They're gamlin," Dallow remarked. "Until now, I would've said they're mostly harmless, except that they're nigh invulnerable."

"*Harmless?*" Crloc roared. He dropped the remains of his fallen friend and pointed. "This is harmless?"

Crloc stormed up to the largest gamlin and swung wide with his sword. Rather than being split in two, the gamlin gripped onto the blade and began clawing its way toward the hilt. Crloc swung his sword back and forth before throwing it down and swatting at the creature with his shield. The gamlin, still covered in its hot dragon innards, leaped toward the troopof soldiers.

"As far as I know, gamlin can only be damaged by magic," Angst warned his friends.

"This is going to be a massacre," Tarness said.

"Do something!" Tori pleaded.

The moment his hands began to glow, Angst wanted to vomit. He fought the emptiness and swallowed back the acid that shot from his belly and burned his throat. Two soldiers were already dead, their armor ripped to shreds by gamlin claws, hot dragonbreath still burning their flesh. A smallish gamlin horted loudly as it jumped over the heads of soldiers and leaped at Victoria. She dropped to the ground and spun about, expertly batting the creature away with her two thin-bladed swords, sending it flying into the air. Angst caught the gamlin in a small air shield to keep it from attacking her again. It hovered over everyone, frantically scratching at its trap.

"No magic!" Crloc marched toward Angst.

Tarness stepped in front of Crloc to block his path, but the angry Captain Guard didn't even slow down. He slammed his shield against Tarness's chest and pushed. Tarness's lips curled in anger, and he swung his sword at his opponent's chest. There was an enormous crack as his sword broke against Crloc's blackened shield. Tarness roared in fury. Throwing his sword aside, he began beating Crloc with his own shield. Both men stood their ground.

"Impossible!" Crloc yelled at Tarness.

Tarness continued smashing at the large man with his shield, slowly inching Crloc away from his friends. Angst shook violently from exhaustion as he focused on the air shield that trapped the first gamlin. He willed it to float over a second gamlin gnawing on the back of a soldier's head then expanded it to encompass both creatures. They rolled within the bubble, fighting and scratching with their long claws. His eyes narrowed in concentration and sweat dripped from his forehead like he was sick with fever.

"I need to get to the others, fast," Angst yelled, panting heavily.

"On it," Hector said with a grin.

Hector dropped his sword and shield. He leaped back, grabbed Dallow's staff and dove into the fray. Hector pried the nearest gamlin from its quarry—a helpless soldier whose chestpiece was ripped to shreds. The creature popped up into the air, and Hector batted it higher with the end of the staff. Angst captured the third gamlin in his trap.

There was a loud crash as Tarness and Crloc's shields met.

Deadlocked and unmoving, both men grunted with the effort. Crloc punched Tarness's shoulder with his sword arm. Tarness winced but remained steadfast. Angst glanced at the two men and, seeing the fierce determination in Tarness's eyes, was amazed that Crloc didn't move.

"Dallow, can you get the other two?" Angst yelled.

Analyzing Angst's air shield and the floating gamlin, Dallow reached out with one arm. He took a deep breath, his brow furrowing in concentration, and a fourth gamlin floated high into the air.

"Nice work!" Angst said. "We need the last one, Hector."

In an impressive display of acrobatics, Hector bounded across the road to land beside the final gamlin. Angst and Dallow moved in as the soldiers scurried away from the dragon carcass, making a clear path for the magic-wielders. The lone gamlin ripped and tore at the bloody leg of a soldier, easily shredding dark armor and the flesh it protected. When Hector kicked it with his boot, the surprised animal spun about, launching itself at him. Hector swung, catching the creature on the end of the staff. It gripped tight, but Hector kept spinning. He stopped suddenly, propelling it high into the air. Dallow captured the gamlin in his shield.

"Now what do we do?" Dallow asked.

"I don't know how to kill them without my sword," Angst said, "so over the edge."

They inched their way toward the dragon carcass, which blocked the path to the cliff. The gamlin clawed desperately against the invisible shield as Angst and Dallow pushed their air traps as far as they could. When they were close enough to feel heat from the dragon's body, the shields hovered just beyond the cliff edge. Angst nodded and both men let go. The gamlin fell, their guttural cries quickly lost to the bridge music and raging waters far below. Angst immediately collapsed in a heap of exhaustion. Victoria scrambled forward and dropped to a knee, resting her hand on his head.

After several moments of catching his breath, he looked up at

Dallow.

"Not bad?" Dallow asked with a smirk, brushing bright blond locks from his green eyes.

"You're amazing!" Angst said with a smile. "Are you hiding a foci?"

"Dallow, duck!" Victoria yelled.

A gamlin covered in liquid fire leaped from the dead dragon's stomach. Without hesitation, Hector batted at the creature. His staff landed with a splash, and hot fiery goo flew at Dallow's face. Dallow screamed in pain and dropped to his knees, clawing at his eyes. The gamlin grunted and horted as it was tossed over the edge of the cliff.

Tarness punched Crloc in the head with all his might, knocking the man to the ground. He spun about and ran to Dallow. Angst scrambled to his oldest friend. He threw off his gloves and wiped desperately at Dallow's eyes, brushing hot liquid from his friend's face and burning his fingers. Angst could smell the singed flesh of his hands and Dallow's face and eyes. He continued wiping away the hissing slag, rubbing it off his hands on the snowy ground until the dragonbreath was gone.

"Please be okay, Dallow," Angst begged. "Please be okay."

"I need water," Hector cried out to the soldiers. "Now!"

A soldier threw a bladder to him. Hector poured it into his hand and splashed at Dallow's face then wiped away the brittle burnt flesh. Dallow was hyperventilating, whimpering with every breath, but the liquid fire appeared to be gone. He covered his eyes with his hands. Hector poured the remaining water on Angst's numb and throbbing fingers. Tarness, Hector, and Victoria stood in a circle around Dallow and Angst, staring down at them helplessly.

"It hurts, Angst," Dallow cried out.

Dallow pulled his hands away from his face and arched his head back. An ugly scar of blackened flesh masked his face from temple to temple. Dallow's eyes were completely gone and his eyelids burned away, fully exposing the darkened, empty sockets. Angst swallowed back his stomach and shook with despair, tears filling his eyes. Hesitantly, he leaned in to inspect the damage, making certain the glowing fire was gone.

"Are you with me, Dallow?" Angst whispered, gripping his friend tight. "Please be with me!"

"It hurts so much," Dallow said quietly before passing out.

36

Dallow lay on a makeshift stretcher carried by Tarness and a burly Rehman soldier who seemed disgusted at having to cart a wielder. But every time the man complained, Tarness would question whether he was getting tired or offer to carry Dallow by himself...if it was too much for the soldier to handle, and they would go on. Angst and Victoria rode close by, watching helplessly as Dallow struggled.

He tossed and turned on the gurney, his clothes damp with sweat as he fought off the pain of burns that had sunk deep into his face. In his brief moments of consciousness, Dallow would mutter words in Acratic before placing glowing hands over his eyes. His friend would moan, or scream, before becoming unconscious. Hours passed, and Angst watched in amazement as sheets of scabbed skin fell away from the wounds, leaving fresh new skin in its place. Dallow was healing himself, but it was an ordeal.

The next time he woke, Angst reached from his swifen to grip Dallow's shoulder. "Is there anything I can do?"

"Leave me alone!" Dallow snapped loudly. His breathing was hoarse, but after a moment he reached back to squeeze Angst's hand. "Sorry. Healing through as best I can. Maybe...maybe you can find Rose a foci and grow them back. Heh. I can heal, a little...my face, but I can't replace my eyes."

"I'll do..." Angst choked up. "I promise I'll do whatever I

can."

Dallow grunted in pain, squeezing Angst's hand so hard his fingers turned red then passed out again. Angst felt responsible for everything. He would have died before putting Dallow through this pain and torture. Was all of this because of his self-indulgence? He felt punished for seeking another foci, though he, too, was dying.

In spite of her anger, Tori continued riding with Angst. Even when things were tough between them, she was there for him. He loved her more for that right now than anything.

"Is he going to live?" Angst whispered in her ear. "Will he see again?"

"I've been trying to see since the attack," she said with obvious insecurity. "It just doesn't work right."

"That's not an answer! Tell me what you know," Angst snapped. "Please."

Victoria sighed, leaning over to touch Dallow's face. She closed her eyes and dropped her head to focus. Her breathing became heavy for several moments.

"He'll live, Angst," she promised. "I know that he will live."

Angst nodded at this and squeezed her free hand. He reached back to Dallow's hand and held it once again.

"He will see again, I think," she said hesitantly. "But I don't know. I don't understand, but I don't see that his eyes will ever be the same."

"Thank you, Tori," Angst replied sincerely.

Dallow woke suddenly, breathing fast. He pulled his hand from Angst's and began muttering in Acratic once again. Crloc was waiting. The large, bearded man rushed over to Dallow and slapped at the glowing hand.

"What are you doing?" Angst cried out. "Leave him be!"

"Crloc, stop this!" Victoria screamed.

"There will be no magics in Melkier!" Crloc reached for Dallow's hands. "This close to the castle, magic is blasphemy!"

Despite his exhaustion and emptiness, Angst reached for his sword. Victoria shook her head, her eyes wide with distress.

Tarness set two handles of Dallow's gurney on the ground and rushed forward to grab the front before the large Rehman soldier dropped his friend. Without warning, Hector leaped from his panther swifen, grabbed Crloc by his steel chestpiece and pulled him off his horse.

Hector landed hard on the ground and tossed Crloc high into the air with his feet. Crloc landed on his face and shoulder with a crash then rolled over onto his back like a lopsided somersault, finishing his acrobatics in an unnatural sprawl. Hector pounced onto the man's chest and placed a dagger firmly against Crloc's neck, cutting off chunks of dark beard in the process.

"No magics!" Crloc croaked.

"You don't want magic?" Hector snarled. His wolf-gray eyes gleamed with hungry anticipation, hackles rising from the base of his neck to the back of his head. "I promise, no magic, and I will still kill six of your men before a single bit of magic is used."

Crloc held out his hands defiantly but now Hector's thumb was deep into the man's vocal cords and he was drawing blood with the dagger. Victoria's long thin blades were out, and she looked ready to leap off Angst's swifen. Tarness stood over Dallow protectively, seeming ready to kill whatever soldiers Hector left over. Dallow's hands covered his eyes as he continued healing them with whatever spell he knew. Angst held his sword aloft shakily, waiting to wield magic until it became absolutely necessary.

"This is your one warning, Crloc," Hector growled. "Leave Dallow be or we will enter Melkier castle without an escort!"

"I'll—" Crloc started to threaten before choking on Hector's thumb. His face turned blue before he nodded his head once in reluctant agreement.

Hector stood, hungrily licking Crloc's blood from his dagger and spitting on the ground beside the man's head. He stormed to the front of the gurney and shoved the big soldier aside to pick it up. Crloc rose shakily, holding his hand against his bleeding neck.

CHAPTER THIRTY SIX

"What are you looking at?" Crloc croaked to no one. "I didn't say stop! On your way to the castle!"

"When this is done, if you don't slap that man stupid," Hector growled to Angst, "crush him in his own armor!"

* * * *

The moment they entered the castle, Angst could hear it: a quiet, distant buzzing that seemed to come from the back of his head. He looked at his friends to see concerned expressions at this new unknown they faced together, but could tell they heard nothing. Victoria turned her head to face him, the angry expressions she'd had for him these last few days replaced with worry. He nodded at her and smirked with the tiniest bit of hope. He could feel it, somewhere in the castle. Dulgirgraut.

There was little time to appreciate the beauty of Melkier Castle. The somewhat casual escort of Rehmans' Charge was now accompanied by a more formal troop of twenty soldiers, which flanked Angst and his friends on either side and herded them through the hallways. They sported the same dark black-blue armor, but a pale yellow and light blue cape also hung from every shoulder. The capes matched banners and flags that fluttered high in the monstrously tall hallways. Inadvertently, Tarness tripped into a guard as he gawked at the lofty arched ceilings.

All soldiers stopped with weapons pointed and, if it weren't for his dark skin, Angst would have sworn his friend was blushing. Crloc pushed his way through the guards, shoving weapons aside like low-hanging tree branches. He eyed the large man cautiously before looking over Angst, Dallow, and Tarness.

"Watch yourselves here," Crloc warned. With a nod to Princess Victoria, he added, "She is the sole reason you are being allowed into the throne room."

Crloc stomped back to the head of the line, and the entourage inched forward again. The sheer number of soldiers with them made it more than apparent that magic was not welcome, and that this stricture would be enforced vehemently.

While the distant buzzing of Dulgirgraut brought Angst hope, it also drained him as he reached out to find it. In spite of the foci's proximity, he was weaker than ever. The emptiness consumed him, and his lip quivered with exhaustion. Tarness immediately gripped Angst's right arm before he fainted. On cue, Hector stepped to Angst's other side and held onto his arm. Victoria looked at them both gratefully, ignoring Angst's embarrassed stare at the floor.

"Why is it every time we visit a capitol city we're escorted by guards?" Hector asked Tarness, as though propping Angst upright was as normal as eating.

"It's because Angst is so dangerous," Tarness said in his deep voice. "Can't you tell?"

Angst could only nod and cough out a chuckle. He felt like he could lose a battle with a feather, and hoped this wave of emptiness would pass before he met with King Gaarder.

They stopped in a passageway before the throne room to enjoy some waiting while Crloc entered the room with the now-unsealed parchment Victoria had given him.

"Her Royal Majesty, Princess Victoria of Unsel," a voice boomed after fifteen minutes of standing.

The throne room was made for giants. Tall archways crisscrossed overhead. Light poured in through stained glass windows depicting epic battles. Pale yellow and light blue banners hung along every wall. In the middle of the room, built on a large, circular staircase, rested a single throne. Guards shadowed their every step, with twitchy hands on hilts and eyes that barely blinked.

"No wonder they're nervous," Hector whispered, analyzing the room. "How in Ehrde could you protect the king when the throne is such an open target?"

They waited at the bottom of the stairs, facing the king of Melkier on his throne. The thin white hair framing Gaarder's wrinkled droopy face was the only thing Angst recognized. In the mere months since his first encounter with the king, Gaarder seemed to have wasted away. He wore a high-necked, light blue

266

robe, which hung loosely from his thin frame. The dark blue doublet with pale yellow embellishments under the robe appeared overlarge and uncomfortable. His eyes were wary and there was no longer welcome in them.

Victoria curtsied low. Hector, Dallow, and Tarness bowed deeply while Angst struggled to nod. King Gaarder stood shakily and walked down the stairway. Crloc stepped forward quickly to offer a hand, which the king took gratefully. He stopped in front of Victoria, bowed politely and then embraced her. Crloc stood behind the old king, at ease and smiling smugly at the young princess.

"You grow more beautiful every time I see you, dear," Gaarder said with a fatherly smile.

"You do me great honor, Your Majesty," Victoria said with a warm blush as she embraced the king. Her cheek brushed against his briefly.

Gaarder stepped aside to stand before Angst, his wrinkled eyes pinching with concern as he looked at the frail figure of the middle-aged man. Crloc tore his eyes from the princess to attend his king closely. He glared at Angst. Gaarder reached forward and shook Angst's hand, looking at the weak grip then looking Angst in the eye.

"You seem to be missing something," Gaarder stated, peering over Angst's shoulder. "I had heard, but that looks to be eating you alive. The dangers of magic, son."

Angst couldn't help but feel a sense of defeat at this statement. Gaarder had seemed accepting of, even interested in, magic when they'd last met. Now he apparently believed it to be evil. Dulgirgraut seemed even farther away than when they'd left Unsel. A wave of nausea and weakness overcame Angst, and Hector's arm was under his shoulder before he could fall. Gaarder ignored this, looking over the others and nodding at them politely before facing Victoria once more.

Gaarder waited. Angst and his friends looked at Victoria, who merely smiled, also waiting. Her eyes and smile were innocent, almost vapid, as though suddenly imbued with patience Angst had never seen. What was this all about? Would her position truly be weaker for asking first? If there were some deeper politics taking place, it was beyond his caring. The king smiled, the princess smiled, and Angst's patience became a lone thread of spider silk strung between them. It dragged on *for-ev-er*. He had to say something, anything, to break the silence. At this thought he saw Victoria tense, and he didn't care.

"I like your castle..." Angst said. He was immediately surrounded by sighs, and Victoria's eyes closed in disbelief. "...Your Majesty."

Gaarder barked out a laugh, patting Angst on the shoulder gratefully. "Thank you, Mister Angst," Gaarder said, his voice scratchy with age.

Had he been thanked for the compliment, or humored for blundering through politics he didn't understand?

"We read the offer from Queen Isabelle," Gaarder said to Victoria, placing his hands behind his back. "The Goyburn Peninsula has been in dispute for hundreds of years."

Angst looked over at Hector, completely bewildered. Hector shrugged, as did Tarness. Dallow's face was pale and he appeared in shock—the sole one of the group, other than Victoria, who understood the ramifications of the offer, apparently.

"The lands are fertile, the port is empty," Victoria said calmly, though she tugged on a curly lock of hair. "This agreement has the potential of placing Melkier at a trade advantage over Unsel."

King Gaarder licked his lips hungrily and rubbed a thumb across the tips of his fingers in anticipation. It was obvious the old man enjoyed bartering. "In exchange, all you want is that old sword?"

"You have it? You have Dulgirgraut?" Angst asked, too desperately.

"Pardon me, Your Majesty," Victoria politely requested of the old king. She turned to Angst with all the patience she could muster. "Shut up."

Angst pursed his lips to hold back anticipation, and Victoria turned her attention back to Gaarder with a controlled smile.

The old king chuckled, his eyes twinkling. "I see," he stated curiously. "Your offer is generous, but to make this decision there's something we need to understand. Is this for him, or for Unsel?"

Victoria gasped, pausing as her eyes flicked back and forth between Angst and Gaarder. She swallowed hard and took a deep breath. "This is for me," she said quietly.

The king's eyes widened briefly. He looked at Angst for a long moment then nodded knowingly. Crloc put a restraining hand on the old king's shoulder, which drooped slightly at the Captain Guard's touch. "I'm sorry you are hurting, son, but we need time to consider," Gaarder said.

Angst smiled weakly and nodded.

Victoria grabbed the old king's arm. "This isn't a negotiation, Gaarder. There isn't much time," Victoria pleaded. "I want...I want this to be peaceful."

"The world has changed since Angst took the great sword as his own," Gaarder stated, shaking his head in frustration. "I respect your request, and I'll admit we are hungry for your offer, but this decision isn't made lightly, or by me alone." Gaarder looked at Crloc, who smirked, eyeing them all imperiously.

Victoria seemed on the verge of tears and, for the first time in days, Angst felt close to her. She was angry with him for Alloria, or something else entirely, but nothing between them had really changed. Her reaction wasn't much, but it was enough, and with a deep breath, he stood straight.

"We promise a response in several days," the king said, looking at Angst.

"Of course, Your Majesty," Victoria replied with worry in her voice.

"Daughter, attend me," Gaarder commanded, pointing with two fingers and beckoning her forward. "I would like to introduce the queen regent—my daughter, Nicadilia."

Victoria's back stiffened at the woman's approach, her eyes growing wide at the title. Angst felt it best to curb his curiosity about Tori's reaction, instead watching the Queen Regent gracefully walk toward them.

A tall, thin blonde wearing a pale blue gown of velvet, she appeared several years older than Angst and draped in everything expensive. Her light blue eyes were sunken in her pale, gaunt cheeks and they flitted over Angst and his friends distractedly. Nicadilia had a permanent sneer lifted high beside each nostril and, at first glance, it seemed her beauty had been lost long ago to pomp and self-importance. But as she approached, he saw that she carried a heavy aura of sadness.

Angst noticed the thirsty look of Crloc drinking her in. The man's eyes flitted from Nicadilia to Victoria, ignoring everyone else in the room. Crloc looked at both women as though weighing livestock to brand, and more than ever Angst wanted to crush the bully where he stood.

Nicadilia glanced over them as she approached. She stopped before Angst and looked him up and down. Angst said nothing—she was a queen like Isabelle and his flirting would only cause more trouble. Nicadilia smiled at him curiously, pausing as if waiting for something. After a brief moment, she turned to face everyone, her nose high and her gaze low. Victoria curtsied politely. Angst and his friends followed her lead with respectful bows.

The queen regent held out her elbow. Like a well-trained dog, Crloc walked to her and interlocked arms. She looked at him without fondness or love, merely nodding when he took his place beside her.

"You are welcome guests at the castle," Gaarder promised. "And I expect you at my table for dinner tonight."

"Yes, Your Majesty," Victoria said with a curtsy. "Thank you."

37

Her soon-to-be royal majesty and princess, Alloria, drew long-nailed fingers up and down the rich armrest of the queen's throne as she settled back into the high-seated cushion. This was arrogance beyond reproach, but still she allowed herself to revel in her victories and languish in potential.

In spite of the late hour, or early depending on your perspective, Alloria was dressed to rule. Her plunging, pale blue corset was cut directly from Queen Isabelle's own style—showing more than enough to be distracting. The dangly sleeves of her fine silk blouse and long silk skirt were bone colored and shone in the torchlight. Her finery was enshrouded in a high-necked brocade cloak that hugged her sides while sitting and flowed dramatically when she walked.

Alloria sat up straight—the bustier provided a great view for onlookers but at the cost of breathing. Fortunately, Vars didn't take notice. He stood several feet away, looking downtrodden. His suit of armor was ostentatious—highly-polished silver embossed with solid gold tree branches that curled about wildly. At this moment, the suit barely seemed to fit the large man as though his depressive state ate away at his stature. He looked old, too old to be alive. Vars's long handsome face was withered with age, the skin hanging helplessly from his chin and neck. A half-wreath of white hair crowned his temples. His peering blue eyes were alert, yet sad around the edges.

After his attack in the hallway, Alloria had taken steps to show him she was more than a pretty face. She had subjugated the old knight, allowing her to focus on more important issues. It was all coming together. She had taken almost everything from her self-righteous all-too-perfect cousin—Isabelle's love and respect, the throne... What else was there?

"I suppose when this is done, I'll need a champion," Alloria said in her airy voice.

Vars did not make eye contact but instead looked down at his left hand, gently rubbing absent fingers with his right. His pinkie and ring finger were gone. Not grotesquely torn asunder, or freshly cut by means of torture; they were simply missing. He looked weakened and confused as he balled his hand into an awkward fist then rubbed the stumps again.

"Did you hear me?" Alloria snapped.

"Um, yes...yes, Your Majesty," he stuttered in shock, forcing his arms to his side and standing at attention.

"Maybe I should *point* a few things out to you," she admonished, directing her pointer finger at him. She stared at her finger mockingly, wiggling it and smiling, before returning her focus to Vars. "You still have that one, don't you?"

"Yes, Your Majesty," Vars said in disbelief before looking at his fingers once more and shuddering.

"I answer only to one," she said, lowering her head and looking at him with a dark scowl. "And that one is not you." She pulled back her threatening finger and whisked long light brown hair from her tan face. She pursed her pouty lips in self-righteous pompiety. "It's simple. I'm needed far more than you are," she stated matter-of-factly. "That's why I will one day be queen, and you will continue to do as I say."

"Of course, Your Majesty," Vars replied. His voice was scratchy and weak but ice cold, barely restraining the hatred behind his glare.

"As I was saying," Alloria said in a singsong voice. "I suppose I will need a champion..."

"I believe I was, um, designated, for that position," he said warily.

"Ha!" she blurted. "No, you will be my Captain Guard...spelled 'lap dog.' *If* you behave."

Vars nodded submissively, swallowing hard at the insult.

"A true champion is one that can be trusted," she continued. "Our relationship isn't exactly built on trust."

"But—"

"You still don't seem to understand our...position," she said. "We agreed to this situation. Did you think to get out of it so easily?"

"No." Vars sighed. "I had merely expected it would be different."

"You don't have to be my lap dog, Vars. Nor do you have to lose anything further," she said threateningly as she glanced at his hand. "This could still be a rewarding way to live."

"To live, Your Majesty?" He balled up his three-fingered hand.

"I believe Angst would be a good champion," Alloria said longingly, ignoring the older man's comment. "And maybe more than that."

"You're kidding," Vars said. "People would never accept a wielder as champion. Not to mention, isn't he old for you?"

"At least he's younger than you. Anyway, he's sort of cute for an older man," she said. "He's thoughtful, he cares, he has power—especially with that sword."

Alloria sounded hungry for something she couldn't have, and Vars rolled his eyes when she looked away. She was now sitting on the edge of the throne and rubbing her hands together.

"And?" he asked.

"It's the last thing Victoria has. I would've taken everything!" Alloria said triumphantly.

"And you believe it will be that easy?" Vars asked.

"I don't believe it will be too terribly hard to sway him," she said, ineffectively tugging at her bustier and staring at her ample cleavage with a smile. "I know Angst is already interested. We've made a connection, of sorts."

"This is all fine if he's not already dead," Vars said with bushy, raised eyebrows. "The chances of him making it back are very slim."

"If it were you, I would agree," Alloria replied tartly. "But I wouldn't count Angst out so quickly."

A young man burst into the room, followed closely by a soldier. Alloria shot up from the throne she shouldn't have been sitting in. Vars reached for his sword instinctively, but she held out a hand to calm him. The teenager leaned heavily against the soldier, appearing to have been dragged over a long distance by horse. Longish brown hair matted with dried blood stuck to the side of his thin, pale face. His wild eyes desperately scanned the room as he clung onto the soldier's arm for support.

Alloria's demeanor immediately changed from self-righteousness to feigned worry. She left the throne and quickly walked to the young man, taking his other arm and steering him to a nearby seat. Panic and gratitude filled his face as he took a long look at the beautiful young woman. She shushed several times to calm him as he patted the chair to make sure it was real before sitting down.

"Apologies, Your...Your Highness," he stuttered.

After he settled into to the chair, she stood upright in all her glory. His jaw dropped helplessly at her beauty, his breaths short and quick.

Alloria smiled appreciatively. She placed a warm hand on his shoulder and looked up at the guard.

"Paul was with the soldiers sent to protect Unsel from, um, the sinkholes, Your Highness," the knight stated, doing a poor job of looking her in the eye. "Mr. Paul said he needed Her Majesty, the queen, right away."

"Thank you." She rewarded the peering soldier with a broad smile. "Young knight, how may we help?"

"I have a message for the queen, Your Majesty," he said nervously, swallowing hard.

Alloria nodded in acknowledgement.

"My...my dad said to deliver it to her," Paul said, choking up.

CHAPTER THIRTY SEVEN

Alloria sat down next to the young man, and his eyes went wide and he licked his lips. She inched closer and put a hand on his knee. "These are trying times, and Queen Isabelle is exhausted," she said in an airy voice. "But I will rouse her from sleep to give her your message."

Paul looked at Alloria, weary from travel and desperate to trust. He glanced over the package of beautiful face with full lips, large breasts held aloft, and warm touch resting on his leg. His labored breathing calmed in her presence.

"Please, Your Majesty, it is desperately urgent," he said, choking on the words as his eyes became glossy. "The hundred knights are dead. Killed by the monsters protecting the approaching sinkholes!" He sniffed hard and his throat tightened as the tears began to trickle down his cheeks. "All of them, and my father." Paul now wept openly at acknowledging the death of his father, completely losing control.

Alloria continued patting his thigh consolingly. "I'm so sorry," she said looking at both the young man and the worried guard. "How is it you are the only survivor?"

The cries slowed as the young man collected himself, his cheeks blotchy from grief and embarrassment.

"I...well...magics, Your Majesty," he explained weakly.

Alloria nodded at him in understanding. "You can wield the magics?"

"Yes, ma'am," he admitted.

"And you destroyed the monsters?" Alloria continued.

"Yes, ma'am," he said with the tiniest bit of pride in his voice. "Only magic could destroy them."

"So you're a hero!" she declared, gripping his thigh firmly.

"Hero, Your Majesty?" the young man said in spite of himself. "I...well...I," he stuttered in disbelief.

"Say no more," she proclaimed. "Vars!"

"Yes, Your Highness," Vars said, now at attention.

"I will pass this urgent message on to Queen Isabelle now." She stood quickly. "You will see our hero to safe quarters."

Alloria leaned forward for all to see and kissed him firmly on the cheek. She then looked at the accompanying guard. "Assist Commander Vars and see our young hero to a safe place," she said, "while I inform Queen Isabelle of the goings on."

"Yes, Your Majesty," the guard said, standing at attention and offering an arm to the young man.

"You both do us honor," she said to the guard and the young man.

Alloria gave Vars a sideways look and quick smile. Paul gripped the guard's arm.

"I will see them to a place safe for us," Vars said, offering a second arm to the "hero."

Alloria watched them leave the room and, in spite of another job done well, she frowned. She couldn't help but ask herself if this was too much, if she was doing wrong. Even though she had agreed to all of this, she still had conscience, albeit a little one. At least she wouldn't have to shoulder any blame, nobody would be missed, or hopefully they would be lost in the shuffle. Most importantly, she would get what she wanted, and Victoria would lose everything.

But, in spite of all, it was messy.

In spite of all, she thought on Angst, and wondered how she could get away with that too.

38

They entered what had to be the longest hallway in all of Ehrde. It practically dripped with pale blue and golden banners that adorned the castle like a circus tent. Light gray veins in the marble floor, wall, stairs, and handrails coordinated handsomely with the decor. Melkier Castle was far more ostentatious than Unsel's, but in spite of the breathtaking garnish, it felt neither warm nor welcoming.

Angst was exhausted from the trip, distraught from troubles with Victoria, guilt-ridden over Dallow's injury, and empty. The emptiness was spreading, and his desire for a foci had grown from mere want to the painful hunger of a starving man. The proximity of Dulgirgraut was the tease of a prize so barely out of reach it seemed to tickle the ends of his fingers. A song whispered in his ear, which was both frustrating and enough encouragement to take another step. Now, more than ever, he needed a friend to lean on.

Hector had taken lead, followed closely by Tarness. The large man kept one hand around Dallow's waist in a clumsy attempt to help him along, but it might've gone smoother if Tarness had just carried him. Dallow's shoulders slumped as he cautiously shuffled his feet along the marble floor, keeping to himself in his personal anguish. Angst was reluctant to bother them with his troubles; his exhaustion was nothing compared to Dallow's sudden blindness. He looked at Victoria hopefully—she always knew what was on his mind, always knew what he needed.

She giggled.

He shook his head in disbelief at Victoria's reaction to their situation but then her smile faded and he realized her eyes were distant and distracted. She frowned and tugged at one of her curly blond locks in frustration.

"What in Ehrde are you doing?" Angst finally asked. "You certainly aren't here with me."

"I'm... just a minute," she whispered, waving a hand at him dismissively. Several moments passed and they turned a corner to walk up a long and wide flight of stairs.

"I was talking to Jaden," she whispered excitedly.

"What?" Angst said, much too loudly. The others attempted to ignore him. "What? How?"

"The earth maiden taught him to speak through stone," Victoria said. "He's been practicing, and we've been talking."

"For how long?" Angst asked as quietly as he could, almost stumbling up a step.

"A week or so," Victoria said, staring at the floor.

Angst blinked in astonishment. How could she have kept this from him? He could have spoken to Heather and let her know he was safe. Victoria seemed to shrink a moment, her head lowering into her shoulders. She looked him in the eyes, and could feel how disappointed and upset he was.

"I didn't know if it would—" Victoria began.

"Heather!" Angst snapped. "How is Heather?"

"I...I'm sorry Angst. He didn't say," Victoria said guiltily.

"You have a way to communicate with Unsel, possibly with my wife, and you didn't tell me?" His whisper cracked in anger.

"It's not like that," she said defensively. "I can't initiate it—"

"I thought you were here for me, for us!" Angst said in a normal tone, whispering now completely gone. He had needed her, and not only was she focused on someone not with them, she had kept something from him. Again. "How long has this been about him?"

"You don't understand!" Victoria snapped. "It's not about

him at all..."

"Now?" Hector asked in a monotone voice to anyone within earshot. "You have to argue now?"

"They seem to be like this all the time," a soldier of the Rehmans Charge interjected.

"You don't even know," Hector said, shaking his head in defeat.

"Are they married?" the soldier inquired, looking back and forth at the arguing pair.

"You'd think so," Hector replied with a sigh.

"While you two have been messing around, I've been in a panic about what's going on at home!" Angst yelled. "You know this but you have nothing to say? You can't even ask?"

"I thought you'd be mad," Victoria said quietly.

"You're right!" Angst snapped. "I am mad!"

"Then why don't you do it?" she replied, putting her hands one her waist.

"Why don't you show me how?" he asked.

"I don't know how!" Victoria said, articulating every word. "I said that already!"

"Then you tell your boyfriend to contact me—"

"He's not my boyfriend," she spat in a shrill voice. "And he's busy..."

Angst breathed flames from his nose and Victoria shot fire from her eyes.

"You must be getting old, Angst," Dallow chided, desperate to change the conversation. It was the first time he had spoken, and it instantly quieted both Angst and Victoria.

"Thank you," Hector muttered under his breath.

"Wh...what's that, Dallow?" He'd been so wrapped up in the argument and his anger with Tori that he'd forgotten all about his friends, and the castle, and the listening ears.

Angst stumbled again, reaching out and finding Victoria, who helped steady him. They glared at each other, and he jerked his arm away from her. Victoria raised both her hands defensively, as though she would never help him again.

"Her Majesty, Nicadilia," Dallow said with a sigh, smiling at the change of subject. "She sounded like someone you would have been, well, more Angst-like with."

"She was a little old for him," Tarness said in his low voice, winking at Victoria.

"Um, well, it's not that," Angst replied, looking at Victoria from the corner of his eye. He ignored her thin raised eyebrow. "She's a queen, like Isabelle, and I didn't want to insult anyone."

Victoria scoffed loudly, and both escort and Rehman soldier turned their heads to look at her. She rolled her eyes. "She is not like my mother," Victoria said haughtily. "She is nothing more than a princess with a fancy title."

The young man escorting them faced forward quickly, unwilling to acknowledge Victoria's comment. The Rehmans' Charge soldier coughed and did the same, wide-eyed and silent.

"A princess?" Angst asked hopefully. "I thought she was a queen."

"What?" Victoria snapped. "Nicadilia is no more a queen than I am. She's a princess in waiting, and that's all. I assume the title was given to her because she's so old."

"Here we are!" the young man interrupted loudly, hoping not to be caught in a conversation that acknowledged the queen regent's age. "Your Majesty's room is here to the right. Mr. Angst, you are directly across from the princess."

"She didn't look that interested in Angst," Tarness interjected.

"She sounded interested," Dallow said with a smirk, reaching out to Angst and patting him on the chest.

"I agree," Hector said. "But the prin...queen regent is a tough bird..."

"Mr. Hector!" the squire said loudly, pointing at a nearby door. "Your room is there. Mr. Tarness yours is across the hall!"

"It would be good for us, Angst, if you were to get to know her," Hector suggested.

"And Mr. Dallow is staying with Mr. Tarness. That will be all!" the squire said with great finality.

CHAPTER THIRTY EIGHT

The Rehmans' Charge soldier bowed curtly to Victoria, nodded at Hector, and accompanied the furious squire back down the hallway. They listened to the squire grumble about disrespect as he turned the corner down the stairway. Angst chuckled.

"Nicadilia seemed, I don't know, sort of bitchy," Tarness said off-handedly. "I typically ignore women like that."

"Not up to the challenge, old man?" Hector teased.

"I've dealt with bitchy before," Angst said, eyeing Victoria.

Victoria's eyes went wide, quickly becoming glossy wet. She sniffed loudly with a deep sad breath.

"How do you deal with bitchy?" Tarness asked.

"You have to be mean. Women like that don't appreciate good guys," Angst said, still staring at Victoria. "I hate it. It's not how I am, but I'll be mean and treat her the way she acts."

"I can't imagine you being mean to any woman," Tarness said with a chuckle.

"We do what we have to," Angst said sadly. "This isn't about you, or me. This is about all of Unsel. Maybe more."

Tarness nodded as he guided Dallow to their room. Hector looked from Angst to Victoria and, shaking his head in disapproval, walked to his room. Victoria and Angst stared at each other. Both looked furious and sad at the same time—on the verge of apology, or battle, or embrace. Neither said a thing, and with a deep breath, they spun on their heels and parted ways to their own room.

39

Melkier dining tables were not the standard rectangle of Unsel or the fantastical oval of Rohjek. The table was an enormous square with a 'U' cut out every several feet, allowing plenty of room for extra food and elbows. This made it necessary for every guest at the table to hop their heavy wooden chairs forward several feet to better tuck themselves into the meal.

Where Queen Isabelle would've been prominently on display at the head of the table, King Gaarder sat in the middle, within the largest 'U', wrapped in tight like a potpie. Crloc and his freshly-Hector-carved beard sat to Gaarder's right, and taller-than-Crloc Nicadilia to his left. An older nobleman sat beside Nicadilia, safely partitioning her off from their estranged guests. Angst and his friends were directed to sit across from Nicadilia, the king and Crloc.

Even sitting, Nicadilia appeared tall. She was as thin as one could get without looking unhealthy, as if her tallness had stretched out every ounce of fat. Nicadilia was thin-lipped and thin chested. Her low cut burgundy dress showed no cleavage and was made for a larger woman. Despite a gaudy display of jewels swirling about her arms and chest, there was nothing flattering about her attire. Her high cheekbones stood out beneath aging skin hungry for sunlight and washed out by pale blond hair. She was not unattractive, but age and a lifetime of looking down her nose at others had turned her into a handsome woman unable to reach the full potential of her beauty.

Angst guided Dallow to his seat before walking around the table. Everyone watched in surprise, and Nicadilia's mouth hung open.

"May I sit next to you?" Angst asked Nicadilia while nodding politely at the older man already sitting beside the queen regent.

"Uh," she replied hesitantly then nodded at the other man to move. "Of course."

Angst struggled to help the old man hop the heavy chair out of his dining alcove then sat and proceeded to noisily hop himself back into the same spot. Heads around the table nodded reactively with every jounce, their eyes wincing at the screeching noises.

"I look forward to learning more about Melkier," Angst said enthusiastically to the queen regent. "I'm feeling better than I have in days, and I'm certain dinner will be fun."

"Yes," she said, her cheeks now a bright shade of red, "fun."

The old nobleman sat between Tarness and Dallow. He looked to his right, his eyes widening at the empty sockets, then to his left and swallowed hard at the enormity of the large black man sitting next to him. Tarness ignored the nobleman, gawking at a woman beside him who was so well dressed for the occasion she was as fancy as the marble floor. Tarness flashed her an enormous grin, his white teeth bright behind his dark lips. She stared up in astonishment and attempted to hop her chair away, as though momentarily forgetting she was stuck in her 'U.' She pulled her right elbow off the table for safety and stared straight ahead.

"That's a very becoming gown, Your Majesty," Angst said quietly to Nicadilia, his brows furrowed with mock-sincerity as he leered at her dress. "Did you make that?" From the corner of his eye, he could see Victoria's shoulders tense with worry across the table.

Nicadilia turned to stare down her nose at Angst with thin, intolerant eyes. "You realize, sir, that I am royalty?"

"Of course," Angst stated with a smirk. "That's why I said

Your Majesty."

As though she had never been teased or taunted in her entire life, Nicadilia almost lost composure. Appearing shocked, she stared at Angst in befuddlement, as though he'd smacked her upside the head. She leaned forward and peered, as if analyzing him for the first time.

"I did not make the dress," she stated flatly. She brushed graying blond hair from her high cheeks as if dismissing Angst like a fly.

"Good, because it really isn't flattering at all," Angst said with feigned relief.

"Pardon?" she squawked, completely unnerved, now looking down at her dress as though she wasn't the one who'd put it on.

Victoria looked from Angst to Nicadilia in astonishment. She glanced at Hector who stared at his place setting, his grin uncontrollably creeping up one cheek.

"I would just feel bad if you were the one who made it," Angst said as sincerely as he could. He whispered loudly, "I can understand if you'd chosen a light blue, or a bright green, but that red... I guess it would be better if it fit. You really look overweight."

Nicadilia stared at her gown, desperately attempting to straighten it out with her hands as though brushing off droplets of water.

A cloud of dark hovered over Crloc, and his nostrils flared. While he couldn't hear all of the conversation between Angst and Nicadilia, he bristled at her reaction. The king held out a reassuring hand, nodding at his Captain Guard to keep the peace.

"Mr. Angst," King Gaarder said, facing him. "Were you aware that my daughter, the queen regent, will soon wed Captain Guard Crloc?"

Angst raised one eyebrow in surprise, leaning forward to look around Nicadilia and the king and stare at Crloc with wide mocking eyes. He then shared that same expression with the queen regent.

"No, Your Majesty. Crloc didn't mention that to us." Angst

looked at Victoria. "Did he say anything to you when you dined together?"

Victoria shook her head quickly, grabbed her goblet of wine and took a long draw. Nicadilia glared openly at the princess, and Crloc slammed his fist on the table. Hector shook his head, his smirk now reaching both cheeks.

"I didn't realize you were royalty..." Angst said to Crloc.

"Would it have made a difference?" Crloc said gruffly.

"I would've bowed after pushing you into the hole I made," Angst said with a broad grin.

Tarness barked a quick laugh, making the woman next to him squeak nervously. Nicadilia chuckled despite herself, avoiding Crloc's stern glare and covering her mouth with a napkin. She caught herself and looked down at her dress once more before glaring at Angst. He shrugged and took a sip of wine, thoroughly enjoying that it was appropriate in Melkier to leave his elbows on the table.

"It has been a long time since this table has seen levity," King Gaarder said with a smile, resting a firm hand on Crloc's arm.

The old king's eyes squeezed shut for a long time, and everyone quieted in respect. When he finally opened them, they appeared glazed over by exhaustion. Table-runners delivered a course of candied meats and pickled fruits while topping off goblets of thickwine. Tarness gobbled his helping faster than anyone. Hector also ate the food quickly, while Dallow savored every bite.

"It's okay to eat," Angst said quietly to Nicadilia. "I swear nobody's looking."

The queen regent placed her fork on the table and stared at her food with wide eyes.

"Your Majesties," Dallow asked. "May I ask you about the dark armor? How does it resist magic?"

Gaarder looked at Crloc, who shrugged dismissively. The king raised two fingers to call forth a squire. He whispered in the young boy's ear and sent him scurrying away.

"It was never meant to resist magics," Gaarder said. "We

were looking for a way to protect our soldiers from drag-onbreath."

The squire returned, handing the king a broken piece of large bone. It was dark, almost black, yet blue when reflecting light. Gaarder handed it across Nicadilia to Angst. As soon as he touched it, he shivered. He held a void in his hand that was both fascinating and nauseating. Angst could have felt the steel of plate, but this was more like a sinkhole sucking at his magic. It was unlike any mineral he had ever come in contact with, and he ran his fingers across it to look for the hole he felt. The king smiled and nodded at his reaction. Without consideration for dinner etiquette, Angst casually tossed it across the table to Hec-tor, who caught it and handed it to Dallow. Victoria's face was in her hands, as though she were a grown-up who had brought her naughty children to a neighbor's party.

"Dragonbone," Gaarder stated. "To protect us from the drag-ons' fires, we harvested bones from their kills to protect us. Coated our soldiers' armor to keep them from harm."

"It makes sense," Dallow said. "If dragons had the same bones we do, the bones would disintegrate in their own drag-onbreath."

"Yes, mi'boy," the old king said. "Who knew it would resist magic as well?"

"So...about the sword," Angst said.

"My counsel has yet to review Your Majesty's generous of-fer," Gaarder said to Victoria.

"We look forward to your thoughtful decision," Victoria said politely.

"So it *is* here," Angst said with a smirk.

Victoria rolled her eyes at his lack of tact, but Gaarder merely smiled. "Yes, Angst, we do have a sword that resembles the one you used to wield."

"Your Majesty, it could save my life," Angst pleaded.

"That is a small price to pay for the safety of our kingdom," Crloc growled.

"Angst is no danger to Melkier!" Victoria said. "We've been

allies for centuries!"

"Allies don't have contested lands," Crloc spat as he stood.

"Melkier is not prepared to support magics!" Nicadilia sliced at the air with her hand.

"What if you don't have a choice?" Hector asked, mockingly rubbing a spot on his chin.

Crloc tried looking at his own chin, touching the spot Hector had cut off. "We've had no problem defending ourselves!" Crloc said in fury.

"That's not what I saw earlier today." Hector peered at Crloc with his wolf-like eyes.

"Enough!" Gaarder yelled in a gravelly voice. "This is time for dinner, not debate. Is that clear?"

The tension dissipated, slightly, but enough remained to make everyone sit and grumble quietly to themselves.

"I don't understand why you people can't see how dangerous you are!" Nicadilia whispered over her shoulder to Angst in an attempt to get in the last word.

"I still don't understand why you wore that dress," Angst replied.

Queen Regent Nicadilia went pale. She stood fast, her chair falling to the ground behind her with a smack. She seemed on the verge of slapping Angst, but instead covered her mouth and rushed out of the room.

Angst caught Gaarder's eye and shrugged helplessly.

The king looked at Victoria.

"I know how she feels," the princess said quietly.

40

Queen Isabelle lay on her side, staring at the fire that popped and snapped as wood settled into the grate. Every night that Victoria was away, she found it took longer to fall asleep—though she knew in her heart that, somehow, her daughter was safe. Isabelle blinked heavily. She hoped the lessons learned on this adventure would sway her defiant daughter to choose the path of queen and not adventurer. It was a gamble, but what choice did she have? It was just as much a gamble to make the young magic-wielder a queen, wasn't it? She had borne a wielder, as though she deserved such punishment.

The queen shut her eyes as she envisioned peeking through the doorway to watch a nine-year-old Victoria on bare feet, her long dark hair pulled into a tight knot. Her linen clothes were baggy and padded to protect her and she had just bested yet another boy while dueling swords. She looked unhappy about it and sighed.

"Tyrell, I'm bored," the young princess whined.

"I see that," Tyrell said as he bent over stiffly and helped the twelve-year-old boy to his feet.

"She cheats!" the burnished-haired boy said, pointing the sword at her. "No girl is that good!"

"Mind your tongue!" Tyrell admonished, slapping the sword away.

The boy lowered his sword slowly, obviously upset at losing

to a girl. Victoria stuck her tongue out at her accuser, making him grip his hilt hard with embarrassed frustration.

"You did well today. Better than you think, son," Tyrell said, patting him on the back.

Isabelle sighed with relief. While she understood the importance of these training sessions, she had feared for the worst sort of accident.

"See yourself home," Tyrell waved the boy off.

"Yessir," the lad muttered, watching Tyrell and Victoria turn their backs on him. The two walked toward the queen's nearby throne.

It was one of those uncontrollable moments that can overtake any child. Jealousy, anger, an almost-fury at the injustice of the humiliation boiled over within him. With barely a sound, the young boy leaped forward, swatting at Victoria's rear with the flat of his blade.

Her heart in her throat, Isabelle started through the door, only to stop when she saw her daughter's reaction. Casually, nonchalantly, the princess unsheathed her sword, blocked his swing and spun to kick him in the gut. The boy crashed to the floor with a groan.

Tyrell stared at the princess in shock, the look on his face a mirror of Isabelle's. He gripped Victoria's arms and spun her about to check for damage. She was so scared at his reaction that she started to cry.

"I'm sorry, he... I... He was going to strike me," she said, the tears pouring out.

Tyrell rested his hand on the princess's shoulder and shushed her gently before storming over to the young boy. He lifted the boy by an ear and an arm. "Do you have any idea who this is, boy?" he barked, his face red with fury. "Do you know what you could have done?"

Now the boy, too, was in tears, and Queen Isabelle stormed into the room.

"What's going on in here?" she roared.

"He attacked her from behind!" Tyrell said, still holding the crying boy by an ear.

Isabelle marched to Victoria, kneeling to inspect her as if checking the flank of a racing horse. The princess immediately stopped crying.

"She seems unharmed," the queen said to Tyrell.

"You see yourself to the kitchens, Samsen!" Tyrell yelled, spinning the boy about and kicking him in the rear. "I'll see to it that you're scrubbing pots for weeks!"

The boy left in tears, bawling his sorrys loudly.

"He didn't mean it, Tyrell," Victoria said with a sniff, her voice thick with guilt at Samsen's predicament.

"You will learn as queen that commanding punishment is often unpleasant, but necessary," Isabelle advised coldly.

Victoria nodded at her mother, understanding but still unhappy with the queen's teachings.

Tyrell took a deep breath and turned to kneel before the princess. He wiped her wet cheeks with the back of his hand and smiled proudly. "You did well, Your Majesty," Tyrell acknowledged. "How did you know to block his attack? He was behind you."

Victoria shrugged. She rubbed her nose on her linen sleeve only to have her arm pulled from her face by Isabelle. Victoria rolled her eyes at her mom and sniffed loudly. She looked at the door Samsen had walked out of.

"I don't think the kitchens are a good place for him," the princess said with a wince, pressing her palm to her forehead. "He'll get hurt in there!"

Victoria began crying uncontrollably and buried her face in the queen's long dress, holding on for her life.

Isabelle and Tyrell looked at each other helplessly.

* * * *

Isabelle blinked rapidly as a handmaiden set another log in the great fireplace. The older woman looked at the queen, worried that she had been too noisy. After hastily brushing bits of bark from her long gray woolen dress, she rushed out of the queen's chambers. Isabelle smiled to herself as she once again dozed into memory-filled dreams of her daughter.

* * * *

The young queen paced on one side of the great hall, while the king hovered over a table at the other. She peered at her husband, both perturbed and full of love. She had cleared her throat loudly, several times, to no avail, as her husband doted on his daughter.

"And you see that, Daddy?" the eight-year-old princess said, tugging on his dark brown beard and pointing at a peninsula between Unsel and Melkier. "You'll lose that if you make your men go over there." She pointed at Rohjek. "But that's okay because I'll get it back!"

"Oh, you will, will you?" the king said, chuckling in his tenor voice. He tickled her sides and smiled at her giggles while eyeing the map. "Hmm. It's possible, but I don't see—"

The third ahem was more of a squawk, both interrupting playtime and bringing focus to the frustrated queen. She held her fists hard against the waist of her green brocade bodice. The king smirked, setting Victoria on the floor and walking over to his wife.

"And how may I assist, milady?" he asked mockingly.

"You really want to host a party for the commoners?" Isabelle asked, tapping her foot in disapproval.

"We would be nothing without those *commoners*, and you know this," he said sternly, itching a spot beneath his crown. "They are the people of Unsel. We have a duty to protect them and to—"

"Fine," she interrupted in exasperation. "But do we have to thank the entire castle staff? Where do we even hold that many people inside the castle?"

"Outside, Mommy!" Victoria said, clapping her hands. "The party can be outside by the big sword! We can make the sword a game!"

The king shrugged at Isabelle, who agreed in her own disgruntled fashion.

* * * *

"You cannot leave the castle, young lady, and that is final!" Isabelle commanded.

"I'm thirteen!" Victoria yelled back, stomping her foot. "I want to see what's out there!"

"You don't need to see what's out there," the queen yelled, her temper rising. "You need to learn your role here!"

"How can I learn to be queen stuck in here? I don't even know what's going on out there!" Victoria said in a high-pitched tone. "I need to know our people, Mother!"

"It's far too dangerous," the queen said dismissively.

"I'll find someone to keep me safe!" Victoria snapped.

"Don't be silly, Tori," Isabelle admonished. "I doubt anyone can keep you completely safe."

"Don't call me that! You can't call me Tori anymore!" she said, her fists clenched.

The queen shook her head in frustration, the weariness of parenting weighing heavily on her shoulders. She took a deep breath and straightened her back.

"I need to get out there now, Mother! We will need them someday, before things get bad!" Victoria pleaded.

"Bad would be another country kidnapping you, or even worse, assassinating you." The queen shuddered.

The young teenager pressed fists against her temples and winced in pain. Her head cocked to one side and she shuddered. "No, bad will be all nations of Ehrde at war and no true queen for them to follow!" Victoria blurted out, her face twisting in pain.

Isabelle's eyes went wide at the odd statement. She wanted to move away but instead moved closer to her daughter. Hesitantly, she reached out to touch Victoria's shoulders, unsure how to comfort the young woman. Before her hands connected, the moment passed. Victoria stared at her mother in disbelief at the offered compassion, as though no strange words of forewarning had left her lips.

"What are you doing?" Victoria snapped. "Mother, just let me out with some guards."

"You will do as you are told, or face the consequences," the queen commanded.

"I'll get out of here one day. I know it," Victoria said. "Even if it kills me. Even if it kills both of us!"

* * * *

Isabelle sat up in a panic. Sweat dripped from her forehead, and wet hair matted her brow. She looked around the empty room, feeling like she was being watched. The memories overwhelmed her. Isabelle had only learned of her daughter's abilities when she reached adulthood. Had Victoria always known the future? The dreams were becoming hazy. What had her daughter said. War? All nations at war? That she would die and there would be no queen?

"Tyrell!" Isabelle screeched at the top of her lungs. "Tyrell!"

41

Angst's room was spacious and opulent, with every amenity a visiting ambassador could desire—and it set his teeth on edge. The white marble walls covered with rich tapestries, the greymaul desk and tables, fresh flowers...in winter? It was too much, and he was antsy enough to pace. Instead, Angst restlessly fidgeted in an overstuffed nap-inducing cush-chair, fighting off exhaustion and listening to his friends banter.

"This is a nice prison," Hector growled, pacing for himself and Angst.

Hector appeared uncomfortably squeezed into the light brown leather doublet he had worn for the dinner with King Gaarder. He seemed restrained by formality, trapped in leggings and boots and finery. Occasionally, he released his clenched hands from behind his back long enough to undo another clasp in the doublet before returning them to their resigned position. When he completed this bit of theatre, he would return to pacing, pausing only to blame Angst with long looks.

"They obviously aren't worried about us causing trouble," Tarness said as he played with a flower-embroidered doily that dripped off a nearby table. "It's that armor. It must be. Is it anti-magic? I barely harmed Crloc when we fought."

"I thought you were going easy on him," Hector said in surprise.

"You're kidding, right?" Tarness replied, cocking his head to the side ironically. "Would you go easy on that guy?"

"Crloc's not that bad," Victoria interjected.

"The armor isn't anti-magic," Dallow said quietly from the bed, rubbing his face with his right hand. "There's no such thing. It's merely enhanced to reject magic. Sort of like an air shield that deflects arrows."

Victoria sat on the edge of the bed next to Dallow, watching over him like a worried mother. She placed her hand on his forehead, not once looking away from the sunken sockets where his eyes had been. His face was pale and damp, and she surreptitiously wiped her hand on the bed.

"I don't feel a fever," she said.

"Thank you, Your Majesty," Dallow said, his voice thick with melancholy. "I'm sure I'll be fine."

Tori looked at Angst, reaching out to him with her eyes. Angst could see her staring from the edge of his vision, but continued looking straight ahead. He completely avoided that side of the room. Still bitter at what he had learned about her constant earthspeak communication with Jaden, he didn't want to deal with Victoria right now. But worse than that was poor Dallow. With enough light from candles and the fire, Angst could clearly see the rough graffiti of scarring across his face from temple to temple. Even Dallow's blond bangs were gone, as were his eyebrows, completely burned away by fire. Angst's guilt was like the quick paws of a wild animal, relentlessly digging at the edges of emptiness already consuming him.

"They've made a lot of those weapons and armor," Tarness said, looking back and forth between Angst and Victoria.

"But how?" Dallow questioned. "You can crush bone with magic, Angst, or you could when you were healthy. Could you manipulate the dragonbone?"

"I didn't try, but I doubt it," Angst said softly. "It felt like nothing…like a void."

"If you couldn't," Tarness asked. "How could they?"

"Dulgirgraut," Angst said. "It's the only thing powerful enough."

"That seems…plausible," Dallow said thoughtfully. "Though I don't understand how."

"I don't understand why Melkier is suddenly against the use of magic," Victoria added. "They used to walk a fine line of tolerance, like Unsel."

"That's a fine line?" Tarness snapped, making everyone's heads turn in surprise. "How many of your friends went to jail for doing what they do naturally—"

"Not now, Tarness," Angst said, instantly defending the princess then sneering at himself for doing so. "I agree with Tori."

"Of course you do," Hector said, rolling his eyes.

"This isn't the time to argue the rights and wrongs of Unsel laws. It's a fact that Melkier allowed the use of magic," Angst said. "Look, I met Gaarder at the party when I first wielded Chryslaenor. He didn't hate magic. He even told me about the sword. Something has changed."

"Nicadilia being named Queen Regent is odd," Victoria added.

"Are you sure you aren't just being critical?" Hector asked.

"That's usually done only when someone has to step in," she observed. "Maybe if Gaarder were incapable of ruling due to health or age."

"He looked at Crloc or Nicadilia every time he had to make a decision," Hector added without breaking stride. "He even surrounded himself with them at dinner."

"There was something very off about Gaarder, about all of them," Victoria said, staring at Angst and hoping he would pick up her cue. "It just didn't feel right."

"At this point Gaarder's never going to give up my sword," Angst interjected, still ignoring the princess. "We need to take matters into our own hands."

"We have to handle this carefully, Angst," Victoria warned. "Melkier is a friend to Unsel."

"What I need to do…" Angst began to explain his plan, as he rocked back and forth to launch himself from the chair. His teeth chattered with exhaustion.

Hector turned about suddenly and walked over to him, resting a hand on his friend's shoulder and keeping him from leaving his seat. "What do you need us to do, Angst?"

Angst's arms shook from the gentle pressure of Hector's hand, and he flopped back into the chair with a frustrated grunt. Angst suddenly hated this chair, and blamed its comfort for sapping every ounce of energy from his body.

"We need to find Dulgirgraut," Angst said.

"I can do that," Hector offered with a sly grin. "Sounds like fun. It's been a while since my spying days. Any idea where it is?"

"It's definitely here, in the castle. Gaarder confirmed it, I can feel it, but that's all I know," Angst said apologetically. "I'd check the ground floor first."

"Why the ground floor?" Hector asked.

"Who could move it?" Angst offered.

Hector nodded in acknowledgement.

"I could go to town and dig up something on Crloc and the queen regent," Tarness offered with a big grin.

"You mean dig up a draft or seven of mead?" Angst asked with a smirk.

"A good brothel is where the best rumors are," Tarness said, feigning great wisdom.

"Brothel?" Victoria asked, judiciously lowering her eyes.

"I meant pub, Your Majesty," Tarness said innocently, though his smile said otherwise.

"I'm jealous," Angst lamented.

"Just trying to do my part," Tarness said in mock earnest as he fought his way out of his own cush-chair.

"I suppose I'll rest in my room," Dallow said pathetically, a slight catch in his voice. "If someone would give me a hand..."

"Actually, Dallow, you need to find out how they made the armor," Victoria commanded. "Maybe the library?"

"What?" Tarness and Hector both looked at her with offended frowns.

"Why would you say such a thing?" Dallow asked, his voice

cracking.

Victoria looked pleadingly at Angst. He could guess her intent and reluctantly sought her eyes for confirmation. She hadn't been checking Dallow's temperature—she'd been attempting to see his future. In spite of how upset he was, this is exactly why he loved the princess so much.

Angst smiled and nodded. "She's right," he said loudly. "Dallow, when have you ever needed your eyes to read?"

"I...well, I..." Dallow took several deep breaths. He reached up to brush away tears that weren't there and sighed. "I'll try," he said after swallowing hard, regaining some composure.

"I think you'll be surprised, Dallow," Victoria said.

"Really?" Dallow said hopefully.

"Believe her," Angst encouraged.

"You know, it just may work," he finally said in rising excitement.

Hector eyed her curiously but said nothing. Dallow sat up and gave the young princess a hug, pulling back suddenly when he remembered who he was hugging. Victoria clapped and giggled at Dallow's reaction.

"My apologies, Your Highness," he said worriedly.

"Shush," Victoria replied, still beaming. She guided his hands to her arm so he could follow her as they stood.

There was a knock at the door, silencing the room.

Victoria's eyes went wide, and she looked at Angst.

He returned her surprised gaze knowingly. "I've got this," Angst said with a cat-like grin.

"When have I heard that before?" Hector said with a sigh.

Angst stood shakily, pushing away Hector's offer to help, and straightened his tunic before walking to the door.

"What are you doing?" Victoria asked.

"Just like you," he said with mock-sincerity and raised eyebrow, "I'm doing my job."

Angst opened the door to reveal Queen Regent Nicadilia and a young page.

42

"My father asked me to make certain your accommodations are acceptable," Nicadilia said, her gaze flitting around the room. "I can come back la—"

"Please come in," Angst said with a flourishing bow, waving her into the room. "My friends were just leaving."

"Oh. Um, thank you." She glided into the room, the young squire following closely behind.

"Would you mind terribly if your man escorted Dallow to the library?" Angst requested.

"It isn't necessarily proper for a queen to be alone with a man in a room," Nicadilia said nervously, looking for judgment in everyone's eyes.

Hector smirked at Tarness, who smiled and winked back. Victoria refrained from scoffing at the self-appointed title and rolled her eyes at the boys.

"You have no need to be concerned, Your Majesty," Victoria said in mock-defense of Angst. "He's married and completely harmless."

"Oh," she said in surprise. "Thank you, Princess. Then, by all means, please take my boy."

The squire looked at Dallow's sunken eye sockets with great concern and didn't move—his legs apparently unwilling to commit to leaving the queen regent's side. Victoria pulled a light blue kerchief from her pocket, rolled it up, and tied it around

Dallow's head. She tugged the edges down to cover most of the scarring.

Dallow touched the kerchief thoughtfully and bowed his head. "I'm honored, Your Majesty," he stated serenely.

"Good luck, Mr. Dallow," Victoria said, squeezing his shoulder.

Dallow reached out for the squire. The boy put Dallow's hand on his shoulder and left the room slowly, followed closely by a watchful Hector. Tarness winked at Angst from behind Nicadilia before exiting the room. Victoria stopped at the doorway, whipping her head about and peering at Angst through cold, slitted eyes. She crossed her arms as if making a stand to stay. Angst stared back. He needed her to leave, and openly wondered if she would tantrum like a child.

Victoria seemed hurt and upset at his thoughts then abruptly chose anger. "Fine!" she said, stomping her foot.

"Fine," he replied coldly.

Tori's eyes were dangerous as she stormed out the room, slamming the door behind her. Angst closed his eyes and took a deep breath. He hated this, hated what their relationship was becoming. She had always been his escape, and now acted more like his wife. When he opened his eyes, he saw Nicadilia looking at him in surprise.

He shrugged. "It's complicated," he explained.

"She's a princess," Nicadilia said knowingly. "It's supposed to be."

"You changed out of that ugly dress." Angst smirked, trying to change the subject. "You look better."

Nicadilia wore a long, light-gray dress of a sheer fabric that clung tightly to her svelte figure. She held her arms high enough to keep draping sleeves from brushing the marble floor. Angst could not see her feet—the meticulously tailored hemline was a mere hair's width over the tile—and she seemed to glide with every step. Jeweled golden bracelets stacked from Nicadilia's left wrist to her forearm, complementing her thick gold necklace and heavy gold tiara. The crown, and title, wore Nicadilia with great comfort.

"I'm not ugly!" Nicadilia said defensively, now looking over him to avoid eye contact.

"It was hard to tell in that dress," Angst said. "At least this is a little better. I think..."

"You are a rude little man." Nicadilia tried to match his insults. "If your room is acceptable, I will take my leave."

"I didn't say the room was acceptable," Angst said coolly.

He took several steps toward the queen regent, looking directly at her. Her back straightened, and she turned her chin slightly away. She obviously didn't approve of anything about him—what he said, what he did, who he was, or what he could do—but still remained in place despite her growing discomfort.

"I...well...I," Nicadilia said, trapped by her commitment to ensure the room was acceptable. "Wielders are not to look directly at royalty."

"Then make my room better, and I'll stop looking at you," Angst said firmly, still making his way toward her.

"Wielders cannot make demands of royalty in Melkier," she stated haughtily.

Angst did not enjoy this game. He took a deep breath, debating on opening a hole in the tile and dropping her several floors. The others were risking their lives, right now, to save his. Hector thought Angst could get information from the queen regent that they would find useful. Despite feeling absolutely no connection to her whatsoever, he would keep trying.

Angst smiled at Nicadilia through gritted teeth. "That's nonsense. If I'm not supposed to *make demands*, or even look at you, then why are you here?"

"You are not to question me—"

"What?" Angst wanted to press his wrist to his forehead and relieve the pressure of her crazy splitting his brain in two. "That's why you're here? To tell me not to make demands or look at you? You're crazy."

With a loud scoff, Nicadilia's eyes narrowed. She floated to the door and pulled at the handle. Just as the door cracked open,

Angst willed it shut, wielding just enough magic to push gently against the metal handle.

"Was...was that magic?" She yanked her hand from the handle and spun about. "In my presence?" She crossed her arms and seemed to be shaking slightly.

Angst carefully made his way to the queen regent, using each piece of furniture between them as a crutch to lean on. "Your Majesty?"

Her face was filled with worry. She seemed to struggle with Angst's very presence, but when he stood too close for everyday conversation, she made eye contact. Nicadilia's eyes were pretty and filled with wanting for everything she couldn't have. She looked at him and her lips thinned. Angst felt like Nicadilia needed something from him, but had a hard time reading her. The queen regent was the model of restraint, a chrysalis that would never open, and above all else, Angst wanted to avoid what could be inside.

"Why are you really here, Nicadilia?" Angst asked.

She looked ready to strike but, at the very last moment, buried her face in his shoulder instead. Angst stood very still, momentarily stunned by this sudden trust from a woman he was certain hated him. He was mostly certain he disliked her too, but here she was, crying in his arms, and what else could he do? He reached around the queen regent to comfort her, which opened a dam of tears she must have held in since birth. With every ounce of patience and courtesy he could muster, Angst inched back toward the nearby cushioned chair—pulling the still-sobbing Nicadilia along with him.

Why, he wondered, automatically patting her back, *do they always cry?*

"I'm sorry if I spoke out of turn?" he asked, not knowing what else he could have done wrong.

Nicadilia lifted her head from his shoulder, her eyes leaking like squeezed sponges. One side of her face cracked a smile, followed soon by the other. After twenty years of marriage, Angst had experienced his share of outbursts by Heather and knew how to turn this around.

"Or was it the eye contact?" he said, hoping it would continue to fend off the tears.

"No, Mr. Angst," she said shaking her head, her pale blond hair flowing from shoulder to shoulder.

"So," he replied. "You were going to tell me why you're here?"

"You remind me of him," Nicadilia said quietly, "so very much."

"Of who, Your Majesty?" Angst asked.

"I had a lover," she said. "He was a short man, like you."

Angst winced. Really? Short? He reluctantly nodded for her to continue.

"I wanted so much for him to be my king. He was wise, and strong, and brash," she said. "Then the dragons came and everything changed."

"What did they change?" he asked.

"I can't really say."

She hesitated, guiltily looking down at the large ruby ring—identical to the one hanging from his neck—decorating her middle finger. The queen regent rocked the ring back and forth with her thumb, and his worry bubbled up through his chest. He was at the cusp of asking about it when she cut off his thoughts.

"He, too, could wield magics like you," she stated, her eyes becoming glossy.

"And that was so bad?" Angst asked.

"Yes," she said, despondently.

Angst bit his tongue, curbing his natural reaction to lash out defensively. He needed her, and holding her like this Angst felt it was time to stop being mean.

"What happened to him?"

"He left us," Nicadilia said quietly.

She looked into Angst's eyes, memories streaming down her cheeks. Angst felt her sadness, and momentarily pitied Nicadilia. He wiped a tear with the back of his hand, and she kissed his fingers. That gentle touch was like an invitation sent to the wrong person. Angst's eyes widened as the queen regent licked her lips and kissed him. He met her lips fully, but every fiber of Angst, other than his mouth, wanted to pull back. He wasn't attracted to this bigot in any way, physically or personally. His kiss was genuine, but his heart ached for someone else.

They stood, inching their way to the bed, awkwardly walking with entangled legs. Angst felt lost—he did not want to have sex with this woman. He didn't even want to be kissing her, and had no clue how he would explain this to Heather. Angst was weak, and tired, and more exhausted than he should've been. When they finally, finally reached the bed, he collapsed helplessly. A heap of old man and exhaustion. She looked down at him with worry.

"I'm sorry...I..." She rubbed his arm. "You aren't okay, are you?"

"It's not you, I promise," Angst explained. "It's the sword... I'm dying."

"No," she said in shock.

"I can't do this," he said weakly. "I'm sorry."

"Don't be. You've done nothing wrong," Nicadilia said. "Will the sword save you?"

"Only the sword," Angst said honestly, hungrily.

Nicadilia looked at Angst sprawled on the bed. He felt a helpless figure, like a turtle lying on its back. She fingered her ruby ring while vacillating between pouncing, or helping, or walking away. After endless contemplation, she held her hand out to help him up.

"You need the sword," she said, "and I know where it is."

43

To say Scar looked pathetic was like describing a murder as being only unfortunate, or a tornado merely unnerving. He lay as close to the fire as possible without cooking himself, his long nose tucked under a paw, barely revealing his eyes. The only way to tell if the puppy lived was by his shallow breaths or the single whiskery eyebrow that lifted inexorably in the presence of food. Every fifth or sixth breath the lab pup took was a sigh, another reminder of Angst that made her smile. Heather avoided looking at the scar along the lab's side, which now appeared thick, wet, and red. Instead, she stared at his barely open eyes, sadly and fondly, avoiding the ruckus of Rook and Janda.

Rook paced the small room, and seemed on the verge of chopping wood once more. His cheeks were red, and stress-induced sweat leaked from his curly hair down the sides of his face. Every thirty seconds or so, he would stop and peer at Janda with a look that screamed "talk to me." Janda would hold one hand to her ear, beneath her bright red hair, with the other hand raised to stop him from asking. He finally did stop, crossing his bulging arms and staring at her with wide eyes.

"One second, butter," she said to Rook. More than a second passed. "Jaden says something's going on at the castle he doesn't understand."

"You can talk to Jaden?" Heather asked.

"I'll explain later," Janda said with a nod, hoping Heather

305

would understand.

"What's going on?" Rook asked, his voice heavy with concern.

"A flag boy came back from the front. Jaden saw him in the hallway," Janda said quickly, trying to relay the full message. "Alloria reported to the queen that there's a battle and they need more men."

"That's good," Rook said excitedly.

"The queen has ordered every soldier in Unsel to march," she relayed to them. "But a man named Wilfred, an advisor to the queen, told her something isn't right."

"I know Wilfred," Rook stated. "He's a friend of Angst's."

"Wait," Heather said dryly. "Angst has friends that are men?"

"Just a rumor," Rook said with a wink.

"There was no seal on the document Alloria brought the queen," Janda continued. "And the boy has gone missing."

"That's it?" Heather asked.

"That's enough," Rook said with a surprised expression. "Has he sought out the boy?"

"Alloria won't talk to Jaden," Janda said, shaking her head. "He's had no luck."

"I don't believe the queen would accept an unsealed document so readily," Rook said in disgust and frustration. "She's never been the same since losing her eye!"

"There's something else," Janda said distantly.

Tilting her head, she stared at Heather, still holding one hand to her ear. Heather pulled and rocked herself to the edge of her cush-chair, knowing from the look in Janda's eyes that this was a message for her. Janda nodded in acknowledgment. Rook had returned to his frustrated pacing.

"Angst is alive," Janda said.

Heather's breath caught, and tears gathered in her eyes.

"He's not well, but he's alive," Janda said. "It seems young Jaden has been in communication with Victoria. They are at Melkier, and Angst feels Dulgirgraut is too."

"Why hasn't he bonded yet?" Heather asked.

CHAPTER FORTY THREE

"How do you know he hasn't?" asked Rook.

"Scar," she said simply, nodding toward the sleeping pup.

Rook looked from her to the dog inquisitively.

"Jaden doesn't know why," Janda said. "It seems there are complications with the king—and his daughter."

"Of course there are," Heather said with a discouraged sigh. "Is she young and beautiful, or do I need to bother asking?"

"Actually, she may be older than Angst," Janda answered.

"Good," Heather said wryly.

"It seems Victoria and Angst have been arguing. A lot," Janda continued.

"Good," Heather said once again with an inward smile.

Both Janda and Rook stopped what they were doing and looked at Heather in surprise. Heather shrugged indifferently, making Janda smirk.

"Can you ask Jaden to pass a message to Angst?" Heather asked.

"Jaden doesn't know the next time—" Janda began.

"Tell Jaden I will make him laugh himself to death if he doesn't," Heather snapped. "It wouldn't be my first time."

Janda smiled helplessly as she passed along this message.

"Jaden would be more than happy to ask Victoria to pass along your message, right away," Janda said with an obnoxious grin.

"Just let him know that we," she said, patting her pregnant tummy, "are fine. We're safe with good friends. All is well. We love him. Hurry up!"

"Your message will be delivered," Janda said.

"Also, let him know I expect to be taught how to do this 'earthspeak' the next time I see him," Heather added.

"He would be more than pleased," Janda said after several moments.

"Really?" Heather asked in surprise.

"No," Janda stated. "But does he have a choice?"

Heather smiled openly at her new friend before resting back into her cush-chair. She looked at Scar, who sighed deeply, one eyebrow lifting curiously then the other, before the lab pup shut his eyes.

Rook had stopped pacing.

"You should go to Unsel," Janda said.

Rook stared at her with wide eyes, surprised by what she'd said, yet excited she knew what he would ask.

"You're nothing more than eye-candy here, butter," Janda said slyly.

Embarrassed, he looked at Heather, who reluctantly nodded in agreement.

"But," he hesitated nobly, "I promised Angst I'd keep you safe."

Janda's hands burst into flames. A small ball of fire bounced back and forth between them. Rook watched the flames dance from one hand to the next, mesmerized by her power.

"I think we'll be okay," she said, letting the flames snuff out.

"Right," Rook said, deadpan. Magic always made him nervous.

"So get out of here," she said with a grin that released him from his duties.

Janda stood and walked to him. She wrapped her arms around him and landed a passionate kiss on his lips, which he gladly returned.

He held her tight. "That's why I love you," he said quietly.

"Oh," she said at hearing those words for the first time. Her voice suddenly became quiet and girlish, and she whispered, "You do?"

"You scare me and excite me. You drive me crazy and inspire me. You believe in me, and already you know me. How could I not love you?"

Janda melted into Rook's arms. "I love you too, Rook." She looked up into his eyes. "Please be careful."

"Only a little," he said. "Just enough to come back."

On this, Rook took his dramatic leave.

Janda swooned, pressing her hand against her chest, holding her heart in place. Heather smiled, loving the moment and hating the loss of passion in her own marriage. It was beautiful and depressing all at the same time. She missed Angst—he felt so far away in so many ways.

Heather waited patiently as Janda stared at the tiled floor, gathering her composure. She understood what Janda faced. Was this the last time she would see him? How long would she have to wait before he returned? Would he be the same when he came back? Heather asked the same questions every time Angst left.

Eventually, Janda straightened and faced Heather enthusiastically, her smile wide and mischievous. "Let me teach you what I know about earthspeak," she said excitedly. "Let's see if we can figure this out together."

44

Dallow shuffled his feet slowly, in spite of the young page's assistance down the hallway. At a faster pace, his shoes seemed to find uneven tile automatically, making him stumble. It was his own fault—without the distraction of friends tending to his every need, his thoughts wandered. Dallow's mind didn't wander aimlessly, however; it sped through a maze of disconnected thoughts and lonely worry.

This injury had cost him more than sight, though that would have been enough. His work was everything to him. His research, his time at the library, his travels to learn more… The palace would have no use for a blind curator. Princess Victoria might be kind enough to insist Dallow remain, but he would be no more than a figurehead. The thought stirred his insides—a mixture of loss and pity smashed together in an apothecary bowl.

This would also be the final leaf off the tree of his marriage. His estranged wife would revel in the ultimate "I told you so." She had already threatened to leave when he said he was headed out for another adventure. Dallow didn't believe her, and mostly didn't care, but he was a creature of habit and didn't really want the marriage to end, simply because he believed it should keep going. She could handle his long hours at work, and tolerated his new tendency toward "adventures," though she hated it, but wouldn't stand or stay for a "cripple."

To rub salt in his fresh wounds, his great reward for the sacrifice of his eyes, his face, and his looks would be loneliness. Angst, Hector, and Tarness cared, even loved him, but they were needed elsewhere. If Angst lived through this, if he actually got to Dulgirgraut in time, the adventures wouldn't stop. He couldn't just set the foci in the corner of his house and ignore the responsibility that came with that sort of power. Angst would continue maiden saving and dragon slaying, and Dallow would be left behind—they couldn't possibly drag him along in this condition.

Another frustrating stumble brought his attention to the tile floor once again.

"Is this actually a tile floor or did you bring me outside?" Dallow grumbled.

"I, um, we are still inside, sir," the page muttered nervously.

Dallow nodded and thought about Rose. He missed her and understood why Angst was so enraptured with Victoria. They were young, fun, beautiful and, most importantly, interested. They would actually react to teasing and flirting, or ask questions as though they cared. Rose genuinely wanted to know Dallow, and he missed that attention. He missed her large eyes, pale skin, and dark red hair. He, more than anyone, understood what Angst was going through—and wished he could convince Hector that their relationship was mostly safe.

The page sighed, and Dallow felt bad. He could only assume he looked like a monster and was scaring the boy. The last thing he needed to do was upset the only set of eyes available.

"You can ask me your questions, young page," Dallow prompted. His voice cracked slightly, having been used only sparingly since the attack.

"Your princess told me you preferred to be left alone," the page replied apologetically. "Um, how did you know I had questions?"

"You keep breathing like you're getting ready to speak," Dallow said with a smile. "And then you sigh."

"Oh. I thought it was magics," he said with some disappointment. "Was it dragons, sir?"

"Yes," Dallow said simply.

"You look healed, sort of," the boy said in confusion. "Does it hurt, sir?"

"Less each day," Dallow said with a wince as he rubbed under the blue blindfold covering both eyes. "Mostly it itches."

"Eeuw," the young page said in wonder. "Please, one moment, sir. We are approaching stairs."

Dallow stopped as the page let go of his arm to walk around to his other side. The page then inched Dallow toward the wall and forward to grasp a railing. They made their way down the stairs relatively quickly with the additional reinforcement, but Dallow stumbled at the bottom and fell to a knee when he tried to take a step that wasn't there.

"I'm sorry, sir," the young man said, hurrying to help Dallow up. "I didn't mean..."

"It's fine, I'm okay," Dallow said, mostly embarrassed. "I was a little overconfident, is all. At least now I know how many steps there are."

"How is that?" the page asked excitedly.

"Counting is the only way I'll find my way around, until I figure out something else," Dallow explained. "Two hundred and thirty seven baby steps down the hallway, and twenty-eight stairs in this stairway."

"Oh," the boy replied in disappointment. "So it's not magics."

"Are you not afraid of magic?" Dallow asked.

"No!" the page said proudly. "Well, yes. Sort of." There was another moment of hesitation then, "Can I tell you a secret?" The boy's voice fell into a whisper. "My uncle could make rain. He was killed by the Rehmans' Charge."

"I'm truly sorry," Dallow said, gripping the young man's shoulder.

"It happened several months ago," the page said sadly. "He was nice to me, and his rain helped a lot of people."

"Magic is like any tool or weapon," Dallow said. "It can be used for good, or for evil."

At this, the page went quiet, tilting his head at Dallow's thoughtful words.

"Are we almost to the library?" Dallow asked.

"Almost," the young man said. "I'm sorry, sir, but you said I could ask questions…"

"Please, call me Dallow," he offered. "Go ahead."

"Mr. Dallow," the page said. "Why does a blind man need to go to the library?"

"I'm not sure," Dallow replied sincerely.

They shuffled for ten long, dark minutes before stopping at the entrance to an enormous library. Dallow took in a deep breath of books and ink, and genuinely smiled for the first time in days. Even without seeing the bindings or the parchment or the printed word, there was a comfort in the smell.

"We're here," Dallow said in relief.

"How did you know?" the page asked.

"Please take me to a chair, preferably one in front of a table," Dallow asked, ignoring the question. "And bring me a book."

The young man helped him to a giant desk with a chair, and Dallow fumbled his way into the seat. After positioning himself, he placed both hands on the desk reverently and waited.

"What, um, what sort of book would you like?" the young man asked.

"Well, let's start with what I came for." Dallow removed the blindfold, exposing his eye sockets. "Bring me books on dragons."

The page choked at the sight of Dallow's scarred face and scurried off. Dallow hated taking the blindfold off—he knew it would scare the boy—but the princess's kerchief was distracting. His scars already itched, and the perfumed cloth tickled his skin.

"Here you go, Mr. Dallow," the page said, placing a large book on the desk and wrestling it under Dallow's hands.

Dallow caressed the leather cover hungrily. He placed one on the binding and rubbed his fingers along the cool, compressed pages. It wasn't necessary, but he opened the book to feel the print as though fondling a long lost lover. With a deep breath, Dallow concentrated.

"Um…um…sir?" the page said in a panic, taking several

steps back. "Mr. Dallow! They're glowing... You, you have eyes!"

Dallow looked toward the boy's voice and saw nothing, but the words from the text flowed into his mind. Dallow wanted to cry, but that ability had been lost too. After several labored breaths, he smiled.

"I can still read," he said, his voice choked with disbelief.

He cataloged the book and a sense of relief washed over him as he took in the contents. With a sigh, he closed the large, leather-bound book and placed his hands on another. He absorbed that one quickly and soon made his way through the stack.

"It seems you can read too," Dallow stated, almost out of breath from excitement.

"Well, yes, I can, Mr. Dallow," the page said proudly. "How did you know?"

"You brought me the books I asked for," Dallow said with a smile. He instinctively tried to wink then sighed to himself once more. "Can you stay for a while?"

"Gladly, Mr. Dallow," the boy said excitedly.

"That's a good man," Dallow said. "I need more. Bring me anything you can find on old history and magic."

"Right away, Mr. Dallow," the boy said.

"Hurry, young man," Dallow requested, finally feeling at home. "As fast as you can bring them to me. I'm hungry, and I need stacks and stacks, as many as you can carry!"

Within minutes, the boy's quick footsteps thudded over the hardwood floor as he rushed back, excited to help his new friend. Just as the page arrived, there was a loud clatter as a stack of books fell to the ground.

"You must be careful," Dallow corrected instinctively. "Are you okay?"

When he got no answer, Dallow stood, and the armored hand of a soldier landed heavily on his shoulder.

"What's the meaning of this? Who's there? What do you want?" Dallow asked.

CHAPTER FORTY FOUR

"It's the Charge," the boy whispered.

* * * *

Tarness was used to quieting a room simply by walking in. His size had always brought him the wrong kind of attention, but he'd gotten used to it. Years of whispers, fearful stares, and even some pointing had been enough to harden his shell. Tarness had been an average-sized boy, but after the other kids stopped growing, he didn't. He was too large to ridicule or bully, but he wasn't immune to the things left unsaid in the wide eyes that followed his every movement.

This night had been a frustrating one. The drinks were watered down, the women ignored him, and his questions went unanswered. There was something about Crloc and Nicadilia they needed to know, but every time he asked, he was quickly ignored. The urge to hurry itched in his veins. He worried that the trail of destroyed tables, stools, and bouncers left behind at various bars would bring attention to his quest. More importantly, Angst needed answers that the evening hadn't provided. And maybe, hopefully, when all this was done, they could find Maarja.

The Stale Talon was different from the other bars he had visited tonight. Not because it was a rickety old dump hidden down a dark city alley and so crammed under a building Tarness had to duck to enter. Nor because it lived up to its name as the acrid stale scent of unwashed ale-spilled floors met his nose. The Stale Talon was different because a dozen men got to their feet as he came in.

Tarness made his way through the standing ovation to wait politely at the bar for several moments before coughing to get the barkeep's attention. The craggy older man ignored Tarness, choosing instead to focus on the mugs he wiped out with a dirty towel. His wiry black and gray hair was unkempt and as oily as the rag he held. He wore baggy brown pants, a blue linen shirt too large for his thin frame, and an apron that must have been held together by cooking oil and ale stains. The barkeep continued scrubbing away, making the mug more greasy than clean.

"A mug of mead, please," Tarness said in his deep voice.

"We're out," the barkeep snapped, slamming the mug on the table and picking up another.

"Then how about some port?" Tarness asked.

"Nope," the barkeep grunted. His voice was high-pitched and whiny. "Out of that too."

"Ale?" Tarness asked, frustrated and thirsty.

"You'll find what you're looking for at another bar," the man replied.

A hand clamped onto his shoulder, and he smiled. He turned to see a tall, sturdy man he assumed was the muscle. The fifth muscle he'd met that night. The man tried tugging, but Tarness ignored the hint and turned back to stare at the barkeep. He was losing his patience.

"I was told what I'm looking for is here," Tarness said, struggling to remain courteous.

"Get this guy out of here," the barkeep told the muscle, completely ignoring Tarness.

The man holding onto his shoulder attempted to yank Tarness from his seat, but Tarness was upset enough that there was no budging him. There was a crunching noise that sounded like wagon wheels on gravel followed by laughter from around the bar. The pull on his heavy cloak began to pinch. Tarness looked over his shoulder to find that the bouncer had changed into a grayish rock, or covered himself in rock. He looked the rock man up and down, unimpressed.

"I'm not leaving until I get a drink," Tarness said in frustration, "or two."

"Fine, we'll do this your way," the stone man grumbled.

Patrons now clapped and laughed, pointing at Tarness, obviously excited that there would soon be entertainment to accompany their drinks. The stone man pulled an arm back and swung, striking Tarness in the chest with a loud crunch. The stone man didn't move as several large cracks crawled up his arm. The bar went quiet, in shock that Tarness hadn't been knocked across the room. Tarness puckered his wide lips and blew, and several pieces of cracked stone fell to the ground. He picked up the man by the waist and threw him down onto the nearest table.

"Hold it, everyone!" the old barkeep yelled. "Before my bar gets destroyed. How did you do that? Nobody can handle a punch from Dusty."

"It's what I do," Tarness said shortly, his nostrils flaring. As he eyed the other patrons, several hands and arms began glowing. They looked ready to attack him at any moment. "I thought this might be a place I'd fit in."

"Did anyone follow you here?" the barkeep asked.

"It looks like someone beat me here," Tarness said, pointing at a tall man in the corner shadows whose eyes grew wide with worry. "You usually host the Rehmans' Charge?"

The spy bolted for the door, but Tarness reached him first. The soldier tried running past, so Tarness slammed a large fist into the side of his head. He tripped and went face first into a support beam. The man collapsed to the ground.

"Is he dead?" the barkeep asked.

"Nah, he's breathin'," a husky voice near the body said. "What do we do with him?"

"We can't kill him," said another patron. "Too many questions."

"But what about Dusty?" the husky voice asked. "His whole family will be in danger!"

Dusty pushed himself up from the table, the stone façade shed. He held his bloodied arm and looked about in panic. "What am I going to do? Where should I go?"

"Go to Unsel, find the Wizard's Revenge," Tarness advised. He tossed Dusty a gold coin. "Ask for Graloon."

"Graloon?" the old man said with a sneering grin. "How do you know that old bastard?"

"He's a friend," Tarness grunted. "Go on, Dusty. Hurry. This one may have friends nearby."

Dusty seemed at a loss for words, merely nodding at the man he'd tried to beat just moments ago. He gripped the coin tight and rushed from the bar.

"What about that mess?" the barkeep said, thumbing toward the soldier sprawled on the dirty floor.

"I'll take him with me when I leave," Tarness offered.

"Thanks… What is it you want, exactly?"

"A drink would be good," Tarness suggested, "and then maybe we can start over."

The barkeep slapped a large mug of mead in front of Tarness. He downed the entire glass and waited for a refill before speaking. The barkeep hesitated, but only until Tarness flipped a coin onto the bar.

"Is that why you're here?" the skinny barkeep asked. "For the mead?"

"Are you kidding me?" Tarness asked. "Does anyone come to your bar for the mead?"

There was some laughter, and Tarness downed his second mug. He wiped his lips with his forearm and slammed it on the bar expectantly, waiting for another quick refill. When it arrived, Tarness stared at it in contemplation. He believed in Angst, and had supported his friend through all of this mess. He wanted the man to live, and he'd worked way too hard for the little guy to die. He would do anything to get answers.

"I need to know about Crloc," Tarness said simply. "And the queen regent."

"There's nothing to tell," the barkeep grunted, waving his arm dismissively.

"See that guy?" Tarness asked, pointing to the Rehmans' Charge soldier lying in his own drool and blood. "That could be every man and woman in here. I really don't care."

"I…" The barkeep hesitated. "I don't know much."

"I don't think we have time to banter." Tarness nodded to the body on the floor. "So out with it."

The barkeep sighed deeply and wiped beads of sweat from his tall forehead. Several customers shuffled away from the guard's body nervously, while others dropped coin on their tables and left abruptly.

"They died." The barkeep's face tensed. "They both died months ago."

"What are you talking about?" Tarness asked. "That's nonsense."

"I agree. Nothing I've heard makes any sense," he said in frustration. "Nicadilia was a princess, promised to wed a nobleman. Crloc was just one of her guards."

The barkeep looked about nervously; several more patrons left, the others looked at the floor.

"Go on," Tarness encouraged.

"They were leaving Melkier," he continued. "Rumor has it to join the king on his trip to Unsel. They were a day behind His Majesty when the monsters came."

"Monsters from the Vex'kvette?" Tarness asked.

"No. It was dragons," he said in a quiet, raspy voice. "It was the first attack by two of the beasts. An entire regiment of soldiers, Princess Nicadilia, and her guards...all burnt to ashes."

"But they're alive," Tarness pressed.

"No, they aren't," he whispered, looking around the room nervously. "They were lost to dragonfire!"

"Then how are they at the castle?" Tarness asked in amazement.

"That's the question, isn't it?" the barkeep asked, staring at Tarness with wild eyes. "After that, everything changed. Wielders were put to death, Her Majesty became Queen Regent, the soldiers started wearing that blasted dark armor, and her betrothed—"

Melkier soldiers poured into the bar, shrouded in the dark blue-black armor. They spread around the room, a sword or polearm pointed at every remaining patron. Four soldiers surrounded Tarness nervously, their weapons at the ready, shaking only slightly.

Tarness smiled at the barkeep and tossed several coins onto the bar before turning around. He raised his arms in feigned helplessness.

"I suggest you all behave before I dent that pretty armor," Tarness advised.

45

Even at night, the castle had more soldiers than shadows, making it near impossible for Hector to sneak about. The bright stone walls and well-candled corridors offered little opportunity to hide. It didn't help that his joints were sore from long cold rides and the abusive years he'd put them through. Crouching at length was near impossible, and in spite of his many talents, becoming invisible wasn't one. This left him with little choice but to acquire a suit of the shiny blue-black armor from an unwary soldier roaming down the wrong corridor at the right time.

The armor fit snugly and felt cold to the touch; the discomfort from wearing it almost made him ill. But everything about Melkier made him uncomfortable. It wasn't only the armor, but the king, the queen regent, that bastard Crloc—every courtesy seemed forced. Through all his years in the employ of Unsel, he had never experienced such passive disrespect. Princess Victoria was treated only barely better than a commoner and was constantly under the rude inspections of Crloc. He gawked at her more openly than Angst. She was too young, or simply too distracted with Angst, to notice.

Hector was still dumbfounded that the princess was here and, of all things, had bested him in a duel. Either he was getting old, which was true, or there was something else. Every time he gave it further thought there was a distraction—an oddly timed attack, or more recently, an argument between Angst and Victoria. This made him sigh deeply.

Hector had been a soldier almost since he'd wielded his first weapon. He'd followed the king blindly, and on His Majesty's passing, supported the queen without question. While he didn't always agree with her decisions, she was a strong leader and Hector supported Isabelle proudly. Victoria was young, and showed potential, but from the first moment Angst had admitted to their relationship, Hector had worried. Somehow, his short, chubby, old friend had a way with women that affected them in ways Hector just didn't understand. No one seemed to be bothered by this. Hector felt he struggled with this concept even more than Heather did, which meant he had no one to turn to with his concerns. The worries rested in a cauldron that boiled over more every day they spent with the young princess.

Normally, he would've let it roll off him like beads of sweat after a well-fought duel. Angst could do what he wanted with whomever he wanted; that was between his friend and Heather. Victoria was different. She was a princess, royalty who would one day be Queen of Unsel. Her need for Angst, her desire for his company, was a crutch that confused her decisions now and would hinder her ability to lead the country one day. In this opinion, Hector stood alone. No matter how he argued, Angst would never understand. His friend was infatuated with her youth and attention without realizing how strong her manipulations were. Angst was too quick to blindly trust, and too needy to be a hero for the princess.

If he could only have convinced Dallow to side with him, Angst might have weighed his decisions differently, but Dallow was more infatuated with Rose than Angst was with Victoria. Where Angst was somewhat used to the attentions of younger women, Dallow was lost in them. The constant bickering with Dallow on this trip, the way he blindly backed Angst as though he understood the ramifications, was so frustrating it made Hector want to leave. Now that Dallow was injured, Hector couldn't even bring himself to argue further.

Then there was Tarness, who accepted and encouraged whatever Angst chose to do. He was so hungry to find someone that he lived through Angst vicariously. Hector hoped when this was over he could help his large friend find Maarja just to gain an ally.

His frustration, coated in a thick layer of anxiety, festered uselessly, and like a good soldier, Hector shook it off to focus on his search for Dulgirgraut. One of the two largest swords in all of Ehrde, and he couldn't find it. It wasn't on display like Chryslaenor, nor hidden in some room on the main floor. The only place remaining was the dungeon. This made some tiny bit of sense because it seemed the only entrance in the castle under heavy guard. He was filled with doubt the sword would be there. As Angst had suggested, it was every bit as unlikely as the sword being hidden away in a distant tower—who would have moved it?

Six guards stood before the stairway leading down. There were only six, which was a relief, especially since none currently held a weapon. They stood at focused attention, hands down at their sides and staring forward instead of being watchful, which was as useless as sleeping. He licked his lips and wiggled his calloused fingers in anticipation. Every fiber of Hector longed to take them down. Even with the armor they wore, four would be incapacitated before he would have to "struggle" with the other two. Hector drew in a deep, controlling breath and decided to attempt tact. He hoped it would fail.

The guards remained at attention on his arrival. Hector smiled inwardly, more than a little grateful at his luck in acquiring armor that paraded a high rank. They saluted with forked hands over hearts, and he emulated their odd motion before passing through the doors. While he had wanted a throwdown, it would have been noisy and, for one, brief moment, he was grateful for easy. Easy was a rare creature he only occasionally met in passing through life.

A long flight of marble stairs brought him deep into the belly of the castle's dungeon. He hated dungeons; no matter how well decorated the entrance, they were almost all the same—seeping into one's pores and sucking life direct from the bone. This one was different. There was an unnatural energy to this dungeon. The hair on his arms rose and goosebumps crept down his back. It wasn't right.

The cave-like corridor under the castle was bright and almost beautiful. Light tan limestone walls reflected flickering torch fire, casting his shadow on dark wooden doors. Hector checked each door as he walked down the long, wide stone hall, confirming each one locked. His teeth buzzed as he approached the end, and an unnatural sound filled his ears. He drew a long dagger and a short sword, holding the dagger down low, almost hidden in his left hand, and the sword high and at the ready.

At the end of the hallway was an enormous blue-black steel door, almost the size of the corridor. The door had enough locks and bolts that Hector wanted to pick them all just to cause trouble. He ignored the few remaining cells and approached the large door. Hector slid a thin black-steel plate aside to look into the room. In the center was a giant stone monument that looked identical to the one in Unsel's courtyard. An enormous sword lay on the ground close to a wall, a glowing green light emanating from the blade.

"Dulgirgraut," Hector whispered. "But how did it get down here?"

Hector spun about when he heard a muffled cry, sword and dagger once again at the ready. It was the first human noise since entering the dungeon, and he cautiously approached the nearest cell door. Hector pulled and found it unlocked; the door swung open with a squeaky whine.

An old man lay on the ground against the far wall. Skin clung to his bones, desperately trying not to fall off. His face was a wasted skull of hunger and anguish. Deeply-socketed dark eyes looked at him, and the man held out a glowing hand. Hector rushed to his side and kneeled.

The man's labored breathing was wracked with pain. He seemed barely able to lift an arm, but still pointed to the far corner of the room. Hector looked over to find a pile of blackened dragon bones. He followed the man's finger to see stacks of armor and weapons leaning against the wall. Some were standard chrome while others were coated in the blue-black.

"Did you do this?" Hector whispered. "Did you make the armor?"

The old man nodded, licking his thin hairy lips. Hector thought for a moment, trying to decide if he should kill the creator or try to save him. There wasn't much man left, and Hector drew his dagger. The man nodded gratefully, desperate for release.

"Rest well," Hector said and, with a swift motion, cut the man's throat.

There was a wet, gurgling sound as the man died in his arms. As he passed, his large dark eyes looked over Hector's shoulder in panic and Hector finally realized his mistake. All his finely honed senses, all the abilities that kept him from being snuck up on, even his heightened hearing, were all smothered by the dark armor he wore. Hector could only think *no* before the pommel of the sword struck the base of his skull. The loud, wet smack was quickly followed by darkness.

* * * *

Victoria slipped into the chainmail skirt, which—at mid-thigh—seemed much too short to protect anything, including her modesty. The chainmail top Crloc had given her looked uncomfortable, and the thought of that cold metal rubbing against her was horrifying. Fortunately, there was a layer of padded cloth beneath the mail. Unfortunately, that cloth only covered her breasts, and barely at that, holding them suspended unnaturally. Victoria's cheeks warmed. Angst was the only person she felt comfortable being naked with, and only because she was sure he didn't care. Tori looked in the mirror. While she wasn't disappointed with the view, she also wasn't comfortable sporting this outfit for just anyone.

She couldn't help but think that Angst would love this, and

hate it. He would gawk at her in this outfit, dousing her with compliments while at the same time desperately lost for words. It made her giggle. Victoria loved her friend so much, and was grateful he understood their boundaries. At the same time, he would hate sharing her with another man. Victoria was so frustrated with Angst it completely distracted her from everything else.

A rapping at her door was followed by Crloc impatiently clearing his throat.

"I'll be a few more minutes," she said, faking enough happiness to muffle her worry.

Victoria reached behind her back and awkwardly gripped the strings for the left and right flap of her top. Looking at the mirror, she sighed. If she left the strings loose, she worried her entire top would fall off. If she pulled them tight, the padding would shove her breasts up and together. There was no winning.

Was this truly what she wanted? Was this really the life of an adventurer? As a group, they had fought and struggled all the way here only to find they would have to keep fighting. It sounded so much more romantic than the life of a queen, but there was no break—it was no wonder Angst always seemed exhausted. But, really, what choice did she have? Everything she did was to save Unsel and, just as importantly, her best friend. He needed that stupid sword to live, and Unsel needed Angst to have the sword, no matter the consequence to her.

When Crloc had come to her room earlier and presented her with the Berfemmian armor, Victoria had been speechless. It wasn't at all like armor. If not for the chainmail, it would've looked like something a woman working a brothel would wear. She would look cute in it, but she also didn't want to wear it for Crloc. Still, maybe she could be like Angst and woo what she wanted. Some sweet talk, a little skin, and a few kisses, since she liked how Crloc looked, would render the location of the blade.

Kisses…why not kisses? Angst had kissed her whore cousin. Alloria wanted everything that was Victoria's. The moment Victoria announced she wanted to adventure, Alloria had pried her way into the queen's favor. As if Alloria would ever be queen. But worse than that was Angst, the one relationship that was genuinely hers. Alloria had brazenly thrown herself at him, and he'd fallen for it! Kissing him, practically naked, with her giant breasts pouring out! Victoria was positive, completely convinced, that she wasn't jealous at all. But Angst would be when he found out she'd kissed Crloc. Thinking of Angst, she pulled the laces tight in frustration, shoving her breasts together in the Berfemmian top, before knotting the back.

"Is everything all right, Your Majesty?" Crloc said from the door once more.

Victoria took one last look in the mirror. She pulled at her long curly blond hair and shook her head. She'd never understood why Angst liked blond hair, but even though he never complimented her on it, it added to her disguise. Victoria looked herself up and down and smiled until she noticed she was barefoot as a peasant. She ran around the room, her feet slapping loudly on the tile.

"Princess?" Crloc said loudly.

The only shoes she could find were her black riding boots. She sighed to herself and rolled her eyes as she slipped them on. They were almost knee high, and even though they helped cover more skin, they looked trampy. At least it was better than being barefoot. She took one last deep breath.

"I'm changed," she said.

Crloc opened the door, stepped into the room, and closed it behind him, almost-slyly locking it. For the briefest of moments, she once again wished it was Angst viewing her in this costume. Victoria could feel nothing from this man, and inwardly cursed herself at her waning ability to wield magic. She could understand if he'd been wearing that armor, but Crloc wore a handsome black leather tunic and gray tights. What was the point of wielding magic if it didn't work when needed?

"You look gorgeous," Crloc said, stepping close. "But not at all like one of the savage Berfemmian."

"Good," she said, her thin brows furrowing with worry. She

wanted to delay the kissing and tried more banter. "Do they really wear armor like this?"

"They do, Victoria."

Crloc didn't use her title, and eyed her hungrily, staring at her exposed flesh. Victoria sought the wooing words Angst might've used, but they were lost in her growing panic. She knew how to flirt with boys, even when she couldn't find the words. Looking down at her exposed midriff, she rubbed her taut tummy.

"How do they stay protected when so much is left uncovered?" Victoria asked.

She looked up at Crloc; he was staring at her hand and stomach. Instinctively, she sucked in her gut before cursing herself for being so obvious. Why did this have to be so hard? She should just beat the man senseless to find out where the sword was, but Melkier was an ally and he was attractive...

"They are the most fearsome of warriors," he said in a low voice. "They only feel it necessary to cover their vitals."

Victoria immediately realized that her coy move of bringing his attention to her uncovered stomach was a mistake as he eyed her hungrily, licking his lips. Her heart raced as he advanced but she only realized she'd been backing up when her shoulders hit the wall. Crloc pressed his lips to hers, and Victoria let herself melt into him. There was one kiss, a second, and then she brought her goals into focus again. She would let him continue for a little while longer then ask about the sword. This might just work! Excited, Victoria kissed him back aggressively.

Crloc rubbed a hand up and down the outside of her left thigh. Her eyes flew open, and she reached down to shove it away. He grabbed her small arms and lifted them over her head, pressing her against the wall. He kissed her neck, making his way to her chest.

"No," Victoria squeaked, trying to pull away from his hold.

"If I were to become king and be rid of Nicadilia, I could take you and become master of two kingdoms," he said in a husky voice between kisses. "Now wouldn't that be a coup."

Crloc pulled her arms together and held her wrists with one of his giant hands, groping freely from her waist to her breasts with the other. Victoria breathed heavily, struggling in vain against the large man.

"I didn't say you could do this," she pleaded weakly.

"I didn't ask," Crloc said, looking deep into her eyes before plunging his face between her breasts.

This wasn't working at all as she had intended. Victoria had never been touched like this. She felt aroused and betrayed at the same time. This was wrong. She was attracted to the man, but his advances were unnatural—rough and aggressive. She needed to find out about the sword...for Angst...for Unsel.

"Wh...where is Dulgirgraut?" she stuttered.

Crloc ignored her, continuing his unwanted groping. He reached behind her and struggled with the strings of her top.

"Stop this now!" she said loudly, inching down the wall away from his hand.

Crloc pulled his face up, lifted his free hand and slapped her.

Victoria cried out helplessly.

"Your coward boyfriend hasn't bedded you yet?" Crloc asked, looking in her eyes for confirmation. He put his hand over her throat. "It makes me glad to ruin you for any man."

"He's not my—"

Crloc kissed her square on the mouth.

Victoria bit hard, drawing blood. The man yelled, jerking his mouth back. He wiped blood from his lip and beard. Crloc looked at the red on his hand with a broad grin then raised it and struck her over and over. Victoria screamed in pain.

"I'll take you, and I'll take you again until you enjoy this," Crloc said.

Her thoughts were lost to panic and fear as the enormous man continued his groping. She wanted to cry, wanted Angst to break through the doors and save her.

Angst.

What would he do? When the statues in that village had attacked, he had said something. He'd said—

Crloc squeezed her breast so hard she squealed. The freak

was enjoying this.

Focus. What did Angst say?

Angst said to bury her panic, all her emotions, that there was always time later to let it out. Bury it, he'd said, so she could survive and do the job. Sometimes, his age was actually wisdom. He was always there for her, even now, and she fought to climb over her panic. Even if she couldn't read Crloc's thoughts, Victoria had been trained to defend herself by one of the greatest fighters in all of Ehrde.

"I'll take you while your boyfriend dies!" Crloc yelled maniacally as he prepared to dive in for more young flesh.

"I don't think so," Victoria said, deadpan.

46

Rook's fingers were stiff and his injured leg reluctant to bend after the frigid ride to Unsel. He dismounted slowly, shoving the reigns of his pinto into the hands of a bundled-up stable boy. The scrawny youngster looked colder than Rook so, rather than exchanging pleasantries, he dismissed the lad with a nod and limped inside. Rook was definitely a summer boy. He would've much preferred to be in a warm bed with Janda—as long as she didn't burn him alive.

Rook removed his gauntlets and tucked them into his belt. He rubbed his numb fingers together for warmth as he made his way down a gray stone alcove. A large crowd had gathered at the castle forebuilding in front of the keep entrance, and he hoped to bypass that swarm of busyness with this lesser used entrance. His hopes were lost to bumped shoulders and the frustrated apologies of servants or guards seeking the same shortcut from traffic.

"What's going on?" he asked himself aloud.

This maze beneath the castle was the main byway for the staff when entertaining guests, but was otherwise empty. Rook passed by numerous adjoining corridors that led to every corner of the castle. The smell of hops from ale storage wafted down one hallway. Mouth-watering roast gently drifted from another and, finally, the heavy scent of oily metal came from a dark corridor where armor and weapons were stored.

Rook hungrily took note of the hallway the roast-smell came from, in hopes of investigating later, before limping up a flight of stairs. At the top was an antechamber with direct access to the temporary throne room. It was large enough to host a dozen people, and often used for servants waiting with food. It even smelled of sweet molasses and ash, Rook assumed from past feasts. The room was sparse, and mostly devoid of people. Two soldiers stood in full plate on either side of the alcove stairway, unmoving in their formal attire, while Jaden rested in a nearby high-backed chair.

Rook forced himself to smile at the young man. He hated the conceit in Jaden's face, and the fact that his curly blond hair was now oddly long. The annoying wielder wore loose-fitting burgundy pants and a tan jerkin that fit his thin, wiry frame tightly. Rook wanted to beat the smug off the man's mouth, but owed Jaden for healing his leg, so he fought back the urge.

"You're finally here," Jaden said in a tired voice. "Oh, that's right, you ride a horse."

"Did you find them?" Rook asked, ignoring the insult.

"No, I've been waiting for you," Jaden replied shortly.

"Did you at least speak with Alloria?"

"No, the coronation is soon and I haven't been able to get her attention," Jaden said with a sigh.

"*That's* why it's so busy. You never mentioned this to Janda," Rook said impatiently. "I thought the coronation wasn't for several weeks."

"I didn't feel it important," Jaden said, rolling his eyes.

"Are you really that stupid?" Rook asked.

"Pardon," Jaden replied, standing with a lazy stretch and walking over to Rook.

"Alloria and the queen could be in danger," Rook tried to explain.

"Don't speak to me like I'm a fool," Jaden said defensively, now at arm's length from Rook.

"What's wrong with you?" Rook demanded. "You were completely different when Angst was here."

"I respect Angst," Jaden said, peering down his nose at Rook with his sharp blue eyes. "You don't even wield magic."

"What does that have to do with anything?" Rook asked.

"Power is respect," Jaden replied in a surly tone. He lifted a pinky. "In this small finger..."

Rook whipped his hand up from his side, grabbed Jaden's finger, and jerked it back. The bone snapped loudly, and Jaden screamed. Rook glanced at the two soldiers guarding the doorway but neither moved, and he smirked to himself.

"If you don't respect that," Rook said, covering the man's mouth with his hand and pushing him back into a chair, "you've got nine more."

Jaden's eyes filled with hate, and Rook's dagger was against his neck even before Jaden's arms began glowing.

"Your wielding better be to heal that finger," Rook growled. "I don't have any more time for your nonsense. I'll gladly kill you now and ask the princess's forgiveness later."

Jaden put one hand on the broken pinky and pulled. He grunted as the finger once again pointed in the right direction then squeezed his eyes shut, concentrating on the magic needed to mend the damage. Rook removed his dagger but didn't sheath it.

"First Angst and now me," Rook said in disgust. "Do you really need someone to beat you down before you respect them?"

"It's how things are done at home," Jaden said apologetically. He suddenly looked lost. "Wherever that is."

"Remind me never to visit. Your *home* sounds pretty messed up," Rook said. "Look, as far as I'm concerned, you can leave."

"The throne room, through those doors, is the last place the boy and the guard were seen." Jaden bent his pinky carefully.

"Fine," Rook said dismissively.

"I want to help," Jaden offered, almost pleadingly.

"Is there anything you can do to locate them?" Rook asked, wiggling his fingers to indicate magic.

"Nothing I've been able to think of," Jaden stated. "I did search through the throne room and extended hallway thoroughly, but found nothing. As far as we know they could be in town."

"You could've just said that from the beginning," Rook said, disgusted.

Jaden stared at him blankly.

"Let me check with Tyrell to see if the guard ever reported back to duty," Rook suggested. He pointed down the stairs. "Maybe see what you can find down there, and we'll meet back here in thirty minutes."

* * * *

Rook spent ten of those minutes locating Tyrell, and another five impatiently waiting his turn in line. The old man had aged these last few months. His short hair was more gray than blond. The skin along his cheeks seemed pulled tight, as though straining to maintain youth and fight back inevitable age. Still, in spite of the dark circles beneath the man's eyes and his tense shoulders, Rook wouldn't even consider dueling Tyrell.

Rook coughed as politely as he could. Tyrell didn't look up from the long list of items on his to do scroll, clicking his tongue as he mentally checked off completed tasks. He did, however, raise an eyebrow in acknowledgement. After another moment of reading aloud, something about pastries, he sighed. "How's the leg?" he said speedily, still staring at the list.

"Fine, sir," Rook said formally.

"Heather?" Tyrell asked.

"She's well."

"Good. Thanks for checking in," Tyrell said. "If that's all—"

"It isn't, sir," Rook said quickly. "I was told a boy and a guard are missing."

"Nothing more than rumor and innuendo," Tyrell said dismissively.

"But the unsealed parchment requesting more troops?" Rook asked in concern.

Now Tyrell looked up, peering down his nose at Rook with fatherly chagrin. After his time with Jaden, Rook was tired of looking up people's noses.

CHAPTER FORTY SIX

"Aren't you supposed to be guarding Heather?" Tyrell asked.

"Yes, but..." he replied hesitantly. "I left her with Janda."

"Considering Janda's troubled past, I would think twice on that decision."

"Her what?" Rook asked.

"I don't have time for this, Lieutenant," Tyrell replied tartly. He leaned forward and whispered, "I'll ask later how you learned about the troop deployment but, to set your mind at ease, there was a seal on the document. It was broken by an inexperienced soon-to-be princess."

"But—" Rook said helplessly.

"No one has reported a missing boy, or even mentioned one arriving at the castle, and the guard in question is AWOL," Tyrell said, obviously tired of the conversation. "The man was about to be discharged due to his poor attendance. In short, he drank too much and had trouble showing up for duty."

Rook's shoulders dropped, and he stared at the floor with a long face. Tyrell smiled genuinely at the younger man. He stepped back from formality for the briefest of moments and placed a hand on Rook's broad shoulder. Rook looked up to see Tyrell nodding thoughtfully.

"Rook, you did the right thing to follow your instincts and bring this to me, but all of this has been accounted for," Tyrell said. "Thank you, son, but we really do need you guarding Heather. If Angst comes back with that sword, the last thing we want is for Heather to be in danger. Assuming Angst is even alive."

"He is alive, sir," Rook said, now whispering. "Angst, the princess...all of them are alive and in Melkier. They think they know where the sword is."

"What?" Tyrell said with wide eyes and a half-smile. "How do you know this? I hope this source is more reliable."

"It's the same source, Captain," Rook admitted. "It seems Jaden has the ability to communicate over a long distance using magic. He informed Janda of what he heard here at the castle, as well as his communications with our team in Melkier. I assume he's talking with Angst."

"Of course he is," Tyrell said defensively. "Who else would he be speaking to?"

Rook looked at Tyrell in surprise, but remained silent.

Tyrell leaned in very close, his lips mere inches from Rook's ear. "Did Jaden report anything on Princess Victoria?" Tyrell whispered.

"She's with Angst, sir," Rook replied quietly. "Her Majesty is safe."

Tyrell's shoulders collapsed, and Rook jerked to position himself for a catch in case the Captain Guard collapsed. Tyrell took a deep breath, stood straight, and slapped Rook on the arm. The man was actually grinning.

"The queen will be very pleased with your report, Lieutenant," Tyrell stated. "Was that all?"

"It seems they've been arguing a lot," Rook said quietly. "Angst and—"

"Even better," Tyrell interrupted, practically beaming. "I'm glad you came to me with this. Please return to Heather and Angst's home, and let Jaden know I need to speak with him immediately after the coronation. It seems he is no longer useless."

"Yes, Captain!" Rook said with a stiff salute.

"Dismissed," the Captain Guard said, returning the salute.

* * * *

The antechamber was the perfect size for pacing. Rook squeezed his hands behind his back as he walked the length of the room. More than anything, he wished there was something physical he could do. A solid workout, like chopping wood or dueling, would set his worries at ease and allow him to think clearly. Something just didn't add up, and he felt he was missing the obvious.

Rook wanted Tyrell's guidance, like when they'd faced Aereon, but the Captain Guard believed nothing was awry. At this point, he would even settle for talking to Jaden again—grill the arrogant bastard for what he'd found out and use him as a sounding board—but forty-five minutes later, the man was still nowhere to be seen. Rook needed to get back to Heather before Tyrell found out he'd delayed.

Rook continued stomping around the small room. It was so frustrating, so upsetting, he just couldn't concentrate. And there was that smell! Molasses and ash…it was too sweet and scratched his throat at the same time, distracting his very breathing. When he returned to the castle, he would have it out with the cleaning staff.

Jaden popped through the door, out of breath, with sweat beading down his forehead. He appeared exhausted and made his way to a chair. Rook eyed the strange man up and down, confused about his condition.

"Are you okay?" Rook asked, almost annoyed by the display.

"I searched every corridor as quickly as I could," Jaden said, frustrated and out of breath. "I used every spell I could think of. I sifted through dust on the floors to find remnants of blood. I filtered all smells with air to find the lingering scent of decomposition. I even sought out remains of water in drying blood. There is nothing down those stairs. I'm sorr—I, well, I did everything I could."

Rook smiled inwardly at the lost apology, and nodded his head in acknowledgement. He was impressed; it seemed Jaden had actually tried.

"You did fine, Jaden," Rook said. "I spoke with Tyrell, and he feels everything is accounted for. I still don't know. Something feels off, but I trust the man."

Jaden looked disappointed but nodded in understanding.

"He ordered me to return to Heather and Janda, and he would like to speak with you after the coronation. He—" Rook stared at Jaden's foot. "What's that?"

Jaden followed his eyes, bemused but unmoving.

Rook rushed over and kneeled, shoving Jaden's foot aside. A tiny, tiny speck of brownish-red rested on the brown tile floor. Rook had to stare to see it, and the more he stared the easier it was to lose sight of. He glanced up at Jaden, who nodded in agreement and dropped to a knee. Jaden's hand began to glow and he touched the dot.

"Blood," Jaden said with an almost-smile. "I'm sure of it."

"Is there more?" Rook asked, his heart now racing.

Jaden stood, both arms glowing brightly. He closed his eyes and spread his fingers out. Moments passed and the glow subsided. He opened his eyes with a look of discouragement.

"Nothing in the tile," he stated. "It could've been from a nose bleed."

"But it's right here in front of us," Rook said in frustration. "How could we miss something so obvious?"

"I wouldn't call that obvious," Jaden remarked.

Something obvious, Rook thought to himself.

He looked around and found himself drawn to the soldiers in armor, still standing at attention. The room was otherwise empty. He walked up to the closest one and saluted. No response.

"Is there a problem, soldier?" he asked in a commanding voice.

There was no reply. Rook looked back at Jaden, who shook his head in confusion.

"I thought the suits were decoration," Jaden said.

Rook rapped on the armor with the back of a knuckle. The knocking did not sound hollow—the metal resonated thickly, as if filled with water. Rook gripped the arm of plate steel and pulled. The suit fell forward and the helm rolled off.

Beneath was a soppy wet head covered in thick brownish goo and sprinkled heavily with ash. Molasses bubbled from the guard's mouth and ears. Now that the helm was removed, the sweet smell of molasses no longer smothered the sickening scent of decomposition.

"Why molasses and ash?" Jaden asked in confusion, trying not to choke on the stink of death.

"It hid the smell well enough that we didn't notice, and the killer had easy access to both," Rook determined. "They use molasses to make ale, and the ash is likely from the kitchens—both readily available down those stairs."

Jaden walked over to the other suit of armor and put his hand on it.

"Don't," Rook said. "We both know who's in there."

"What do we do?" Jaden asked.

Servants of all type poured out of the stairwell, ignoring the armor, the body, Rook, and Jaden. They held candles, and decanters of wine, and towels, and flowers. There must have been forty people moving through the antechamber, rushing to the throne room as quickly as they'd entered.

"Nothing," Rook said, his shoulders dropping. "It's too late. The coronation is starting."

47

"It's here, Angst. In the castle," Nicadilia said consolingly. "I want you to have it. I want you to have Dulgirgraut so you can live."

Nicadilia pressed her lips hard against his, her tongue reaching out hungrily. Angst didn't want to kiss her, Nicadilia wasn't his wife, but he couldn't turn away from her attentions. He needed the sword. He was too exhausted to find another way, and Nicadilia's tongue was far too aggressive. She was so unlike Heather, who was passive-aggressive, or Victoria, who was aggressive only for "cute boys." A small part of him actually appreciated the attention. She put her hand on his chest and squeezed.

"Come," she said invitingly as she pulled away from his mouth. "Come with me."

"Where?" Angst said weakly.

"To your great sword." She offered a supporting hand. "Let me save you."

Emptiness encompassed Angst. It was now the sort of illness that left you so weak you didn't even have the energy to vomit. Every movement made Angst's muscles shake uncontrollably. He shivered without the accompanying cold. He took her hand and stood from the bed. The room spun about in a pot of vertigo. Angst was too embarrassed to tell Nicadilia to leave him be, and steadied himself with all of the pride he had left.

340

CHAPTER FORTY SEVEN

"Please," he said too desperately. "I need it...the sword."

"I will bring you to it."

The room momentarily became dark as though the guilt from her kisses had sucked the remaining strength from him. More than anything, Angst wanted this to be over. For the first time in his life, he just wanted to die. He felt the nearly undeniable temptation to let it all slip away. Unsel could fend for itself; his friends would be safer without him. But then there was Heather, and the baby. And Victoria needed him.

He nodded reluctantly. "Let's go."

She put his arm over her shoulder, which was awkward because Nicadilia was so much taller. In spite of the difference in height, she still glided. Angst smiled inwardly at this observation, and chuckled to himself. He stared at the ruby ring, which she wore on the hand clasped around his chest. Like a drunkard, Angst fumbled with his own necklace, digging into his tunic. He pulled out Alloria's ring and smiled at it, thinking about the beautiful young woman who'd given it to him. He held it up.

"It looks just like yours," he said in a raspy whisper.

Nicadilia almost dropped him. She shoved Angst against the wall, leaning him beside the door, and lifted her own ring next to the one around his neck. They were identical, and she sucked in her shuddering lips.

"Did he... Who gave that to you, Angst?"

"Alloria," he said distantly. "She's so pretty."

Nicadilia drew in a deep breath then smiled. "Is she still alive without her ring?"

"Yes." Angst nodded. He felt disconnected, almost drunk, and pressed his fingers to his lips. "Very alive."

"Walk with me, Angst," she said with newfound courage. "I'll bring you to Dulgirgraut."

"You are so kind, Nici," Angst said. "Thank you."

Nicadilia winced at the nickname as she struggled into the hallway with Angst under her arm. Loud noises and a muffled scream came from behind Victoria's door as they passed.

"What was that?" Angst asked. "Is she all right?"

"She's being taken care of," Nicadilia said.

"Oh," he said, completely befuddled.

"You weigh a lot for someone so short," Nicadilia grunted.

"...only short on the inside," he muttered as they struggled down the stairs.

The journey from his room to the dungeon entrance was a dizzying, nonsensical trip. Random muscles throughout his body twitched of their own accord. His vision went in and out of focus. Angst kept thinking of waking up with Victoria naked, and then she was gone and he was alone. He thought of Heather, and his children, and Scar. Nothing made sense. There was a blur of guards, and finally a long set of stairs leading down into a limestone cavern.

"I hate dungeons," Angst muttered.

"Can't you feel it?" Nicadilia asked, ignoring him, forcing happiness into every word. "Dulgirgraut!"

He sought the great blade with his mind, reaching out to the end of the dungeon. It was so very close. Another set of arms helped him down the hallway. He tripped along helplessly as they directed him into a cell. His arms were lifted up into shackles and when Nicadilia let go, he hung from them painfully. The tiniest amount of power trickled into him, like a single drop of water squeezed out of a rag. It wasn't even enough to catch his breath but, maybe, barely enough to keep him alive a while longer.

"Angst, you have to help us," Nicadilia said in a voice that was almost sweet.

"I can help," Angst said nobly, his blue eyes rolling in his head. "What do you need?"

"Do you see the armor over there?" she asked, pointing to the far wall. "Cover it in dragonbone."

"No...no magic," Angst slurred. "I can't."

"Focus, Angst," she said loudly. "You can!"

Angst pointed his shackled hand at the armor but nothing happened. He began to slip away into the inviting darkness. Nicadilia nodded toward a nearby guard. There was a loud scream.

"Dallow?" Angst asked, opening his eyes.

Dallow's scream was soon accompanied by another, deeper moan of pain.

"No," Angst pleaded, now standing on his tiptoes. "Tarness!"

Nicadilia nodded once more but nothing happened. She shot a cool look at the guard, snapped her fingers and pointed down the hallway.

"What's going on?" she demanded.

"He's killed two guards with his legs, Your Majesty," the soldier said. "Broke their necks."

"Shackle them," Nicadilia commanded.

"We've tried," he said in desperation. "No one can get close enough."

Angst smirked to himself, knowing that Hector was somewhat safe, but Tarness and Dallow were in danger. And what of Victoria?

"Where's Tori?" he said between strained breaths.

"She'll be joining your friends," Nicadilia promised, "after Crloc has had his way with her. Didn't you hear her screams from the hallway?"

"No," Angst pleaded, pulling weakly against his chains.

Now, more than anything, he wanted to bring the entire castle down. He wanted to destroy everything, kill everyone. Like everything else, the wish was hollow.

"You can save them, Angst," she said tenuously. "Imbue our armor with the dragonbone. *Now!*"

It took every ounce of energy to direct his right hand toward the far wall. As he summoned magic, it glowed a faint blue, and the inviting power of Dulgirgraut tickled his periphery. In exhausted desperation, Angst grasped the mineral from one of the dragonbones piled against the wall. The dark, cold void sucked the energy from him. Angst wanted to stop, but Tarness and Dallow still screamed in pain, and who knew what Crloc was doing to Victoria. What they'd planned for Hector.

The bone was cold and slick, a sucking emptiness that made

his mind recoil. No matter how hard he tried to wield the minerals in the dragonbone, they wouldn't change. The screams were unrelenting. Angst didn't have the energy, or the power, needed to do this.

"Bring a bone to me," Angst commanded, his voice shaky. "I have to touch it."

Nicadilia nodded to the guard, who brought Angst a black bone the size of his arm, putting it in his hand. Angst could feel its grainy nature, but couldn't make it move until he understood. He drew as much power as he could from Dulgirgraut and filled the porous bone with magic, saturating every crevice and valley with the green power of the foci. Angst squeezed the darkness out like juice from a lemon.

Dusty remains of the dragonbone fell to the floor like sand, leaving a floating glob of darkness. The small blue-black cloud floated over a nearby piece of chest armor. It slowly melted away, pouring into the plate chestpiece. The armor shivered as the darkness infused into it. When it finally stopped moving, it was no longer bright silver but the blue-black sported by all Melkier soldiers.

"You did it!" Nicadilia said, kissing Angst on the cheek. She slashed the air with her hand and the screaming stopped.

"Why?" Angst asked. "Why are you doing this to my friends?"

Nicadilia's eyes were wide with crazy. Her left hand rubbed violently over the large ruby ring on her right, as though scrubbing away a maddening itch.

"Leave us!" Nicadilia screamed. *"Now!"*

The guards abruptly scurried out of the room. More guards from the hallway followed in a loud clanking of armored steps.

"This is your fault!" she spat in a dark whisper. "You did this!"

Nicadilia gripped Angst's cheeks in one hand and directed him to look at a nearby corpse he hadn't noticed until now. A man his size, whose life was sucked from him. His skin was so thinly draped over his body that, even dead, he looked in pain.

An ugly splatter of dried blood covered the man's chest from a gaping cut across his neck.

"I loved him!" she screamed. "I loved him, and you killed him!"

"How did I kill him?" Angst asked helplessly through pursed lips pinched by her fingers.

"Magics! Your magics!" she screamed maniacally. "So you will pay the price!"

"I liked the kissing better than the crazy," Angst replied in exhaustion.

"More armor, Angst," Nicadilia demanded. "Now, or your friends will be punished."

48

There was a loud thud, and Nicadilia's eyes rolled into the back of her head. She dropped unceremoniously to the ground.

"Consider that an act of war!" Victoria said angrily to the crumpled body.

Angst stared at his friend, first with gratitude then worry and, finally, shock. She had done it. Victoria was the only one free, but it had cost her. An ugly red welt spread across her right cheekbone. Dried blood covered the side of her face along her jaw where blows had cut her skin. Angst felt guilt for not being there and pride that she'd battled her way to him.

He took in the rest of her and completely forgot about the emptiness consuming him. The chainmail top she wore presented her breasts as if on a platter. Victoria's thin midriff was bare, and her waist barely covered by a chainmail skirt that reflected the light from nearby torches. Angst didn't know what to say—it was almost better than seeing her naked. She chuckled at his thought then winced from the bruising.

"Your jaw seems to have become unhinged," she said quietly.

Angst closed his mouth, swallowed back the dryness, and let his eyes shut. They wouldn't open, but that was okay. He still saw Victoria in that little bit of chainmail armor. She looked so pretty, and he was so tired; it was perfect fodder for dreamtime. He drifted off.

"No, Angst!" Tori yelled, dropping to a knee and shaking

him.

Angst hung from the shackles, unmoving, his body dead weight against the chains. She placed a hand on his cheek and felt nothing. Almost nothing. She frantically looked around the room, desperate for help. Victoria started to cry helplessly.

"Not now," she wailed. "We were so close!"

"What's going on?" Hector grumbled from a nearby cell.

"He's... I think he's dead," she blurted.

"Wouldn't be the first time," Tarness said from another cell. "Get us out of here so we can bring him to the sword."

Victoria didn't want to leave him, she felt so helpless. She shook his hand and patted his face. He had to wake up; she didn't want him to die angry at her. There were so many things left unsaid. If only she could will him to live...but that was impossible. This wasn't what she had wanted for their future.

"Now, Princess!" Hector commanded. "While there's still time!"

Victoria reluctantly pulled herself away from Angst. Numbness overtook her as she fumbled with keys she had taken from a guard killed on the dungeon stairway. She walked into one of the prison cells and released Tarness from his blue-black shackles. He completely ignored Victoria's attire, pulled her quickly into his giant arms then took the keys.

"Go to Angst," he said in a low voice.

She nodded and ran back to Angst, tears streaming down her cheeks. Tarness released Hector and Dallow, and they followed him to Angst's cell. Nicadilia lay on the dungeon floor in a sprawl. Angst hung limply from the shackles, Victoria's wet cheeks pressed against his. Hector glanced at the princess's garb and shook his head as he rushed to Angst. Dallow leaned against Tarness, who waited at the entrance, watching the hallway.

"How is he?" Tarness yelled over his shoulder.

"Dead," Hector stated in a monotone voice, his hand against Angst's chest.

Victoria let out a bawling cry.

"Victoria..." Hector said politely, hoping she would contain her grief.

She continued crying loudly.

"*Your Majesty!*" Hector screamed.

"What?" she screamed back.

"You take Dallow. *Now!*" Hector commanded. "Tarness, help me bring Angst to the sword room."

Tarness looked almost as upset as Victoria. Helping Dallow along, he seemed on the verge of tears, or breaking something. Victoria was reluctant to move until Tarness practically shoved her out of the way to unlock Angst's shackles. He lifted Angst's body like it was made of air, and followed Hector out of the room. Victoria placed Dallow's hand over her shoulder and joined them.

"What are you wearing?" Dallow asked, jerking his hand back.

"Not much," she said, returning his hand and patting it reassuringly.

They stood in front of the door to Dulgirgraut's cell impatiently as Hector analyzed the locks. He rubbed a finger along the scar on his jaw as he sifted through memories of lock picking from his younger years. Victoria walked up to Angst with Dallow close behind. She reached out and held his lifeless hand. It was cold and clammy, and Victoria shuddered helplessly. Dallow patted her shoulder consolingly.

"Dallow," Hector said, "We're in front of a door that has about a dozen different types of locks."

"Describe them to me," Dallow said, his eyes already glowing as he sifted through the volumes of information in his mind. "Quickly!"

Tarness looked at Angst's hand in Victoria's then looked at the princess, longing for his friend to be alive. She looked at him helplessly and shook her head no, confirming that Angst was indeed dead. Every muscle in Tarness's body clenched with anger.

"Well, the first lock looks traditional," Hector said. "I see a circle on top of a tri—"

348

CHAPTER FORTY EIGHT

"No!" Tarness yelled so loudly they all looked up. *"I said no!"*

Tarness shoved Angst's body to Hector, who struggled to keep him aloft. With a deep breath, Tarness launched his hands forward, burying his fingers deep into the steel of the door. He grunted as he kept pushing them inward until the steel gave way. With an angry roar, he gripped hard and pulled back, wrenching the enormous door and hinges from the limestone frame. Rubble fell to the ground. Hector and Victoria pulled Angst's body safely away, in wide-eyed shock as Tarness threw the round door down the hallway. It crashed and rolled noisily until embedding so deep into a distant wall, it would rest there forever.

Dulgirgraut lay on the floor in a pile of dust. At one time, it might have rested on a marble pedestal in the center of the small circular chamber. The pedestal appeared to be made by the same people who had created the monument that held Chryslaenor. Victoria entered the room, followed by Dallow and Hector. They circled the small round chamber as Tarness came in, carrying Angst. He gently laid Angst's body beside the giant blade. Nothing happened. The large man placed Angst's hand on the hilt. They watched breathlessly, and still nothing happened.

"This is your job, Tori," Tarness said.

"What?" Victoria said quietly.

"Angst doesn't ever seem to completely die," Tarness explained. "If this sword doesn't wake him, you have to."

Victoria rubbed her hands together and pressed them to her chin. She looked at Hector and Dallow, who were both nodding in confirmation. She approached Tarness and Angst.

"All those things you wish you'd said before he died," Tarness said so quietly only Victoria could hear. "Everything you wish could happen but never will...every truth you hide from Angst, and from yourself. Tell him now, or we lose everything."

Victoria looked at Tarness in tearful panic, pleading with her eyes for a way out that he couldn't give.

"More than anything, Angst wants to be a hero," Tarness said. "Angst needs to know that he's your hero, and more."

Her Majesty, the royal Princess Victoria, dropped to her knees and gripped Angst's hand in desperation. She hated this with every fiber of her body. Sharing her feelings, telling the truth about them, even to a dead body, even to someone she loved, was more than she could bear. Holding Angst's hand did not help. Victoria frantically searched the room for a way to avoid all this.

"What are you afraid of?" Tarness said.

"I…it's just that I…" Victoria said helplessly.

"I love Angst," Tarness said sincerely.

"As do I," Hector said unabashed.

"So do I," Dallow agreed. "He's my best friend. I've always loved Angst."

Victoria's heart raced in panic, snatching her breath. Beating on bad guys was so much easier than this, but Angst was dead and she couldn't even feel him. She leaned forward and whispered.

"What's she doing?" Dallow whispered.

"She's bringing him back to life," Tarness said quietly, his large eyes filled with hope and desperation.

Victoria continued to whisper in Angst's ear. Nothing happened. She fell across his chest and cried, her mail skirt rustling as she shifted her body. She pulled herself up, took a deep breath, whispered in his ear one more time. Gripping Angst's chin, Victoria turned his face toward her and kissed him firmly on the lips.

49

Isabelle's white hair was so tall it towered over a pale green collar that rose from her shoulders and framed her head from ear to ear. Several well-placed curls dangled over her jewel-adorned ears, barely held back by her ruby-encrusted crown. The queen's face was painted thickly enough to almost hide the scarring around her fake right eye. She breathed deep, fighting against her restrictive corset. Pale green stitching appeared chiseled into the white brocade of her bodice. She peered over the crowd with every ounce of regality she could call forth.

The makeshift throne room was nothing more than a too-large hallway, which now barely contained the assembly of noblemen and women, foreign dignitaries, watchful guards, and a certain pensive bewilderment. Unsel had long expected that Victoria would one day become queen—an assumption blindsided by this jarring coronation of a virtual newcomer. Royalty and wannabes had scrambled through weather to squeeze into this small space for a glimpse of who would potentially hold their future.

The hall was split into three almost-distinct corridors separated by smartly placed marble columns. To Isabelle's left sat foreign nobility, ambassadors, and honored guests from outside Unsel. On her right, were nobles of the local variety. Lords and ladies who all fell under the queen's rule.

The center was mostly clear, making a path for the princess-to-be. She wore white on this day—a long flowing gown of silk

351

and satin, a demure shield that hid everything Alloria. She hated it. The dress wasn't bold, or shocking, or exciting, and she felt squeezed into being something she wasn't. She'd worn it not by choice but by command. Isabelle wanted everyone to see this moment as a new beginning, a clean slate for Unsel. Nothing could be cleaner than this dress.

A brass quintet played quietly as she took slow, meaningful steps down the long aisle. Rays of cold light shot in through the windows, reflecting off her dress harshly, making her radiance appear forced. She looked from the left aisle to the right, smiling graciously as she sought accepting eyes.

Instead, she found cool courtesy, polite smiles, and reserved concern. There wasn't a single source of uncontrolled excitement anywhere in the room. Even Vars... Ivan's father stood at attention, his hands behind his back. He nodded once, urging her to continue as expected, but offered no further sign of enthusiasm.

She was so desperate for love and acceptance that her heart began to race. Her feet faltered, and her breath hitched in her chest. Her eyes sought the throne. The queen was stoic, unmoving, as she waited. Alloria finally found Tyrell, who gave her a warm smile. The old man didn't hate her. In spite of his concerns, he was the one person to offer an ounce of acceptance. His smile was enough that she could swallow her panic, catch her breath, and continue the long slow walk to the throne. Alloria looked at Tyrell once more and hoped he didn't see the guilt in her eyes.

* * * *

It had been, perhaps, one of the saddest moments Janda had experienced. She had walked in with a small plate of carved meat for Scar and set it down. In spite of the lab's illness, he always somehow found the energy to eat, yet this time...he remained still. Janda kneeled to wake him, gently rubbing the dog behind his ears. The lab pup didn't move, didn't breathe.

Janda had shot Heather a panicked look, unable to speak for the catch in her throat. That was hours ago.

Heather held Scar in her arms, rocking back and forth with tears streaming down her cheeks. The dark, furry body—even its curious eyebrows, or the tail that was always good for a wag or two—was still. Heather wiped the tears away with her free hand while aggressively petting the dead animal. Janda stood with her arms behind her back, at a total loss for what to do. Heather's ability to affect the emotions of those around her made Janda cry as well, and Janda hated crying.

Eventually, she forced herself to leave the room, and then the house. Anything to get far enough away that tears didn't overwhelm her. The onslaught of raw emotion was taking its toll, and she found herself unable to find consoling words.

She paced back and forth along a twenty-foot length of Angst-carved path, letting the cold air seep in and cleanse her thoughts. Snowflakes gently tickled her arms, the crystalline shapes resting on her pale skin for an instant before melting away—their uniqueness gone forever. Janda was grateful for the moment of clarity, to finally feel free of Heather's influence.

Heather was convinced Scar and Angst were linked, since he had healed the pup with the magical sword. She was also convinced they had shared the same fate; now that Scar was dead, so was Angst. The burgeoning despair was so great Janda could feel the edge of it twenty feet away from their house. She had to convince Heather that Angst could still be alive, before the sadness swallowed Heather whole.

Janda took one last breath of sharp, cold air and walked back inside, bracing herself for the wave of mourning. She began sniffing the moment she entered the house, and by the time she arrived at the main room, tears filled her eyes.

"Maybe," Janda choked. "Maybe this doesn't mean what you think it does."

"He's dead," Heather said quietly. "Scar is dead, and Angst is dead as well. I don't know what I'll do without him, Janda."

Janda collapsed beside Heather. Putting an arm around her

friend's shoulder, she wept uncontrollably.

* * * *

Panic was the only thing keeping Rose awake. She was cold and wet, certain that a thin layer of ice now coated her very bones. The long ride on the back of this terrible monster through the stormy ocean was beyond nightmare. While the creature was a continent, large enough to ignore the constant onslaught of twenty-foot waves, Rose was not.

Another wave crashed into Rose, her legs flew out from under her, and she clutched Chryslaenor with both hands. Desperate for air, Rose breathed in salt water yet again. Choking to the point of gagging, she knew she would drown this time. She longed for a break from the madness, but didn't want to die. Rose only wished for one brief moment to catch her breath.

The waves passed, but instead of relaxing, her heart raced, painfully beating against her chest in a bid for freedom. She collapsed, gripping her chest with her free hand, desperate to keep her heart in place. Chryslaenor wiggled, and her bleary eyes grew wide as ooze poured from the wound.

A long, thin tentacle, no wider than her leg, slapped nearby, seeking the parasite. Several more shot out of the ocean, forcing Rose to scramble behind the great blade to avoid their touch. The tentacles lashed randomly across its back, like a horsetail swatting flies.

Moments passed and they finally pulled away, mercifully retreating to the dark choppy waters. Rose kneeled carefully to keep from moving the sword. She covered her eyes with one hand and sobbed, while the other remained glued to the hilt of Chryslaenor.

In spite of the storm and the waves, she could hear crashing water. When the noise became almost unbearable, the creature stopped moving. Rose wanted to weep, but decided she was too exhausted. Could things possibly get worse?

Rose stood on thin, shaky legs, and turned to face the noise.

The view was surreal. A hole in the ocean. Water poured into it from every direction. An enormous, round waterfall into nothing. It didn't even make sense. As Rose inched forward for a better look, Chryslaenor fell.

Blood gushed from the wound. A dozen tentacles shot out of the water, hungrily seeking the source of injury. They flailed recklessly, relentlessly. Rose tried to run, pulling Chryslaenor with her cold-numbed arm. The foci allowed Rose to drag it closer to the waterfall, leaving behind a scar of oozing blood.

50

"What are you doing?" Tarness asked.

Victoria pulled back, while Angst remained unmoving. She looked at him with furrowed brow, surprised her kiss hadn't woken him. "I thought you said—"

"I said to wake him," Tarness said with wide eyes, "not make out with him."

"This is exactly what I've been talking about," Hector ranted. "Nothing they've been doing is appropriate. She's royalty, and he's married!"

"It's not like that," Victoria said in frustration. "I just thought—"

"I'm sure she just misunderstood, Hector, and now isn't the time for your bitching," Dallow said, ignoring her. "Things aren't always what they seem."

"What they seem?" Hector asked, pointing. "What did that seem like to you?"

They kept arguing, Hector upset about how inappropriate her relationship with Angst was. Dallow convinced Hector just mistook their friendship for something else. Tarness wanted both his friends to leave Angst and Victoria alone. Victoria glared at Angst, embarrassed that she had kissed him, furious that the kiss wasn't enough, and now upset at what the others were saying. She was so angry, she shook.

Victoria stood and stared down at her best friend. *"Wake up!"*

she yelled as loudly as she could. The arguing stopped, everyone quieting instantly. She lifted her foot high and stomped hard next to Angst's head. *"Now!"*

His eyes opened, staring up at her like a newborn. Angst tried to sit up and found he could only do so with her assistance. He looked down at his hand resting on the giant sword then up into Victoria's eyes, and smiled.

"Thank you for saving me," he said in a scratchy voice. "I love you too."

"I don't know what you're talking about," she replied, looking at the others in embarrassment.

"I'm going to be okay," he said assuredly. "But it's time."

Victoria's face went immediately from embarrassment to worry. "I'm going to lose you," she whispered, reaching out to hold Angst's hand.

He shivered in anticipation, his heart skipping a beat as though he was asking a girl to dance for the very first time. Goosebumps covered his arms. A foci, Dulgirgraut, was everything he wanted, and everything he wanted to avoid. It held the power he needed to live, to save those he loved, but also carried with it a great curse of responsibility. Angst had never expected that with Chryslaenor, but hoped he was ready for it this time.

"I don't think I can see you anymore when you're bonded to a sword." Victoria said. "Do you have to bond? Are you sure it's what you want?"

For a moment, this too-brief moment, she was his again. They had grown so close this adventure, and then things had fallen apart, further than he would ever have feared. The tension between them represented a loss that hurt like an open wound. Feeling this connection one last time was almost enough to convince him to try carrying Dulgirgraut without bonding, but this adventure had proved to him their closeness was fleeting. Bonding with the sword would be, should be, forever.

Her lip quivered at his revelation, and Angst gripped her hand, grateful that she was with him.

"I want this more than anything," he said, looking into Victoria's eyes.

Victoria nodded in resignation, saddened by his response, then stared at the dusty floor.

"Well, almost anything," Angst said with a wink.

"What?" She lifted her head, surprise in her eyes.

Angst smiled at Tori as he pulled his hand away. He gripped the small thin handle of the enormous blade. The chamber dimmed as though Dulgirgraut was soaking up every particle of light. From nowhere, a cool breeze gently tickled the torches around the cell, making them pop and crackle loudly. Angst lifted the sword from the ground, waking the great blade from its slumber.

Dulgirgraut glowed with a soft green light, so refreshing it was like an invitation to take a dip in a cool pond on a hot summer day. Angst let the light flow from the sword and encompass his body. He rested the tip of Dulgirgraut on the ground but held the hilt high overhead until the sword was perfectly vertical.

Angst had waited too long before bonding with Chryslaenor. There would be no waiting with Dulgirgraut, no hesitation. He sought his friends about the room, making brief eye contact with each of them. Tarness nodded at him with a broad tearful smile. Hector's head bobbed up and down slowly, while Dallow smiled toward him blankly. Finally, Angst looked at Victoria, who was worried to the point of tears. Angst gave her a forlorn smile, took a deep breath, and closed his eyes.

"Yes," he said in a voice not completely his own.

He relaxed, forcing his muscles to unclench as much as he could, and let it happen. All his concerns about whether the bonding could take place were immediately gone. Dulgirgraut searched his mind for that place Chryslaenor had originally bonded and found it. Within moments, Dulgirgraut was attempting to fill in the space, but the foci wanted a trade. It wanted a piece of Angst before completing the connection, but there was nothing left to give; the trade was uneven.

"No!" Angst cried out in surprise.

The bonding felt like hot sharp spikes slowly pressing into

every pore of his skin. He started to shake., but what felt like mere shaking to Angst appeared as madness to his friends.

Victoria watched in horror as Angst contorted and blurred. His face would pause for moments, showing pain, and then pleasure, and then agony as the foci attempted to take a part of Angst that was no longer there.

"This isn't right," Victoria yelled. "I can feel it! Hector, this isn't right. Make it stop!"

Without question, Hector leaped to tackle Angst and was immobilized in mid-air. As if his attack was a trigger, a translucent green circle expanded from the sword—like an air shield everyone could see. The shield reached Hector first, throwing him against the wall, then slowly pressed the others away from Angst and Dulgirgraut. Tarness fought against the invisible barrier, his anger growing as he struggled. Sweat from his forehead trickled back as though he stood in a great wind. He fought harder and roared loudly until green light flashed from the blade and tossed him back. The barrier continued to grow, even after they were against the cell walls, the green power crushing the life from them.

"Please, Angst," Tori whimpered. "It hurts."

This wasn't working. Bonding hadn't hurt last time. His friends were in danger, in pain, but there was nothing he could do. His brain was on fire, burning through his eyes like a madness that couldn't be controlled.

"That's enough!" Angst yelled.

He pushed against the energy, drawing it into himself. Dulgirgraut fought for more of him, while Angst struggled internally to fight the foci. The green hue slowly became darker. His friends screamed in pain as they were forcefully crushed against the walls.

"There isn't anything left," Angst pleaded. "It's all I have to give!"

Cracks appeared in the stone around the room, and chunks of doorframe flew out into the hallway. Everyone's heads turned, they were no longer able to face forward as their cheeks pressed into the wall.

In his brief time with Chryslaenor, Angst had found an understanding with the great blade. In an odd way, they had become companions, as though the sword was a living entity. The foci seemed to have goals, and needs, and a will of its own. This realization clicked in Angst's mind, and he met Dulgirgraut's will with his own. The glowing hue about them fluctuated from green to brown. Still, his friends writhed in pain. This had to end. With all his strength, he willed the sword to be his own.

"That's enough! We have work to do!" Angst yelled at the sword. "*Now!*"

The foci succumbed to Angst's will, and the brown hue surrounding Dulgirgraut became a dark red.

Angst's friends dropped to the floor. They looked up to see Angst still, no longer a vibrating figure of blurred images. With one hand on the blade and his head lowered, he took a deep breath. He smiled when he opened his eyes. Victoria gasped at what she saw.

"That was exactly what I needed," he said with a grin.

* * * *

A hush covered the room in a blanket of anticipation as Queen Isabelle placed a gem-encrusted silver tiara on Alloria's head. The newly adorned princess was radiant, her honey-brown hair rested in curls on her shoulders. Her full lips were painted bright red. Long thin diamond earrings trickled from her delicate ears. Alloria's white gown fit form and shape as though painted onto her slender body.

Alloria nodded at Tyrell politely before turning to face the queen, dropping low into a curtsy. She looked up at Isabelle, who beckoned the young princess to rise. Alloria turned on her heel to face a hall crowded with nobles and regals.

"Her Majesty, the Princess Alloria," Isabelle squawked, introducing Alloria as though she had become a different person.

The applause was polite, almost enthusiastic but not quite ingratiating. Alloria swallowed hard and burdened her full lips with a newfound princess smile. She had hoped for the roof to shake from clapping. Secretly wished for young women overwhelmed with jealousy to pass out in the aisles. Half-expected a dozen suitors to drop knee and propose their hand and lands. Instead, she was greeted with polite applause. A coldness met her eyes as she peered over the crowd.

One way or another, they, too, would soon be hers.

* * * *

"Things between us haven't been right for a long time, and I didn't even get a chance to fix them," Heather said between sobs, holding Scar's body close. "I'll miss him so much."

Janda cried helplessly in the thralls of Heather's ability as she kneeled with her arms wrapped around her. Eventually, Janda's arm began to tingle as though falling asleep, and she pulled away, having to fight Heather's influence for every inch. She opened her eyes and tried shaking the sleep out of her arm. Janda's heart began to race and she started pulling Heather's hand from Scar.

"What?" Heather snapped.

"Look!" Janda pointed down at the lab's scar.

Heather stopped petting his coat and leaned forward to inspect the scar. Tiny burgundy bubbles boiled and popped along the injury. A small green cloud emerged from the old wound, slowly expanding around the dog. The bubbles became larger. Scar still did not breathe. The bubbles crept underneath his fur, reaching out to his paws, his tail, and head. Parts of Scar began to enlarge unnaturally.

"We need to get him out of the house," Heather said in panic, dropping the quickly-growing lab on the tile floor. "Now!"

Janda nodded silently and pushed the dog's hindquarters while Heather pulled his paws. They slid him down the hallway as the green cloud and burgundy bubbles forced Scar to grow larger. His eyes still shut, the dog breathed, yipping and moaning while one leg twitched uncontrollably.

Scar was almost the size of a full-grown horse and getting larger fast, his fur transforming into sharp needles.

"Ouch!" Janda yelled, jerking her hands back. She licked blood from her finger and looked to Heather for guidance.

"We need to hurry," Heather pleaded, her face a storm of hope and worry.

Wrapping her hands with the end of her skirt, Janda continued pushing. The entrance was only feet away as they struggled with the growing dog. New legs pushed grotesquely through Scar's side. They were stopped halfway through the doorway, as the dog was too large to fit through. His four eyes opened. They were an ominous, dark red.

"What do we do now?" Janda said, out of breath, pressing her bleeding hand hard against her skirt.

Janda scrambled over the dog, careful to avoid the spiky fur quickly growing into daggers. The creature's breathing was rapid, and as she cleared the entrance to stand beside Heather, Scar barked. The house shook.

"Run!" Heather yelled as she turned to the door.

* * * *

Rose stood on her tiptoes at the very edge of chaos, staring at the round waterfall. She glanced over her shoulder to see dozens of tentacles lashing out. Her heart raced painfully, and she clawed at her chest in desperation. The tentacles were coming closer.

"This is your fault!" she screamed at Chryslaenor.

Black lightning grew from the blade, biting at her hand and striking the creature she stood on. It shuddered in pain. More of the hairy tentacles shot up from the water and began their frenzied search, now even closer.

"I hate you," Rose said to the blackness. "You're holding me, and Chryslaenor, captive, and I'll do everything I can to stop you. Starting with this!"

CHAPTER FIFTY

Rose took a deep breath, ran to the end of the monster, and leaped over the edge of the waterfall.

51

Angst walked to Victoria and reached out to help her up. She shakily took his hand and stood. Victoria held onto his hand, squeezing with all her might, concentrating to find something. Her thin brows furrowed with concern, and she looked at Angst as though she didn't recognize him.

"With all my power, I will let you in," Angst whispered.

She continued to grip his hand and, after several moments, her eyes filled with tears. "Maybe there is something?" she lied with a fake smile.

"Don't worry about us, we're fine," Hector sniped, standing on his own.

She ignored Hector, staring up at Angst with a quivering lip. "No, you're gone," she admitted. "I can't feel you anymore."

"I swear you still know me," Angst pleaded. He let go of her hand and tapped a finger to his forehead. "Concentrate. Focus. Wield your power, don't just assume. You can still see me."

Victoria shook her head in consternation. She placed a hand on his cheek and tilted her head to one side quizzically. "Maybe…a little," she said hopefully. "But your eyes..."

"What's that about his eyes?" Dallow stood by the wall, dusting himself off.

Tarness and Hector approached Angst, staring at his eyes. The iris was still blue, but the pupil was now a dark burgundy.

"His center is red, almost brown," Hector told Dallow.

"That's amazing," Dallow said. "I've never heard of anything like that in my life."

"Looks sharp," Tarness said, slapping him on the arm. "Alloria will like it."

"Really?" Angst asked hopefully.

Victoria slapped him hard on the mouth and stomped out of the room.

"What was that about?" Hector asked.

"It's complicated." Angst hefted Dulgirgraut and set it on his back. It locked into place as though held by an invisible sheath, now resting over his left shoulder instead of his right where Chryslaenor had sat.

"Isn't it always, with you?" Dallow quipped. "How do you feel?"

"Back to normal," Angst said with a knowing smile.

"Normal?" Dallow asked.

"Well, all things considered," Angst replied with a chuckle. "I don't feel like my head is going to split open anymore, and I don't feel...empty."

"Good," Dallow said, sounding hopeful. "So..."

"Let's go find Rose." Angst patted his friend on the shoulder.

They followed Victoria out of the chamber to find King Gaarder storming toward them with a troop of Rehman soldiers in their shadowy blue armor. His cheeks were dark red, and his white hair whisked back as he led the men. Gaarder pointed at the sword towering over Angst's shoulder. The soldiers pompously ignored the dusky burgundy glow surrounding Dulgirgraut's blade, taking a defensive stance as they stopped to face Angst and his friends.

Behind the king stood Captain Guard Crloc, holding Tori by the back of her neck with one hand. He squeezed tight enough to make her wince. A bitter grin accompanied his sneer as he gazed at her exposed flesh. He pulled her head close and took a deep sniff of her hair. His cheek was bruised and dried blood covered his chin where Victoria must have gotten the better of him earlier.

365

"Put that sword back now!" King Gaarder commanded. "Or your princess dies."

Angst's right eyebrow raised in surprise. He looked back at his friends with their weapons at the ready and shook his head. They lowered their weapons but didn't sheath them.

"This is your one chance to stand down!" Angst offered to the king. "Lower your weapons, let the princess go, or Melkier will never be the same."

The king peered at Angst, assessing his opponent. Gaarder looked at the man and the giant sword he wielded. He looked to his Captain Guard for advice.

"Would you like me to snap your girlfriend's neck?" Crloc growled at Angst.

Angst ignored Crloc, continuing to gaze at Gaarder. Then Angst's hands began to glow.

"Kill her," the king commanded, slashing at the air with his hand.

Angst's eyes flashed red, and the soldiers behind the king flew into the walls. Angst reached out to their bones, and they screamed as they became flush with the rock-hewn corridor, as if pulled into the stone. Crloc's grip around Victoria's neck was wrenched open, his armored fingers spread wide apart and at unnatural angles. Crloc refused to cry out, but it was obvious his fingers weren't supposed to bend that way.

Freed from his grip, Victoria stretched her neck from side to side then calmly walked to Angst.

"Pig!" she snarled at Crloc before facing Angst. "I think you should kill him."

"I thought Melkier was an ally?" Angst asked.

"After treating me like this?" Victoria asked in surprise.

Angst pulled his gaze away from King Gaarder and looked at the Captain Guard with disgust. "If I had more time, I'd slap you to tears," Angst threatened. "But I've learned that won't beat sense into you. I'm trying to be...a better person."

"Coward." Crloc smiled triumphantly.

"Angst?" There was disappointment in her voice, and Tori

cocked her head and looked at him in surprise. "Do you see what he asked me to wear?"

"You did put it on…" Angst chided.

"What was I supposed to do?" Victoria snapped. "I was trying to save your life!"

"You could've said no."

"What, you don't like me in this?" she asked.

"It's not that…" Angst said, staring at her angrily.

"Not now, kids," Hector grumbled.

"I told you! Your boyfriend is a coward!" Crloc yelled. "That's why she gave in to m—"

Angst willed Crloc's jaw shut. He stared at Victoria in panic, guilt-stricken that he hadn't been there to save her. That he was led past her room and didn't even stop to help.

"He tried to rape me, Angst," she said quietly. "I got away, but only barely."

The blue hue around Angst's hands and the burgundy glow in his eyes flared dangerously as he set his jaw and turned his gaze on Crloc. The large Captain Guard with his large beard seemed a statue, locked into place, his joints unmoving. Angst stepped closer, a burgundy hue glowing brightly around Dulgirgraut. Angst placed his hand on Crloc's dark armored chest and closed his eyes in concentration. Nothing happened at first as he struggled with the dragonbone imbued within the armor.

"It's just another mineral, Angst," Dallow advised quietly. "You did it once already."

Angst felt the metal, felt his will sinking into it as if it were made of snow. A shadowy blue drip fell from Crloc's left elbow like water, followed by another. Every one of the Rehmans' guards gasped in surprise as the dragonbone melted away from the Captain Guard's steel, dripping to the floor like fresh paint in a heavy spring rain.

"No!" King Gaarder pleaded, pulling Angst's arm desperately. "You can't do this! You don't know what danger this brings!"

Within moments, the blue-black protection was gone, leaving

a traditional, tarnished chrome and steel suit of armor—free of resistance from fire, or magic. Angst continued staring at the man. Crloc's eyes grew wide with panic, and he whimpered through his closed mouth.

There was a loud pop followed by a crack. Crloc's eyes rolled into the back of his head. Angst stared at the man's legs, which made a disturbing grinding sound loud enough that Victoria covered her ears. Instinctively, Dallow looked away. Crloc began to shorten as the now-silver armor compressed, slowly crushing him. When it became too much, Crloc finally screamed through his forced-close mouth, his eyes crazy with panic and pain. King Gaarder covered his face with both hands, and Angst's friends turned away—all save Victoria, who smiled wickedly at the Captain Guard's ordeal.

After long minutes, the popping of bones, wrenching of metal, and screaming of man stopped. Crloc continued to stand, but he was now five feet tall—a full head shorter than Angst—and an odd sight, with arms and torso too long for the rest of his body. Angst approached the Captain Guard and pushed on his chest. The man toppled backward and fell to the stone floor with a crash, no longer understanding where his center of gravity was. Angst concentrated, and with one final push, Crloc's armor flitted away to sand, leaving him in dirty undergarments.

"What...what did you do?" the king stuttered, looking at Crloc in shock. "Your magics shouldn't have affected his armor! Guards!"

"We came in peace," Angst said through gritted teeth. He grabbed the lapel of Gaarder's tunic and pulled him close. "I asked for help because I trusted you! You hurt my friends...you hunted and killed people just because they could do magic!"

"This is what we had to defend against," Gaarder yelled, pointing at the soldiers stuck in the wall. "That armor is the only thing keeping them at bay! It's the only thing keeping us safe! You don't understand!"

"Magic is the only thing that will keep your kingdom from being destroyed!" Angst said in a cold, deliberate voice.

CHAPTER FIFTY ONE

Angst threw Gaarder aside, pulled the giant sword from his back and drove it into the ground. The king shuddered in spite of himself. Angst leaned against the blade, his head lowered. Gaarder and his soldiers struggled to move forward, but found their legs locked into place. Closing his eyes, he concentrated for several long minutes. Oily darkness leaked from the Rehmans' Charge still stuck into the wall, puddles on the ground like juice squeezed from lemons. Long moments passed before Angst finally opened his eyes.

"Let's go. We need to find Rose," Angst told his friends. "We've wasted too much time here."

"What did you do?" Gaarder asked.

"I've removed the dragonbone from your soldiers' armor and weapons," Angst replied matter-of-factly. "All of them. Every single one."

"No! You...you don't understand what you've done!" Gaarder said in a panic, grasping Angst's arm in desperation. "We're defenseless! You've killed us all!"

"I'm saving you, whether you like it or not!" Angst replied, yanking his arm from the old man's grip. "You no longer have any defense against magic users, so you'd better make peace with them fast if you want someone to defend Melkier."

Gaarder's face paled with fear. His lip quivered, and the great king suddenly seemed very old. "The armor wasn't to protect us from the magic users!" The king sounded mad. "Without it, we'll be overrun! They will destroy us!"

"Then I would recommend that you start apologizing to wielders, and making friends quickly." Angst looked around at the guards in disgust. "They're your only hope."

Angst walked past the king, closely followed by his friends. Victoria stopped in front of Crloc and kicked him in the crotch with all her might. He screamed loudly before passing out.

"Bitch!" she yelled at the fallen man, spitting in his face.

Angst walked back, gripped her behind her elbow and pulled her down the hallway. "Feel better?"

"Maybe just a little," Victoria said, her eyes boiling with fury.

"I thought you were trying to become a better person?"

"Only a little better," Angst said with a smirk. "These things take time."

The room shook violently, dust and small stones falling from the dungeon ceiling, creating a cloud. The shaking abated for a moment. Angst looked at his friends, and every eye looked back at him accusingly.

"Can't you make that thing stop?" Tarness asked, pointing at Dulgirgraut.

"It's not the sword this time," Angst said. He looked back at Gaarder.

"I told you! I told you and now it's happening. They know….they know we're defenseless," Gaarder muttered. "There will be hundreds."

"Hundreds of what?" Hector growled.

The king looked at Hector with wide, crazed eyes.

"Dragons," he whispered.

52

Alloria curtsied respectfully to the crowd before moving to stand to the left of Queen Isabelle. Tyrell stood behind the queen austerely, his stiff white tunic and gray leggings handsomely complimenting her attire. He feared none in the castle enough to don armor for this affair. A thin steel longsword rested across from his able right hand. Piercing gray eyes darted over the busy crowd in impatient focus.

Isabelle leaned forward to stand until Tyrell gently pulled her back.

"Aren't we done?" Isabelle whispered over her shoulder.

"Soon, Your Majesty," Tyrell replied with a tolerant smile. "You agreed to personally receive ambassadors from Meldusia, Nordruaut, and Fulk'han—each of whom is here for the coronation."

Queen Isabelle looked at her Captain Guard with displeasure, as though this was his fault and she intended to hold him responsible. Tyrell merely shrugged before standing upright. Without waiting for any acknowledgement that she was ready, Tyrell signaled the crier, whose yell made several in the room jump with a start.

"Ambassador Jintorich of Meldusia," the crier announced from the hall entrance.

Curiosity turned every head in the giant hallway. Each step the Meldusian took brought loud clacking sounds into the otherwise quiet space. Those standing along the outer edge of the room lifted on tiptoes to better see the sight. Observers close to Jintorich didn't bother to hide their shock as jaws unceremoniously unhinged and eyes widened at his passing.

Isabelle forced herself to smile, an unnatural act. It looked as though her ears were tugging her painted red lips back in an uncomfortable arc. The Meldusian was no taller than her knee. In spite of his height, the "man" was wide and bulbous. His nose and cheeks were round and reddish, like strawberries not quite ripened. Jintorich was almost bald, and his forehead protruded as though he wore a helmet. His ears were thin and tall as his head, coming to a point, with tufts of hair framing their edges. He wore white robes of rich fabric with vertical rows of soft leather insets. Jintorich had no shoes—the clicking apparently came from his incredibly thick toenails, which curved over the front of his toes like armor, tapping on the floor with a clicker-clack. He stopped before the throne, and with some assistance from his toothpick staff, he bowed low at the waist, his tiny white terrycloth robe creasing over his feet. Long thin wisps of brown hair flipped over his forehead.

"Your Majesty," Jintorich said in a loud, high-pitched voice. "It is my sincere honor to make your acquaintance."

"It is our honor to receive you, ambassador." Isabelle nodded. She forced herself to blink, certain she hadn't since he'd entered the hall.

Jintorich looked at her with tiny black eyes that twinkled mischievously. He smiled and reached into a pocket. Nearby guards readied themselves, hefting polearms and swords as the Meldusian pulled out a small box.

Isabelle rolled her eyes at the soldiers, and Tyrell shook his head and sighed.

"I'm certain the queen is in no danger," Tyrell said wearily. "So please stand down."

The nearby soldiers shuffled their feet in embarrassment as they relaxed, still eyeing the visitor in apparent disbelief.

Jintorich's plume of dark brown eyebrows lifted high in delight and his ears drooped. "Are all of the West so fearful of change, Your Highness?" Jintorich said pleasantly.

"My apologies, ambassador," the queen said, her painted cheeks flushing. "The changes have been many and the frequency great. We weren't completely prepared for how much change to expect."

"Of course, Your Majesty," Jintorich stated with a diplomatic nod of his large head, and then jovially replied in his high-pitched voice, "we were even more surprised than you!"

The queen's eyes widened at his direct response, and she politely chuckled with him before becoming serious. "Can we assist in any way?" Isabelle asked sincerely. "Is Meldusia in need of aid?"

"Thank you, Queen, but we manage. Unsel and Meldusia have enjoyed a long friendship," Jintorich acknowledged, holding the box out to her. "We are, indeed, grateful for that relationship."

Tyrell intercepted the small wooden box, inspecting it briefly before handing it to Isabelle.

"As are we," she replied. She opened the box and immediately oohed in spite of herself.

The flower broach was made from five small red dragonscales held together by tiny silver chains encrusted in diamonds. The center featured a sizeable diamond, large enough to make Isabelle's mouth twitch hungrily. The delicate craftsmanship was unsurpassed, and it required a great amount of self-control to return it to its box instead of dashing from her throne to change into appropriate attire and wear it. With a sigh, she handed the gift back to the princess.

"For your Princess Alloria, in honor of her coronation," the small man said enthusiastically. He rose onto his thickly-nailed toes and looked about the room.

"A very kind gift, ambassador," Alloria said gratefully, tugging the box from Isabelle's reluctant grip. "It is quite beautiful."

"We had heard the same of you, princess, and thought it appropriate," Jintorich said, still looking around—almost, but not quite, turning his back on the queen in an effort to see.

"Is there something we can help you find, ambassador?" Isabelle asked stiffly.

"I'm sorry, Your Majesty," Jintorich replied. "Height was never an advantage my people enjoyed, and even less so now. I was wondering, if it pleased Your Majesty...I would very much like to meet Mr. Angst."

Isabelle's back stiffened as if she'd been slapped in the rear. She swallowed hard and glanced back at Tyrell, who shrugged in surprise at the request.

"Angst is on a mission for Unsel, ambassador, and his exact whereabouts are unknown," she said tersely, her voice pitching almost as high as Jintorich's. "Is there something we can do for Meldusia?"

"We believe we have identified another foci, like his great blade, and seek his guidance," he said with an oblivious smile.

"Oh, of course," Isabelle said in surprise. "We are hoping he will be back within several weeks. You are welcome to be our guest while waiting."

"You are too kind." Jintorich smiled and bowed. "At your convenience, Your Majesty, I would enjoy the opportunity to discuss other matters as well."

"I would love to breakfast with you in several days, ambassador," the queen offered.

"That would be quite lovely," he said, bowing once more. "With your leave."

The queen nodded and the small, bulbous ambassador waddled to her left. He found an empty chair, upon which he climbed and perched to watch from a better view.

"Ambassador Maarja of Nordruaut," the crier yelled at Tyrell's behest.

Isabelle was irritated at Tyrell's rush to see the visitors without her lead, though secretly grateful to finish this quickly.

Maarja entered the room, mostly covered in white furs and soft tan leather. Her tanned skin and platinum blond hair made her beautiful face that much more striking. Two lines of white paint stretched from her eyes over her cheeks. She towered over every guard, and her hands were large enough to crush the head of any soldier. In spite of her great size, she appeared nervous, as though attempting to tread lightly on another's property. The difference in size between the Meldusian and the Nordruaut made her entrance shocking.

"Your Majesty," Maarja said in a husky voice, dropping to one knee and placing her hands on the hilt of her daggers.

Tyrell immediately turned to the nearby guards. "Leave your weapons be," he whispered, "unless you want her to feed them to you."

Maarja lifted her head, barely, and winked at the Captain Guard in acknowledgement. Tyrell's eyes widened in surprise that her hearing was so keen. Maarja let go of her daggers and spread out her arms in a wide, welcoming gesture.

"Please tell us your story, young Maarja," Queen Isabelle stated as she opened her arms respectfully.

Maarja remained kneeling so she could look at Isabelle eye-to-eye. She studied the other woman, inspecting the queen up and down. She immediately noticed the scarring and false eye, and nodded respectfully.

"Good hunting, Your Majesty?" Maarja asked.

Several in the hall gasped at this question—the queen's eye was never mentioned—but, to their surprise, Isabelle did not react harshly.

"It was a good hunt, and a story I will gladly share in the future," Isabelle said calmly.

Maarja smiled at this and nodded once in respect then handed the queen a large bundle wrapped in soft leather. Tyrell took the bundle and untied the straps to reveal the white fur of a snow fox.

"A rare gift, indeed," Tyrell said respectfully, handing one of the furs to Alloria.

"Thank you," the princess cooed, petting the luxurious fur.

"Are you a mate of Angst?" Maarja questioned Alloria.

"*No*, of course not!" Alloria blurted out, but after seeing Tyrell's calming hand, she gentled her response. "I mean, Angst is a dear friend. Why do you ask?"

"In my brief time with him, it seems you would be a woman he would want to mate," she stated. The large woman sighed, sounding exasperated. In a discouraged and rushed sentence, she quickly said, "IseekcounselfromAngst."

"Did you say, you seek Angst's counsel?" Isabelle said, her throat constricting once more.

"Yes," Maarja replied, visibly distraught.

"Angst is away on a mission," Isabelle replied tersely, gripping the ends of her throne's armrests.

"I'll wait," Maarja said.

"May I ask why you need Angst?" the queen asked.

"Eastern Nordruaut will soon war with Unsel," Maarja stated matter-of-factly.

Noisy speculation immediately filled the hall as dozens of attendants raised voice to question this new threat.

"I've been told there is one who would soon challenge Angst for the right to battle," Maarja continued.

"Oh, of course," Isabelle said, as her insides collapsed in panic. "I'm certain Angst will accept that challenge—if not, Unsel will meet you on the glorious battlefield."

Maarja suddenly stood, making everyone but the queen jump in surprise. She seemed excited by Isabelle's offer, as if she had been bestowed a gift. "The battle will be great, Your Majesty!"

"It will be a battle for stories," Isabelle said, standing with raised fist over her heart.

Maarja looked ready to hug the queen in her excitement, but instead fought to restrain herself.

"Please be our guest until Angst returns," Isabelle requested calmly as she sat back on her throne.

Isabelle gestured toward the spot where Jintorich rested. Maarja bowed her head and walked over to the small man. She looked at him curiously, and at his beckon gently shook hands. She immediately smiled with fond respect, in spite of his size.

CHAPTER FIFTY TWO

"Enough waiting!" boomed the Fulk'han Ambassador as he stormed into the room.

Five Fulk'han escorted the Ambassador into the hall—two gray men and three brightly colored women.

"Who allowed five into the throne room?" Tyrell asked a nearby soldier.

With a nod, the soldier left ranks to seek an answer.

The men appeared practically identical, light gray and covered head to toe in armor that looked as though bones had grown outside their body. The women were sex. Each a different color—pink, bright blue, or purple. Slightly darker hair seemed to pour from their heads, falling long to the back of their knees. Cat-like tails rose up and down their calves seductively, and all men in the room breathlessly followed every curvy cat-like step. The five strode to the throne, the lead gray man bowing as briefly and curtly as the tiniest of sneezes from the smallest woman on Ehrde.

"To what do we owe the honor?" Isabelle said drolly, reluctant to welcome the Fulk'han's rude demeanor.

"I am Ambassador Boiter," he said curtly. "And I am here for Angst."

"Is anyone here to see me today?" Alloria whispered to Tyrell.

"Angst is on a mission, but I'm sure when he returns—" the queen began.

"When he returns, he will be taken into our custody," the Fulk'han ambassador advised her. He pulled a parchment from a round leather case at his waist and read: "The Fulk'han Empire does hereby place Angst, Hector, Tarness, and Rose under arrest for the murder of our lord and savior, Ivan," Boiter yelled.

Maarja looked at Jintorich, who appeared in shock and gripped his short staff tightly. She took a step closer to the nearest Fulk'han.

"Deemed guilty by the high command of Fulk'han, these perpetrators will be returned for incarceration and execution, or war with Unsel is imminent."

Isabelle's pressed her hand to her mouth thoughtfully. Tyrell reached for the parchment and handed it to the queen. She reviewed it, immediately confused by the illegible scribbles. It was nonsense, but she nodded diplomatically and handed the scroll back to Tyrell.

"My council will discuss your demands, ambassador—"

"No!" he commanded. "The accused will return with us or I will return with their heads!"

With the suddenness of a cat, Maarja leaped into the air, grappled the Fulk'han ambassador around the neck with her enormous legs, and spun about. There was a loud snapping sound, as if someone had broken a piece of wood. Maarja rolled to stand, flipping the gray man's carcass over to an empty area far beyond the throne.

53

They had sprinted from the dungeon and abruptly stopped just outside the exit. Victoria looked at each of them impatiently. Angst and Tarness were resting on their knees, panting heavily. Dallow held onto Tarness, breathing fast but still upright. Hector seemed fine, rolling his eyes at the others.

"My heroes," Victoria said sardonically.

"I've been sick for a month!" Angst said, excusing himself, gulping down large drafts of air like it was his favorite mead. "This...sword...is...heavy."

"No, it's not," Victoria snapped. "You know better than to lie to me."

"I thought you couldn't *read me* anymore?" Angst half-whispered between hungry breaths.

"I know you that well," the princess said, also whispering.

"Dallow is slowing me down," Tarness explained.

"Don't blame me," Dallow said, letting go of Tarness to adjust the bandage covering his eyes. "The blind man is keeping up fine."

The castle shook so violently that Victoria and Dallow dropped to their knees. Tarness tipped over, knocking Angst to the floor. When the quake abated, Angst rolled over and looked at Hector, who remained standing in a half-crouched position.

"How many dragons would it take to do that?" Tarness asked.

"All of them," Dallow said in concern.

379

"While you girls are resting, I'm going to run a quick errand," Hector said over his shoulder. "Meet you at the entrance." He took off at a sprint.

Tarness looked at Angst curiously, but Angst merely shrugged, unsure what his friend was up to.

"Let's keep going," Angst said, standing cautiously. His knee felt twingy, and he favored it as they made their way to the castle entrance.

"What's wrong now?" Victoria asked.

"It does that sometimes," Angst said under his breath. "I'll shake it out in a minute or two."

"Are you all old?" Victoria asked in exasperation.

"No!" Angst and Tarness said defensively.

"Yes!" Dallow replied.

"Ugh!" Victoria said, rolling her eyes before leading them out of the castle.

"If you think we should go faster, you can carry us," Angst teased.

There was a haze of dust on the floor, as if the hallway had never been cleaned. The castle guard carefully guided staff to safety, ignoring Angst and his friends as they made their way through the chaos. They squinted as they exited the castle into the bright early-winter day. Angst peered across the city of Melkier to see a dark red blob in the distance. The large dragon hovered at the edge of the city like a fly preparing to join a picnic.

"Oh good, there's only one," Angst said in relief.

"Are you kidding?" Victoria asked.

"It's hard to see from here," Tarness said, "but that thing is enormous!"

"We'll be fine," Angst said. "Where's Hector?"

"Here," Hector grunted, dragging a large bed sheet filled with their armor and gear. "I think this is everything. I found it while looking for your sword."

"You're the best!" Angst complimented as he maneuvered into his greaves.

CHAPTER FIFTY THREE

"Yes," Hector replied. "I am."

After suiting up, Hector nodded toward Victoria, who had remained in her chainmail top and skirt. Goosebumps covered her fair skin, and she shivered slightly in the cold air while looking at the large dragon.

"Tori?" Angst asked. "Aren't you going to be cold?"

"Of course I'm cold. It's freezing!" she said with a defiant shiver.

Victoria rolled her eyes at the concerned look on Angst's face and picked up her red cloak from the sheet containing their armor. She clasped it around her neck and stuck her tongue out at Angst.

"Better!" he said with a smile. "Let's go be heroes!"

Upon summoning, his swifen instantly appeared, strong, no longer marred by sickness or insecurity. The ram was once more cast of solid steel, shining bright in the reflection of the morning sun. Dulgirgraut the Defender had covered the creature with an extra coat of heavy armor and a thick layer of confidence. A gentle burgundy hue now shone from the crevices of its muscles. The ram breathed in heroics and exhaled bravado, and Angst mounted it with all the conviction of destiny.

Tori glanced back at Hector with concern. He stared at the swifen in disbelief and shook his head from side to side. Before she could voice her worry, Angst pulled the princess up to mount in front of him. Looking at his friends—Hector on his panther, Tarness and Dallow on Tarness's stallion—he nodded once, and they rode.

The city shuddered again, as if afraid of the lone dragon waiting in challenge just outside its periphery. In spite of his not-as-keen-as-it-used-to-be vision, Angst could make out great bursts of dragonfire from the creature. Angst felt anxious at their slow pace. He knew he could push the swifen, all their swifen, to ride fast—just as he had when they'd chased magic—but there were still people in the streets...

"We should ride faster!" Hector yelled.

"Who do you want to trample?" Tarness asked, pointing

around at the crowd.

They continued to ride, and the blob of dragon grew quickly. From a mile away, Angst couldn't even guess the dragon's size.

"How big is that thing?" Angst asked in awe. "We aren't even halfway there."

"I tried to warn you!" Victoria yelled.

He sought Dulgirgraut for answers, but the foci remained silent. He cocked his head to one side, attempting to delve deeper into the sword. A cool barrier prevented all communication— Dulgirgraut offered no assistance, not even music like Chryslaenor. It seemed he had all the power yet none of the knowledge.

"What's wrong, Angst?" Victoria asked.

"The sword. It's different this time," Angst said. "Something isn't right...wait, how do you know?"

She looked down at her hands in concentration, and a gentle pink hue surrounded them. Angst quickly covered them with his own so the others wouldn't see. It would be so much easier if they knew, but it was Victoria's secret to keep.

"You're doing it," he said proudly.

They stopped as the city became grass and field—their eyes wide and jaws agape. The dragon was so enormous it didn't fit in his vision. It made the dragon from the Great Bridge of Melkier seem a child in comparison. Though if this were the mother, it wouldn't be the mother of just one dragon—it would be the mother of all dragons in all time.

The red scales were so dark they seemed brown. Protruding ridges about the dragon's scale shot out like enormous stalactites. Great wings beat with such effort large trees were felled as though thrashed by tornados. A storm of snow and dust clouded the ground in gusts with every flap.

They all stood in awe of the dragon's size and ferocity. They shared a shiver, and not one of them was able to speak, reliving the dragonfear they had already experienced at the bridge. Angst turned his head from side to side as he took in the wingspan, which stretched the length of the city. If this wasn't everything dangerous, Angst would have sat down and watched in amazement. This titan, this dragon, was every gorgeous unmitigated disaster that Ehrde could deliver, and a fascination to his eyes.

"Looks like this is a job for Angst," Tarness said enthusiastically as he reached over to roughly thump Angst's shoulder.

Angst urged Victoria off his ram swifen then dismounted. He stared at the creature, dumbfounded, before looking to Hector for guidance.

"Well, now what, genius?" Hector asked, looking up at the giant red beast.

"You're not helping," Victoria said.

"What does that thing tell you to do?" Hector questioned, ignoring her as he nodded toward Dulgirgraut.

"Nothing," Angst said in exasperation. "I feel healthy. I feel power similar to Chryslaenor, but communication is gone. It's like this foci is ignoring me."

"Try harder," Hector commanded.

Angst took Dulgirgraut from his back, holding it high as he could. Chryslaenor would have been aggressive, urging Angst to shoot lightning while flooding his mind with spells and ideas to put him on the offensive. Angst concentrated, focusing all his will on the blade, struggling to attack the giant dragon with something. Anything. The foci glowed a dull red, but nothing else happened. Moments passed, and he lowered the tip of the foci to the ground.

"It seems that Dulgirgraut doesn't like lightning," Angst said in frustration. "I'll have to take the fight to the dragon."

"Maybe you need to hurry up and make friends," Tarness teased.

"Tarness could be right," Dallow said.

"But there isn't time," Angst worried. "I don't know if it's broken, or if I'm broken, but it will have to wait. We need another plan."

The ground shook, and Tarness looked about inquisitively.

"What's wrong, Tarness?" Hector asked.

"Where are the earthquakes coming from?" Tarness asked. "I

thought it was maybe from that dragon landing—"

"Good question, but one disaster at a time. Angst, you need to destroy that dragon," Hector said. "What about the Ivan thing? Slice that dragon up like strips of steak!"

"Mmm, steak," Tarness said.

"Bad idea," Dallow said quickly, touching his face. "If lava comes gushing out, there's no telling if Angst could protect himself, us, or the rest of the city."

Angst nodded in agreement and looked at Victoria. Her face was paler than usual, and she shook her head, agreeing with their assessment. She stared off at the dragon as though analyzing the creature, but Angst knew she was trying to read the future when her eyes glowed pink.

"Close your eyes," Angst whispered.

"The bones," Dallow said, "destroy the dragon's bones. It won't be able to fly. It will just collapse in a heap."

"That I could do," Angst said smiling excitedly and patting Dallow on the shoulder.

"You'll have to touch the bones," Victoria advised, finally opening her eyes and looking at Angst.

"But I was able to remove the black from all Melkier armor without touching it," Angst said. "I've got this."

"I hate it when he says that," Hector grumbled. "We should probably find cover."

Angst lifted a hand now glowing dark red and the ground rumbled as a rocky barrier rose and formed a half-dome. There was enough space to protect his friends, and it was thick enough to take damage.

"I'll be right back," Angst said cockily, but when he tried to step away, Victoria held his arm.

"Please be careful," she said.

"What could possibly go wrong?" Angst asked.

She looked at him dryly.

Angst walked away, holding her arm until it became her hand and then her fingers. Her fingertips escaped his, and he took a deep breath. It was brave time, and he reached out with the sword, carving a circular swath of rock around him. With a noisy crunch, a six-foot chunk of ground lifted into the air.

He focused on anchoring his feet to the platform while flying toward the enormous dragon. He had, so far, gone unnoticed. Angst concentrated, urging his transportation to one side, and found it sluggish to maneuver, like trying to force a boat sideways. He pushed harder, finally using air to budge it and felt like he was shoving a tree. The gigantic dragon's head whipped about to face him, and Angst reared back at a snail's pace. Wet fire shot from its mouth, barely missing Angst as he forced the platform higher into the air.

Streams of fire blasted again and again. Angst could only go up, down, or forward. This wasn't the same as battling Ivan—the platform just wouldn't maneuver. One hundred yards away would have to be close enough. Angst sought the dragon's bones. He forced the platform to rise just in time as dragonfire shot from the great wyrm's enormous diamond-shaped head. Angst could feel the bones, could feel their pores, and willed magic to fit into each one like a puzzle piece.

Time slowed as he drew magic from Dulgirgraut and willed it into the bones. When he'd poured every ounce of magic he could into the dragon, when everything finally clicked into place, Angst urged the blue-black bone to dust. The dragon roared and, with surprising speed, spun in mid-air, swatting Angst with its tail. The blow tossed him off his rock platform, which fell and smashed into pieces. Angst plunged toward his friends.

"Dallow, Angst is falling this way," Hector said quickly. "Can you make a cushion of air about ten yards ahead of us?"

"Twenty," Tarness said.

"Ten will be fine," Hector replied.

"Done!" Dallow nodded, his eyes glowing bright white behind his bandage.

Angst dropped to the ground, crashing hard on the frozen earth, completely missing Dallow's shield. He bounced once and skidded into the air-shield barrier.

"I told you twenty," Tarness yelled.

Tori ran to Angst, sprinting past Hector as he reached out to hold her back. Angst lay still, and Victoria kneeled roughly, skinning her bare knees. She ignored the pain and grabbed his shoulders, trying to shake the unconscious out of him.

"Angst?" she shrieked. "Are you okay?"

He opened his eyes and inhaled deeply. "Ouch," he let out with a squeak.

Hector and Tarness arrived at his legs, pulling him back toward the barricade. Angst had his hand glued around Dulgirgraut as though in shock, dragging it with them.

"What are you doing?" Victoria demanded. "He could be hurt!"

"Better than being dead," Tarness yelled. "Look up."

The creature's body was now vertical and its wings beat slowly as it reared its head back. It took a deep breath, and Victoria ran with them. A gush of dragonfire was accompanied by a horrific gurgly scream. They sprinted behind the half-dome barricade just as the lava struck.

"Ergh," Dallow yelled. "Trying to reinforce with air, but—" Dallow grunted loudly, collapsing to a knee. Tarness put a hand on his friend's shoulder. "I'm all right...just too much." Dallow panted, attempting to catch his breath.

"You're doing great!" Tarness said as he watched streams of lava flow around them in a wide arc.

"Angst, what happened?" Hector asked, ignoring Victoria as she kneeled beside Angst with her hand on his chest.

"I can't make the platform change direction," Angst said.

"What about using air to maneuver it?" Dallow suggested.

"I tried," Angst said.

"Were you too far away to destroy the dragon's bones?" Hector pressed.

"No, but I think Victoria's right," Angst acknowledged. "I need to make contact with them."

"See," Victoria said, kneeling beside Angst. She placed a hand on his face in hope of reading his future. "You should always do what I say."

"But I didn't have to touch everyone's armor to remove its protection," Angst said, wincing from the fall.

"When you first expunged the blue-black from the bone," Dallow said. "Did you have to make contact?"

"Yes," Angst said.

"You can remove the protection if it's already been separated from the dragonbone," Dallow explained. "But you need to touch the bone to remove it from the source."

"But I can't get close enough," Angst complained. "I think the sword hates me."

"We don't have time for that," Hector snapped. "We need to figure out how to get you closer."

"Can we survive another blast of dragonfire?" Tarness questioned. "We're surrounded by lava now..."

"Not unless you guys suddenly figure out how to make air shields." Dallow said through gritted teeth, sweat beading his cheeks. "I don't know how I'm holding the lava back."

"I know how to get to the dragon," Angst said.

Victoria pulled back her hand and immediately shook her head. Angst rolled the top half of his body to one side, and grunted as his back popped loudly. He rolled to the other side and pushed himself up to standing. Angst took a slow step toward her.

"No, Angst," Victoria whispered, moving back.

"Why feathers, Tori?" Angst asked as she shook her head.

Everyone looked at them in confusion, but Angst ignored their stares as he kept moving forward.

"No!" she yelled, her back pressing against the air shield.

Angst popped that bubble of appropriate, placing his hands on Victoria's cheeks. He stood so close their noses almost touched. He stared her in the eye. Victoria breathed quickly, looking from side to side for an escape. Angst appeared on the verge of kissing her.

"Oh, not now you two," Hector said in disbelief. "Of all times..."

"Victoria," Angst said, loud enough for everyone to hear. "Why does your swifen have feathers?"

Tarness let out a low whistle, and Dallow smiled broadly.

Victoria blinked several times before her brows furrowed in anger. She slapped his hands down and struck him across the cheek.

"I knew there was something," Hector said under his breath.

"You just put them all in danger," Victoria spat. "Mom will kill them if they know."

"We'll all be dead if you don't help," he said more gently. "I'll ask again, why does your swifen have feathers?"

"B...because she has wings," she said. Her face was panic-stricken as she looked at the wary gazes of their friends. "I don't even know if she can fly."

"Maybe if we summon her together," Angst said hopefully.

Victoria nodded slowly, her face brightening as she began to understand. Angst picked up Dulgirgraut and placed it in that familiar spot between his shoulders. He wished he had guidance from the sword. He remembered the chase to Unsel, wishing and willing his friends to follow closely behind him. That push was what she needed. Angst stood behind Victoria, embracing her with his hands touching her bare stomach. He placed the side of his face next to hers and concentrated. A burgundy cloud enveloped him.

"Do it now," he said distantly.

Victoria spoke the spell in Acratic, and the unicorn appeared in its pink, feathery glory. Heedless of the danger or urgency, Victoria leaped forward to hug the creature on tiptoe, one leg bent at the knee, her foot lifting into the air. Angst opened his eyes to watch and swore the poor swifen sighed.

"You've got to be kidding me," Hector said.

"Really?" said Dallow with a chortle as Tarness continued to whisper a description in his ear.

Victoria hopped onto her swifen's back, and its golden hooves struck the ground with anticipation. Reluctantly, Angst mounted the petite creature, doing his best to adjust Dulgirgraut.

She looked back at him with a smirk. "Ready?" she asked, almost squealing with excitement.

"Sure," Angst said with a deep wary breath.

Great pink, feathery wings unfolded and began flapping gently. Victoria clapped in excitement and squeed loudly as the swifen lifted off the ground.

"You two...well, I don't even know what to say," Tarness sighed. "Be careful."

"Don't worry," Victoria yelled over her shoulder. "We've got this!"

Angst smiled proudly despite himself.

"Oh please," Hector said discouragingly. "Not her too."

54

"Yeaaaaah!" Victoria yelled, reveling in excitement and freedom as the pink, feathery unicorn dove between streams of dragon fire.

Angst gripped her waist in panic as she piloted the unicorn with reckless abandon. His leg muscles were quickly exhausting from straddling tight during the several upside-down loops she'd performed in conjunction with almost uncontrollable giggles.

"Did I ever say thank you?" Victoria yelled over her shoulder, the ends of her long blond hair whipping his face.

"No," Angst yelled against the wind. "For what?"

"This!" she declared, her broad mouth wide with smile.

"The swifen?" he asked.

"No," she said. "All of this! The adventure, the freedom…this was everything I wanted!"

Angst strained to listen as the rush of air crashed against his ears. His large red cloak flapped wildly, but her voice wasn't clear at all. The wind pulled tears from his eyes as he squinted to watch their approach.

"You're welcome, Tori," Angst yelled, as warmly as he could.

"I love you!" she yelled.

"I love you too!" he replied, momentarily forgetting his panic. Could it all be right again? "Let's go kill a dragon!"

She laughed maniacally as the unicorn adeptly hopped over a

stream of dragonfire. When they neared the dragon, it whipped around again. With the speed of thought, the pink flying unicorn dove out of harm's way, barely avoiding the giant horns protruding from the back of the dragon's head. A bright pink glow surrounded Victoria's hands. He could only imagine her glee at this, and she nodded agreeably at his thoughts. Magic wasn't just happening for her, it wasn't just coming naturally like breathing, Victoria was truly wielding it.

"You need to jump off when we reach the base of the neck..." she explained loudly.

"What?" Angst asked.

"... then leap off the end of the tail when you're done!"

"That's it?" Angst asked.

"Don't mess up or we all die!" she said, suddenly serious.

"Really?" he asked.

"Yes," she answered. "I don't think that will happen, but it could. You have to trust my cue!"

"You're cute?" Angst was so frustrated; he had never thought his hearing to be a problem. "I trust you!"

"Then hang on," she said with determination.

Angst squeezed onto the unicorn with his sore legs and gripped Victoria's tiny stomach as tight as he dared. The dragon's head swung about and snapped at them, but not before they dropped twenty feet, making Angst's stomach lurch into his throat. The dragon made Ivan seem small, and they were so far from the ground Angst could hardly catch his breath. He looked straight ahead and concentrated on being a hero.

"Be ready!" she yelled.

Angst pulled Dulgirgraut from his back, grimacing at the blade's stubbornness. The blade would not speak to him, but still glowed a bright burgundy in anticipation of the coming battle. Victoria guided the unicorn to swoop up once again and circle over the dragon's enormous head. The snake-like pupil in a yellow eye followed their every move.

Starting above the dragon's head, the unicorn flew inches above the neck, racing for its back. Angst took a deep breath.

Leaning on Victoria's shoulders as gently as he could, he pulled his knees up to the swifen's flank. She pushed against his hand to provide support, shaking under Angst's weight. Carefully, as slowly as he dared, Angst stood on unsure legs.

Angst leaned forward, putting his left hand cautiously on Victoria's shoulder. His knees shook, and his heart raced in panic as he looked down. A glimpse of Ehrde below showed patches of farm and city in a way Angst had never imagined. He swallowed hard, and his grip became slick with sweat. His stomach churned and nausea crawled up his throat as his view of the long fall was replaced by the dragon's dark red neck of hard protrusions. The dragon was a city in itself, and Angst wondered how he could possibly run from front to back in time to keep Victoria safe. But it appeared wide, and solid. With a deep breath, Angst jumped.

"Not yet!" Victoria yelled after him.

The hard landing jolted every joint of every bone. The dragon's neck was slick, and his twingy knee buckled as his feet slipped out from under him. Angst found himself rolling over the edge of the beast. He grappled desperately, trying to yank his arm free from the entrapping cloak that wrapped around him like a cocoon. Angst slid fast and caught a glimpse of the ground below right before landing hard on an outcropping of scale. Panic flowed through his veins, and he sat up quickly. Cold, wet wind blasted his face and his feet hung over the edge, but at least he still had Dulgirgraut in his grasp.

The wyrm's large head rolled from side to side like a snake in water, desperate to find a means to rid itself of the intruder. Angst stood cautiously on the dark red protrusion and looked up to see a rocky formation of uneven growths forming a pathway up. His friends were in danger, Melkier was in danger, and he had to hurry. Angst placed the great blade between his shoulders and scurried up the slick scale. It felt like scrambling up shale on a mountaintop, and he often lost his footing as he made his way.

Angst pulled himself up to the dragon's dark red neck and crawled across it carefully until he reached its broad back. He stood slowly and sought his footing. He faced the tail, the wind now crashing against his back, and the dragon rose and fell with every beat of its large wings like a plank on stormy waters. Bracing himself, Angst ran along an obstacle course of rock-like outgrowths. He watched his footing while seeking loose scale and focused on running as fast as he could, but the end of the dragon seemed just as far away. How long could Victoria maintain the flying unicorn without him?

Angst tripped two-thirds of the way along the dragon's back, landing hard on his chest. He pushed himself up to his knees, taking a moment to study the red surface. The dragon's flesh was coated in thick leathery rock, which was made up of layers upon layers, like a fungus. There was no vulnerable spot, no fleshy opening, no obvious target, and Angst grunted as he stood, placing Dulgirgraut on its tip.

A loud grinding sound followed sparks where the sword touched dragonscale. Angst leaned over and picked up a chunk of scale carved off by the foci. Had the foci done this itself? Was it attempting to help? There was no time to waste in wonder. He lifted Dulgirgraut by the grip once more and swung hard. Sparks flew with every lash of his blade, dislodging large pieces of red dragon. As he carved deeper, the dragon began to take notice. It writhed in fear, shuddering like a wet dog then spinning about in mid-air. The dragon flew straight up before diving straight down.

Angst continued digging the grave, his eyes glowing red as he anchored his armored feet to the creature. Every shake, every rise and fall, was a new heart attack. Weak with panic, he lost himself in chopping away and dislodging more scale. After removing more than three feet, Angst finally found something fleshy. Without hesitation, and with all his might, he drove Dulgirgraut into the dragon's back.

Dulgirgraut sank into the dragon and continued sinking until it met something solid. Angst could only hope it was bone. The dragon continued shifting violently from side to side, trying to shake him like an untamed stallion. Bright golden lava squirted from the opening Dulgirgraut had created. Angst closed his eyes and concentrated, filling the dragon's bones with magic again. With his mind, he sought every opening, every pore of every bone throughout the titan. The dragon's wings slowed and faltered, as though carrying a weight too heavy for a dragon the mere size of a castle.

The creature fought, jerking back and forth in anger, knowing that something inside wasn't right. Angst struggled with patience as it took time to fill the giant with magic. When, finally, magic reached into the entire creature from tip to tail, he willed. Dust. Sand. Erosion. Particles. Angst couldn't will the dark bone away, but he could disintegrate it to the finest amount of nothing in existence. With the most pathetic of squawks, the largest dragon ever crumpled and fell.

Angst yanked Dulgirgraut from the wound, and slapped it between his shoulders as he tried to run along the dragon's back. Lava shot out of the gaping hole, chasing Angst while he scrambled away, grasping onto protrusions as the beast spun out of control. When he finally reached the tail, with all the hope and trust he could gather, Angst leaped into the air.

He landed hard on the back of the unicorn and clung to Victoria so tightly she winced.

"I'm here," she grunted. "You did it! We did it!"

Angst forced himself to loosen his grip so he wouldn't hurt her. He looked at the dragon, watching as it fell helplessly to the ground. An empty red bag of writhing muscle and fiery anger. The dragon landed hard, and a mass of glowing ooze spread from its red body.

"You did great, Tori!" Angst yelled, relief starting to set in. "Let's check on the others."

The unicorn swifen gracefully swooped down to their friends behind the large stone barrier Angst had created. Each of them smiled proudly, and gratefully. Annoying pellets of sleet dropped from the sky, hissing noisily as they landed on the distant dragon.

"What took you so long?" Hector grunted with a smile, holding his hands over his eyes to protect them from the annoying rain.

"He jumped too soon," Victoria teased, dismissing her swifen. She shivered for the first time as the excitement abated and sleet pelted her bare arms and torso.

"I what?" Angst asked, quickly removing his thick red cloak and wrapping her in it.

"You didn't wait for my cue," Victoria elaborated. "Thanks."

"You didn't say anything about a cue!" Angst retorted. "I thought you said you were cute! I already knew that."

"So it worked?" Dallow asked, hoping to interrupt a new argument.

"Couldn't have done it without you, old friend," Angst admitted, hugging Dallow affectionately.

"Let's go see the damage," Tarness said excitedly, patting both Angst and Dallow heavily on their shoulders.

They left the safety of the barrier, carefully tiptoeing around the steaming gobs of cooling dragonfire. The lava hissed as it fought the cold air and ground. When the dragonfire became too thick, Angst finally set the tip of Dulgirgraut to the ground and created a path with a shield of air.

"Handy," Hector quipped as he cautiously walked along the new path.

They stopped a hundred yards from the titan, unable to tell if it was alive or dead. Large masses of dark leathery scale rose and fell from breath or death. Glowing yellow and orange lava poured through crevices between the dragon's scales as it collapsed in on itself. The mass of body gave up in stages—the back, the chest, the wings, all fell into the lava, melting away in the hot, angry dragonfire.

Angst and his friends stood in awe, holding their hands in front of their faces to protect them from the intense heat emanating from the dragon's remains.

"What's that?" Hector asked in a gruff voice, coughing from the dry heat.

"What do you see?" Dallow asked.

"Just a dark blob in the middle," Tarness stated. "Almost like a bubble in that lava, but it's growing."

"We should go now, Angst," Victoria said, worriedly patting his arm.

Instinctively, Angst wielded Dulgirgraut and took several steps forward to shield his friends. The dark shadow slowly rose over the dragon carcass and moved toward them as though walking up a flight of stairs. The blob took the shape of a man, and a maelstrom of darkness roiled between ever-changing cracks of red and orange. As if birthed from dragonfire, the enormous man-shape grew to full height and walked toward them. He was as tall as the element Earth, a giant statue of dark heat and molten lava. A gentle blue flame coated the creature like a skin, and bright yellow light shone from behind his face to portray eyes, mouth, and nose. Angst refused to cover his face from the sapping heat, standing defiant with foci in hand.

"What is this?" Hector yelled.

"It's the element Fire," Victoria said simply, sliding cautiously behind Angst.

"Yes, young Princess," Fire stated, his scratchy voice crackling like a bonfire. "You!" Fire yelled, pointing at Angst with a thick cloud of sleet-melted steam rising from his arm.

"Me?" Angst looked over his shoulder innocently before returning his gaze to the giant element.

Fire stood a mere fifty feet away, and was so hot Angst's sweat evaporated as it left his pores. The element was black as pitch, black as coal, but his bitter, yellow eyes were hot, hot fire.

"You! You mortals! You humans killed my host! You killed my first child!" Fire screamed in fury. "I will take my due!"

55

Jaden sat in the antechamber, irritable from having to wait and annoyed by Rook's constant pacing. The large man had moved chairs out of the way to make the most use of the room, pausing only occasionally to inspect the guard's body further. It was disgusting and odorous, but Rook insisted on leaving it for evidence. Jaden wanted to argue, but his stiff pinky convinced him otherwise.

Jaden was on the verge of giving up his attempts to prove himself. He was completely lost in this strange land. Where had he come from? Why was he so adept at magic? Jaden didn't even know if he was a good guy or a bad guy. Everything felt off, and since arriving at Cliffview, he had done nothing but fail, over and over again. This wouldn't have bothered him so much if he hadn't just failed the one person he wanted to impress above all others.

"No matter what's going on, you have to tell my mother about what happened to Alloria in the hallway!" Victoria had insisted, talking to him angrily through earthspeak. "Tell her that if she doesn't listen to you, I'll come back and tell everyone in Unsel what I can do!"

He couldn't stand the queen, but the more conversations he had with Victoria, the more drawn in he was. Jaden's past was wispy memories, like smoke from dying embers, but he knew he had never felt this way before. Victoria's beauty, her poise, her smell, obsessed him. He longed to talk to her when they were apart and hurt when their conversations were over. But it seemed that every time their communications were cut short, it was because of Angst.

Angst hated him or, at the very least, didn't trust him. Every look Angst gave him was cold and his jaw seemed constantly set in frustration—making Jaden even more defensive. The old man couldn't be jealous of his accord with Victoria, not when Angst held her heart. They were best friends, and who was Jaden but one more guy with a crush? He'd rather ask the queen's permission to court Victoria than Angst's, but one day soon, he thought he would have to face them both. He shuddered. The responsibility of wielding a foci seemed easier than having to broach the subject of love with both of them. Maybe flirting was safest.

Several screams came from the temporary throne room, and Jaden sat up and rushed to the door, jiggling the handle helplessly. Was this one last chance to prove himself?

"It's locked," Jaden said. From behind the doorway, there was the crash of weapons, followed by battle screams and panicked yells. It sounded like war inside the large hall.

"Don't you wield magic?" Rook yelled, shoving the young man aside and kicking the door open.

Someone had let crazy loose in the throne room. Dukes and ladies rushed out, fleeing from the battle, followed closely by servants. A group of soldiers circled the main event, protecting the innocents running away, but mostly staring in awe as they waited to arrest those final few fighting. They framed the outside of the fight, creating a thin wall between the brawlers and the royalty, both defending and trapping them against the wall. One large gray man covered in bone and a pink scantily clad woman with her cat tail fought an insanely tall Nordruaut woman. Soldiers struggled to keep a second, purple Fulk'han woman away from the queen while Tyrell battled a muscular gray man in boned armor.

Rook continued elbowing through the crowd until he wedged himself between several guards. Jaden trailed close and, from over Rook's shoulder, saw the most amazing sight. A tiny bulbous ball of a man leaped from the floor, jumping off the Nordruaut woman's shoulder and launching himself at the pink woman. The little guy thrust what looked like a tiny staff at her face; it flashed brightly on contact, making her reel back, screaming. He then sprung off her forehead to land back onto the Nordruaut's shoulder. She eyed the small man protectively before pummeling against the gray man's shield with her bare fists, denting it with every thundering blow.

Tyrell battled his own gray man who appeared almost identical to the first, save for white marks roughly painted across his bone armor. The creature was filled with bravado, taking wild swings and expecting his great strength to overpower a master of the sword. Tyrell ducked and parried expertly, stabbing and slicing, delicately seeking the weakness in the bone plate armor. Trickles of gray blood dripped to the floor, unnoticed by the attacker.

"Let's go!" Jaden said, anxiously pressing against Rook.

"Soon," Rook said, holding up his hand for Jaden to wait, his eyes analyzing the fight.

Jaden didn't understand but followed Rook's lead, biting on his lips impatiently. He held onto Rook's arm as he watched the fight, distractedly thinking of the ideal spell that could end this mess. The mess became messier. Jaden felt Rook tense, and focused on the fight in time to see a soldier in front of the queen skewered by a large curved dagger. The purple Fulk'han woman licked her broad lips with a hungry smile as she pulled her blade free.

The Nordruaut roughly threw her gray man aside, attempting to make her way to the purple Fulk'han. The gray man slammed into Tyrell. His attacker swung down hard, sinking his thick, arched blade deep into Tyrell's arm. He roared in pain, instinctively pulling back. Tyrell made eye contact with Rook and Jaden, shaking his head.

"No!" Rook yelled, ready to attack.

Jaden followed Tyrell's cue, throwing his free arm around the large man, struggling to hold him back. It was like restraining a wild bull as Rook wrenched and elbowed.

"You said to wait," Jaden whispered loudly in Rook's ear. "You were right!"

"Enough!" yelled the gray man towering over Tyrell, his curved sword pointed at the man's neck.

Fighting stopped. Maarja released a strangling grip from around the pink woman's neck, letting her drop helplessly to the ground. The woman lay on the tile floor, both hands cradling her neck as she rediscovered the greatness of air.

"It's time!" the gray man standing over Tyrell yelled over his shoulder.

The purple woman facing Queen Isabelle snarled in frustration before pulling away and spinning on her heel. She ran out of the room, knocking over several guards en route.

"You made a grave error, Your Majesty," the man yelled. "Killing our Ambassador was a mistake, but sending your entire army into battle was greater still."

"What is this?" Isabelle screeched.

The gray man smiled at Alloria. Queen Isabelle turned her head to look at the young princess. Alloria was cool, contained in an envelope of knowledge that none in the room expected. She nodded at the Fulk'han slowly, as though this was part of a greater plan.

"You have left your capital unprotected." The man laughed. "As I speak, Fulk'han troops are marching the streets, killing your people, and your scant, remaining soldiers."

"No," the queen said pleadingly. "Why?"

"Why?" the gray man yelled. "You sent spies into Fulk'han! They killed our Takarn on the cusp of our rebirth as a nation of power!"

"They weren't spies," Isabelle pleaded. "Your Takarn...Ivan was nothing more than—"

"Silence!" the Fulk'han gray man spat as he cut her off. "Unsel is now ours!"

A dozen Fulk'han soldiers marched into the hall, their weapons dripping in red. Six giant gray men circled the outskirts of the room while the others marched through to the center. They stopped before the queen, pointing polearms and swords at the guards shielding the crowd. One Fulk'han placed his polearm on Rook's shoulder.

Rook counted quietly in whispers.

"What are you doing?" Jaden asked.

"Counting the different ways I can kill this bastard," Rook replied under his breath.

56

"We had no choice! That thing was going to kill us!" Angst yelled desperately, holding Dulgirgraut aloft with one hand while reaching behind him with the other to protect Victoria.

"I don't think it's listening," Tarness said.

Fire stopped his approach, turning his sooty head about. Blackened lava rose slowly through his constantly roiling body, reaching his head to disperse in the blue flame surrounding him. A thick layer of choking ash hovered about the element, landing heavily in each footprint like dirty snow. Fire took several steps back to the dragon and kneeled to pet remnants of the beast like a dog passed. Gripping a horn of the half-dragon head, he held it aloft and stared at its hollowed eye socket.

"You killed my child!" Fire roared with the ferocity of a volcano. Flame and lava shot up from small cracks in the ground, sleet hissing all about him as the very earth around Fire heated with his anger.

"That was one ugly child!" Angst quipped.

It was all the element could stand. Fire screamed, spinning about and leaning forward to face Angst. A beam of white heat shot from the element's mouth, leaving Angst scant seconds to erect a shield of air. Even with Dulgirgraut's help, he was barely able to protect his friends from the blast. It wasn't a mere gale of fire, it was a constant battering and Angst lost footing as he struggled to keep his ground. Another stream of blinding fire blasted from the element's mouth and hands as it dropped the dragon's head and strode toward them.

"You think that foci protects you?" Fire taunted between attacks.

"We're still here," Angst replied, taking another cautious step back. He held both hands outward, protectively guiding his friends back as well.

"So I see," Fire continued, his voice crackling deeply. "You think you can take me?"

"Your brother Magic wasn't so hard, and I understand he's the worst," Angst taunted. "What are you...second in line? The one that's almost as powerful as Magic?"

"Ooh," Victoria said worriedly. "That was the wrong thing to say."

The stream of fire and lava was ferocious, and Angst could feel his shield cracking as he continued to protect his friends.

"Why do you say that, Princess?" Tarness asked. "What makes you think you even have a clue what's going on—"

"Your mom didn't hate you," Victoria said, facing the large man with a stern gaze. "She left you behind because she had no choice."

"What?" Tarness asked, stuttering weakly. "How do you know that?

"She knows," Angst said over his shoulder, "everything."

"Magic lives, and hates you almost as much as Water—though I doubt any of us hate you that much," Fire warned. "How does it feel, Angst, to be hated by almost all elements?"

"Like this!" Angst yelled as he willed the ground beneath the element to disperse.

Fire dropped out of sight, falling into the hole Angst created. It wasn't near the size of the sinkholes attacking Unsel, but large and deep enough to swallow the giant, living element. Angst took a moment to look back and face the distraught, exhausted, panicked faces of his friends. Angst smiled at them hopefully, baring his teeth with all the cocky he could muster before looking forward once again to see a black and bluish hand crawl from the abyss he had created.

"Run," he yelled, as he expanded the hole.

His efforts only delayed the inevitable. Fire laughed, continuing to move forward as lava rose from the hole, pushing the element out. Angst stood his ground while his friends retreated. He reinforced the shield of air, protecting himself from the advancing element and sought help and intelligence from Dulgirgraut, only to be disappointed again. He continued to retain the power without the knowledge to wield it, and hoped Fire was unaware of his dilemma.

"If all you've got is some hate, I'm pretty sure I can handle that," Angst replied defiantly. "I've been married for a long time!"

The ball of flame came from Fire's entire body. It was the same height as the element, three times as large as Angst, and enough to encompass all of them. Angst threw out a bubble of air to surround the fireball, hoping to slow and smother it. Even with all Dulgirgraut's power, it took every ounce of his considerable will to disperse the missile. A pile of hot coal and cinders dropped mere feet from them.

"Not impressive at all. That took you far too long," Fire said, still walking toward him. "Did you not bond, or does that foci hate you like everyone else?"

Fire threw three more balls of flame in succession. Angst felt a hand on his shoulder again, and knew it to be Dallow. His friends had stopped retreating, each of them reaching out with magic to help him stop the element's attack. Angst stopped two of the fireballs, Dallow and Victoria stopped the third.

"You learn quickly," Dallow said to the princess.

"That's because she's amazing," Angst stated.

Angst went on the offensive. He willed the ground to rise beneath Fire, throwing him up in the air and back toward the dragon's carcass. Angst drove his will to create a mound of earth. Stone and dirt landed on top of the element, covering it in an ever-growing pile. Angst stopped and all went quiet, leaving only the sound of sleet hissing on lava.

CHAPTER FIFTY SIX

"No way it's that easy," Tarness stated.

"Keep backing away," Angst advised, his voice scratchy as he swallowed dry, hot soot.

"Where to?" Tarness asked. "Unsel?"

It could have been laughter, the crackling sound of a forest fire, or lava destroying everything in its path. Fire stepped through the pile of dirt and stone as though covered in mere feathers. It was as if nothing had happened.

"I thought you wielded a foci," Fire said dismissively. "Has magic become so weak, or is it just you?"

"We'll keep doing this until you are finished!" Angst yelled.

"You don't even understand!" Fire roared. "I am finished!"

The element lifted both arms out horizontally, his hands pointed upward and his head lowered in concentration. Shadows rose in the distance, dozens of shapes in dozens of sizes. They flew about recklessly as they approached like an angry swarm of bees.

Dragons.

Dozens of dragons flying toward them. Red and brown and dark and gray, all with bright yellow eyes and hungry expressions. The dragons appeared large, though none as large as their mother. They carried the weight of revenge, an inspired ferocity.

They wanted nothing more than to destroy everything, starting with Angst.

"You killed their mother, and now they hunger for you," Fire taunted. "How can you do it, Al'eyrn? How can you protect your friends, and this city, from my wyrms while fighting me?"

A fireball the size of the mother dragon, larger than Melkier castle, grew from Fire and slowly flew at them. The moment was surreal. This was no mere mushy fireball haphazardly sewn together from old spells long forgotten. This was the entire innards of a volcano, a piece of the sun, and it moved so slowly it seemed they could run away but the ball of flame was so large there was no time to get free.

"I can't stop this one!" Angst yelled, gripping Dulgirgraut's hilt as though throttling the foci.

Dallow's hand was still on his shoulder, and he knew the others remained behind him. This was a losing battle, and Angst was desperate for his friends to run. He threw air and earth at the fireball to no avail. The ball of flame continued toward them, and in spite all his efforts, in spite all of the power from Dulgirgraut, there was nothing he could do to stop it.

Yards became feet, feet became inches and just before the mass of flames ripped apart the fragments of Angst's defenses, the fireball smashed into a giant stone statue. Angst stopped moving back, stopped tripping awkwardly over his friends. Rock and sand from the impact pelted his air shield, shooting fast enough that they would have ripped Angst and friends apart. Angst looked up to see the familiar stone woman standing tall before him. Earth.

"This is how he protects himself, brother! Angst does not stand alone!" Earth roared, lifting her arms as though directing a choir.

The ground around them, the entire city, shook violently. Gamlin of all sizes leaped from the ground to attack the dragon horde. They bored into the flesh of the young dragons, ripped away the scale of elders, and fought through dragonflame to attack the rest. For every dragon supporting Fire, three or four gamlin attacked.

"No!" Fire yelled.

"Yes!" Angst replied, his jaw setting in anger.

"That's where the earthquakes came from!" Tarness said with a worried smile.

Angst and his friends threw more mounds of dirt at Fire. Earth assisted, creating a whirlpool of ground beneath the element's feet. Fire sank into the whirlpool, but the ground burned as it succumbed to his lava.

"This is beyond us, Angst," Dallow yelled. "Their fight isn't ours!"

"I agree!" Hector said. "This war has nothing to do with us. We need to get out of here!"

"I won't argue," Angst stated. "I can't protect everyone. But where do we go?"

They were surrounded by madness. Gamlin were pulled apart by dragons. Dragons were split asunder by gamlin. Earth and Fire came to blows, punching and clawing like angry children. Angst, Dallow, Tarness, and Victoria continued willing their tornado of lava and earth beneath the elements.

"Run!" Earth yelled.

"Where?" Angst asked.

"Enough!" Fire roared, lifting a hand high into the air. "I'm not limited to Ehrde! I'm not one planet! I am all of them!"

Angst and his friends looked up into the blinding sky. A bright ball of flame streaked toward Ehrde, growing as it approached. It was the source of all power and chaos combined in a singularity.

"Eat a star!" Fire said to Angst.

"Protect yourselves!" Earth yelled as she pulled at Fire's arm.

57

"What are you doing?" Earth yelled in panic, her voice loud enough to make Angst's eardrums vibrate painfully. "Do you want to destroy the entire planet?"

"I will not lose to this human, sister," Fire retorted. "Nor to you!"

The star roared loudly as it plummeted to Ehrde. The sound shook the very innards of their ears like a thundering waterfall gone mad. Angst could only imagine how panicked the people of Melkier felt. He was bad at measuring from a distance, but as it came closer, the star appeared roughly the same size as the great dragon he and Victoria had killed. Which meant it was massive.

"But you shall kill so many," Earth said, genuine concern in her gravelly voice.

"I couldn't care less," Fire said sharply. "These humans you fawn over are like parasites. Kill a few, and more take their place."

"Stop this madness, or my gamlin will destroy every dragon in your flock," Earth warned.

Fire laughed at this hollow threat, his lava-formed body churning wildly.

"I will merely create more," Fire finally said.

Earth marched forward and drove two balled fists directly into the other element. Fire tried to pull back but the darkness churning through his body expanded. Soot that normally left his body in dusty clouds now fell to the ground in solid chunks. Dark rock poured into the element as he struggled to push away. Fire screamed as his body was cooled by the injection of new minerals. Bright light shot from his hands and eyes, blasting at Earth relentlessly.

"We need to get out of here!" Victoria pleaded, pulling desperately on Angst's arm.

"Where do we go?" Hector asked helplessly, looking up to measure how much time remained before impact. "Even on swifen we can't ride fast enough to run from a star!"

"It's got to be a night-stone," Dallow said. "Stars are much larger, and couldn't possibly get here that fast."

"That doesn't help," Tarness grumbled. "It's still enormous."

Brainstorming was nigh impossible as their eyes flitted upward nervously. Angst sought his friends for advice. Tarness and Victoria continued staring at the sky falling. Hector looked at Angst and shook his head.

"Can you slow it?" Dallow asked. "Can you give Earth a chance to beat Fire?"

Angst grimaced at the thought. Earth had fought them this entire trip, attacked them at every step. She'd covered people in stone and sent them to kill Angst and his friends. She'd almost succeeded at killing Victoria in the sinkhole. But here she was, protecting them from an element Angst had no chance of destroying with a broken foci. It made no sense.

The elements were damaging each other. Chunks of stone flew from Earth's marble façade, and tiny cracks glowed bright, dripping with hot lava. Fire shuddered violently, unable to melt all the cooling stone and dirt Earth forced into the element's body. It was almost too much for Angst to fathom, and his mind numbed trying to comprehend this madness. He swore to himself that if he were able to help her, if he could buy Earth enough time to destroy Fire, he would do everything possible to finish the job Fire had started and destroy her too.

"Fine," Angst said coldly.

"If it's a night-stone, and not actually a star, it will be made of rock," Dallow advised.

"How does anyone know this?" Tarness asked in panic.

"It's only theory," Dallow answered sheepishly, "but small, oddly shaped rocks have been found embedded in large craters. Many feel they come from up there, so we call them night-stones."

"Go on," Hector encouraged. "Quick."

"Alchemists believe stars are made of fire, so if it's a star we're all dead. And I mean everyone in Ehrde," Dallow said analytically. "If it's a night-stone, it will be element covered in fire. Reach deep and you'll find what you need."

Angst looked to Victoria for some hint that this could possibly work. The worried look on her face said everything, either she couldn't see what was going to happen, or she could and it was going to be bad, but he had to try. Angst pulled his arm free from Victoria's grasp and wielded Dulgirgraut once more. His burgundy pupils glowed brightly as did the light surrounding the foci. Angst pointed the blade at the night-stone and reached with his mind. It was like shoving his hand into boiling water, but when he finally reached in to his elbow, he felt rock.

"It's a night-stone," Angst grunted.

"Push, Angst," Dallow encouraged.

Angst pushed, and forced, and grappled with every ounce of magic he could draw from Dulgirgraut. He leaned his left leg forward, and locked his right as though attempting to topple an invisible wall. There was no stopping the night-stone, there was so much fire surrounding it Angst struggled to find minerals he could anchor to. Angst fought, pushing so hard his entire body tensed and his back strained painfully. The night-stone slowed, but so very little.

Angst grunted with every breath and shook with exhaustion. First his lip quivered, and then his fingers. A muscle in his leg shuddered as fatigue devoured him whole Hector described this to Dallow.

"Pull back, Angst," Dallow yelled.

An entire layer of marble surrounding Earth had chipped

away, like skin fallen to expose muscle. The fine details of hair and nails were gone, the toga Earth wore was no longer recognizable; she was a thinner, roughly carved statue. A patchwork of her former self. Fire suffered in similar fashion—a lopsided shape of man, missing a bite from his head and half his torso.

Tarness dropped to the ground, shaking and covered in sweat. Victoria kneeled beside him and placed a hand on his temple.

"Tarness?" Hector asked.

"He's burning up," Victoria shared.

"He's in shock, or dehydrating, or both," Dallow said.

Angst drew magic from Dulgirgraut with great desperation. He wasn't merely hungry or famished; he was starving for power to slow the giant fiery stone that plunged from the sky. He screamed in anger and frustration.

"This fight is done!" Fire declared.

"No!" Earth and Angst yelled simultaneously.

Earth's left arm dropped to the ground, shattering into tiny pieces. Fire, now much smaller and thinner, redoubled his efforts. An angry crack appeared at the base of Earth's neck, crawling up to her temple. Lava dripped from her eye like a tear as a third of her head landed on the ground with a loud thud. She pulled what remained of her stumpy hands free from Fire's body.

"Bury yourselves, Angst, as deep as you dare," she cried out desperately. "Now!"

Without hesitation, Angst stopped pushing the night-stone. Drawing together the last of his strength, he dug a hole in the ground beneath them, using the rubble to create a protective dome. Mounds of earth and layers of elements rose over them in an arc of protecting shield. His last view of the sky was fire. After putting Dulgirgraut behind his back, he turned around with his arms wide and attempted to tackle everyone to the ground. When they all landed, when everyone stopped squirming, Angst created the largest, thickest, strongest air shield he could while continuing to tunnel deeper, throwing piles of dirt and stone over them.

"I'm so sorry," Angst said, grateful that at least nobody saw the tears streaming down his cheeks. "This isn't what I wanted. I'm so sorry."

Earth turned away from Fire, diving to cover the mound over Angst and his friends, bridging herself over them for protection. Some of the remaining gamlin disappeared into the ground for safety. The star, the giant night-stone, landed with the sound and ferocity of cataclysm and nightmare. A hot, blinding flash of light was soon followed by a circular blaze of wind and fire that destroyed everything in its path. The gamlin that remained above ground, along with the dragons flying to escape, all burned away like dry leaves in a forest fire.

Angst panicked in the smothering confines of their earthen protection. Victoria gripped his arm with thin fingers and whimpered, but he couldn't console her. Every ounce of his concentration went to keeping the barrier up. The ground shook and their bunker heated from the blast above.

"Dallow, reinforce my air shield before we cook!" Angst said.

"It will use up too much air," Dallow replied in concern. "We'll run out!"

"But we will be dead before we have a chance to breathe it!" Angst yelled. "Do it now!"

* * * *

Above ground, an unnatural quiet had replaced the chaotic battle. Thick ashes slowly drifted to the crater left by the night-stone. Sleet began to fall as though it was finally safe to leave clouds. The thin, broken element of Fire stood in a pile of ash and rock. Smooth blackened stones fell from his body as he continued to disgorge the minerals Earth had forced into him. He surveyed the damage, bright light shining from his smile. Everything was dead. Dragons, gamlin, Earth. All that remained was an ashen scar carved deep into Melkier.

"Do you see what you made me do, sister?" Fire said to nobody, reveling proudly in himself. "I had to kill you. I had to kill most of my children, and yours, as well as these pitiful humans…all for what?"

Fire looked about at the devastation, smiling to himself at the chaos wrought this day. No life remained and Earth was destroyed. This was indeed a good day…but then it was always a good day when everything burned.

"You have once again placed your faith in these humans, and to what avail?" Fire asked. "All that is left is this nothing that surrounds us."

There was no reply as the world was quiet save the constant drumming patter and sizzle of sleet on hot lava. Fire nonchalantly strode over the battlefield to find half of Earth's face. He picked it up, but it was nothing more than a statue now—the remaining eye and half a gritty mouth were unmoving.

"Goodbye, sister," Fire said to Earth. "I'll see you in two thousand years."

He tossed the broken head to the ground. It rolled several times to land face up, staring vacantly at the sky. Fire looked about one last time before melting into the ground, disappearing into a thin whirlpool of lava, leaving behind darkness, and dust, and ash.

58

A shadow fell across the fake throne room as large gray Fulk'han men and their pastel-colored escorts strode into the room. The gray men eyed the few soldiers of Unsel, sneering down their tense anticipation with a sense of ownership. Rook could barely contain himself, a spring coiled so tight it could snap, or launch, without warning. Jaden had given up holding the man back, staring at Tyrell for a sign.

Tyrell gave him nothing, his fading focus on the queen as he gripped his bleeding arm. The sword master had paled and appeared too woozy, even for the blood gently leaking from his wound. Isabelle shot sidelong glares from the newly crowned princess to the gray man who now seemed in charge. Her bearing was one of impatience, and in spite of the imminent takeover, it was obvious she didn't intend to relinquish her throne.

The Fulk'han who took lead walked to her, his shoulders held rigid with pride and his left arm covered in scars. He appeared larger than the others, with almost every bone and ridge of his exterior painted white or black. Isabelle wondered if this indicated rank, or kills. He glared at the guards standing in front of her protectively but otherwise ignored them. The leader looked the queen up and down before turning dismissively to face Alloria. He bowed his head in a gesture that was almost polite.

"The Fulk'han Empire is grateful for your assistance, Majesty," he boomed for everyone in the hall to hear. "But the time of Unsel is now past, and you will soon join the rest of the guilty as we decide the best use for your resources."

Jaden was surprised she didn't flinch at the inclusion or the incrimination. Alloria quickly searched the room for help, but all eyes were cold and accusing. She ignored the glares and continued searching.

"Am I not to rule Unsel?" Alloria asked, finally meeting the leader's gaze.

"You will manage Unsel as we incorporate your nation into our empire," he replied proudly.

"I don't understand," Rook whispered. "Why does the queen remain silent?"

"She keeps staring at Alloria," Jaden replied. "I think she's waiting for something."

"Who are you to make these new demands?" Alloria asked.

"I am Guldrich," he replied. "General of Fulk'han."

"This wasn't the agreement," Alloria said, taking a challenging step forward.

"The empire's needs have changed," Guldrich said.

"What needs?" Alloria asked. "I agreed to be allies, nothing more."

"You think we would trust your treacherous ways with leadership?" he asked. The large man beat against his bone armor twice with a balled fist to get her attention. "You are a nation of spies and destroyers. You are godkillers and don't deserve to be called allies."

"That's your final word?" Alloria said coolly. Her eyes locked onto the back of the hall, and she barely suppressed a grin.

"Be quiet, child, before I make you my consort," he said down his nose with a loud sniff.

Alloria's full attention was on this leader. A funny grin crawled across her face, and she laughed out loud. A genuine belly laugh that made her grip her stomach. She appeared mad, or at the very least, unthreatened. The gray man looked about, confused and embarrassed, as though his very manhood had been questioned.

She caught her breath and raised a hand. "I'm sorry," she gasped. "That was unexpected. I bed with men not freaks."

Guldrich shook with rage, his hand clenching into a ball.

"Now, Vars!" she yelled.

"What?" the Fulk'han questioned in shock.

Vars ran into the room with platoons of soldiers, inciting war and wielding chaos. The Fulk'hans at the back of the room were shred like helpless cattle, instantly torn to pieces, unable to defend against the sheer mass of attackers. With the energy and power of a younger man, Vars sliced wildly with his great sword. The light blue head of a Fulk'han woman flew from her body, wincing as it was thrown hard against a nearby wall.

"I've got to get some of this!" Rook said.

Rook leaped forward, grabbing the throat of the nearest gray man with his bare hand and tearing it out. The beast dropped his polearm, desperately scratching at his missing flesh before collapsing to the stone floor. Rook threw the mess of flesh into the eyes of another gray man before picking up the polearm and skewering him.

"Me too," Jaden agreed. "You kill those two, I get the rest."

Jaden studied the room, identifying where every Fulk'han stood. He concentrated, reaching out with his mind. A bright orange glow surrounded his arms, making everyone nearby step back nervously. A gray man saw the glow and launched into the air. He screamed loudly as Rook's polearm expertly drove between protruding ribs in his armor. Rook flung the dying man aside and brandished his sword.

Rook stood before Jaden protectively as the younger man continued reaching out. Three more Fulk'han took note of the scream, turning away from the approaching Unsel soldiers.

"You have to do it now!" Rook commanded.

Jaden grunted from the effort as he let loose his spell. Dozens of Fulk'han soldiers cried out. Just as Angst had slammed Jaden deep into the ground, Jaden drove the Fulk'han knee deep into the marble floor of the throne room. All of them, instantly stuck, every single Fulk'han locked in place. Jaden collapsed in exhaustion.

"Nice work," Rook said, patting him on the shoulder. "You did it!"

"Finally...something right," Jaden whispered, gripping his racing heart. He saw stars and breathed fast, desperately trying to avoid passing out.

"Kill them all!" Isabelle finally spoke.

"Wait," Alloria interrupted, pointing at her 'consort.' "Keep him alive."

With a nod from the queen, order was returned in blood and death. All other Fulk'han were summarily executed, and every death left a body that fell back or leaned forward grotesquely, unable to completely fall over due to Jaden's entrapment. Within minutes, the battle was over and the Unsel throne was free from conquest. Before Isabelle could ask why Guldrich should be allowed to live, Alloria marched forward.

She lifted her dress to reveal a long, thin dagger strapped to her leg. She unsheathed it, driving it deep into the unsuspecting gray man's side. He screamed in pain but, trapped in the floor, couldn't defend himself. The soldiers protecting Isabelle grabbed his muscular arms to keep him from beating the young princess. She wiped the black blood covering her hand onto her adversary then spit in the large man's face.

"You'll die for your treachery!" Guldrich yelled.

"Vars!" Alloria called.

The large man in his bulky, decorative plate armor pushed his way through the mess of crowd and soldiers. He walked to the princess and lowered his head respectfully.

"Majesty?" he asked.

"Remove his tongue," she commanded.

"Wait," Isabelle yelled.

Vars immediately gripped the gray man's jaw to pry his mouth open. He unsheathed a sick, angry dagger while wrestling the man's tongue free with his armored hand. Without remorse,

Vars shoved the dagger into the man's mouth and carved out Guldrich's tongue. He pulled on it roughly, cutting at a remaining string of muscle and flesh until the tongue was removed. The gray man gurgled a scream, yelling profanities nobody could understand as blackened blood poured from his mouth.

"I hope you know how to write," Alloria said coldly. "To tell your *Emperor* of only one country this: you are not welcome in Unsel. His treachery, his attempt to coerce and control has failed. Just as we killed your *God*, we will kill each of you. From this point on Unsel is at war with Fulk'han. Brace yourselves for what you have wrought this day, because it is the end to everything you hold true and safe."

The Fulk'han were silenced, but the room erupted. Lords and ladies, soldiers and knights, all cheered at the princess's defiance. The corners of her broad lips curled. Finally, the reverence she had sought during the coronation. Alloria did her best to ignore the cheers while continuing to stare down the helpless man.

"Vars," she commanded.

"Yes, Your Majesty," he replied, standing at attention, dropping the tongue to the floor with an unceremonious splat.

"Cauterize this thing's mouth so it doesn't die," she stated firmly. "Then have him escorted to Rohjek. If they haven't been compromised, release him to their company so he can deliver my message."

Vars bowed deeply, though his eyes were flat and cold.

"Jaden," Alloria called out. "Please come forward."

Rook assisted Jaden to his feet, helping the weak man through the crowd.

"Yes, Your Majesty," Jaden said, almost whispering from exhaustion.

"Please release this Fulk'han," she requested.

Jaden nodded and took a deep breath. Grateful there was only one, he set the gray man free. Alloria smiled in appreciation while Vars escorted the lone living Fulk'han from the makeshift throne room. She spun about and dropped to one knee before Queen Isabelle.

"Please forgive me, my queen," Alloria pleaded. "It happened so fast, I worried for your safety."

"The rest of my kingdom?" Isabelle asked. "How does it fare?"

"You ordered me to send all troops to defend our borders against the monsters and their sinkholes," Alloria said quietly. "I failed to do this. When I learned of the attempted coup, I held them back and sent them to protect the city. Unsel is safe. I'm sorry for not heeding your commands."

Isabelle stared down at the young princess and placed a thoughtful hand on the woman's honey-brown hair. She patted it in consideration, smiling proudly.

"Now you see," Isabelle squawked aloud, looking over the crowd. "Now you see why she is your princess. Now you see why she is my true heir. Trust her, trust this hero of Unsel, for she has saved us all. Alloria has preserved life as we know it."

The room erupted once again in cheers and applause.

Jaden looked at Rook with a smirk as he clapped encouragingly. Rook clapped politely until he heard a loud retching. The Captain Guard was leaned over, holding onto his knees. Rook made his way to the older man quickly.

"Poison," Tyrell whispered, sweat pouring from his forehead, "...in the blade."

Rook helped Tyrell stand. Queen Isabelle pressed her way through the guards and placed an arm on her champion's shoulder. He bowed his head then looked into her eyes. She smiled warmly, acknowledging his success in battle and thanking him without words. If one were to stand close to Tyrell, closer than appropriate, as close as the queen stood, you would have almost seen him smile too.

"See him to the infirmary," Isabelle commanded of a nearby soldier.

The queen took several steps to Maarja and Jintorich, who remained on her shoulder. She looked at the two of them, inspecting both as if deciding their fate.

Isabelle sighed deeply with both respect and resignation.

419

"Thank you for your assistance, friends," she said politely. "Please find comfort in your rooms. We will meet later so I can thank you more formally."

"Thank you, Your Majesty." Maarja nodded then turned and made her own path through the crowd. "I'm impressed," she said to Jintorich. "You fought fiercely."

"We make a good team," Jintorich said proudly from her shoulder. "I can get down…"

"You may do as you choose, my friend," Maarja said respectfully. "You are welcome to stay."

Jaden elbowed his way to get to the queen.

"Your Majesty," he pleaded. "Please, a moment."

She ignored him.

"I have a message from your daughter," he said, a little too loudly.

Isabelle stared at him coldly, her patience at an end. There had already been too much for one day—too much magic, too much fighting—and she'd had enough. Her missing daughter, the adventurer who hadn't come home, dared send a message through a wielder?

She pulled out a finger and unleashed her onslaught on the young man. "No! No, you don't have a message from my daughter!" she screeched in her highest voice. "There are no messages I want to hear from her! That is enough magics for one day in my court! Do you understand?"

Without waiting for a response, Isabelle stormed from the room.

Jaden swallowed hard, feeling very small and alone as the crowd dispersed. He could hear his own breathing, and a grotesque scraping sound as soldiers attempted to pry Fulk'han bodies from the floor behind him. In spite of his efforts and his desperate desire to please the princess, he had failed at the one task she had asked of him.

He ground his teeth in frustration as he asked himself, what would Angst have done differently?

59

"Angst." Victoria choked on the thin air. "We need to get out. I can't breathe."

"Nothing left," Angst tried to explain. He had buried them too deep; he could barely draw enough power from Dulgirgraut to maintain their protective dome. "I can't push us free."

There was no reply. He flexed the arm Victoria held onto and felt no response.

"Anyone?" Angst pleaded.

Still no answer.

Had he failed? After all this, was there nobody left? He sobbed, fighting for air, for magic, for power from Dulgirgraut. It wasn't enough. There was nothing left. What an awful way to die—killing his friends in a desperate attempt to bond with this broken foci. Lost and forgotten, buried deep in the ground. If only he knew earthspeak, he could've apologized to Heather for his folly.

Bright spots blinked in the distance. This was the end; he was passing out.

There was a muffled crunching, like someone eating stale bread. The sound grew louder, and pebbles broke through his air shield, dropping onto his face. His magic must have been fading. Fingers gripped his arms.

"Tori, is that you?" he choked out. "You need to cut your nails."

The only reply was a deep horting sound. A gamlin pulled

421

and tugged at his arm. Angst gripped tight to Dulgirgraut with his other hand. Rock and dirt scratched and slid against his face, tearing at his cheeks. He wanted to scream, plead for the creature to stop, beg for the nightmare to end. The gamlin continued dragging him while another pushed on his feet. And then, air. Sweet, delicious air, as the gamlin popped out of the ground dragging Angst along.

Angst coughed as he drew in desperate, hungry breaths. He rested on all fours as the ground, almost too hot to touch, sapped his remaining strength.

"The others," Angst pleaded. "Save my friends."

He fell over onto his side and passed out.

* * * *

Angst woke to find his friends lying beside him. He groggily rolled over, pushing himself to his knees. The ground was still hot, and his mouth dry as drought. Angst tried calling out to Victoria, but his throat was filled with painful cracks. He slowly crawled to her, shaking her arm. She grunted and Angst closed his eyes as relief and gratitude swept through him in a dizzying tide.

He pressed on to his friends, shaking each of them while regaining some of his own strength. His gauntlets were gone, and the ground was hot enough to loosen the pores on his hands, making the ash feel clingy. With every other crawl, he brushed ash and dirt from his raw palms onto his muddy cloak. It was uncomfortable, but it didn't matter. They lived, somehow. Had the gamlin really saved them?

Angst stood on shaky legs then leaned over to pick up Dulgirgraut. With his hand outstretched, he hesitated. The blade had saved his life, but failed him throughout the battle. He needed it to live, but he hated the foci for its reluctance to help. Still, what choice did he have? With chagrin, Angst lifted the sword, placing it between his shoulder blades. He hoped it wouldn't be needed for a very long time.

Angst looked about at the devastation as his friends regained consciousness. They were in the center of a crater miles around with edges so high they blocked the distant castle. The sleet had been replaced with flakes of cool snow that melted instantly on the ground. The melt had gone on long enough that patches of ground were slick, and Angst shuffled his feet slowly to keep from falling.

He tried to help Victoria up only to have his hand pushed away. Angst instinctively worried that he had upset her.

"Stop it," she replied, reading his thoughts.

Angst nodded as he helped Dallow while Victoria assisted Hector. Tarness was the last to stand. The large man looked near death. His eyes were yellow, and skin peeled from his thick lips. Tarness constantly licked them, his hands shaking as he brushed dirt from his face.

"Why are we alive?" Hector asked in his gruff voice, already standing straighter than everyone else.

"Gamlin," Angst answered. "But I don't know why."

Hector nodded in understanding. They looked about warily. The crater was a small glimpse of the devastation wrought by the warring elements, and they were all anxious to leave.

"Which way to Unsel?" Angst finally asked.

Hector looked up into the sky and gauged their position.

"This way," Hector stated. "Follow me."

Angst threw Dallow's arm over his shoulder and stumbled along in Hector's wake. After walking for ten minutes, Hector stopped and pointed. Directly ahead, a large, gray stone rested in the middle of the blackened, muddy pit. They approached cautiously as it was the only remains amidst all the damage. The rock was curved, like a waning moon. A singular orb protruded over a roughly carved slit that at one time could have been a mouth.

"Earth," Angst stated coolly.

The eye opened, making everyone jump. It blinked rapidly, as though shaking off the shock of being only part of a head. The mouth, the half slit, opened. Tiny pebbles fell from its broken crevice with every movement, dropping to the muddy ground like spilled blood.

"Angst," she said in a weak, gravelly voice. "You live."

"Barely," Angst said. "But yes, we still live."

There was no reply. The mouth opened and closed unnaturally, like a fish out of water, and Earth blinked slowly.

"I suppose I should thank you," Angst said. "Your gamlin saved us."

"Good," she said quietly. "They are trustworthy companions. I am glad you survived."

"Are you?" Angst asked, handing Dallow off to Hector.

Angst kneeled beside the giant half head of Earth.

"Why do you say that?" she asked defensively. "I have been protecting you—"

"You tried to kill us!" Angst spat. "Your gamlin have been attacking Unsel for months!"

"They did no such thing," Earth said defensively. "Not a single human was killed."

"You tried to kill Victoria," Angst yelled, pointing back at the princess. "I was barely able to save her from the sinkhole you created."

"You do not know what you speak of," Earth replied. "Water hates you more than anyone. She probably set the trap for you and your princess."

"What of those poor people you covered in stone?" Angst asked. "Cooked alive, and then you forced their bodies to attack us!"

"No!" Earth said. "I covered those poor people to protect them from dragonfire. I know nothing about this attack!"

"Lies," Angst argued. "All of it!"

"Angst, you do not understand," Earth said. "I have always believed in humans. I try to protect them, despite their insolence and foolish nature. Angst, I intended you to be my host. You wield mineral so beautifully, so naturally, you could have been my champion."

"I would never be your champion!" Angst yelled.

"I know this," she said sadly. "But still, you could..." Pebbles fell from the missing half of her mouth with every word spoken. Her head began to collapse in on itself. Victoria put a calming hand on Angst's arm, but he pulled it free.

"Your host? Are we nothing but tools for you?" Angst went on, ignoring her statement. "You elements see us as insects. Something to manipulate as a part of your game."

"Some do, Angst," Earth agreed.

"I've had enough! I'll be the host for humans!" Angst declared. "The champion for wielders!"

"There is no such thing! No host for humans!" Earth chuckled.

"There is now," Angst stated coldly. "As far as I'm concerned, one down, four to go."

Earth didn't reply, closing her one eye as if finished. Little of the head remained—an oval that outlined the eye and mouth. Angst walked away, waving for his friends to follow as he headed once again in the direction Hector had suggested.

"I hope one day you understand, Angst," Earth said weakly. "Maybe this will help..."

Angst stopped with a sigh and turned around to look at the head of Earth one last time.

"What?" he snapped.

"My gamlin," she replied. "The remaining gamlin are yours."

Everything went dark and Angst winced as he felt a pinch in his mind. He swallowed back bile that burned his dry throat. Opening his eyes, Angst found himself on one knee, unable to speak, the palms of both hands shoved against his temples.

"To the winner go the spoils," Earth stated matter-of-factly. Then quietly, so very quietly, she murmured, "I could still win."

"What's this?" Dallow asked.

"I don't know." Angst rose with renewed energy and returned to the head. "What are you talking about?"

Earth said nothing, the head now still as a stone. It was too much. Too much frustration, too much unknown, too much failure... He kicked and stomped in anger, finally wielding

Dulgirgraut and hammering against the statue head until nothing was left but rubble. His tantrum abated, he leaned against the sword, rubbing tears from his eyes. Victoria looked at Tarness and Hector helplessly.

"Feel better?" Hector asked.

"No," Angst said with a sob, wiping streams of tears from his eyes. "Maybe. A little."

Victoria walked to him and gripped his hand. She pulled Angst to follow.

"Come on," she said. "Let's get out of here."

60

Angst felt stunned, as if he had suffered a blow to the head, and his friends appeared similarly distracted. They had witnessed great displays of power that were far beyond comprehension, and each of them struggled with it in their own way. Victoria pulled loose strands from her curly blond hair. Hector spun the point of a dagger on his hand, flipping it around the back of his knuckles until the handle landed in his palm. Tarness chewed ferociously on nuts from a pouch around his waist. Dallow's eyes glowed white behind his bandage, cataloging everything that had happened as if writing his own book. They waited, and Angst knew he needed to help them focus on something; his friends needed a goal above all else.

"Rose," Angst said. "We need to find Rose."

"Yes," Dallow said hopefully, his eye sockets dimming as he lifted his head.

"Hector, how long do we have before the sinkholes reach Unsel?" Angst questioned.

"A couple of weeks, Angst," Hector said, catching the handle of the dagger between two fingers and tossing it up into the air. "We should probably go back now, unless you know where Rose is?"

"I don't," Angst said, "but I do have an idea."

"I've heard that before," Victoria said, rolling her eyes, letting go of her hair and pulling the two red cloaks tight around her.

427

"We need to set up camp," Angst suggested. "Somewhere safe...away from here."

"South," Hector advised. "Melkier soldiers will be looking for us eventually, and would expect us to head north toward home."

"Let's go," Angst ordered.

They turned about, following Hector southward at a brisk pace for several minutes until reaching the crater wall. The mud and stone had melted and then hardened, creating a thick layer of blackened tile shards. It would have been impossible to scale with bare hands, but the swifen scrambled up the edge with sure feet. At the top of the wall, everyone looked back at the devastation. The crater reached the castle. The night-stone had destroyed half of Melkier city. Angst wanted to weep, but couldn't. All his emotions seemed to ball up and wedge in his chest.

Victoria patted his arm gently. "It wasn't your fault."

"Maybe," he replied with a grimace. "But I won't let this happen again."

* * * *

They rode hard for several hours, avoiding main roads and towns. The sleet and snow meant sloppy conditions, often slowing their passage to wherever Hector was leading them. Angst was cold, but refused to take his cloak from Victoria. The frigid air might have bitten, but the numbness helped him focus. So much had gone wrong, so many lives lost. They had won the foci, but at what cost? Dulgirgraut either didn't work right, or was so different from Chryslaenor that Angst had a long way to scale up its learning curve.

"We should stop here," Hector grumbled. "Before it starts to sleet again."

Hector had found a mostly dry clearing surrounded by thick pine and low-hanging asten trees. The woods provided ample cover for a small campfire, and the tree line would help protect them from blasting winds that could sneak up on them in an open field.

They dismounted and began removing satchels from the swifen. Victoria kicked sticks and rocks away from a spot near the campfire Tarness was building.

"When you're done, Tarness, would you mind helping me set up my tent?" Victoria asked.

"Of course, Your Majesty," he said, stacking several dry sticks to a point.

"That won't be necessary," Angst said.

"Pardon?" she asked haughtily.

"You can stay in my tent tonight," Angst offered, his shoulders already squaring off for a confrontation.

"I'll be fine on my own, thank you," Victoria said coolly, continuing to kick uncomfortable rubble away from her ideal camping spot.

"I need you to stay with me tonight," Angst asked. "Please."

"No."

The others were visibly uncomfortable, shuffling their feet and staring at each other from the trenches of another argument.

"Why now, Tori?" he asked, his jaw setting in frustration. "Of all nights, why do you have to ditch me now?"

"Angst," Dallow pleaded. "Can't you just let it rest?"

"No, Angst," Victoria said.

"I just got my ass stomped by a giant man who is constantly on fire!" Angst yelled, his hands shaking with anger. "Can't you please be here for me?"

"She said no, Angst," Hector said, grabbing one of Angst's hands in an attempt to calm him down.

Angst's eyes flashed red, and Hector immediately let go and took a cautious step back. Angst squeezed his eyes shut and clenched his hands into fists, taking several deep breaths to calm himself.

"I was going to let Tori explain later, when she was ready," Angst said quietly.

"Angst?" she asked.

"It's part of what she can do," Angst continued. "When we sleep next to each other, we share dreams."

"Really?" Dallow asked, his interest piqued.

"Usually I can't remember my dreams, even the foci dreams, but with Tori I can," Angst continued. "That first night she came into my tent from the storm, we dreamed of Rose. That's how we knew she was safe."

"So she is okay," Dallow said with great relief.

"We dreamed of her back in that town...the one where we stayed at the inn..." Angst sought the name but couldn't remember. "Anyway, now that I'm bonded to a foci, I'm hoping we can pinpoint where she is."

Victoria sighed. "Fine."

"So, you want me to believe the reason you two have been sharing a bed is because you can remember your dreams?" Hector said with a raised eyebrow.

"What exactly is it you do, Victoria?" Dallow asked, ignoring Hector.

"I'm a seer," Victoria explained quietly. "I can see people's lives, their past, their future, or in some cases futures."

"Futures?" Tarness asked.

"The path isn't always clear, and lately what I can do hasn't worked very well," Victoria said forlornly. "So I see several futures that could happen. Sometimes I can choose the path."

"I wonder why it isn't working," Dallow asked. "I suppose with the introduction of the foci and elements...there's so much going on, who could possibly know everything that could happen?"

With the suddenness of a springing mountain lion, Hector threw a knife at Victoria's chest. She caught it expertly and chucked it to the ground, the knifepoint sticking into the root of a tree between his feet with a vibrating thud.

"More than a seer, you have foresight too. Which explains a lot...like, how you beat me," Hector said with a smile. "But you wouldn't have caught that if your abilities weren't in check."

"That was a dangerous way to test her," Angst said, furious at

Hector.

"She already tested herself when we dueled, Angst, so calm yourself," Hector said, raising a hand.

Angst cocked his head warily, but remained beside Victoria.

"That was brave, Your Majesty," Hector said with great respect. "Dueling me, and not knowing whether or not your foresight would work when we fought."

"So do you know what we're thinking now?" Tarness asked in concern, conspicuously not looking at the shiny mail contraption holding her breasts aloft behind the cloak.

Victoria laughed out loud and winked at the large man. "Sometimes it's not too hard to figure out," she said. "But if I concentrate, when I'm close to someone, then yes."

"And you still hang out with him?" Tarness asked, jerking a thumb toward Angst.

"No kidding!" she proclaimed.

Everyone but Angst joined her in a brief round of laughter, while he blushed uncontrollably.

She placed a forgiving hand on his arm. "He's actually harmless, most of the time," Victoria said with a droll smile. "But you can't always control yourself in your dreams."

"Hey!" Angst said defensively while everyone laughed again.

"I'm kidding," she said. "Why don't you set up our tent before I change my mind?"

Angst looked lost, or ready to break, too sensitive to the teasing. He couldn't shake off the destruction they had witnessed in Melkier. He had just bonded with a foci, and barely regained his life in the process. He had lost the fight with the element Fire. Angst worried about Heather and felt helpless, unable to protect her. It was all too much, and Victoria gave him a genuine hug, long and meaningful, while he regained his composure.

"Gross," Tarness teased. "I'm going to collect firewood."

"Still, that just isn't right," Hector said, shaking his head. "I'll see what I can find to eat."

When Victoria finally pulled away, Angst nodded gratefully. He avoided eye contact while unfolding their tent.

"Some hero," he said in a small voice.

"You're doing great," she answered sincerely. "You're my hero, Angst."

"Yeah?" he asked, standing up a little straighter.

"Of course you are, silly," Victoria said, almost rolling her eyes.

"Your Majesty?" Dallow asked. "I don't mean to interrupt."

"You're not interrupting, Dallow," Victoria replied. "You want to know about your eyes."

"Yes," Dallow said hungrily.

"I kept trying to see in Melkier." Victoria walked over and held his hand. "In spite of Hector's confidence, I don't completely understand.

Dallow licked his lips in anticipation, his breathing irregular as he concentrated, trying to control it.

"I don't know what will happen with your eyes," Victoria said finally.

"Oh," Dallow replied, sounding distraught.

"But somehow you will see again!" Victoria said hopefully. "Of that, I'm sure."

"How?" Dallow's grin was wide, and he gripped her hand tight. "When?"

"I don't know how, Dallow," she answered. "But I think it could happen tomorrow."

61

Unsel

Tyrell entered the infirmary with the help of a guard. The smell was normally enough to keep him away, even when ill or injured. The pungent odor of medicines overlaid with a thick scent of sickness and decay was poorly masked by a potpourri dish that only made things worse. The room seemed deafeningly silent after the recent battle, and Tyrell all but collapsed against a nearby table. He refused to lie down in front of the soldier, hating the weakness he'd already displayed.

"Go get the physician," Tyrell muttered around a thick tongue, pushing the man away. "She's probably tending to wounded in the hall. Tell her it's poison."

"Right away, Captain Guard," he said, his face concerned.

The soldier rushed from the room. Within seconds, there was a crash in the hallway followed by a grunt. Undoubtedly the guard or physician tripping over one of the surgery pans. He wished she would be careful, and hurry. He rarely fell ill, and the kingdom faced far too many unknowns for him to be confined to bed rest. Whatever poisons were slowing him, the physician would have a cure. Tyrell sluggishly turned his head to greet her, gripping his stomach to keep his insides inside.

Vars stood at the entrance, his blade dripping fresh blood, his lip twitching as a malevolent grin spread across his long face. Tyrell sighed helplessly, too weak to even wield his sword, too

433

close to death to speak.

"The physician won't be coming," Vars said. "But I'm sure you've figured that out already."

Melkier

King Gaarder took a long draw of warm thickwine. He felt cold, and weak. His old hands shook as he emptied the last of the bottle into his goblet. Gaarder's tongue was dry and heavy from drink, and his heart weak from the death and destruction under his rule. Half his city was gone; the devastation wrought by dragons and magic had literally reached his doorstep. All Gaarder could see from the entrance of Melkier Castle was wasteland, and crater. When they'd shut the castle doors, shadows of guards were burned into them.

He had lost his tears and succumbed to a sort of emotional exhaustion. Gaarder's heart wrenched painfully with every breath, and each drink numbed his pain so barely. Crloc had been right about the dangers of magic, but even he couldn't have foreseen such raw power. How could they possibly defend themselves now? At this point, there was nothing left—no kingdom, no hope, only survival.

Nicadilia floated into the room, closing the door behind her. She smiled at her father before nervously inspecting their surroundings. They were alone.

"My daughter," Gaarder slurred weakly. He waved her over. "Join me for a drink."

Nicadilia walked to her father and glanced at the bottle. "The wine is gone, father," she said. "There's nothing left."

Gaarder burst into tears. Dropping his goblet to the floor, he covered his eyes in shame. The goblet dented on impact, and the last of the thickwine ran onto the tile floor.

"I was a fool," Gaarder sobbed. "Crloc was right, but so was Angst. Princess Victoria came as an ally, and now we either go to war with Unsel, or we surrender."

"No!" Nicadilia yelled. "We cannot surrender!"

"It's time we set aside our pride, Nici," Gaarder said. "While our kingdom still remains at all intact."

Nicadilia swallowed hard and reluctantly leaned forward to give the king an awkward hug around his neck. Her ears buzzed loudly, and the ruby ring on her finger glowed. It urged her to squeeze harder and tighter.

"What is this?" Gaarder asked, looking down at the ring.

"I can't," Nicadilia said aloud to the ring, hyperventilating from panic. "He's my father."

There was a dark whisper in her ear. "He was."

Nicadilia tried pulling away from the embrace, but her hand thrust forward to his chest like a talon. It gripped through the king's soft tunic hard enough to pull at the flabby skin beneath. Black sparks from the ring dove into the king's heart. Gaarder writhed in his chair, grasping at her hand but unable to move it. The queen regent pulled at the gripping hand with her other, desperate to stop the attack. A bright red hue surrounded the ring, and the king's heart raced faster and faster under her fingertips. The old man pushed at her arm and his feet flailed helplessly, until he stopped moving entirely.

Rohjek

Five Unsel soldiers waited at the Rohjek border with a Fulk'han prisoner in tow. A gag was tied tight around the Fulk'han's mouth, and heavy rope bound his hands behind his back. He looked angry and leaned to one side as though favoring a wound.

Three Rohjek knights of the Red Brigade approached fast, the hardened red leather of their chest armor easily visible. They stopped barely across the border and saluted politely, their hands flaring upward over their right eyebrows.

"We received your message but hours ago," a Red Brigade knight stated. "This is your prisoner?"

"Yes, Guldrich here needs an escort to Fulk'han," the Unsel soldier replied. "He carries a message for their leader, from Princess Alloria."

The soldier from Unsel dismounted and handed the reins of Guldrich's horse to the Red Brigade knight. The knight nodded politely as he stared down the prisoner.

"Is there anything else we need to know?" the knight questioned.

"Ah, well, his tongue's been removed," the soldier said. "And he's been stabbed between his ribs. Honestly, I'm surprised he lives."

The Fulk'han struggled in his ropes, yelling loud enough that dark, bloody spittle drooled down his gray chin.

"These Fulk'han are formidable," the knight remarked. "How fares Unsel?"

"Unsel remains steadfast," the soldier stated proudly. "As always, we appreciate the support and assistance of Rohjek."

Each side saluted before the small band of soldiers from Unsel rode off at a gallop. The Fulk'han waited until they were out of sight before yelling at the brigade knights and struggling against his restraints. The leader of the knights dismounted and untied him.

"Is it true, that you are without a tongue?" he asked.

"I wath," the Fulk'han said with a wince. "Itsh almotht grown back."

"Unsel is lost to us then?"

"For now," the Fulk'han stated bitterly.

Guldrich rode his horse around the Red Brigade soldiers, like an animal set free. Drool and blood from his mouth made him appear ravenous as he stared after the Unsel guards who had delivered him. Guldrich spat on Unsel ground before crossing the Rohjek border and galloping off to Fulk'han.

Nordruaut

Niihlu stood before the wall of a large glacier. He stared down at the long handle of an enormous axe sticking out from the wall unnaturally. The great, curved blade could be seen deep within the frozen confines of the wall. Niihlu braced himself for the cold as he removed his furs and leathers. Powerful young muscles contracted in the sub-zero conditions of northern Nordruaut.

"How did you know this would be here?" King Rasaol of Nordruaut asked the tall, thin man beside him. "No one hunts this far north."

"I know things, Your Majesty," the man replied.

The man looked oddly out of place among the accompanying Nordruaut horde on their wooly bookeen mounts. He wasn't quite as tall as the Nordruaut, but stood just shy of seven feet. The man could have been a hundred, or no age at all, with his bald head and hairless face. He was garbed in long brown robes, which flailed about wildly in the northern winds.

"Niihlu has defeated many to wield this foci," Rasaol said. "He is a mighty hunter. Will he live?"

"Eh." The man shrugged. When he saw the king displeased at this response, he embellished. "He was not born to wielding a foci, but I have conditioned him to do so. It will be damaging, but he is my test."

"We cannot be weak before our enemies," the king said thoughtfully. He looked at Niihlu and nodded.

Niihlu shivered, naked in the icy grip of winds and winter. He gripped the long handle of the foci, it sang to him shouting its name *Ghorfjend The Blitz*. Its power flowed through his veins like streams of ice.

"The foci is mine!" he yelled victoriously then paused. "Wait, what is this?"

Shards of ice formed over Niihlu's hand, crawling up his arm and across his chest. He instinctively pulled his head back as a sheet of ice covered his neck.

"This is why he had to be naked," the old man said calmly.

Niihlu screamed for a moment as an icy shell formed around his mouth and over his head. It enveloped his body, and Niihlu remained unmoving, a frozen statue.

"He is dead?" the king asked, astonished by the sight.

"Maybe," the old man replied. "This is where it gets interesting."

A crack like thunder made the otherwise sedate wooly mounts shuffle nervously. Several more followed, and bits of ice chipped away from Niihlu. The wall split down the center, large shards breaking away, each landing with a noisy thud in the deep snow. The split grew wider until the giant axe could be pulled free. The ice around Niihlu shattered, shooting in every direction.

"That's why we aren't standing next to him," the old man stated, brushing away chips of ice.

Niihlu turned to face the other Nordruaut and held the weapon high in triumph. They cheered and yelled at his success. Niihlu approached the king, who gasped as thin sheets of ice formed about the Nordruaut's naked body and fell to the ground like frozen sweat. The blade of the great battle axe hissed and smoked with cold demeanor. A white light surrounded it, far brighter than the snow. All watching Nordruaut winced at the blinding weapon.

"This doesn't feel right!" Niihlu grimaced.

"You weren't meant to wield it," the old man replied.

"I'm so cold," Niihlu yelled. "It hurts."

"And it always will." The old man smiled. He waved his hand dismissively and a dark vortex appeared. He stepped into it and was gone.

Vex'steppe

Maudusta was one hundred and seventy three. An old man by any measurement in Ehrde, and as Iroquia of the eight tribes, he was the eldest to reign over the tribes of Vex'steppe. In spite of the tight, curly white crown of hair surrounding his bald black head, the wrinkled dark skin on his face and hands, and his thin bare arms, there was a deep and powerful energy he contained that none would challenge.

The night brought cold in the desert, and he stood like a

young man, naked save his waist wrappings. He breathed deep of the dry, dusty air. He longed for his wife, the beautiful Driandra, former Iroquia of the Berfemmian female tribes who had provided him so many sons and daughters before she passed. He dug his bare toes into the still warm sand and sighed deeply, staring into the brazen starry skies that covered his desert end to end.

All was silent. There wasn't a single whisper in the quiet sands to alert him, but experience had taught him to know the air, and it moved wrong. Maudusta gripped his stadauf tight—the twin-bladed staff crunching loudly as he placed it firmly in the sand. He squeezed the staff harder, feeling the carvings in the white decorated handle. Maudusta lowered his head and concentrated.

"I won't be killed by you, or your daggers, ANduaut," he said.

"I know your weakness, old man." ANduaut's voice echoed in the sands from everywhere and nowhere. "You will die by my hand, and as your son I shall become Iroquia."

"My son was lost weeks ago to the great battle of sea and wyrms," Maudusta said sadly. "You who came back are not the same person with your red ring. You are no longer my son."

Maudusta ducked as a dagger flashed where his head had been. He struck out with his stadauf, only to split the open air. He listened, and felt, waiting for ANduaut's next movement.

"I'm still your son and it is time for you to pass," ANduaut's voice surrounded him. "Now!"

A blade bit Maudusta's side, and blood trickled down his waist. There was pain in his abdomen when he reared back to avoid another strike. Maudusta stood erect, his stadauf perfectly vertical to Ehrde, and listened. He heard the gentle whoosh of steel and lifted the staff to block.

"Impossible," ANduaut said.

Maudusta swung at the source, striking deep into a second attacker. His son had not come alone. He lifted up with all his strength, ignoring the sloshy sounds of tearing skin and gut.

"It is only impossible that you are here, my son," Maudusta said calmly. "You and your *friend* died, and you must die again to be at peace."

The end of Maudusta's weapon dropped to the sand. A great darkness formed around his son's companion, now visible in the brightness of the moon. The man looked hopeless, and desperate. He dropped his dagger and reached out to Maudusta.

"It's so cold," he pleaded. "Please don't let the Dark Vivek take me."

"Your choice is made and is not mine," Maudusta stated. "The darkness you represent is just the beginning."

The second attacker disappeared into a dark smoky vortex, gone forever into a ruby ring that shattered to dust. Twin daggers thrust deep between Maudusta's ribs, and he arched his back in pain, refusing to scream.

"I'm sorry, father, but this is our way," ANduaut said, ripping the daggers free. "It is time for you to pass, and the tribes to war."

62

"What is this? What's going on?" Angst asked.

They floated over the Vex'steppe desert, looking down at the half-naked body of an old, dead man.

"Niihlu has a foci? Gaarder is dead?" Angst continued.

"We're dreaming again," Victoria said.

"But this isn't a foci dream."

"No, Angst, I don't think it ever was," Victoria said.

"These are your dreams, Tori?" Angst asked. "This whole time we've been sharing in your dreams?"

"Yes, Angst," she said apologetically. "This is why I didn't want to share a tent. I have no confidence in what I can do, and I wasn't sure my dreams would work. I didn't want to disappoint you."

"I'm not disappointed," Angst said. "I don't understand why we didn't go into a foci dream, but if all we've seen is true—"

"I believe it is," Victoria said.

"Can you bring us to Rose?" Angst asked. "We need to find her."

"I've never been able to control where, or when, I'm taken in my dreams," Victoria explained. "It just happens...oooh, like now."

The desert faded away.

The home of Angst and Heather

441

Heather and Janda hid behind nearby trees, watching, and waiting for a sign from Scar. After shrinking to puppy size again, he lay unmoving in the destroyed doorway of the cottage. Heather took cautious steps around the tree, poised to leap to safety in spite of her pregnancy.

"Do you think that's a good idea?" Janda asked.

"I have to know," Heather said.

Pulling her shawl tight around her arms, Heather cautiously approached Scar. When she saw the lab breathing, she rushed to his side and dropped to her knees. The red welt from his namesake looked irritated—the scar appeared fresh from belly to back along the pup's ribs. Heather patted his head gently, and Scar's tail wagged. She looked back to smile at Janda and noticed flames hovering over one of the woman's hands.

"Just being careful," Janda said guiltily.

"Thank you, dear," Heather said with a smile. "But if Scar grew to full size, I don't think even your fire could help."

"Right," Janda said, letting the flame extinguish.

Scar lolled his head from side to side groggily before coming to. He stood on wobbly legs, sneezed, and shook as though covered in water. Heather looked at Janda and shrugged as the lab pup regained composure. Scar turned around and sniffed Heather, his tail wagging wildly—once again a happy puppy. Heather patted him on the head then stood with Janda's help.

"Such a relief," Heather said gratefully.

"I'm sorry about your house, Heather," Janda said.

"It won't take long for Angst to fix," Heather said. "I'm just so glad Scar's alive."

"I guess that's good news," Janda said hopefully. "That means Angst is alive too, right?"

"Yes," Heather said with a sigh. "I believe so. I can't imagine what he's going through though."

Scar licked at a paw and then at his back, turning around as though chasing his tail. He snapped at the air then snapped again as if he hadn't quite caught something. The pup ran off toward the nearby woods, stopping mid-way to spin around several more times. He continued snapping at the air as though biting at an annoying fly.

"What's he doing?" Heather asked.

Scar began to grow as if danger was approaching. When he became half the size of the house, he pounced onto nothing and shrank again. He continued snapping, and growled.

"I don't understand," Heather said worriedly.

"We should go in the house," Janda suggested.

"No." Heather pulled Janda's sleeve and pointed at the ground. "Look."

A small bubble rose from the pavement, followed by several more. Foam covered the ground as if the earth was a dishtowel being squeezed clean. Larger bubbles formed around Scar as he bit and wrestled with each one.

Heather pulled Janda hurriedly toward the road. Scar saw them, leaped forward with a wagging tail as if ready to accompany them then spun about to snap at another bubble. The puppy grew, and barked so loudly it vibrated in her bones.

Janda summoned her lioness swifen and looked at Heather expectantly.

"I don't know how," Heather said desperately.

They inched over to a nearby stump so Heather could wrestle her way onto the creature. Janda mounted quickly behind her and brought the swifen about so they could watch. Scar continued to battle with the bubbles, and himself, as though fending off madness. He leaped from one end of the clearing to another, changing sizes, snapping at unseen bubbles. He stopped, half the size of the monster he could become, and looked after Heather with sad eyes.

Scar barked one loud warning. It was enough, and Janda reared her swifen about and took off at a frantic pace. After several minutes she slowed, her hand burning bright for warmth and light. Heather listened, but the sound of Scar's barking was now distant.

"That poor thing," Janda said. "I feel like we should go back and help."

"I wouldn't know what to do," Heather said sadly. "We'll have to wait for Angst."

Janda wondered to herself—if this was happening to Scar, what was happening to Angst? She kept quiet, nodding with a forced smile.

"We should go to Unsel and wait for him to return," Janda suggested.

"Let's go to Graloon's," Heather agreed.

She looked back once more to hear the lonely wail of the giant monster dog she'd left behind. Heather patted Janda gently on the shoulder, and they rode toward Unsel.

Unsel

Isabelle sighed deeply as she finally approached the hallway to her room. It had taken everything she had not to ask the guards for help. Instead, she had dismissed them. Tyrell was off to seek healing, and she wanted nothing more than quiet and solitude to settle her nerves.

She glanced around quickly, found the hallway to her room empty, and immediately began pulling pins from her hair in a very un-queen-like fashion. It was her kingdom, and her castle, and she had earned the right to some impropriety. She smiled to herself—it was a small reward for being correct.

Alloria was the right choice for princess and, one day, queen. Although she hadn't consulted Isabelle with the treachery threatening Unsel, Alloria had done the right thing and saved the kingdom. It was a relief to know there was a responsible princess as her heir, one she could trust to lead Unsel. Tomorrow, she would sign the papers making it formal. She sighed happily to herself at this thought as she opened the doors to her room.

Her handmaid had failed to light candles or lamps, and the room was mostly dark, save for a small fire in the grate. Isabelle closed the double doors behind her, picked up a nearby candle and walked toward the fire. Resting on the floor in front of the fire was a dark, oblong object. Isabelle slowed.

"What is this?" she questioned loudly.

Isabelle kneeled before the object and placed her hand on it. Hair. Her heart raced as she pulled it around to see in the dim firelight.

"No," she pleaded desperately. "Tyrell, no!"

She took a deep breath to scream, but was stopped by the long fingers of a strong hand covering her mouth. Isabelle flailed her arms, letting go of Tyrell's head and trying to beat at the man standing behind her. She reached over her shoulders to grab at hair, but there wasn't enough. She pushed with her legs only to feel the cold steel of armor against her back.

"Just relax, Your Majesty," Vars whispered. "You may have died in your sleep, but Unsel is in good hands now."

63

Epilogue One

Victoria cried inconsolably, rocking back and forth in a ball between Angst's arms. Through her wracking sobs, he could hear Tarness and Hector shuffle anxiously outside their tent. He was at a loss for what to do, or what to say, and did his best to console the princess by patting her hair and holding her tightly.

"Angst," Tarness said carefully, his voice hushed and deeper than normal. "Is she okay?"

"Yes," Angst said, looking at her. "I think."

Victoria's eyes were dark and wet with tears, a sunset of red blotched her pale skin beneath them. She looked up at Angst with mournful eyes before losing herself to uncontrollable tears again. Angst made more vain attempts at consoling her as she rested her forehead on his shoulder. What had happened? He struggled to recall. It was a blur—their dreams strung together like wisps of white cloud in a blue sky.

Angst squeezed his eyes shut in concentration. He remembered being everywhere. He remembered a Fulk'han prisoner, and Niihlu of Nordruaut, and Tyrell...and...and Isabelle. His mouth dropped open, and Angst sucked in air as the dreams came back. Victoria sought his eyes again as realization struck.

"Oh, Tori," he said sadly, holding her even tighter.

Another wave of heavy sobs overtook her when she realized

446

Angst understood, and remembered everything that had happened. He didn't dare question whether it was real, or if it could have been a mistake. Somehow, Angst knew, and judging by the conviction in Victoria's grief, she knew as well.

Minutes passed, and the heat of a rekindled campfire warmed his back through the tent. Victoria pulled away from his embrace and lay on her side, curling into a protective ball. He covered her with blankets, and kept patting her back consolingly.

"Go," she said in a thick voice. "Tell the others."

"Are you sure?" Angst asked.

"They have to know," she said quietly. "Tell them all of it."

Angst left the tent, surprised to find it still night. Warmth from the fire barely held back the cold winter air. Hector paced and Tarness waited, almost holding his breath. Dallow wrung his hands together. Now that they all knew what the princess was capable of, they understood the gravity of her outburst. Angst pressed through his friends to stand before the fire.

"There's been a coup," Angst said. "I don't remember it all clearly. We can ask Tori for more details in the morning."

"In Unsel?" Dallow asked cautiously.

"Everywhere," Angst said.

"What?" Hector said in shock. He stopped his pacing and walked to Angst.

"Gaarder is dead. Melkier's now ruled by Nicadilia and Crloc," Angst said, though he still couldn't wrap his brain around the enormity of it all. "Rohjek is consorting with Fulk'han. Even the tribes of Vex'steppe have been seized. I don't remember everything, but...I think all of them have been taken."

"Unsel," Hector questioned. He gripped Angst's shoulder and pulled him around. "What of Unsel?"

64

Epilogue Two

Alloria sat on the throne and leaned back into it. The room was finally quiet. The last of the thin-faced coroners had left with Fulk'han bodies in tow, guards had been dismissed, and Isabelle had finally turned in for the night. Alloria patted her plain, unbecoming white gown, and couldn't wait to be rid of it. If she was forced to wear something so uncomfortable, it should've at least been flattering. She sighed as she tousled her honey-brown hair. It was only a matter of waiting, which she hated.

Not only had she done everything she had been tasked to do, she was now considered a hero of Unsel. With Isabelle's recognition, she had earned everyone's respect. It was far more than she had expected, or even hoped for. It was just as the Dark Vivek had advised.

Vars strode into the room, his thin gray hair high and tight over his long wrinkled face. He wore his stodgy old armor—polished silver decorated with brightened gold leafy flourishes. Vars's hands rested behind his back as he slowly made his way to Alloria. His face was stoic, not a hint of success or failure in his posture. Not a single speck of red tarnished his armor, and she wondered if he had stopped to polish it.

"I have been in contact with the Dark Vivek," Alloria stated.

CHAPTER SIXTY FOUR

"It seems most of the coups have been successful, though not all."

"Oh?"

"Rohjek and Fulk'han have become allies," Alloria said. "We ignored Meldusia, as they're harmless. There's been nothing from Angoria, yet."

"Did we have any success?" Vars asked sternly.

"The king of Melkier is dead, as is the beserk tribal leader of northern Vex'steppe."

"What of the Nordruauts?" he asked coolly.

"They now have a champion, one who wields a foci," she said with a smile. "Eastern Nordruaut is with us."

"Very good," Vars said. "That's worth much. The Vivek must be pleased."

"Dark Vivek," she corrected.

"Is there really more than one?" Vars asked.

"I haven't questioned," Alloria said. "You are welcome to."

Vars looked down at his missing fingers and shuddered in fear. He shook his head.

"How fares Tyrell?" she asked.

"A lone Fulk'han beheaded the poor Captain Guard," Vars lied smoothly with raised eyebrows.

Alloria looked momentarily saddened or guilty. Tyrell was the one man who'd believed in her, and it was unfortunate that he'd had to die.

"Second thoughts, milady?" Vars asked.

"There is no room for second thoughts, Captain Guard Vars," she said calmly. "And Isabelle?"

Vars pulled Isabelle's crown from behind his back and casually tossed it toward her. It landed on the tile with several clinks before sliding neatly to Alloria's feet. The large ruby centerpiece of the main spike was cracked in half.

"Long live the queen," Vars said with a smirk.

About the Author

David J. Pedersen is a native of Racine, WI who resides in his home town Kansas City, MO. He received a Bachelor of Arts degree in Philosophy from the University of Wisconsin - Madison. He has worked in sales, management, retail, video and film production, and IT. David has run 2 marathons, climbed several 14,000 foot mountains and marched in Thee University of Wisconsin Marching Band. He is a geek and a fanboy that enjoys carousing, picking on his wife and kids, playing video games, and slowly muddling through his next novel.

To learn more about David and his writing please visit his blog:

www.gotangst.com

Angst and his friends return in the sequel:

Drowning in Angst

Available now!

41659862R00255

Made in the USA
San Bernardino, CA
04 July 2019